THE WOMAN ON THE BENCH

ELIOT STEVENS

INKUBATOR
BOOKS

Published by Inkubator Books
www.inkubatorbooks.com

ISBN (eBook): 978-1-915275-97-4
ISBN (Paperback): 978-1-915275-98-1
ISBN (Hardback): 978-1-915275-99-8

To Sofia

1

Her voice. That's the first thing. Not her body, not her scent. It's the sound of her—that soft, fathomless voice. The sort of voice that beckons you from the edge of dark woods.

'Hey.'

That's all. A simple greeting, but spoken intimately, as if to a friend. No, not a friend: an *accomplice*. A co-conspirator.

But this, my attempt to describe her voice, comes later. First, it's just me. An awkward me, trying to conceal the sneaky cigarette I'm puffing on, swallowing the smoke, choking back the cough. I turn instinctively, half-expecting to see my wife standing there, eyes sad rather than cross, her words unspoken but loud nonetheless. *You're smoking again.*

But it's not my wife, although they do sound similar. In fact, this is my first conscious thought: *she sounds exactly like my wife.* And they really do sound alike. Sensual sirens.

She, this other woman, steps out of the shadows and into the weak light, like a character on a stage. Like someone not entirely real.

I blow out the smoke, catch my breath. I'm trying to look

relaxed, cool-guy-having-a-smoke sort of relaxed. As opposed to the relieved-it's-not-my-wife variety.

'Hey,' I echo, with a nod.

She holds up her own cigarette, rests it between her lips. When she speaks, the tip wiggles up and down. 'Light?'

'Sure,' I say, reaching to my pocket. And as I do, I study her. She's beautiful. Petite, dark hair, wide eyes. I find the lighter, and she leans into the light of the small flame. Her skin is smooth, flawless. She has the eyes of someone who smiles often. We're alone, out here. It's unsettling to be alone with someone beautiful.

'Thanks,' she says once her cigarette is lit. She leans back, waves the smoke away. When she sets her eyes on me again, there's a spark shining in there.

'I scared you,' she says. It's not a question.

I laugh. 'Was it that obvious?'

'Yup.' She takes a puff, nods towards my cigarette. 'Not supposed to?'

I peer down at its glowing end and shake my head. It's my third one this week. Not too bad. 'No,' I say. 'Not really.'

Someone has turned up the music inside. It's a track I don't recognise. I stopped recognising songs around about the age of thirty. The baseline thumps inside my chest. Hers too, I imagine.

'Oh well,' she says, her lips curling upwards, with a light, carefree shrug. That's it. No judgement at all. Just plain, simple, spontaneous acceptance. It's nice.

We share a moment's silence. Comfortable silence. She leans against the wall, this stranger, the same way I am, and looks up towards the sky. It's night-time, the city lights drowning out the stars. Light pollution, they call it.

I sneak a glance at her body. My eyes hesitate on her narrow waist, the curve of her hips and back. I have thoughts. When I look up again, she's looking back at me. I'm pretty sure my face has gone red. I take a quick drag, the smoke drifting into my right eye. It stings, but I pretend it doesn't. I fumble for words, come up with a rather lame, 'So, you're a friend of Jackie's?' I hardly know Jackie, our host. I'm a friend of a friend.

She doesn't answer immediately. For a second, her expression seems to be saying, *I saw you looking at me.* And then, just maybe: *And I don't mind.*

'Sort of,' she says, 'I'm here with Michael. You know him? Tall, blond hair? He's wearing a leather jacket.'

A ridiculous, pointy prickle of jealousy somewhere inside my chest. Of course she's here with someone. We're in our late thirties (although she might be slightly younger), someone like her is unlikely to be single.

'Um, not sure,' I say, although I've already forgotten the bloke's name and description. I'm finding it hard to focus on anything else but her.

'It's odd, isn't it?' she says, waving a hand towards the door we both walked out of, to stand here in this ill-lit back garden. Beyond that door, the party continues. 'Making new friends as an adult. Feels like there's no point.'

I nod, chuckle. I agree. In fact, I'm quite sure I've often stated the same myself. I have the same friends I've had since the age of twelve. Colleagues, acquaintances: I sometimes refer to them as *friends* too, but it never rings sincere when I do. Then I wonder if she means *us*, if she's confessing to me that she doesn't really want to know me, so no point in pretending. Except, that's not how it sounds, at all.

I'm about to reply when someone else steps out. Before I realise, my hand darts behind my back, concealing the cigarette. We go quiet, and I can't help feeling like we're both irritated by the intrusion. Not only on account of my smoking, that is. We've been interrupted, but there's also a strange feeling of having been *caught*.

A large, precarious figure in a suit a couple of sizes too large stumbles through the door. A man, who only notices us at the last second. When he does, he jumps, letting out a little high-pitched squeal, then immediately fixes his expression, gives us a cross-eyed, blurry smile. He walks past us hurriedly, almost trips on his own feet, laughs an apologetic little laugh, then, to the relief of all parties involved, disappears through a small gate in the garden fence.

We share a quizzical smile, and, suddenly, looking into her eyes (perhaps because of the beer), I feel like leaning forward and telling this complete stranger that I think I'm in love with her. I have no idea why, but the thought is there. Gabbie, Ed's wife, says it's all down to my star sign—I'm a Pisces. Apparently, we are slaves to beauty. All it takes to steal a Pisces man's heart, she says, is a pair of beautiful eyes and a perfect figure. Some might say the same goes for any man. I'm not sure what I think. I tend to tune out when someone mentions star signs. Especially if that someone is Gabbie. At times I wonder how someone like Cecilia, my wife, can stand her.

My smile turns stiff.

My wife.

I'm a grown man. Married. I'm not a smoker—not *really*. I'm not someone who chats up strangers. What am I doing out here, with this woman? What am I thinking? I should be inside, sitting beside the woman I married. Holding hands, chatting with the others. Whispering familiar words in each other's ears. Giggling at inside jokes, the sort no one else gets. Yet I'm here. And I'm not entirely sure I want to leave.

I clear my throat. Am I coming across as nervous? It's been so, so long since I've felt the need to impress a woman. Seduction—hard work, that.

'I'm here with my wife,' I blurt out nonsensically. Immediately, I scan her face for signs of disappointment: eyes drifting downwards, maybe, or a twitch of her lips. There's nothing. At least, I don't think there is.

'Oh,' she says. 'Okay.'

I feel like an idiot, although she's not looking at me like that. In fact, she's not looking at me at all, now. Her eyes are fixed on the tip of her cigarette, brushing it against the brick wall of the house, shaping the ash into a fine, pointy tip. Glittering specks fall to the ground, veering from bright red to nothing, and vanish into the darkness.

When she turns, she's smiling again. 'Hiding that from her, are you?' she says, nodding towards my own cigarette.

'Yes,' I say. 'She thinks I've quit.' According to Cecilia, to what I've led her to believe, I've not touched a smoke since she got pregnant. And it's mostly true. It's just, sometimes I'll have one. Nothing wrong with that.

'She shouldn't get you to lie to her,' the woman says in a soft voice. There's a sudden shift in her expression. She's serious now, compassionate. I frown, surprised. It sounds exactly like the sort of mental gymnastics I might come up with to exonerate myself. Turning the blame the other way: I'm lying to my wife because *she* forces me to. The way this woman says it, though, it sounds true.

'You should tell her,' she adds. 'Without apologising. Just tell her. Or don't, but don't feel too guilty about it, at least.' Again, that conspiratorial smile spreads gently on her lips. Her teeth are large and white, almost childlike. 'But whatever you do, stop having heart attacks every time someone walks past.'

I laugh. There's something about her body, her posture, that makes me want to hug her, now. That would be wonderful.

Before I can add anything else, she flicks her cigarette carelessly away, a small eruption of bright sparks where it hits the ground. She turns towards me, her hand outstretched. 'Have to go. My name is Alice, by the way.'

I shake her hand. My wife's hands are soft, delicate. Hers feel strong, energetic.

'Mark,' I say.

She lets go, and I have the impression her fingers linger on my palm, caressing it. I might be wrong.

'Mark,' she says, straightening her back and affecting a formal tone. 'It's been a pleasure.' A beat, a smile. 'It truly has.' She adds this as if surprised. Happily surprised.

'Same here,' I say, and it doesn't sound half as true as it feels.

She waves a little wave, turns on her heel and walks back through the door. My eyes hesitate where they shouldn't. Before stepping back into the house, back into the shared, noisy space of the party, she throws one last glance at me.

Alice, I think. I mouth the letters, silently, liking the way my lips, my tongue, move when I do it. It's a strange name, if you think about it.

Alice.

A name that is almost a whisper.

2

I step back into the throng, the noise and chatter hitting me like a damp gust of wind. I wade through the bodies, speaking into my phone, my features twisted as if I can barely hear anything.

I time my pretend conversation to end just as I approach my wife and friends, in the little corner of the vast living room we've cut out for ourselves. I linger for a second, making sure I'm heard by our little party.

'Yes,' I say loudly, a finger poked inside my free ear. 'OK... yes. Listen, mate, I'm back inside, can't hear you. Ring you tomorrow, OK?'

Cecilia gives me a little inquisitive look, *Who's that?* I roll my eyes, mouthing, *Work.* 'All right then,' I say, bringing the call to an end. 'See you Monday. Bye. Yeah. Bye.'

I let myself drop onto the wide sofa, beside her. Air hisses out of the cushions. 'Sorry, had to take that,' I say, wondering whether Cecilia can detect the scent of tobacco, if she knows there was no call. I feel her eyes on me, but I avoid them, leaning forward to pick up a drink from the table.

'All OK?' she asks softly. Before I turn around, I take a long swig of beer, hoping it will conceal the smell.

'Yes, just Senesi. All good.' Senesi, the Italian fashion designer, is our largest account. A Sunday evening call about them seems believable. She says nothing, but leans her head against my shoulder. Perhaps to sniff me. My wife always smells wonderful.

'So, we were talking about that time at Pete's,' says Clyde, leaning towards me. By the look on the others' faces, I suspect he was the only one talking about it. His eyes are watery, his face puffy and red with drink. He's aged a lot worse than the rest of us. 'What were we... eleven? Twelve? Anyway... it was me and you and, yeah, Pete. His dad was out, but his mum, she...' Clyde keeps talking, but the others have started muttering amongst themselves. Clyde raises his voice, trying to make himself and his uninteresting story heard.

I throw a casual glance around the room. Youngish parents with tired eyes, trying to convince themselves coming here was worthwhile. There are also slightly more energetic couples, the type who aren't quite ready for kids yet. Single people, too, most of them men. They drink hard and laugh loud, feeling sorry for those among us who have to wake up at night to tend to our children (I'm not among them), or are forced to endure the dubious joys of monogamy. These single men and women, they flash their smiles, act youthfully, hint to all the fun they're having at this stage in their lives. They look rather sad.

I scan the crowd in search of the woman. Alice. There's no sign of her.

A gentle squeeze on my knee. It's Cecilia, subtly calling my attention back to Clyde.

'... and she walks in, screaming—and I mean *screaming*—saying, "*I told you not to go through your father's drawers, didn't I? DIDN'T I?*" But us two,' he continues, slapping my shoulder and wiping a tear from his eye, 'we was rolling on the floor, clutching our bellies. In tears, we were. Remember? Remember, Mark?'

Clyde has the vivid memories and attachment to the past of those whose life has amounted to little. I laugh, shake my head in an ah-the-good-old-days sort of way, return his friendly slaps. I have no idea what he's talking about, no recollection of that event, at all. I love Clyde, so I put up with him.

'Anyway...' sighs Philip from across the coffee table we're all huddled around. His mouth is twisted in mild disgust as he looks at the still-chuckling Clyde. 'I did my TED talk last week.'

Philip—handsome, charismatic, confident. He's the mirror opposite of the twitching, overweight, balding Clyde sitting beside me. Philip is an artist. An actual *artiste*, who somehow has managed to gather a small but growing cult following. Not quite as influential as he'd have you believe, certainly not an A-lister, but he's making a comfortable living with his art. One side effect of his career is that he's constantly accompanied by striking twenty-somethings. I glance at the one he's brought tonight, try to recall her name. She's perched on the armrest at his side, hands entwined with his. I never remember their names, but no point, really. He's not the sort to commit to anything. Especially when it comes to sexual partners. Next party, it'll be someone else.

'Oh!' Gabbie says. 'Right, your TED talk! How'd it go?'

'Oh, you know,' he says nonchalantly. As if he hadn't raised the topic himself. 'Nothing special, really.'

'What was your topic?' my wife asks as she leans forward to pick up a pistachio from the bowl on the table. She sounds genuinely interested.

This irritates me. I smile and say, 'Yes, what was it about?'

'*The Work of Art in the Age of Mechanical Masturbation,*' he says. No hint of irony. I know for a fact he's actually saying it in italics. 'It's a contemporary take on Benjamin's seminal work,' he adds.

Clyde is fidgeting. The sofa squeaks under his considerable mass. Philip is about to add something, when he butts in, asking, 'TEDx, wasn't it?'

Philip turns his head towards Clyde, barely. 'Sorry?'

Clyde clears his throat. 'TED *ex*, wasn't it? The, what's it, independently organised talks? The DIY sort, right?'

Philip is uncomfortable. He clears his throat. 'Yes, it was, but—'

'Oh, nononono,' Clyde says, raising a beefy hand in the air. 'I'm not saying it's any less impressive than a real—I mean *normal* TED talk. Sorry, go on.'

The smile I was wearing suddenly feels like a genuine one. I almost pat Clyde on his fat back. Yes, I do love him. Even if he wants to sleep with my wife. Most people do.

'It was *awesome*,' says the leggy twenty-something. She's chewing gum. 'Phil's talk, the things he said about art, they were...' She hesitates, a frown on her forehead. '*Awesome*, yes.'

Now Philip seems irritated by both of them. He runs a hand through his thick blond hair, sits back into the armchair, distancing himself from everyone else. 'Anyway,' he concludes, 'you can watch it online.'

Gabbie peers down at her watch and lets out a little gasp. Brushing crumbs off her dress, she turns towards Ed. 'Better get going, can't afford the babysitter for another hour.'

Ed nods, eyelids heavy. 'Yup,' he says, 'this is us.' He glances across the chattering, swerving crowd with mild, almost detached, curiosity. Ed is a good man. A happy man.

They rise, and as they do, my wife says, 'We'd better go, too.' She always does this when we're out. Cuts the evening short, decides we must leave. It's not like I'm particularly enjoying the party, but still. *We'd better go?* Why? It's not late, my glass is still half-full. Most of all (although I'd never say this to her), there's no child waiting for us back at home. No overpriced babysitter. It's just us.

'Sure,' I say. 'Better go.'

We say our goodbyes. Philip and his girl are staying on. Surprisingly, Clyde stays on too. He's desperately scanning the guests, hoping he might get lucky. I hope he does. The instant the rest of us walk off, Philip and the blond retreat to a secluded corner, hands all over one another, giggling like teenagers. Clyde is left on his own. We're slowly making our way through the room, towards the front door. More farewells are exchanged. As Gabbie thanks our host for a *fantastic* evening, I turn back and study Clyde. He stares into his glass for a long beat, then downs its contents. There's noise and laughter all around except in his corner.

I'm suddenly struck by the absolute certainty that, one day, Clyde will do something extremely stupid. Something terrible, unforgivable. At that moment, he happens to look up, meeting my gaze. I wave to him from across the room. His wide, childlike smile makes something in my chest twitch.

'HERE IT IS,' says Gabbie as their minicab appears. We're standing outside, our breaths turning into white puffs in the chill night air.

My wife hugs Gabbie goodbye. 'Send little Lilly our love,' she says. 'Tell her Aunt Cecilia will come and visit soon.'

Aunt Cecilia. Every time she says that, I turn slightly stiff. Uncle Mark, Auntie Cecilia. Parents by proxy. Non-parents.

'Will do,' says Gabbie as Ed opens the cab door for her. She waves and gives us a little, high-pitched *Byeee*. Ed raises a sleepy hand. 'See you at the office, mate,' he says, ducking into the cab.

We stand there for a second, my wife waving. I can just about make them out through the rear windscreen, Ed and Gabbie, their heads touching. As the cab leaves, he turns and lays a sleepy kiss on her forehead.

We walk towards our car. I throw a quick glance at the party house, hoping to catch a last glimpse of the woman called Alice.

'What is it?' Cecilia asks me. My wife's questions are never casual ones. She stares at me with her wide, pondering eyes, their expression posing multitudes of other, unspoken questions. No one has eyes like hers.

I notice I'm lagging behind her, so I step up to match her pace. 'Nothing,' I say. The lights of our car flash twice as I press the unlock button on the keys.

She's the woman I married, the one I love. At times, she's someone I barely recognise.

'Nothing. Let's go.'

3

A t home. I'm in the bathroom, sitting on the edge of the tub, hunched over my phone. The water in the sink is running. I want it to sound like I'm busy in here.

I open Philip's Facebook profile (his pic shows him bare-chested, walking across a white canvas; his feet have been dipped in blue paint, and they leave messy prints on the material). Doing my best to ignore his narcissistic status updates, I click on the *Friends* tab. He has more than two thousand. I have one hundred-something.

The phone's screen is suddenly populated by names and faces of strangers. Some have changed their profile picture to a country's flag, following a recent terrorist attack. Doing their bit.

I scroll down, trying to find her, but there are simply too many people among Phil's friends. I filter by name, and seven Alices come up. Among them, a bearded man in his seventies, wearing a wig. No sign of my Alice, though.

My Alice. Calling her that, summoning her in my mind

with that possessive, makes me feel slightly insane. Insane and quite pathetic.

Browsing back to the friend list, I spot Jackie, our host. (In her profile pic, she's wearing a Karl Marx T-shirt, a champagne flute held casually in one hand, covering her smiling lips with the other). I tap her name, and her profile page appears. Alice might be here, given she was invited to Jackie's—

'Will you be long?'

Cecilia. She's standing just outside the door, her lips almost touching the wood, by the sound of it. I feel the sudden urge to shout, to tell her it's awful to tell people to hurry when they're in the loo. Everyone knows that. For all she knows, I'm here sitting on the toilet. She should respect that.

'Be out in a sec,' I say, no trace of irritation in my voice. I sense her presence beyond the closed door, her pausing, wondering. The water from the tap has been running too evenly, I think. My silence has been too deep, I think. Suspicious.

There's a shuffle of feet against the floorboards as Cecilia heads back to the bedroom. I peer down at the phone, at Jackie's stupid digital persona, her stupid 'friends', her stupid interests and pics and quotes.

What am I doing?

I'm a grown man. A married man. Not the sort of man who does *this*. I stand up, pocket my phone, a sudden pang of guilt and shame in the pit of my stomach. No, I'm not that sort of man.

I brush my teeth in a hurry, eager to slip into bed next to the woman I married.

. . .

WE LOST our child eight months ago. I'm not entirely sure that's the right way of putting it. My wife was six months pregnant when she had a miscarriage. It was a boy. We don't talk about it, but we do think about it, each in our separate silences. When I do, I refer to it as *the thing*. It's a euphemism, a cowardly defence mechanism. I wonder what mind trick my wife uses when considering our own personal tragedy.

Ewan was my choice of a name. Hers was James. We would lie on the sofa on lazy Sunday mornings, still in our pyjamas, listing all sorts of names, good ones, bad ones, the old-fashioned and the trendy, the maybes and the definitely-nots, mocking the hippie parents who went with things like Ocean or Sparrow. Love came so easy, back then.

Unfortunately, love doesn't prevent you from doing evil things.

Stop it—you're not that kind of man.

'I want this to be his bedroom,' she'd said when we first found our house. This house. The room was south-facing, the soft light of the English sun shining on the bare walls. A guest bedroom, for a very special guest, one we would introduce to the world. Ewan. Or James. But definitely not Ocean.

By the fifth month, the room was ready. I'd put all my effort into making it the dream room for a child. Each wall was painted a different colour (happy, vibrant colours, just like our boy would be), with one featuring a rather impressive portrayal of a castle, including a fire-breathing dragon, a trapped princess and a fearless knight. Silly amounts of toys were already piling up in all corners, ready to be unwrapped by small, wrinkly hands. If those hands were too small, mine would help tear the paper. I'd also stuck those star-shaped stickers on the ceiling, the ones that glow at night. I pictured myself sitting beside his cot, telling him stories of stars and dragons and wonder. I pictured a happy family. I pictured many things.

All that is gone now. After the medical procedure, a week later perhaps, I found Cecilia standing in front of the open door, not quite able to step inside. 'What are we going to do with all this?' she asked me, her voice broken.

I put an ad in the local paper, posted something online. There are parents who can't afford this stuff; giving it away seemed the right thing to do. It felt right. It felt wrong.

Whenever someone came along to collect one of those toys, one of the million newborn accessories you never even knew existed until you're about to become a parent, my wife found an excuse to get out of the house: I'll pop out and get some fruit. We've run out of milk; I'll be right back. Or simply, I'm going for a walk.

The young couples who came round were always very appreciative, some of them thanking me through flowing tears. They sometimes sneaked quizzical looks my way, the obvious questions floating in their eyes, but not spoken. *Why are you doing this? Why are you giving these things away? What happened?*

What happened?

There's no way I can answer that question. I know people who have been through the same thing and got over it. Some eventually had children, others didn't, but they got over it. With us, it's still very much happening.

The hardest moment was when they carried away the cot. I watched as a nice twenty-year-old man, a young father, struggled to get it through the doors of the house on his way out. I watched, smiled politely, but didn't lend a hand.

These are my thoughts these days. They are also my wife's, I believe. But having the same thoughts hasn't brought us closer. It's a bit like those magnets, where equal charges push them apart. At least, I think these are her thoughts. She's become a mystery to me. I enter the bedroom and look at her long, slender body lying on the bed. Her eyes are shut. Is she sleeping?

Moving as quietly as I can, I get into bed. Sometimes, I wonder if the loss of our child was a punishment for what I did. Killing, betrayal: these are the sorts of things that warrant terrible punishments, aren't they? I wonder that now as I lay my head on the pillow. When I reach out and turn the bedside light off, my wife's voice is that of a ghost in the darkness.

'I love you,' she says.

'I love you,' I say.

4

The BeeCreative offices are located in a fancy building in an even fancier part of town. Management likes to put on a rugged start-up vibe for the place, one that contrasts harshly with its luxurious surroundings. I wear a suit to work. Board members would like me to wear a hoodie.

I step into the lift, followed by a couple of young IT guys. Lanky, thin-limbed, with protruding Adam's apples. They nod to me, then proceed to ignore me completely. I know for a fact they earn as much as I do. They've worked for us for less than a year. The older of the two appears to have yet to develop facial hair.

'Big day today.' It's Bill, close colleague and manager for the Senesi account, standing in front of the lift doors as they open. He's sweating even though we're in winter. He's holding two cups of coffee, offers me one. I grab it as the two geeks step out and vanish down a corridor, chatting about cryptic computer matters.

'Cheers,' I say, taking a sip. Single-origin, fair-trade coffee.

From Ethiopia, I believe. Delicious. Possibly the only thing BeeCreative does well.

Bill starts walking towards Meeting Room A, his pace brisk and nervous. 'Morino was in touch, they're eager to see our latest campaign launch concept,' he huffs. 'Says he hopes we don't fuck it up.'

'Encouraging,' I say. Morino is a bastard. As our liaison at Senesi, he represents our most important client. And knows it full well.

We walk through the desks and chatter of the large open space section of the office, where fifty or so BeeCreative employees are already at work. On the far end, a sign on the wall invites everyone to *Be(e)Creative: Write Something!* I think they stole the idea from the Facebook offices, in their early days, so not creative at all. The irony of it is apparently lost on management. It's depressing, but not quite as depressing as the messages employees have felt obliged to scrawl across the wall's surface. *I'm buzzzzzing to get to work!* by someone called Meg always makes me mildly depressed when I happen to read it.

'They'll be here at half-ten,' Bill says, opening the door of the meeting room.

Meeting Room A has ample glass panel walls, the letter *A* reproduced all over them in a variety of fonts and sizes, and offers a spectacular view of central London. This is where we've been spending most of our time, Bill and I, the last few weeks, preparing for the launch of the new Senesi collection: RomAmor, a rather unimaginative combination of the words *Roma* and *Amor*. There's something depressing about designing a marketing campaign for clothes you'll never really be able to afford. Not if you want to eat, that is. Or smoke, for that matter.

'We've narrowed down the choices for the main campaign

slogan to three,' Bill says, shoving aside mounds of paper to make room for his laptop. He flips it open and pulls up a slide presentation. 'They're all shit. But it's the sort of shit Senesi likes, so that's what we're going for.'

I nod, take another sip of coffee while he tries to find the slide he's after. 'When it comes to shit copy, we're the best,' I say. This comment doesn't elicit so much as a smile from Bill. We feed off of sarcasm and caffeine at BeeCreative.

I realise I'm nervous, despite acting relaxed. There are dozens of other agencies ready to snap up Senesi, and if this launch doesn't go as planned, our Italian friends might very well turn to them.

'Thing is,' Bill continues, poking away at the keyboard with fat sausage fingers, 'Malcolm over at Legal thinks we have to tone it down...'

He keeps going, but I realise I'm not listening. Something has occurred to me: maybe Ed knows who that woman, Alice, is. I fight it, I really do, but it just won't let me be. I wonder, at times, if we have any free will at all.

'Hey, Bill,' I say, interrupting him. 'Is Ed in?'

He frowns. 'Ed?' he asks.

'Yeah, my friend Ed. From Accounting, you know, the one with—'

'I *know* who Ed is, Mark,' he says, in a half-growl. 'What I *don't* know is why the fuck you're thinking about your little mate Eddie-Edds while we've got *this* to deal with.' He jerks his head towards the monitor.

I raise my hands in the air. 'I know, I know. It's just... I need to have a word with him. Quick, I promise.'

Bill shakes his head, blows out hard through the nose. 'Yeah,' he says finally. 'He's in. Got here early.'

'Great. Be right back.'

As I head through the door, I look back at Bill. He's

tapping his finger on his watch, a menacing look in his eyes. I give him a cheeky thumbs-up, which only seems to anger him further.

Ed is sitting at his cubicle, hair messy and eyes puffy. I notice his shirt is creased (he's among those of us who refuse to adopt the silly T-shirt-and-hoodie dress code. Another reason I love him).

'Little princess keep you up, did she?'

Ed's head snaps around, startled, as if I've just awoken him from a deep sleep. When he sees it's me, he extends a hand in a limp high five.

'Yup. Very much so. Three a.m., bouncing and laughing. Full of energy, that one.' He says this without the faintest trace of annoyance. In fact, he says it with a smile.

'Enjoy the party last night?' I ask, leaning against his desk. I want it to sound casual. Something inside me is turning, shuffling around uneasily, accusingly.

He nods. 'It was all right, wasn't it?' He rubs his hands against his tired face. Then it suddenly lights up. 'Hey, did you catch Clyde's whole *Was it an independently organised TEDx thingy, or a real one?* Oh man, Philip's face. Priceless.' He laughs.

We both chuckle. Ed, Philip, Clyde and me—friends since primary school. We love to hate on Phil. He's always been too handsome, too lucky.

'By the way,' I say, swallowing a sudden lump in my throat. Why am I doing this? 'Um, do you know that woman who was there... what was her name...' I pretend to hesitate, trying to recall. 'Oh, what was it?' I close my eyes, pinch the bridge of my nose. 'You know, shortish, dark hair... *Alice!*' I say triumphantly after what I believe is a sufficiently convincing pause. 'Alice, yes. Know her?'

A smile creeps across his lips. 'Marky, Marky, Marky,' he

says, shaking his head and waving an accusatory finger at me. 'Lost her number, have you?'

Thing is, Ed is joking. He knows I'd never cheat on Cecilia, so this is all just play. As I say, he's known me since childhood. Apparently, that's not long enough to know what someone is capable of.

'Yeah,' I say, playing along. 'Threw it away, actually. Thought I was above that sort of thing. Turns out I'm not.' I want this to ring fake.

He taps two fingers against his chin, turns pensive. '*Alice*, you say?'

'Yeah, friend of our host, I think. Came along with a bloke, but I can't remember his name.'

'What does he look like?'

'Don't know. Didn't see him.'

He gives it some thought, then shakes his head. 'No, sorry. I don't think I know any Alices. Definitely no one at the party called that. What was it about? Maybe I can get in touch with Phil, ask him whether—'

'No, no,' I say, slightly too fast. I slow down, act indifferent. 'No worries. It's nothing important. It was just... Cecilia is looking for a new hairdresser, and this Alice mentioned something about her sister opening a salon.' I roll my eyes. *Women, eh?* It sounds dull enough to be true, although I feel uneasy mentioning my wife and Alice in the same sentence. 'Not important. I might get in touch with Phil,' I add, waving the matter away.

A message pops up on Ed's screen. 'Ah, sorry, mate,' he says, 'I have to reply to this.'

'No worries.' I look down at my watch. 'Better get back to it, too. Senesi are on their way.'

'Ready for 'em?'

'I'll make sure they think I am.'

Another brotherly, childish high five, and I walk off.

'Mark!' Ed calls out. 'Beers Friday, right?'

We try to meet once a week-ish, the four of us—although Phil rarely turns up anymore—for a few pints and a chat. Ed cherishes these evenings. He's a family man, but even family men need time off every now and then. *Especially* family men.

'Sure,' I say. I envy Ed. I wish my smiles came as easy as his.

As I step back inside Meeting Room A, Bill holds up a finger, inviting me to shut up. He's on the phone. His features are scrunched, fuming. His tone is mellow, professional.

'Of course,' he says, with a smile in his voice that somehow doesn't make it to his lips. 'Absolutely no problem, Luca. We'll be here. Sure. Sure. OK, later then. Bye.' Then, as soon as he's tapped the button to end the conversation, 'Fuck him, arsehole cunt. Thinks we've got nothing else to do but hang around and wait for him.' He scoffs so hard, he almost spits.

Luca is Morino. It took six months for Bill to move to first-name terms with him. Before that, it wasn't *Mister* Morino: it was *Signor* Morino, by explicit request of Morino himself.

'What's up?' I ask.

'He says he's busy, won't make it here until twelve thirty.' He shakes his head. Bill always looks like he's suffering from a massive headache. 'Oh well, we've got more time to work on the copy, at least.'

I peer over at his open laptop, to the words that appear on the screen. Three meagre sentences, brainchildren of our wordsmiths over in the copywriting team. Brain*farts* would be more accurate.

RomAmor. Wear love.

RomAmor. The essence of Italy.

RomAmor. Elegance has a new name.

They're poor. Very poor. Although, as Bill pointed out, it's the sort of thing Morino likes. Bland, predictable, uncreative. I suddenly picture the silly stylised bee in our logo giving me a thumbs-up and saying, *Bland, predictable, uncreative? The perfect job for BeeCreative!*

I try to visualise Morino as he contemplates the proposals. Given what I know of his tastes, I suspect he'll go for the first one. *Wear love.* I make a mental note to present it last.

'OK, let's take a look at the visuals,' I say, taking a seat at the large wooden table in the centre of Meeting Room A. It's 'rustic', that's to say it's full of splinters, unvarnished. I suppose there's some sort of statement being made here, although I can't quite understand what it is.

'They're equally shite,' says Bill. He really is full of enthusiasm this morning. He shifts the laptop so it faces him, and begins thumping the mousepad. Bill's impatience with computers is matched only by his ignorance about their inner workings. He types with two rigid index fingers sticking out from raging balled fists.

When the images appear on the screen, I'm actually quite impressed. Predictable settings, perhaps (Coliseum, Pantheon, that sort of thing), but the photographer knows what he's doing: The RomAmor-clad model is captured casually walking past the city's landmarks, in the dead of night. The atmosphere is sensual, enigmatic, refined. To my surprise, I like them.

'They're quite good,' I say.

Bill grunts. 'I s'pose they could be worse,' he concedes.

'Might have a tough time getting the copy to fit them, in terms of theme.' Usually, the copy comes first. Once it's been approved, everything else kicks off—visuals, website landing pages, banners, etcetera. But with Senesi, you sort of have to improvise.

I reach out, flip through them. 'Yes, we can work with these.'

'Gotta work on the copy though. They're his sort of thing, but not strong enough.'

'Yes,' I say. 'He might like the first one, but the others need work. Let's get a couple of the copywriters over.'

Bill brings up the Skype window. 'I'll call Werner, the German copywriter. At least he knows how to bloody spell.' Werner's English grammar is far better than that of any of our British born-and-bred copywriters.

While Bill deals with that, I pull out my own laptop and power it up. I feel slightly nauseous. It's not the Morino thing. It's Alice. Rather, it's *me*, trying to track down Alice. It feels a bit like a joke, like something I wouldn't really pursue (not me).

But I *did* go so far as inquiring about her with Ed, didn't I?

Stop it, I say to myself. *Get this silly thing out of your mind.* All of a sudden, it feels like I actually can. This thing with this Alice person (what thing, really?), it's just stupid. Immature. I'm a grown man. A man in a suit, for crying out loud, wearing a wedding ring. My attention turns to it. I twist it around my finger, feel the pressure of its smooth surface against my skin. I've always liked wearing it. Being a man-with-a-wedding-ring. It gave me confidence, made me feel like a *man*-man. A proper one. It used to, in any case.

OK, stop this now. Now. You know where this can lead.

The door opens behind us. I turn around, expecting to see Werner, the copywriter who can spell. But it's Annie, a clever young intern. She's balancing a tray with two steaming cups of coffee on it.

'Thought we'd need some more,' says Bill.

'Can I help?' Annie asks eagerly, nodding towards the screens as she places the paper cups on the table. She often does this, tries to make herself useful. I feel a bit sorry for her, this bright girl who aspires to work here. *Aspires* to. Incredible.

'No,' Bill says monosyllabically, without looking away from the screen.

Annie's smile droops slightly.

'Actually, Annie,' I say, desperately trying to come up with something for her to do. 'Could you pop over to the graphic designer teams? Tell them to start thinking something up for Senesi? They'll find the photos in the shared Dropbox folder.' This task will take her about three minutes. It's clearly pointless, I could do it myself without leaving the meeting room, but she seems to appreciate it. Her face lights up again.

'Sure,' she says. 'I'll get right to it.' She turns to leave, but when she's halfway through the door, she stops, slaps her forehead. 'Mark,' she says, digging into her pockets, 'here, I almost forgot.'

'What is it?' I ask. Beside me, Bill snorts. He's eager to press on with the task at hand.

'Oh, just... someone downstairs. They left a note for you.'

'A note?' I frown. When was the last time I received a note? Annie pushes a folded piece of paper into my hand, then heads off again. 'If you need anything, just call,' she says with a wide, hopeful smile.

'*If you need anything neh neh neh,*' Bill echoes below his breath in a mocking falsetto once she's left. He shows no interest in the note I hold in my hand. 'Can we crack on with this now, Mark?'

'Yes,' I answer. I'm not entirely sure what he just said. I'm busy staring at the sheet of paper sitting in my open palm. It's folded in the middle, lengthways, and the corners match up perfectly. Minute bumps in the surface gave me an upside-down, mirror image of the words scrawled within. There's something about it, both simple and unsettling.

Inside, this:

A little bird told me this is where you work.
Fancy a coffee?

-Alice.

Heart thumping, I run my eyes along these few lines, first hurriedly, then slowly, tracing the contours of her handwriting, looping around the *l*s, blinking at the dots above the *i*s. I succeed, but only just, in stopping myself from bringing the note to my nose, probing for any trace of her scent.

There's guilt, too. It's noisy, but distant, like a coming storm. But it ain't here yet. Here, it's just sunshine and joy. I'm fifteen again, thrilled by the inexplicable mystery of a woman wanting to spend time with me. If Bill weren't here, I might be jumping up and down.

Before I know it, I'm standing. My hand is pressing against the glass door, pushing it open.

Bill throws a pen on the table, hard, and it clatters over the edge. 'Oh, what *now*?' he asks.

'I need half an hour,' I say.

Bill's jaw drops. Not figuratively: it actually drops. He stares at me with wide eyes, lips unable to form a sentence. I look away, because I realise I might burst out laughing. Which, given his mood, would be rather unwise. 'Be right back,' I add.

'Mark. What. The. Fuck,' he says. But I'm already through the door.

In the corridor, I bump into Werner, the literate copywriter, on his way towards Meeting Room A. 'Bill's waiting for you,' I say. He's about to reply, slightly startled by my brisk pace. I walk past him. It all seems so meaningless all of a sudden. Senesi, the new collection, my job. All of it insubstantial.

Offices, doors, people, desks, voices, phone calls. They all flash past, like weightless annoyances. Someone calls out to me; I don't stop. I'm in the lift, not entirely sure how I got here. My thumb presses the ground-floor button again and again, even as the lift begins to move. I realise I'm smiling.

It's just a coffee, I tell myself. *A fun, innocent coffee. Nothing wrong with that.* Something inside me (something I shut up very quickly) says the coffee isn't the problem. My smile might very well be, though.

It's innocent, I insist. Just a coffee.

I turn towards the mirror, check myself out in the reflection. I fix my hair, set my shoulders. I like what I see. A handsome, if not stunning, man in his late thirties. In a suit. A confident man. A man who smiles. Would my wife recognise me now?

A hushed *ding* tells me I'm on the ground floor. The doors part with a hiss, revealing the bustling lobby. A scattered crowd is transiting here, coming, going, all very busy. Expensive shiny shoes. Expensive casual T-shirts. Expensive designer handbags. People talking into phones. Others are escorting important clients. A glimpse into the dynamic world of free trade and business.

I peer beyond. Towards an opening door, where a body I hardly know, but somehow already know so well, is just leaving. I run, *run*, towards her, muttering apologies to those I shove aside, unable to take my eyes off her. She's stopped just beyond the entrance, on the equally crowded pavement outside. I watch as she turns left, then right, undecided maybe. Not quite knowing where to go now that I haven't shown up. This woman has come for me. I watch her, her dark hair, her mesmerising figure. The way she bites her full lips, momentarily lost in thought. The way she turns when my fingers brush against her shoulder. Somehow, I'm there, standing beside her. I'm still smiling. Now she is too.

'Hey,' she says.

5

I once read in some silly article that you should never take someone out to dinner or to the cinema if it's your first date together. You can, of course, but it might work against you. What you want to do (the article claimed) is share a thrilling experience: a roller-coaster ride at an amusement park, or go rafting maybe. That sort of thing. Why? Because, according to this particular hack, the rush your date will feel will somehow get muddled up in their mind and be interpreted as arousal. You'll leave a mark in their subconscious—all that heart-pounding euphoria, that breathless giddy feeling, associated with you, forever.

My heart is racing now. I am surprisingly euphoric, although I hope it doesn't show. We're not whizzing by on a roller coaster—we're simply waiting in front of a busy coffee stand a couple of streets from my office. Standing there with yet another cup of steaming coffee in my hand, and this is the giddiest I've been in... who knows how long? It might just be the caffeine. I doubt it.

'Bit creepy maybe?' Alice says, then rests her lips against

the rim of the cup, their corners curled in a smile. 'Me turning up at your office like this? Did I unsettle you?'

I love the word *unsettle*. I love that she'd go for it.

'Yes,' I say. 'You're creepy. And I'm unsettled.'

She giggles. 'Let's walk,' she says.

Let's walk. And it's as simple as that. Walk we do, through crowds and voices, to nowhere in particular. I catch glimpses of people, both men and women, sneaking glances at us. We look good together. I feel tall, handsome, charming. Alice is wearing a short, plain grey skirt, and a red shirt. Her thick black hair sways gently with every step. Her beauty has me smiling. The rhythm of our pace is hypnotic. Sometimes I lead, but mostly she does, like loose dancers who are in no particular hurry.

I think I should ask her how she found out where I work. I recite the words in my mind (*How did you know?* or, *Who told you?*), trying to articulate them in such a way that they don't sound harsh. But no, I can't. It's too predictable, too normal. That's not what this is about. It's not what *we're* about.

'Quit smoking yet?' I say.

She laughs. 'Working on it.' She raises a hand, points towards a bench by the river. 'Let's sit there.'

She sits on the right, I sit on the left. Between us, our two steaming coffees.

There's a brief pause, but it's not uncomfortable. Before us, the Thames flows grey and fast.

'Mark,' she says, a finger pressed against her cheek, lost in thought. Trying the word out, as if tasting a wine. 'Hm.' She crosses her arms, puts on a frown and, in a mock-angry voice, says, '*Mark!*'

I laugh, raise my hands. 'You got me.'

Next, she opens her mouth in an O, presses her open palms at its sides. 'Oh *Maaark!*' She stretches my name to three syllables, shaking her head in surprise, eyes wide. 'You shouldn't have got me *that*. Why, it's *far* too expensive!'

I was taking a sip of the coffee as she said this. My stomach contracts in a fit of laughter. I try to contain it for fear of spitting out the coffee. Which, of course, makes it worse.

Alice seems pleased with her childish little game. I wonder what the next inflection is going to be, when she gently lifts her coffee, moving it out of the way. She shuffles closer, eyes fixed on mine. Her scent fills my nostrils, my mouth.

We're inches away. She lays a hand on my knee and whispers, with a rich, creamy voice, 'Hmm, *Mark*.' Her eyebrow rises ever so faintly as she says this.

My name on her breath, the closeness, her hand on my body. I'm suddenly flooded with images of breathless sex and knotted sheets. Which, I suspect, was her precise intention.

Or perhaps not. She throws her head back and laughs. Lips red, teeth white. I laugh too, slightly uneasily this time.

'Yes,' she says, nodding approvingly. 'I like it. Good name.' She seems to find the compliment amusing and lets out a little giggle. 'Good name,' she says again. 'A *man's* name.' She considers my suit. I straighten my tie, suddenly self-conscious. 'A man who dresses like a man,' she adds with a smile, looking up at me. Her eyes are so clear, so *unencumbered*. I see the cloudless sky in them. 'I like that, too.'

She slides away a little, picks up her coffee again.

I wish we were alone. Far from the city, somewhere intimate, with no appointments to attend. This desire is so strong I almost say it out loud.

Alice has closed her eyes. She tilts her head back slightly, a gentle breeze catching a lock of her hair.

'I miss the sea,' she says with a little sigh.

'I have a place by the sea,' I say before I even realise. It came out fast, almost desperate. It doesn't matter, she seems to appreciate the fact.

'*Really?*'

'Yup.' I take a sip of coffee, stare at the river. Images of Lilac House flood in. Alice and I walking along the beach, barefoot, shoes dangling from our hands. The rustle of the pebbles under our feet. Then, later, the two of us in the cottage, in front of the fireplace. I feel an unexpected rush of adrenalin.

Even in my enthusiastic state, I can't get myself to speak the obvious follow-up: *want to go?*

(*I'm not that kind of man.*)

When I turn back towards her, I notice she's looking at my hand, the one holding the cup. But no, it's not the hand—she's staring at my wedding ring. I hunt for traces of sadness, but there are none. Not even remorse, the guilt people should feel when flirting with someone who is married. But there is *something.* Her eyebrows are drawn close, like someone trying to solve a riddle, or piece together the clues of some deep mystery.

Alice tears her gaze from my finger, clears her throat. I happen to do it at exactly the same time, an echoed, throaty awkwardness. And just like that, that awkwardness is gone. We both laugh and shake our heads. I wish I could hold her hand.

I'm thinking about a weekend away from it all, alone with Alice, at Lilac House. It's our little place in Dorset: stone walls and green grass and, a minute's walk away, the restless waters of Blackwood Cove and the sea.

'That would be nice,' Alice says. She's reading my thoughts. I smile because, yes, it *would* be nice. My heartbeat picks up, I hold my breath. I'm about to say it, to invite her over, as if I were a single man, as unencumbered as her eyes are. As if that house were mine alone and not the getaway my wife and I have shared so many times before. We used to be so happy, in Lilac House.

I'm about to utter the invitation, when Alice suddenly stands up, her perfect figure now vertical. Her waist is level with my eyes. I want to reach out and kiss it. Or bite it.

'Shall we do this again?' she asks.

'That would be nice,' I say, echoing her words from moments ago.

'I gotta rush,' she says, without looking at her watch. I notice she isn't wearing one. 'Have a wonderful day, Mark.'

'Likewise.' I begin to stand, but by the time I have, Alice has already set off, walking fast.

I fix my eyes on her, the swaying hair, the toned legs. Her scent is fading too quickly. *Please turn around*, I think, childishly, incapable of looking away. She's about to vanish into the crowd, but just before she's swallowed by the flow of pedestrians, her head spins round. I watch as she brings two fingers to her lips and blows me a kiss.

IT'S TWELVE THIRTY. The Senesi people are likely already in the office. I check my phone and see three missed calls and a long string of foul messages from Bill. For some reason, it doesn't bother me. In fact, the only thing I can think of, looking at my phone, is that I don't even have Alice's number.

It's okay, I suppose. There's something magical about not knowing how to contact her. Like something from another era. At the same time, I can't help but feel a slight panic, a sharp longing already setting in.

I clear my thoughts. It's okay, isn't it? I don't really need to get in touch with her. Despite this feeling in my chest, it was just an innocent coffee with a nice woman. A pretty woman. We hardly even talked.

I look up and happen to notice a car going a little too fast.

The driver, a man in his forties, is distracted, going through the glove compartment, eyes off the road. My eyes shift to the right, closer to me, and see a little old lady crossing the road. She hasn't noticed the car racing towards her. Her face is pointed downwards, towards her hesitant feet there, carefully measuring out each step. She's holding two oversized shopping bags in her hands.

A brief instant in which time appears to stop for everyone else but them. The nervous man at the wheel and the small lady in his way. Neither have noticed the other.

Before I know it, I'm shouting, 'Watch out!' and leaping into the road. I grab the lady and pull her backwards, towards me, her frail body falling into mine. She smells like tobacco and talcum powder.

The driver's heard my warning. His face turns almost comically pale as he stares through the windscreen and sees where he's headed. He brakes hard, and the tyres let out a long, anxious screech. People's heads turn towards us. Someone screams.

The car comes to a shaky halt only inches from us. The man in the car looks at me with terror and bewilderment in his eyes, jaw hanging open. He blinks, unbelieving, then shakes his head apologetically. His lips articulate a feeble, 'S-sorry.'

'You saved my life,' the old woman says. She's holding one hand pressed against her chest while clasping my arm with the other. She looks at me with the strangely childlike eyes of the elderly. Tears are gathering inside them.

'*You saved my life!*' she calls out, louder now.

'It's nothing,' I say.

'*Nothing?*' she wails incredulously, turning to the people gathered on the pavement nearby. 'You... saved my *life*.'

I kneel down to collect a few things that have fallen out of her shopping bags. The little old lady is describing the event to the bystanders. As she does, she refers to me as a 'hero'.

Pride balloons inside my chest, like a searing sun. I'm slightly embarrassed, but this feels nice.

'Good job, mate,' a young man calls out. He shoots a dirty look at the driver, who's still too baffled to know what to do.

I place the woman's items in her bags, then pat her delicately. 'I'm glad you're okay,' I say.

'Thank you... thank you,' she says, now through tears. She nods thoughtfully and adds, 'You're a good man.'

As I walk off, I feel the eyes of the bystanders on me. I turn towards the bewildered driver and say sternly, 'Drive carefully.' Someone actually cheers. I feel like a knight in shining armour, walking off towards the sunset. All wrongs righted in my wake.

You're a good man.

Yes, I am.

6

W hen I step into the meeting room, I'm twenty minutes late. Bill greets me with a hate-spewing smile. 'Ah, Mark, welcome.'

The two teams sit on opposite sides of the large conference table. Two of ours (three, now I'm here) and three from Senesi.

On our first meeting, I was expecting them to turn up looking like the cast of *The Sopranos*. Mainly because the Italian mob is known to appreciate Senesi suits. I pictured them as loud, brash, overweight. But they weren't anything like that. Senesi's people are placid Italian men, with small builds and soft voices. They smile often. None of our clients are quite as meticulous about their work as they are. They're nice people.

All of them except Morino, of course. And, unfortunately, he's the only one who matters.

'Sorry I'm late,' I say, without providing an explanation. It might be because of Alice, or my heroic life-saving feat, but I feel slightly giddy. My heart is bursting with unexpected confidence.

The Italians say hello, seemingly undisturbed by my late-
ness. Morino, on the other hand, dips his chin almost imperceptibly, lips twisted in a cold smirk. I know I've offended
him. Right now, I don't care.

'We've been through our first two copy proposals,' says
Bill, nodding towards the screen. Beyond the words, his tone
is informing me that we're screwed.

Morino lets out a sigh. 'I must say, Mark, we're not
impressed.' By that, he means *he's* not impressed.

Werner, the copywriter, squirms in his seat. His eyes are
fixed on the table, and he looks no one in the eyes. The poor
kid is terrified.

'I see,' I say cheerfully, looking Morino in the eyes. He's a
small, neat man, emanating natural elegance. His hair is just
a faint shadow above the ears and neck, while a wide bald
patch reveals the taut skin on his head. His face is a collection
of minute features: sharp eyes, sharp lips, sharp chin. A face
that can cut. He wears his suit as if he were born in it.

'Do you want to pick it up from here, Mark?' Bill asks me,
perhaps as a punishment for being late.

'Sure,' I say, still staring Morino in the eyes. Bill slides the
laptop towards me. The presentation slide contains the third
slogan proposal. Our last hope. It's not projected on the
screen yet. An elegant font declaring

RomAmor. Wear passion.

Weak.

I tap a quick rhythm on the table with my fingers,
weighing my options. I'm aware of the silence in the room.

'No,' I say, shutting the laptop. 'We're not going with that.'
Eyes dart towards me. Even Werner is shocked enough to
look up.

I join my index fingers and rest them on my lips, as if

deep in thought. Truth is, I've decided to wing this. Turning towards our guests, I ask, 'May I speak honestly?'

Morino gives a little wave of the hand. 'That would be a first at BeeCreative,' he says with a chuckle. 'Please do.'

'Right. These slogans are based on your input, *Signor* Morino.' I give that *Signor* my best. A hesitation in his stern look suggests he appreciates it. 'But,' I continue, 'your input is bad.' There's a collective intake of air. Terrified glances darting from me to Morino and back, stirring the atmosphere in the room like a sour cocktail. I push on. 'They're worse than bad, sir. They are off-topic. Unrepresentative of the Senesi brand and of this collection. Bill—' I turn towards him. My movements feel smooth, dance-like. I decide to involve him. Perhaps so he can share the victory if my little stunt works out. Or maybe just to see him agonise at the idea of being associated with whatever it is I'm about to say. 'Shall I go with our *own* idea?'

Bill trembles a nod, barely concealing a frown. 'S-sure. Go ahead.' *What the hell are you doing, Mark?*

'Thanks. *Signor* Morino, as we see it, this collection is about sophistication.' I begin pacing around the room, hands open, as if to pluck the fruits of inspiration from thin air. 'It's about taking your time. About choosing meticulousness over haste.' I have no idea what I'm saying. Except maybe I do. 'It's about confidence in the time-tested values of tradition, sobriety and taste. It's a refusal of anything done just for the sake of it, with no thought or commitment.' Morino is staring at me intently, one hand on his chin, the other wrapped around his narrow chest. He likes what he's hearing, but he's not made his mind up yet: is this just marketing bullshit, or is there something to it?

We're about to find out, I think. *Me included.*

It's time to come up with the slogan. The single line of copy that will make or break this account. 'The RomAmor collection isn't mere fashion wear,' I say. 'It's a lot more than that—it's *passionwear*.' I quite like this, and I could stop here, but I keep going. 'Boiled down to its very essence, it tells us one thing, and one thing alone...'

A long pause. I have no idea what it is until it flows through my lips.

'*Don't just do it. Do it* Italiano.'

Silence.

It's a silence we're used to, one in which things could go either way. The tense seconds preceding the client's verdict. Until then, our ideas are neither good nor bad, approved or discarded. They live in a Schrödinger's cat marketing wasteland.

'RomAmor passionwear,' whispers Morino. It's like Alice tasting my name earlier, feeling it roll off her tongue. 'Rom-Amor passionwear—don't just do it, do it Italiano...'

He sniffs, twitches his mouth. Then, gradually, a creeping smile lights up his features. Across from Morino, Bill has been holding his breath so long, his face has turned red. 'I think we have a winner, Mark,' Morino says. His tone is that of someone conceding defeat. 'I have to admit, I like it.'

'You-know-who might complain about the "just do it" reference, cause a bit of a storm, but there's no such thing as bad publicity, is there?' Bill says, relief flowing off him in waves.

Everyone stands. Hands are shaken. When it's my turn to exchange a handshake with Morino, he leans close and whispers, 'BeeCreative being creative, for once. Good work.' I accept his words with a smile.

Once they've left the meeting room, Bill collapses into a chair. He looks at me and shakes his head. 'Not sure how you pulled that one off, Mark. Not sure why you'd stroll in here half an hour late, smiling like you just got a blow job from Ronald McDonald'—he lets out a long whistle—'but if this is what happens when you do, well, please go ahead, mate. Fill yer boots.'

'Will do.'

Bill's smile is darkened by a frown. 'You're acting strange, my friend. You gone insane or something?'

7

On the train. The ride home is a strange one today. Coming down from this morning's high, things appear quite different. The carriage sways and, with every jittery motion, so does my view of things—Alice the intriguing possibility, the temptation worth pursuing. And then: Alice the unforgivable waste of time. The path best avoided.

It's almost an hour's ride home. I try to get comfortable in my seat, sneak glances at my fellow travellers. I'm sitting between a teenager carrying a large cello case and an elderly black woman in beautiful African garb. Our bodies rock gently from side to side.

The boy opens a book of sheet music and begins to read it the same way I'd do with a novel, his foot tapping the tempo lightly against the floor. I glance discreetly at those symbols, that alphabet of sound, and envy him a little for understanding them. He has a neat haircut, this boy, an almost perfectly straight line cutting horizontally just above the clean neck. He's, what, sixteen? A difficult age, but he seems quite comfortable in his skin. I wonder why he chose to play a classical instrument rather than an electric one, or some music software on the computer.

His phone buzzes in his pocket (I like him even more, now, for muting it on the tube). He glances at the name on the screen and lets out a brief, annoyed sigh. 'Mum, I'm on the tube,' he says, picking up. 'On my way back, OK? Yes... pasta is fine. Yes... *Yes.*' He hesitates briefly, then adds, 'Love you.' Before putting the phone away, he taps the settings and mutes it completely, disabling the vibration. When he opens the sheet music again, I feel his muscles relax.

I close my eyes. For some reason, I conjure up an image of this boy's mother. I'm sleepy, and she comes to me as someone from the fifties, like a woman from one of those old ads, those old-fashioned tins of chocolates. A white apron and a crisp, light blue shirt beneath it. Blonde hair. Unreal, almost farcical. She's making dinner for her son, and she's proud of him, you can read it in her movements. I want to tell her she's right, that I too would be proud, because her boy has a healthy interest in music, he's quiet and polite, and although there's no way for me to know, I'm sure he's talented too.

Then my mind's eye focuses on this mother's face. To my surprise, it's Cecilia. A happy Cecilia, greeting me—her husband, and now the father of this young musician—with a wide smile and a soft embrace. 'Welcome home,' she says to us both. 'Welcome home.'

The voice on the speakers announces the current stop, and I realise I must have fallen asleep, because the boy is gone. I crane my neck, try to spot him on the platform outside, but all I see is blackness and the jagged reflections of the remaining passengers. We depart the station and head on, and that vision of Cecilia as a happy mother haunts me, tempts me with the possibility of it. There is a set of words and actions, of motions and thoughts that can still bring us together. That can still make us parents.

The train is approaching my stop. I stand in front of the doors with my briefcase in hand. I feel a quiver in my leg, where Alice laid her hand this morning. When she touched me there and said my name and I could almost have kissed her.

I can't do this, I think. *I can't do this.*

For the second time today, I tell myself to forget this woman. She's been a beautiful distraction, a thrilling thought, but this is not who I am. I'm a married man. A married man who saves old ladies, at that.

I walk through the station and catch a glimpse of my face in a window. My eyes are puffy and my hair unruly. Cecilia sometimes says that exhaustion suits me, makes me sexier (she used to, anyway). In the lift on my way to the coffee with Alice this morning, I saw the reflection of someone eager for novelty. This, now, is the weary face of a committed husband. A trustworthy one.

A pleasant breeze welcomes me outside the station as I make my way home. It's a short walk, five minutes through quiet streets with lush green hedges, family homes on either side. Suburban mums, dads and children, getting ready for dinner.

The thought occurs to me that I should grow a beard. I always thought I'd grow one once I'd become a dad. Not sure why, my father never had one. But maybe I've got it the wrong way round—maybe, it's not fatherhood that leads to a beard, but the opposite. Perhaps if I grew one now, it would somehow magically unlock fatherhood, help us become parents. Happy ones.

The house is close, just round the corner, and I'm walking faster now, heels loud against the pavement, suddenly eager to be with Cecilia. Here it is: the front door. I thrust the key in and step into the house as if propelled by a wave, like a harbinger of good news—*Things will be all right, Cecilia. I shall grow a beard, and we shall have a child, and we will be happy again.*

The house is in shadow.

'Hello,' I say merrily, but the smile on my face has already cracked. The happiness I felt but an instant ago is fading, rapidly deflating inside my chest like a balloon. The atmosphere in our house can do that sometimes.

Cecilia is lying on the sofa. She mumbles a greeting, without looking up. Standing in the entrance, I take my jacket off, undo my tie, and study my wife. All I can see from here is her long hair cascading from the armrest, a knee rising halfway along the sofa, a foot resting on the opposite armrest. Pieces of her. I can't see her face.

Cecilia goes through intensely sad days at times. I don't know if *depression* is an appropriate word to describe her state on these occasions. It might be. I round the sofa, and there's something in the way her body is arranged on the cushions that gives me pause. There's an eerie stillness about her, and for an instant, Cecilia looks like a corpse.

'I think I might grow a beard,' I say, still trying to keep up the merry tone. It's meant to come across like one of those quirky, unexpected things you say to someone you love. Like in the early days: all the effort I put into dazzling Cecilia, with the turns of phrase, the little surprises. They used to make her smile. Now, she throws a detached look my way, then pulls out her phone and starts flicking through it. Its light is cold, hollow. 'Don't be stupid,' she says.

I don't know why, but her dismissing this little idea of the beard really hurts. I stand there, feeling this silent rage poke about inside me, rubbing its sharp edges against my stomach. I walk to the wall and flick the light on, relieved to see the shadows vanish. How can she just lie there in the darkness?

What has she been doing all today? Sometimes I wish she had a proper job. Independent art curators have too much time on their hands.

I sit down beside her. She shifts her legs out of the way, making room for me, then rests her feet in my lap. It could be a tender gesture. It could simply be a mechanical one. I lean forward and kiss her delicately on the knee. My lips press against her perfect skin, and I'm not sure what I feel. What I *should* feel. We hardly touch each other since we lost the baby.

She's staring at the screen, head resting against a cushion. I wonder what my body feels like to her. It's a strange sort of proximity we have. One made of immeasurable distances.

Out of nowhere, I remember the old lady, my heroic life-saving feat from this morning. I consider telling Cecilia about it, but I'm afraid the story might fall flat, leave her indifferent, so I stay silent.

'Rub my feet?' she asks, and I do.

I place my hands on her left foot, begin working it with my thumbs. Tendons shift and skin slides beneath them. I knead and stretch gently and suddenly feel very alone. For an instant, my fingers are wrapped tight around her ankle, and I wonder what it would feel like if this were her throat.

8

It's been three days since my meeting with Alice. I haven't heard from her since our coffee on the bench. Sometimes, it's a relief. But I catch myself at times feeling a restless, shapeless longing, a void in my stomach.

At lunchtime, I decline an invitation from Bill and a few others on the Senesi team and sneak out alone. I walk through the multitude of suits and ties and casual clothes and think I'm just as faceless as they are today. I wouldn't notice myself if I walked past.

I order a coffee at the same kiosk I visited with Alice, still expecting her to pop up and flash her heart-warming smile. We'd slip straight into the comfortable, flirty happiness we've shared, as if we hadn't been apart for more than five minutes. I know we would. I look out for her, my body almost sensing her presence, almost *knowing* she'll turn up any minute now.

She doesn't.

Our bench is taken by two kids with skateboards (*our* bench?), so I take the one beside it. The coffee is good, the river dark.

It's at times like these, when I'm alone and unseen, that I start thinking about Claire.

The *other* woman.

'MARK?'

I was sitting in the arrivals at Edinburgh Airport, distractedly reading a mystery novel. I kept having to go back and read the last sentence, lulled into a half-sleeping state by the silence surrounding me. I'd flown in on the first daily flight from London, and the waiting area was surprisingly deserted. Outside, the skies were grey, rain pattering against the broad windows. Other than the occasional shuffle of feet and the buzz of strollers on the linoleum, a padded quiet filled the space.

Then my name and that question mark. Looking back, I picture this moment as being full of meaning: my name called into question, and with it my identity, my self. The uncomfortable doubt that shakes all your certainties—*who am I?*

None of this crossed my mind back then, of course. I simply looked up and saw Claire Anderson for the first time. She was standing there, a hand extended, a smile on her lips. There was mischief in that smile. At least, so it seems now. Pearl white teeth, blonde hair, a prosperous figure wrapped in office attire. She had the sort of face you can't help smiling back at. The glowing pinks and reds, the conspiratorial eyes. I stood and shook her hand.

'You're taller than I thought,' she said. That's all it takes to win my approval: a compliment. I can be weak.

'Sorry I'm late. Got caught up in the office,' she added. Then, noticing the book in my hand, 'Any good?'

'Great, actually. A classic—*Strangers on a Train*. You read it?'

Claire looked at the title on the cover, a single, perfect wrinkle creasing the smooth skin between her eyes. She shook her head. 'Nope. Never heard of it. I was just being polite. I'm not really the book type.' She laughed, and I couldn't help but laugh too. I'm fascinated by people who have no interest in reading.

'Better get going,' she said. 'The Simmons InfoSystems meeting is scheduled for three thirty. We've got a few hours to get ready.'

I'd never been to the Edinburgh office (haven't been back since), and the prospect of working alongside people I'd only ever exchanged emails with made me uncomfortable. I rarely *connect* with people. But Claire... she had a way of making you feel instantly welcome, comfortable. There was something in the milky quality of her skin, the friendly smile, her generous bosom that made you want to be close to her. Not exactly (or not only) in a sexual way. She was magnetic. I could see why the execs had picked her to handle the important American client.

We stepped out into the rain, and Claire waved to a car waiting nearby. As it approached, I noticed the hideous green and yellow of the BeeCreative logo on its side. We both sat in the back, my case between us.

'Well, I hope you appreciate the warm Scottish welcome,' she said with an apologetic smile.

'Actually, I find it quite... cosy.' It was true.

Claire laughed. A loud, untroubled laugh that made dimples blossom on her cheeks. 'Well,' she said, eyes locked onto mine, 'you're easy to please.'

I returned an uneasy smile, not quite knowing what she meant by those words. Was this innuendo of some sort?

Looking down, I noticed she, unlike me, was wearing a wedding ring. For some reason, I felt relief.

I shouldn't have.

. . .

ONE OF THE two skater boys scrunches up a can of Coke. The metallic sound tears me from my daydreaming. I'm not in Edinburgh anymore, I'm back on the bench by the river.

Bending his skinny arm back, the boy hurls the tin towards the Thames. He doesn't throw it hard enough, however, and it falls short, striking the pavement. The other one laughs a croaky, mocking laugh, and they get up to leave.

When they've gone, I peer over at the bench they were sitting on. Throwing a quick, guilty look around me, I get up and walk towards it. I try to look casual, but my steps feel awkward, ashamed, as if what I'm up to were clear to anyone watching.

(What *am* I up to?)

I sit on the bench, and holding my breath, I move my hand to the spot where Alice was sitting the other day. I run my fingers along the wood, feeling the bumps in its uneven surface, trying to capture the ghost of her presence.

Wait. What am I doing? I'm not fifteen, for Christ's sake.

I know nothing about this woman. What if she's a psycho? It is a *bit* weird how she tracked me down so quickly, so eagerly, isn't it? Would that be OK if she were man? It's the sort of thing a stalker would do, isn't it? Show up at your office unannounced, having only met you once. What if she *is* a stalker? What if she's playing some twisted game with me?

But that's a whole load of *if*s. How likely is it, really? OK, I don't know her well or anything, but she simply doesn't strike me as, well, a nutcase.

Still, even setting aside the stalker scenario, I shouldn't really be here, sighing over a woman like this, should I? It's ridiculous. She's clearly not that interested in me, anyway. Otherwise, she'd have shown up, right? Three days and not a word.

I open my eyes and look down at the bench. It's covered in key-scratch etchings declaring love or hate or simply 'fuck'— fuck this person, this team, this political party. Jagged lines and splinters.

I have to get back to the office, I tell myself. But as I stand, one of the messages on the bench catches my eye. I hadn't noticed it, at first, because it's been traced where I was just sitting.

It takes me a second to understand what I'm looking at. When I do, my heart skips a beat. Or three. There, not etched but written out in black marker, I read these words:

Nice coffee, wasn't it?
Same time next week?

-Alice

Minutes later, I'm walking back towards the office. My pace is fast, the grim London skies suddenly beautiful.

I had no pen, but below her message, I scratched a trembling:

Yes! -Mark

To do it, I used the keys to the house. The one I share with my wife.

9

Pub night tonight. My phone rings as I'm about to open the front door of the King's Head. It's a message. I tap through and see it's from Ed.

Lilly's come down with a bit of a cold. Don't think I can make it tonight. Sorry, mate.

I sigh and slip the phone back inside my pocket. My hand is still resting on the thick wooden door. It's open, but just a crack. I consider turning back and going home. Phil won't have bothered turning up, I'm sure of it. So that would leave me and Clyde. Alone. A mildly depressing prospect, if I'm honest.

I clench my teeth, hesitating. Thing is, I'm restless. Some previously untapped source of energy seems to have burst into my system ever since reading Alice's message engraved in the bench. I can't sit still. The idea of spending another evening on the sofa, next to a silent Cecilia (she's been colder than usual lately), is daunting. Almost as daunting as spending it with Clyde.

A pang of guilt hits me. This is *Clyde* I'm talking about. One of my closest and oldest friends. There was a time when I valued friendship above all else, now here I am, trying to find an excuse to stand him up. I square my shoulders, push the door open, and step into the sour air and clatter of the King's Head.

Clyde is sitting in front of a half-drunk pint. He's bent over his phone, bearlike, looking gloomy. He's wearing a faded T-shirt, the large bulge of his belly resting in his lap. As I watch, he mumbles something to himself. Clyde always wears cheap clothes. Everything he owns is cheap, trashy, second rate. Even the phone he's peering into. When did things go wrong for Clyde? I don't know. I look at him and realise that, if I didn't know him, he might strike me as a weirdo. Someone to avoid.

'Hey, buddy,' I say, walking up to our table. It's always the same one, in the far corner, by the window. When he sees me, his eyes fill with what appears to be genuine relief. 'Hey! Good to see you, man. Good to see you.' We clasp hands, pat backs.

'Let me get you a pint,' he says as I sit down, shifting his considerable weight. 'Be right back.'

It's a busy night at the King's Head. It's not a fancy place, nor a particularly popular one, but it attracts people of all ages. The music isn't too loud, and the atmosphere is warm. It's a nice place to hang out.

I realise my knee is bouncing up and down, and I keep rubbing my hands. I'm excited, and I can't wait for next week, my next coffee with Alice. Right now, while Clyde is away fetching my drink, I'm simply bursting to tell him all about her. All my thoughts seem to veer towards her, no matter what I'm doing. I can't, of course, but that's how I feel.

When he returns, he's carrying two beers, although the one he left at the table is still half full. 'So it's just you and me,' he says in a jolly tone. He raises his glass, and I bump mine against it. 'To us.'

I take a long sip. The cool beer feels good, a mild sedative for my excited state. 'So,' I ask, wiping away a beer moustache, 'how're things?'

'Oh, you know.' Clyde brings a balled fist to his mouth and lets out a quiet burp. 'Same old, same old.'

I nod and I smile, and wonder what the heck we're going to talk about, when—there it is again—that urge to talk about Alice, to share this electrifying load with someone. This is dangerous.

A pretty woman in her thirties walks past our table. She has long dark hair that sways gently with every step. She smiles a polite smile at us and walks up to a small group by the bar. Clyde's looking at her.

'Pretty, eh?' I say, with a nod in her direction. It's not the kind of comment I'd usually make, but if I can't talk about *the* woman, talking about this woman might provide some relief.

Clyde's eyes dart towards me, surprised. I throw up a hand. 'Hey, just pointing out the obvious. Pretty woman. That's it.'

He hesitates, studying me. 'Yeah. She is.'

I'm not quite sure why he'd react like that—as if I'd offended him. I know he fancies Cecilia, always has, so he can be protective about her. But still.

I watch as he leans his elbows against the table, opens his mouth to talk, then shuts it again, picks up the glass.

'What is it?' I ask.

'Well, it's just... I mean, tell me if this is out of order, mate, if you'd rather not discuss it...' Small beads of sweat have formed on his forehead. He's been avoiding my eyes.

'Go on. It's all right, I'll tell you. What is it?'

'I was just wondering... you know... um...' He's really having a hard time with this. I extend my hands towards him, inviting him to continue. He gives it another shot. 'I... just wanted to ask you, mate... how things are going. Between you and Cecilia, I mean.' Having spoken, he immediately reaches out for the glass again, takes an eager drag. Washing away the words.

Why would he ask me that? I wonder. Something inside me also wonders: *Does he somehow know about Alice?*

I try to read his expression, interpret it, but all I see is sweat and nerves and unease. I speak, my voice level. 'Everything's fine.' I take a sip of my own beer. 'Why?'

Clyde digs his nail into the table and starts scratching at it. When he talks, his eyes are still averted. 'I know it must have been... um, *difficult*, what Cecilia's been through—what you've *both* been through,' he corrects himself quickly. 'I was wondering if maybe, you know, you might give it another go. For a baby.' After that last word (baby), he goes for the glass again. Takes a long, gurgling drag.

There's a moment's silence. Uncomfortable silence. I'm not sure how to reply to him. Nor am I sure why he'd ever ask me such a question. I'm reserved. He knows I'm reserved (all my friends do) and that this isn't the sort of thing I like to talk about. Especially during what is meant to be a merry night out with a mate.

I clear my throat. 'No. Not at the moment, in any case.'

(This is an understatement, because I've lost count of how long it's been since I last had sex with my wife. I feel it might just continue this way indefinitely.)

'Oh. OK,' he says with a little shrug. Now he's acting as if it was just a casual question. Why is he asking me this?

'Why are you asking me this, Clyde?'

He looks at me like a rabbit caught in the headlights. An obese rabbit. Then he immediately focuses his eyes on the glass. He rubs the condensation off it with his sausage thumb. 'I thought maybe you'd like to talk about it. That's all.'

'I don't. Not really.'

''K. No worries.'

We let the chatter of the pub fill the silence for a while, and I know this is more uncomfortable for Clyde than it is for me. I'm inflicting it on him. I watch him squirm, shuffle his fat arse in the seat, scratch imaginary itches, twitch his nose. I could stop this at any moment, but I let it hang, this silence, this punishment. Clyde is vulnerable—he needs allies, friends. He's desperate for friendship.

'Tell me about one of those times we went camping,' I say, an apology of sorts in my voice.

He reacts exactly as I thought he would: a hesitant look my way, a smile tentatively spreading on his lips. Then he starts talking.

As always, I can't remember much of the story he's telling me. I wonder how it is that Clyde knows the child me better than I do. There's not much in the *Times we went camping* drawer in my memory. I know we'd sometimes be invited to the place Phil's parents had out in the Cotswolds, and we'd set off with tents and sleeping bags, setting up camp some-where in the vast garden there, but I don't have a specific recollection of any of those nights.

I feel myself nod and smile and laugh.

10

'One for the road?' Clyde asks. We've been here for almost two hours now, and I'm beginning to feel tired.

'All right.' The tingling excitement summoned by Alice's message has been tapered by Clyde's intrusive question, but it's still there. One more beer will help calm my nerves. 'I'll get it,' I say.

When I walk back, two pints in my hands, I catch him staring at the pretty woman from earlier. I feel a new wave of energy and optimism—in a world in which beautiful women left messages on riverside benches, things *can* be good. I have an idea.

'OK, listen, Clyde,' I say, sitting back down. 'You go and talk to her. Go now.'

He tears his eyes off her and frowns. 'W-what? Who?'

I take a swig. 'Oh, come on. She's beautiful, go for it.'

He laughs, but there's a hint of hurt feelings somewhere in there. As if suggesting that *he* could chat *her* up were an insult to his intelligence. 'Mark, listen—'

'No,' I interrupt him. 'You listen. She's single. No wedding ring, no boyfriend, by the looks of it.'

He shakes his head, chuckles a sour chuckle. 'Look at me, mate,' he adds, waving a hand in front of his belly.

'Well? Here's what I see: a guy who doesn't conform to stupid fitness models. A confident guy. You're large, comforting, *solid*. Not some scrawny little wimp.' I point a finger at his stomach. 'That right there says *I'll protect you. I'll hug you. A man with a belly is a caring man. A man with a soul.*'

He looks at me in disbelief, a half-smile on his lips. I press on. 'I feel like hugging you myself most of the time. In fact—' I plonk my beer on the table and grab him in a tight man-hug. And right then, perhaps because of my Alice high, I know what I'm saying is true. Clyde, whom we all secretly look down upon, would be a great husband. His huge mass feels like home. Broad shoulders and comforting rolls.

He laughs into my shoulder and returns the hug.

'Right, so,' I say, back in my seat. 'Let's do this.'

'Oh, Mark, I don't know...' He looks towards the woman. She's listening to her friends talk, a placid smile on her face. There's a controlled elegance in her movements that I find appealing.

'Listen, all right? Listen. Think of the best pickup line you've ever heard. The best.'

He rubs his hands over his eyes. 'I don't know. I honestly have no idea.'

'From a film, even. Doesn't have to be real life. What's a good line from a film?'

He picks up his beer, then something occurs to him. He smiles, sets it down again. 'Actually...'

'Go on,' I say. 'Thought of one?'

'I think so. It's yours. A line you used.'

I wasn't expecting this. 'Me? Really?'

'Yeah, mate. Serious.' He pauses, then adds, 'I always

envied your way with women.' I can't help but notice the resentment in his voice.

'Well... OK, then. What line was it?'

'We were at a party once. We were, what? Eighteen, nineteen? Anyway... we just got there, and we were making our way through the crowd, to get to the drinks. And you, oh God, how did you come up with it? So you're walking along in front of me, and this gorgeous girl, she was going in the opposite direction, staring at her phone she was, bumps into you, almost spills her drink.'

'Yeah? I can't remember this.'

'Yup. Anyway, she looks up, a bit shocked. And for a second I think she's about to tell you to watch where you're walking, say something bitchy like that, you know? But you speak first. No hesitation, you just go for it.'

'What did I say?' I'm genuinely curious. Again, it seems my past is preserved, complete, in a box in Clyde's mind.

'You said, "Oops. It's awkward when you bump into your next boyfriend, isn't it?" Bam. Ten minutes later, you were snogging on the sofa.'

I laugh, surprised. 'Really?'

He nods. 'Yes. That's you, Mark. A lady's man.'

'A lady's man,' I echo, but for some reason the words don't seem to fit me. I might have been, once, a little bit (and nothing like Phil, by the way), but not anymore. *This* me, the married me, the one who has let Cecilia define me, could never do that—dropping one-liners on passing women.

(*I'm not that sort of man.*)

I cough. 'That *was* me,' I say, wiggling my ring finger in the air.

'Oh sure, sure,' he says, raising his palms in the air.

(*Not that kind of man? What about Claire?*)

'Anyway,' I say, shaking uncomfortable thoughts away. 'There it is. You have your pickup line. Except, maybe,' I add, looking towards the woman. 'We should update it a little. We're in our late thirties. Let's go with *husband* instead of *boyfriend*, all right?'

He sighs. 'I don't know, mate. I—'

'I know. Now put that beer down, take a deep breath, then just get up, walk past her, close enough to bump into her, and deliver the line.'

He's looking at her, and I know he's actually considering it.

'Ten seconds,' I say. 'It's ten seconds of your life, my friend. And you know what? I bet it'll pay off. I bet tonight you'll end up with a gorgeous woman. And she with a great guy.' I lean forward, pat his lap. 'You deserve it, my friend. Go for it.'

His eyes float back to me. I can almost see the courage surging inside his chest. An excited smile twists his lips. He breathes a little heavily through the nose. 'All right,' he says finally. 'Fuck it.'

'Yes!' I cheer.

Clyde takes a long sip of beer, then stands. I watch incredulously as he makes his way towards the woman's little group of friends. He's large and clumsy and unattractive, but he's my friend. I know the woman is out of his league, but, at this very moment, I believe he can do this.

I hold my breath and watch him. There he is now, a couple of yards away. His stride slows down for a second; there's a hesitation.

Go on, go on, I cheer him on in my mind. He does. I watch as he straightens his back, squares his shoulders, and continues.

He follows our little plan—he walks past her, close, and lets his shoulder gently bump against her.

She doesn't turn. She just keeps chatting with her friends.

At this point, Clyde is lost. I see his confidence start to

crumble. He's stopped, standing behind her. He turns to me, instinctively, a desperate look on his face, *What now?* I stare back in horror.

One of the woman's friends, a short guy in thick glasses, notices Clyde standing there, behind her. Before Clyde can do anything, the short guy nods in his direction, and the group turns towards him. They fall silent.

The expression on the woman's face isn't hostile. A quizzical look, a hint of a smile. I see Clyde relax slightly. He clears his throat and attempts a smile of his own. I can't hear him from over here, not clearly, but I know the line.

'Oops,' he starts. 'It's awkward when you—'

At that exact moment, someone drops what sounds like a hundred glasses to the ground. They shatter loudly. Heads turn, conversations falter. The woman and her group of friends all seek out the source of the noise—it's a barman, who is now bobbing his head up and down, palms up, apologetically, kneeling to collect the fragments.

I look back at Clyde. He's still there, mouth half-open. The woman and her friends return their confused gazes to him. She leans forward, towards him, eyebrows raised. I cup a hand behind my ear, desperate to hear what she's about to say.

'Sorry, I didn't catch that,' she says. Polite.

'Oh,' Clyde says. He throws a quick glance my way, then stares at his feet. 'I was just saying that... erm...' He gathers what remains of his courage, then looks her in the eyes, a dimwit smile on his face. 'It's awkward, right? When you, erm, bump into your ex-husband? *Next* husband, I mean.' He swallows. 'Right?'

Two of her friends exchange a baffled look. The woman frowns, genuinely confused. I watch as she pushes a lock of hair behind her ear and begins to say, 'Sorry, I don't—'

But Clyde has clearly decided to end this. He goes, 'Hahasorrybyee!' Just like that. One word. His face is bright red, his eyes a bit crazy. He then turns on his heel and walks back to our table.

I can't quite think of what to say. Suddenly, I really want to go home.

'You should have done it,' he says finally, without looking at me.

'No, mate. I'm married.'

Later, walking home, a misty drizzle sets in. My mind, eager perhaps to forget Clyde's performance, turns to the thoughts I'd tried to dismiss.

SCOTLAND. It was still raining. Claire and I had spent hours trying to get our Simmons InfoSys pitch just right. We sat close, in a little meeting room inside the cosy BeeCreative Edinburgh offices.

Just as I finished reciting my part (she said I had to step in at the end, because, in her words, 'Men will let women convince them, but they need another man to seal the deal'), the office phone rang.

'Yes?' she said, picking up. The voice on the other end was distant—little croaking sounds I couldn't decipher. I resented the person it belonged to for interrupting us. I leaned back in my chair, realising how close we'd gravitated while talking.

'Hm-hm.' Claire nodded, then frowned. I watched as her eyes grew wide with incredulity. She looked at me, still holding her phone against her ear. She shook her head slowly, her face filled with a smile that suggested something had gone wrong. Yes, she was the sort of person who smiled at adversities. I suppose she never had to confront real suffering. Or maybe she was just a genuinely happy person. Or a superficial one. I don't like thinking about her, now, so it's hard for me to tell.

Her lips mouthed something, but I missed it, because I was focusing on their fullness rather than the message.

I shook my head apologetically—*Sorry?*—and gestured for her to repeat.

She covered the speaker with one hand. 'It's InfoSys. They say they can't make it. The meeting's off!' she said, in a little squeaky whisper.

I thought of Bill, back in London. If something like this had happened there—an important international meeting cancelled at the last minute by the client—he'd have been shouting and sweating and swearing. But here was this young woman smiling it away, amused rather than upset.

'All right. Yep. Sure,' she said into the phone, then hung up. For a long beat, we sat there looking at one another, me mirroring her expression. We'd spent hours prepping for this. All for nothing.

'When's your plane?' she asked.

'Ten tomorrow morning.'

'We have lots of time to kill, dear colleague,' she said. 'Fancy a drink?'

THERE'D BEEN TOO much time and too many drinks. Thinking back on it now, I see glimpses of pubs and bars, tables and bottles, Claire's Cheshire cat smile hovering behind them all.

I've done what I can to erase from my memory the words that were spoken between us that night. Not that they were particularly meaningful, mind you. In a way, they meant nothing. In a way, we could have sat in silence, or skipped the preamble altogether, let the future happen.

It had been after the third, fifth or whatever bar that we stumbled into that chilly Edinburgh night, lights swirling around us, the pavement shifting under our feet. That was when Claire slipped her hand into mine. There was a little, fleeting squirm in my belly, a half-hearted hesitation. It faded fast.

Our laughter was too loud, but it sounded nice at the time. Her body was as unsteady as mine, and I remember looking down, trying to find my balance by studying the ground, and seeing flashes of her short skirt and bare legs, stumbling more than walking, beside me.

'There,' she said, at one point, raising a finger. I followed it and saw a photo booth standing in a shadowy recess along the street. The wording above the entrance said:

Passports and moments to remember.

'Come,' she said, clutching my hand with both of hers, tugging at me childishly.

I gave in (of course I did). She shifted the grimy curtain aside, and we stepped into the tiny space of the photo booth. I sat on the swivel stool, Claire on my knees, the soft weight of her body pressing against me. We were giggling, our faces flushed and red.

'How does this fucking thing work?' she said, slurring her words, trying to fit coins into the slot. Some fell to the floor, went wheeling outside. We laughed as if this were the funniest thing in the world.

'There we go.' The screen before us lit up and began displaying instructions. A few seconds later, a cold metallic voice began a countdown.

'Ten! Nine! Eight!' we called out in unison. Just before reaching zero, I wrapped an arm around her waist, and she laid her head against mine.

FLASH.

Both of us laughing, caught unaware despite the count-down. Our eyes were looking in different directions, but our alcohol-fuelled smiles were eerily similar.

FLASH.

This time, we're both looking into the lenses. There's little depth to the image, and it sort of looks like my head is growing out of her shoulder.

FLASH.

Claire with her cheek against mine. We might be mistaken for a happy couple.

FLASH.

We're kissing. Feverish, unsmiling kisses. Hungry hands exploring skin, bodies rubbing against one another.

We must have stumbled from there to my hotel, or caught a cab perhaps. I can't remember.

On my plane back to London the following morning, I sat staring outside. I wondered if there had been any way to avoid what had happened. Fate had simply guided me towards its inevitable path. Or... perhaps not. Perhaps fate had nothing to do with it. I had planned it, maybe. Or, at the very least, been open to the possibility.

Cecilia was five months pregnant at the time. Two weeks later, we'd lose our unborn child.

I often think about it as a punishment. One I deserve. After all, a man who cheats on his pregnant wife isn't fit to be a father, is he? But if that is the case, why did Cecilia have to suffer too? She was innocent.

A few days after returning home, I found the strip of photos from the booth. I'd tucked it deep inside my wallet, but I couldn't remember putting it there. A shiver ran down my spine, and I couldn't help looking over my shoulder to check whether Cecilia was there. I knew she was out. Yet I had to check.

Standing in the garden, where I'd been trying to fix the sprinkler system, I studied our faces, mine and Claire's, with mild disgust. This was before losing the baby, but I already hated myself for my infidelity.

I went to the kitchen and pulled out the food bin from under the sink. I folded the photo strip over and over, pressing hard, making it smaller and smaller, wanting it to disappear. I tore it to pieces and threw them into the revolting tepid mess of food waste. Helping myself with a spoon, I mixed it all up to hide the shreds.

Nowadays, I try not to think about all that. But at times, I find myself wondering about Claire's husband. The *other* wronged party, alongside Cecilia. I have no idea what he looks like, what his name is. In these fantasies, he has a thick black shadow for a face. I imagine him somehow finding out about that evening, about his wife and me. Then—especially at night, when Cecilia is asleep beside me—I picture him, heartbroken and filled with hatred, coming in through the door to kill me.

11

Toys strewn across the floor. They catch the eye at random, unexpectedly—a doll with long, stringy hair sitting on top of a small wooden train. A piece of blue chalk, half-crushed to dust. A rubber duck, its face covered in lipstick. Drawings, too, and pencils. Tangles of colour and thick lines, too much pressure applied to the paper.

Beneath this layer of childhood trinkets, a house that is trying its best to appear tidy. A fruitless effort, if an honest one. Chaos. But the sort of chaos that is full of promise and possibility.

'Oh *welcome*,' says Gabbie, sighing through a smile and laying a kiss on Cecilia's cheek. 'Excuse the mess,' she adds carelessly, waving a hand in the air.

'Hey, mate,' says Ed, slapping my arm. 'Good to see you.'

We're at their place for Sunday lunch. We come here every couple of weeks or so. I don't particularly enjoy it.

'Where's the little princess?' Cecilia says, producing a present from her handbag. It's wrapped, the bright colours of the paper mirroring those of the entertainments on the floor.

'Oh, you shouldn't have,' says Gabbie, shaking her head. 'She's been a bit of a brat this morning.' Then, turning towards the kitchen, she calls out, 'Lilly! Come and say hello to Auntie Cecilia and Uncle Mark!'

And there it is. *Auntie Cecilia and Uncle Mark.* I wear my smile as best I can.

Lilly walks into the living room on her tiny arched legs and the unwavering confidence of someone who knows they're in charge. Her face and hair are matted with flour, and she's holding a wooden cooking spoon in her hand. A tiny frown creases her forehead as she surveys us. Her lips form a perfect pink O.

My heart melts. She's adorable, this little girl is, and she fills my heart with joy and longing in equal measure. I know that Cecilia, beside me, is feeling the same. She gets down on her knees, holds the gift towards the girl and says in a sweet, happy voice I only ever hear when she's talking to Lilly, 'Who is *this* for...?'

Lilly's eyes brighten up, and her lips curve into a tiny, toothless smile. She runs towards my wife. Just as she's about to reach us, her balance fails her, and she lands on her bottom. The fall is softened by the bulge of her nappy. She stares at us for a second, back perfectly straight and tiny little legs stretched out in front of her. Her mouth opens, and she lets out a heart-warming croaky giggle. We all laugh, these tall people whose job it is to entertain and adore her.

'Come here, you!' Cecilia says, scooping her up in her arms. She rubs her nose on the baby's full cheeks before smacking a big kiss on them.

'Peppa Pig?' Gabbie asks us as she nods towards the package.

Cecilia dips her chin, without looking away from the girl in her arms. 'Of course. We know it's her favourite.'

'Come on through.' Ed gestures towards the dining room. 'Gabbie made lasagne.'

Lilly suddenly looks up, shaking her head. Her face is the picture of indignation.

'Nonono!' Gabbie says quickly. 'Not *me*. Lilly did. I just helped out a bit,' she adds, shaking her head and rolling her eyes. Lilly seems satisfied by the correction and returns her attention to the wrapping paper.

'Fancy a beer? Wine?' Ed asks me as we make our way, tiptoeing carefully through the toys on the floor, towards the dining room.

'Beer sounds good.' I turn around and notice Cecilia is still in the entrance, Lilly in her arms. The child is holding the little Peppa Pig toy in the air, with her wrinkly fingers wrapped around it. Cecilia is just standing there, eyes shut, nose against that soft, immaculate skin.

I feel like doing the same to her—embracing my wife, holding her in my arms, savouring the scent of her. Telling her that we still have time, we can still mend things. Have a child of our own. At one time, I might have been able to do such a thing. Not anymore.

I turn around and follow Ed. 'Yeah. Beer, please.'

ED AND GABBIE'S dining room is narrow, offering barely enough room for the table and chairs, with large windows facing a tiny, neat garden. Little Lilly sits in a highchair, squeezed between her parents. They each take turns at feeding her. Some of the food ends up in her mouth, most of it splattered on her bib.

'Sorry about the other night, at the pub. I just couldn't make it,' Ed says, without looking at me: he's busy doing the 'aeroplane' with Lilly's spoon. He makes the sounds and all. She's not impressed.

'No worries.'

'Who came?'

'Just Clyde.'

Gabbie snatches the plastic spoon from her husband's hand, as if to say, *You're not doing it right*. Before starting her own version of the aeroplane, she asks, 'How's he doing? He didn't look too good at that party the other night.'

I sigh. 'Oh, you know.' They nod. They know.

Cecilia trains her eyes off Lilly's face for a second. 'He should try to find a woman.'

'Yeah, like *that's* gonna happen,' says Gabbie, with a mean little giggle. She can be a bitch.

'Don't say that,' says Ed, snatching the spoon back.

'Well, okay,' Gabbie concedes half-heartedly, taking a sip of wine. 'But he *has* let himself go... and it's not like he was all that to begin with. Plus, he's hopeless with women... ever heard him trying to chat one up? *Hopeless.*' Sometimes I think she *is* a bitch.

Ed tsks, shakes his head.

'He's sweet though,' says Cecilia. She says it in a soft voice, then nods. 'I can see it happening.' This surprises me a bit. She isn't as harsh as Gabbie when it comes to Clyde, but neither is she usually so tender.

'Yes,' I say, smiling at my wife (but she's already looking at Lilly again). 'I agree. There's someone for everyone, and all that.'

'Phh. Whatever,' says Gabbie, grabbing a glass of wine and wiggling two indifferent fingers in the air.

I consider telling them about Clyde's gaffe at the pub. It would make a decent story, get a few laughs. But Gabbie would say it proves her point (which it sort of would), and I don't want to give her that satisfaction.

There's a second of silence, other than the low hum of Ed's voice mimicking the sound of plane engines.

I realise I don't want to be here. It's more than that, actually—I actively *want to not* be here. For a second, I want it more than anything else.

Where would I want to be? On the bench, with Alice. The image of those words etched into its surface (*Same time next week?*) floats into my mind. I feel the excitement bubbling up in my stomach. I *wish* I were there now. Like a child, I wish.

'Ah!' says Ed. 'That reminds me. He called me the other day. Clyde. He sounded *really* nervous. Told me there was something urgent he had to tell me about.' Ed frowns, takes a sip from his beer. 'I was caught up with little Lilly, so I told him I'd call him back. Haven't got round to it yet.' He looks at me, slightly concerned. The way a good friend would be. 'Any idea what he was on about?'

I try to think. Clyde *did* look a bit weird the other night, down at the King's Head.

While we talk, Lilly starts whining. She doesn't want her food. It's a sweet, tender cooing. I suppose it can become irritating after a while. I read somewhere that toddler's cries are designed by nature to drive their parents crazy, to ensure their attention is drawn to the child's needs. But I like it.

'Not sure,' I say to Ed. 'I doubt it was any—'

'Oh, just *eat*, will you?!' Gabbie cries suddenly, throwing down the spoon, which she's apparently taken back from Ed. It strikes the table, sending gooey filaments of mashed veggies flying all over the place.

Lilly starts crying instantly. It's a heartbreaking, desperate cry. Her mouth curves downwards, and her eyes fill with tears. All her toddler confidence and command vanish in a flash. Now she's a trembling, scared, hurt little child. I feel the sudden urge to slap Gabbie in the face. I don't.

There's a brief, tense silence while Lilly sucks in air for the next round, and I see her minuscule pointy tongue quiver almost comically. I'm surprised, as I always am, to remember that some expressions are innate. We are born with that sadness in our facial muscles. That downward slant of our lips, the scrunched-up eyes. And little Lilly's eyes, now, are filled with what appears to be boundless sadness and disbelief.

Why are you making me sad? her face is asking. So simple, so honest. How much human interaction leads to this question?

I throw a glance towards my wife. Is this what she reads in my eyes? What I read in hers?

Why are you making me sad?

Gabbie's fury dissipates immediately. 'Oh sorrysorry*sorry*, darling. Wait a second.' She reaches into her pocket while Ed tries to comfort his daughter. He does it with a smile, fascinated, as I am, by this tender display of desperation.

'It's all OK, little Lilly. It's all OK,' he says. His voice sounds wonderful. I wonder if I would sound quite as good, quite as believable.

Gabbie produces a smartphone, places it in her daughter's hands. 'Yes,' she says, 'I know, I know. We're terrible parents. Don't judge us.'

The crying stops. Lilly slides her wrinkly index finger across the screen, unlocking the device.

'She can use the phone?' asks Cecilia, bewildered.

Gabbie laughs. 'You joking? Look... she can find the YouTube icon... there you go. Then she'll scroll until she finds the cartoon she wants to watch... yup. Amazing, right?'

We all nod, although I sense Cecilia, next to me, disagrees.

'Yes, we're terrible parents,' says Gabbie, in a way that suggests they're not, really. 'But it works wonders. Stick a phone in their face, and they turn quiet in no time.' A cartoon's jolly tune plays from the phone, crackling a little through the speakers. Lilly's gaze is entirely focused on the moving images, a delicate line between her eyebrows. The sadness, the despair have vanished just as fast as they appeared. Gabbie laughs and shares a smile with Ed. We smile too. I find myself thinking it's lazy of them, to outsource tantrum management to a phone. But then again, who am I to say?

WE'RE IN THE GARAGE, Ed and I, sipping beers. It's a small, messy space, a safe harbour for everything that belonged to pre-marriage, pre-fatherhood Ed. His man cave. Dusty board game boxes, band posters, his vinyl collection. It somehow mirrors the colourful chaos of Lilly's toys upstairs. Older, faded, but serving the same function. I have no way of knowing if this is the case, but I can picture Gabbie nagging at him to get rid of *all that rubbish in the garage.*

I'm leaning against a table, while Ed is crouching on the ground, diving through an old cardboard box. 'You won't believe it,' he says excitedly. 'I found it the other day... I thought of setting it aside, but I was afraid I'd forget where I put it, so I just left it in here... oh, *where* is it?'

'Take your time, mate,' I say. I'm feeling it again—that urge to talk about Alice, the same I felt with Clyde the other night. I shuffle around, set my shoulders, this new wave of excitement making me feel restless. *Same time next week.* I know I'll be counting the hours.

Here I am, a married man in a family home, thinking about another woman.

But it's all innocent, isn't it? I remind myself that nothing's happened; nothing will. It just feels good, that's all.

'Ah, here!' Ed says triumphantly, holding a white envelope in his hand. He stands up, slapping dust off his trousers. He's smiling ear to ear as he hands it to me. 'You won't *believe* it.'

I open the envelope and let its contents slide out. It's a

photograph, an old one. I struggle for a second, trying to make sense of what I'm seeing. When I do, I can't help letting out a little chuckle of disbelief.

'Fucking hell...'

'Yup,' says Ed. 'Look at your Batman T-shirt, mate. You look like a right idiot.' He laughs and takes a swig of beer.

It's the four of us: Ed, Clyde, Phil and myself. Aged thirteen, maybe fourteen. We're standing not far from where we are now, just down the road. The colours have faded a little, but not too much. 'Fucking *hell*...' I say again. 'I mean...'

My gaze goes to myself first, as it does. A handsome boy is staring back at me; it's my face, minus the lines and wrinkles, the stubble, the years. I'm smiling, pointing at the Batman logo on my T-shirt. Not as handsome, of course, as Phil. It's eerie, looking at him: the sculpted cheekbones, the confident, detached air. How does a kid that age pose like that? He's taller than the rest of us and, unlike us, isn't pulling a silly face or smiling. This boy I'm looking at, he'd fit right in on a boy band album cover. In fact, that's probably where he thought he belonged.

And there's Clyde. Already then, the ugliest, the least fortunate of the gang. He's fatter than us, although apparently happier. His smile is the widest, the most enthusiastic, spreading sincerely into his chubby cheeks. For some reason, it pains me to look at him. The optimism in his young face seems so misplaced now. That trust and love for his friends (minus, perhaps, Phil) make me cringe now. We, his mates, have all moved on. Clyde, on the other hand, seems to still be living in the faded world of this picture, fat piling on fat, hair vanishing, sitting around wondering where all his friends have gone, why they haven't turned up yet.

Ed, I hardly look at. In a way, he hasn't changed. He's a man, and a good one at that, but there are no surprises here.

The nerdy boy in the picture was always going to deliver, become a quietly happy, responsible adult.

Before handing the image back to him, I let my eyes scan my own childhood face again. Is there something shifty about the boy I see? Is he trustworthy? Is he the sort of boy who turns into a good man?

Is he?

Ed takes the picture and places it carefully in a plastic folder he dug out from somewhere. 'I thought you'd like it. I'll make copies, hand them out to the others too.'

He says that, and I thank him, but I'm not entirely sure whether I like it. Some people look back on their childhood and get all emotional, feel pangs of longing. Me, I feel nothing.

'That would be lovely,' I tell him.

UPSTAIRS, Lilly and Cecilia are playing on the carpet in the living room. Gabbie is taking a nap in a nearby armchair, her chin resting against her chest. She's snoring lightly.

'OK, we'd better get going,' I say, low enough to sound like I'm trying not to wake Gabbie up, but loud enough to do so. I succeed, and she shudders in the armchair, sits up bewildered, wiping a string of saliva from her chin, letting out a loud, 'Eh?'

Cecilia looks up at me, twists her lips in a mock-sad face, her lips curved downwards. 'Already?' she asks, in a sing-songy voice, before smiling at me.

I look at her there, amidst Lilly's little world. My wife is all smiles now. Beautiful, radiant smiles that make me want to love her. That make me think she deserves a child, because she'd be a wonderful mother. Much better than the annoying woman my friend married.

I'm suddenly struck by the silly fantasy of travelling

through time, going back, all the way back, and undoing the tangle of events that led us together, my wife and me. Never talk to her that very first time. Never charm her (it's funny to think I was ever capable of that). Then love her from a distance, with my secret knowledge of what life would have been for us—nothing much, really, other than pain. Which is a lot less than she deserved. A lot less than either of us deserved.

'I'm afraid so,' I say, smiling at little Lilly.

We gather our things, say our goodbyes. I tell Ed I'll see him at the office, while Cecilia and Gabbie embrace. Then my wife and I kneel to hug Lilly. She cries a bit, doesn't want us to go. She clings onto Cecilia's skirt with her miniature fists until Gabbie picks her up and begins to soothe her. 'Auntie Cecilia and Uncle Mark will be back soon,' she says cheerfully.

They stand at the door, wave as we leave. I wonder if they pity us, this childless couple. They're aware, like all our closest friends are, about the loss of our child. Perhaps they sigh and shake their heads. *It's sad, isn't it? Those poor things. And they're so good with kids.*

'All OK?' I ask Cecilia as we make our way. I regret it immediately, but there it is.

Her head snaps round, the gentle smiles all but gone. 'Why wouldn't it be?' she says. We both know why.

In the car, I switch the radio on to drown out our silence. For the millionth time, I wonder what sort of father I would have been. It's odd—I'm never quite sure.

What I *am* sure about, though, is the sort of father I wouldn't be like. Courtesy of my own.

12

I picture him now as I drive: my father. His slim, sickly frame. His scowl, his nervous, calloused hands. Most times, they were wrapped around a drink. Scotch, usually. I could smell it in the flying spittle, in the rancid breath and harsh words he'd hurl at me and my mother when he'd had too much to drink. Often, the beatings would follow—a string of punches and slaps and kicks and resentment. His strength was surprising, drawn from somewhere other than his slender arms: from an awareness that he'd failed, that'd he'd been given the opportunity for happiness, a healthy child, a good wife, but he had squandered it all.

I remember dreaming about the day I'd be taller than him, stronger than him. Lying in bed, trying to distract myself from the bruises and the pain, and playing the scene in my mind: him about to strike Mum, me grabbing his fist in mid-air. His surprised look, the realisation that I had outgrown him, that he could no longer knock me about. Tasting the impotence Mum and I had had to swallow for so long. And, finally, my punch meeting his jaw.

There was much more to him than that, of course. But it

was (and still is) too painful to consider. Even then (how old could I have been? Twelve?) I could read the traces of someone else beneath the temper and the alcohol. Someone overwhelmed and sensitive and weak. Someone ashamed of what they were doing, but incapable of making amends. Someone not all bad.

One night, I heard him sulking in the kitchen. He never cried, not openly. And although I'd spied tears in his eyes at times, I'd always assumed they were just another inexplicable effect of the booze. But this crying was new. I slipped out of bed and tiptoed down the corridor to the kitchen. To my surprise, there was no whisky on the table. Just my dad, alone, staring straight ahead, crying. He didn't seem drunk. It was difficult, seeing him like that.

I turned around, suddenly desperate to leave, and to my horror a floorboard creaked loudly under my foot. When I looked up, he was staring at me, his eyes enormous and flowing with tears, lips twisted horribly. He didn't move, didn't say anything. He just shook his head ever so slightly, still looking at me, and I think there might have been an apology of sorts in that look of his. But who knows? Some men's lives are so solitary, so unhappy, that communication is simply impossible. I remember feeling pity and rage and love for him, but had even fewer ways than he to show it. I gave a little nod, then walked stiffly back towards my bedroom. The episode was never mentioned again, by either of us.

He died three years later. Pancreatitis, it was. I thought Mum and I would finally get to live happy lives together, freed of his dark, unwelcome presence. But he'd taken it all out of her. A few years later she died too, without ever quite knowing how to enjoy our new, normal family life. I was twenty-two (oddly, this was something that brought Cecilia and me close when we met, the two of us both being young adult orphans). I try not to think about my dad.

Looking back, I suppose alcohol was to blame for a lot of his, and our, unhappiness. But it doesn't really make any difference. At his funeral, I squeezed out as many tears as I could, then buried my face in Mum's arms and breathed in her scent.

13

When we get back from Ed's place, Cecilia retreats to her study, saying she has an exhibition to organise, next week, and wants to get a head start. She often seeks solitude after she's been playing with Lilly.

'Tea?' I offer.

She shakes her head. 'I'm all right,' she says, answering a different question.

'I'll put the kettle on, let me know if you change your mind.' I hesitate for a second, my eyes lingering on the woman I married. There are things I know about her, things that enchanted me when we first met. Little titbits of information that have faded over time. Unexpected ones: I know, for example, that she loves the idea of sitting in one of those American diners, the kind you see in films.

'I'd like to sit there,' she told me once, 'with a coffee and a slice of cake. Not in a city. I'd like it to be in one of those lonely places in the middle of nowhere. With wide horizons, you know?' She'd smiled at me, embarrassed by this small confession. 'You know the sort of place I mean?'

I did.

She has a picture in her study. I'm looking at it now. She saw it in a magazine, found the photographer's details online. He was so happy someone had shown interest in his art that he sent the print over, free of charge, accompanied by flowers. Roses. It made me slightly jealous. But I have to say, the photo is impressive. It's one of those diners, the ones in the middle of nowhere. I doubt Americans can understand the appeal they have to our European minds. They speak of a freedom we're not familiar with, with our narrow horizons, our lengthy history.

In the photo, five booths, set against the wall-to-wall windows. A man sitting at a table, a plate of what looks like scrambled eggs pushed to one side, for the benefit of a newspaper spread out before him. Reading intently. There are wrinkles in his forehead. Two women: one of them a waitress. We can't quite make out the name on the tag pinned to her chest. She's carrying a large pitcher of coffee, apparently walking towards the other woman.

It's this other woman who catches your eye. In her late thirties (and you get the sense they've been a tough thirty-plus years), sitting at a far table, chin resting in her palm. She's gazing outside, towards one of those North American stretches of nothingness: a road (or *highway*), a desert, the horizon.

At times like these, I catch my wife looking at the picture, her expression mirroring that of the woman at the far table. Both lost in thought. Both, maybe, planning to leave.

It's two a.m., and I can't sleep.

My mind wanders from images of Ed's happy family to Alice and our upcoming meeting. I'm jittery, restless. Finally, I can't take it any longer, and I get out of bed. I move silently, trying not to wake Cecilia. It's raining, the moon is wrapped in cloud, and I can't see her face. I think she's sleeping.

The door to the room that was meant for our son is closed, as it always is. I consider opening it, stepping inside, seeing what effect it has on me, but I think better of it.

The treads creak softly as I walk downstairs. I pick up an umbrella, grab a coat from the hanger by the front door, and step out into the drizzly night.

The crisp cold feels nice on my skin. My slippers sink into the wet grass, and the thin blades tickle my bare ankles as I walk around the house, away from our bedroom window (I wouldn't want Cecilia to look out and see what I'm about to do).

I scan this corner of the garden, looking for a specific stone. They all look the same in the darkness... ah, there it is. I kneel down, flip it over, and fish a small plastic bag out of the hole beneath it. Inside are a pack of cigarettes and a lighter.

I light up, then put it all back as it was. I've got mud on my fingers now, so I run them through the grass in an attempt to get it off. Doesn't really work.

The rain picks up, rattling against the umbrella. I hop awkwardly to the wall of the house, standing in the two-foot-wide stretch of dry surface. Droplets fizzle on the tip of the cigarette, but it stays lit. I close my eyes and inhale deeply. It doesn't taste good, not as much as I'd hoped. It's not relaxing, standing here in the cold and the rain, puffing on this. It's just stressful.

Will Alice turn up? If she does, will we sit at the same bench and chat? Perhaps I should suggest a restaurant. But that's risky... it would have to be far from the office. Wouldn't want anyone I know running into us, a married man dining alone with a beautiful woman, and getting the wrong idea.

But *would* it be the wrong idea?

And: would I sleep with Alice, betray my wife, given the chance? It's not something I've asked myself, not explicitly. I summon her in my mind, the narrow waist, the curve of her back, the way her full lips spread in a smile.

I haven't slept with my wife since we lost our child. We don't talk about it, but it's there. I sometimes wonder if it's the same for other couples: has their married life become loveless, too?

I take a long, deep drag from the cigarette. The smoke fills my lungs. I consider, uneasily, the question of whether Cecilia feels sexual attraction for other men. Does she catch herself picturing someone else, his body?

The thought angers me. I bring the soggy cigarette to my lips again, inhale, and suddenly feel a searing pain between my index and middle fingers.

'*Fuck!*' I shout, shaking my hand violently and sending the cigarette stub flying. I've smoked it down to the filter, the glowing tip burning my fingers. 'Shit,' I say, lower now. There it is, lying in the grass. I consider stepping on it, squashing the damn thing, but I can't leave it there, Cecilia might find it. I crouch down under the partial cover of the umbrella, cursing silently, and pinch the cigarette from the ground. Now I'm going to have to—

A noise. Distinct, despite the rushing rain: a low cough, a sniff.

I freeze. Someone is in the garden, I'm certain of it. Just round the corner of the house from here, below the bedroom window.

My mind rushes to Cecilia first—is she standing there, accusatory in her nightgown, watching me smoke? But no... she would have called out, said something.

No. It's someone else. There's a stranger in our garden.

My heart starts pounding in my chest as I dash towards the source of the noise. I feel scared, brave, ridiculous.

There's an intruder on my property, and my wife is alone in the house. I have to do something. Do something in my slippers and pyjamas, but do it nonetheless. Could I use the umbrella as a weapon? Should I stop and grab a heavy stone? No time.

I reach the corner of the house and consider shouting a warning, but I don't want to alert this person. The prospect of spying on them, catching them red-handed, is too strong.

Holding my breath, I stick my back to the wall and take a peek.

Nothing, at first. The sheets of rain, the tree in the garden, the wheelie bin. Then... yes, a figure on the road. Running— running away from my garden, it would seem.

I make a run for it, too. Two strides in, and the umbrella gets tangled in a bush. I curse, pull hard, decide to drop it. The rain soaks me instantly. I dash forwards, slipping and sliding in the wet grass, arms jerking outwards, trying to maintain a semblance of balance.

'*Oi!*' I shout. But not too loud because, insane as it sounds, I don't want Cecilia to wake up and ask me what I was doing in the garden in the first place. I don't want the neighbours to see me in my pyjamas.

The figure is running, and I think that perhaps he heard me, was alerted when the stupid cigarette burned my fingers. I'm almost on the pavement when my foot slides on a muddy patch in the garden. It's like running on ice. My leg flies forward and up, high enough for my hamstrings to burn with pain. Suddenly, there's no ground below me. I come crashing down on my back, head slapping the mud, filthy water drenching my clothes.

I scramble to my feet, irritated, pissed off, moving on all fours at first, trying to make up for the precious seconds lost. But when I reach the road, the intruder is gone. Vanished.

I stand there panting, consider chasing him. What about

the car? I could jump in, catch up with him like that. But I'd have to run inside and get the keys first. Who knows where he could have got to by then.

'Damn,' I say to the empty street. '*Damn*.'

Head low, fists tight, I walk back towards the umbrella. I have to collect my stupid cigarette before going back inside and somehow getting all this mud off me. I try to remember where I'd dropped it. Was it after I began my failed chase, or before? Hard to tell.

I spot it lying on the ground under the tree. I bend down and pick it up and... stop.

This isn't my cigarette. This one is only half-smoked. I squint, bringing it close to my eyes to inspect it. It's wet, covered in dirt, but I can tell it's not been lying here for long.

Whoever the person in my garden was, they were smoking it.

I slowly collect the umbrella, pointlessly holding it over my head (I doubt there's any way I could get any wetter than this), still studying the cigarette. And there's that thought again, that nagging possibility: *What if Alice is a stalker?* Or worse maybe. She could be a dangerous psychopath. A charming, beautiful, dangerous psychopath.

I squint in the dim light from the lamp posts, the cigarette pinched between my fingers. I can't find traces of lipstick on the filter. But does Alice even wear lipstick? I can never tell unless it's those bright red ones. Also, the rain might have washed away any trace of it.

I stumble around for a while, looking for my own dog-end. When I finally find it, I walk to the back of the garden and throw them both as far as I can.

Back inside, soaked through and covered in mud, my heart sinks at the thought of having to shower. I look at my watch—2:38 a.m. Won't be getting much sleep tonight.

'What happened?'

Cecilia's voice startles me. She's standing halfway down the stairs, shoulders hitched up and arms wrapped around her waist, as if cold.

'There was someone in the garden,' I say before I can think of anything else. I feel I should walk up to her, comfort her, but I don't want her to smell the cigarette smoke on my breath. So I just stand there, looking more pissed off than I am, shaking my head and cracking my knuckles.

'Really?' she asks, an eyebrow raised.

'What do you mean *really*?' I say. 'Yes, *really*. I heard noises, didn't want to wake you up, so I went to check myself. There was someone there, standing outside.'

'Did you see him?' she asks, and I can tell from her voice that she's not entirely convinced. She suspects I was outside for a sneaky smoke.

'Yes!' I say. 'I chased him, too. Got really close, but I was wearing *these* fucking things'—I point a threatening finger to my slippers—'and couldn't make it. Bastard got away.'

I'm getting angry. It's not just the mild disbelief in my wife's eyes, it's also the feeling of not being able to deal with some stranger entering our property. Of being an incapable husband in the eyes of my wife. To her, now, I'm either a liar who's come up with all this nonsense just to sneak out for a smoke, or a man who let an intruder get away.

'What did he look like?' Cecilia asks, taking a step towards me.

'What?'

'You said you saw him. What did he look like?'

'I... I don't know. I mean, I got close, but he was running. And it's raining; I didn't get a close look at him.' The truth is, I saw him from a distance. Little more than a human shape, really. I couldn't even say what colour clothes he was wearing. 'He was wearing a black coat, with a hood,' I say, just to say something. 'His face was covered.'

'You got close, almost caught him, but didn't see him?'

'*Yes,*' I say, exasperated.

Cecilia looks at me with those sphinx's eyes of hers. She stands there, slender and ghostly beautiful, her high cheekbones and patrician forehead assessing me.

'Should we call the police?' she asks.

'No, I think I scared him off for good,' I say casually, slipping my drenched coat off. I hope this makes me sound manly enough. Just the other day, I was saving a little old lady in the streets, being cheered by passers-by. And look at me now.

'It's okay,' she says, moving towards me. Her voice is gentle now, comforting. She begins to open her arms, for a hug perhaps, but I don't want her to pick up the scent of smoke. If she did, she'd just assume I was lying all along. Which I *am*, but not entirely. Maybe that's precisely why she wants to get close.

'I need to shower,' I say brusquely, dodging her. It feels bad, leaving her standing there, but I do.

Under the steaming hot jets of water, I try to recall the glimpses of the intruder, piece them together. I have very little to work with, scattered images of someone running under the rain. Fragments.

Except I can't quite shake the feeling that there was something familiar about that figure, its movements. Something I *recognised* in him.

Or her.

14

'Bad news.'

That's how Bill greets me as I step out of the lift and into the BeeCreative offices. It's Monday morning. My stomach is prickling with excitement and unease at the prospect of meeting Alice, and the last thing I need now is office panic. Still, he's handing me a cup of coffee, so it isn't all bad.

'Go on,' I say, joining him as he walks through the chattering corridors. Bill never seems to stand still; he's always in motion, in the middle of something. His conversations too, they never quite begin. He sweeps you up in his whirlwind of concerns, leaving you wondering just how you got there.

'PimpPro.' He spits the name out with disgust. 'His label, they want an idea to promote his latest single. No brief, nothing. By twelve.'

I laugh. 'Of course they do. Have you assembled the team?' We have a team that works on music industry accounts.

'I got Jayesh, Linda and Sven.'

Hopeless, all three of them. Jayesh is a graphic designer

who I suspect is colour blind. Linda is, for whatever reason, an art director who thinks Picasso is her mum's old car. And Sven, a something-strategist: he seems to believe that one can conceal the sound of one's farts by coughing loudly. One cannot.

Not exactly the A-Team. But hey, this is BeeCreative.

'Everyone else is busy on the new Dr Street album launch,' Bill continues as he shoves his way through the office like a menacing tide. *'Dr Street! PimpPro!* Can you believe it? What happened to *real* music, Mark? That's what I wonder every fucking morning. I really do. It's sad, if you think about it. What happened to...' He mumbles the rest of the sentence, shaking his head. His concern seems sincere. Stress isn't a condition for Bill. It's a lifestyle.

We reach the meeting room. I see our three young colleagues squirm in their seats when they notice Bill approaching. Before entering, he leans against the glass door, huffing and puffing. Turning to me, he whispers, 'If anyone in there suggests a viral video, I'm going to lose it, Mark. I really am.'

'I'll bear that in mind.'

Bill frowns. 'What's up with you?'

'What?'

He looks at me suspiciously, waving two fingers up and down. 'This. You're all done up.' He sniffs. 'Cologne too... you seeing a woman or something?'

Is it that obvious?

I keep my cool. 'No, Bill. Just you,' I say, blowing him a kiss.

He sighs a heavy sigh and pushes the door open. As he enters the meeting room, I think I hear Sven squeak with fear.

. . .

ONE HOUR in and we've got nothing. That's usually how it is with our brainstorming sessions. A wasteland of withered ideas.

'How about...' Sven says, leaning forward, all his little brain cells hard at work. Everyone's tired eyes drift towards him. '... how about we take, like, a community approach... like the good he does for the poor... like, you know, like...'

I know I'm going to slap you if you say 'like' one more time.

Linda lights up at the idea. 'Yes!' she exclaims, clearly believing we're onto something here. 'We could get him to turn up at, I dunno, a youth club in east London or something. Somewhere *really* depressing, you know? And...'

Both Sven and Jayesh are nodding now, wide-eyed and smiling with excitement.

'And,' Linda continues, 'he could donate something. Money or something, you know? Maybe a gym. Or—'

'Or musical equipment!' exclaims Jayesh, Pythagoras-like. 'You know, 'cause he's a musician and that.'

'Hardly,' Bill says to himself.

'Awesome!' says Linda. 'So... so... hang on.' She's really thrilled now. She blinks hard, holds the palms of her hands up, as if to slow down this outpour of genius. 'Let's milk this. Make it better. Not only is it, you know, a poor area and all that he's helping... it could be someone whose voice needs to be heard... like, like...' She frowns, deep in thought. So do the other two.

'Women?' suggests Bill. I can hear the rage bubbling inside him. But these innocent souls genuinely think he likes the idea.

'Women!' they all cry out at once, looking at each other with the same elated expressions.

'We could brand him as a women's rights activist!' says Linda.

They're all very pleased with themselves.

'You know,' Sven says seriously, 'social issues, human rights stuff, it's totally trending right now.'

Bill raises an eyebrow. 'Human rights are... trending?'

Sven closes his eyes, nods knowingly. 'Totally.'

'Great idea, Bill. Great idea. Really,' says Jayesh. For a second, I fear he might try to fist-bump him. Luckily for all of us, he doesn't.

Bill turns red. They mistake this for a sign of modesty, the poor things. 'Why, thanks very much,' he mutters. Then, rather theatrically, he turns his eyes to the ceiling and scratches his chin. 'Hang on a minute...' he says. 'I just realised something.'

'What, man?' asks Jayesh.

Bill slowly balls his fists and starts breathing heavily through the nose. '*Women*,' he growls.

'Yes,' says Sven. Not quite as confident now.

'G-great idea, man,' Jayesh insists.

'*WOMEN?*' Bill slams his fist on the table, making them all jump. 'Women's rights *activist*? The guy,' he roars, 'calls himself PimpPro. *PimpPro.*' Bill stares at them in fury and disbelief, chest heaving, tendons taut. 'You know what a *pimp* is, right? Someone who *exploits* women, if anything, you utter gits!'

They curl up in their seats, terrified. I sometimes wonder how it is that BeeCreative ever got to be one of London's most successful ad agencies. Astounding.

Bill flops back in the chair and sinks his head in his hands, exhausted.

I sneak a glance at my watch. Coffee is in twenty minutes. My coffee with Alice... our second date, if you can call it that. Despite the trepidation, I'm twitching with excitement. I keep patting down my tie, stretching out my trouser legs. Will she even show up?

Alice, the beautiful temptress. The innocent distraction. Or, possibly, the deranged stalker.

I know I should ask her about it. Find a way to make it sound like a harmless question. *Are you a stalker? Were you hanging about in my garden last night, by any chance?* Yeah, right.

In the meeting room, everyone is silent, mulling things over. Bill's hand still covers his eyes. I see his lips move silently, likely whispering all sorts of profanities, cursing the day he took this job.

A movement from Sven catches my eye. I see him raise a finger in the air, like in school. He's hesitant. I watch as he frowns, gathers courage. Looking at Bill with fearful eyes, he says, 'What... what about a viral video?'

Oh *God*.

I SLIP out of the meeting as soon as I get the chance. Bill's not happy, of course, but I tell him I have some stuff to work on for Senesi. He reluctantly agrees.

The desperate eyes of the young PR professionals in the meeting room follow me, silently begging me to stay, protect them from Bill's wrath. I feel a mean little tingle of satisfaction at waving them goodbye.

Turns out it *is* going to be a viral video after all. No one's sure about the content yet, but that doesn't really matter. As soon as it's online, we'll turn to one of our trusted clickfarms to generate one hundred per cent artificial likes and shares online. 'The numbers don't lie,' we'll tell the client. Oh, but they do.

Making my way towards the lifts, I spot Werner—the non-illiterate copywriter—approaching me, seemingly about something urgent. I pretend not to see him and pull out my phone, ready to engage in a fake, and very heated, conversation with an imaginary someone.

Just at that moment, the phone rings in my hand. I jump, startled, and almost drop it.

The screen tells me it's an UNKNOWN CALLER.

Alice.

I can't help but smile. But then I wonder, *Is she calling to cancel our date?* The prospect of that fills me with a strange hollow feeling. I watch the phone ring, hesitating for what feels like a whole minute.

It's OK. Just pick up. Even if she is going to call it off, she cares enough to warn you about it.

Only a hidden corner of my thoughts wonders how she got my number. I'm not sure if I find it more flattering or disturbing. I swallow, bring the phone to my ear.

'Hey,' I say. It comes out a bit funny, deep and porn star-like.

'Hey?' Her voice is amused. I can hear the smile in it.

'What a surprise,' I say, cupping my hand over the phone. It's noisy in here.

Silence. Then, 'A nice one, I hope.'

I'm about to say something, but my words are plucked from my lips, my smile frozen. This isn't Alice's voice. It's my wife's.

I look around, desperately trying to find a way out of this conversation. But everyone's busy. Even Werner has given up on talking to me and has left.

'Of course it is,' I say, painfully aware of the shift in my tone. 'I'm a bit busy at the moment, but—'

'I'm in the area,' Cecilia says, not hearing, or not caring. 'My meeting ended early. I thought it would be nice to have an early lunch together.'

My mouth opens. Nothing comes out.

'Unless you're too busy, of course,' she says after an expectant pause. She's frowning, offended. I can picture it as clearly as if she were standing right here.

'No*nono*,' I say hurriedly, racking my brain for a way to please my wife while not standing Alice up. 'It would be lovely. Really.'

'Great. Shall we meet at—'

'What about the Founder's Arms?' I say quickly, before I even know if it's a good idea. The Arms is a stone's throw away from the bench. Perhaps, my muddled brain thinks, I might be able to see them both. Alice first, then Cecilia. 'Where are you now?' I ask, eyeing my watch. My meeting with Alice is in ten minutes. I could at least see her, tell her I'm busy with work or something, apologise and leave.

'Ah, perfect,' says Cecilia. 'I can be there in five minutes. I was taking a walk along the river.'

My heart sinks. 'Fantastic.'

'See you there, then.' She actually sounds happy, which makes me feel like a bastard. Am I?

'Yes, OK, great. Bye,' I say and hang up.

Damn.

I WALK through the lobby feeling absolutely lost. I don't know whether to walk slow or fast, or whether to turn back. I stand on the threshold, eyeing the pavement like someone who's just been through a lobotomy. People mumble their irritation as they brush past me, eager to get out.

On the street, London is loud, busy and indifferent. I stumble along, wondering what I should do.

You shouldn't be dating another woman, for a start.

But I'm not *dating*-dating, am I?

I curse, irritated at Cecilia. But there's more than just irritation. There's surprise, even a hint of joy. A bit like receiving an unexpected letter from an old friend. I can't even remember the last time she surprised me, turning up for a lunch together. Definitely not since *the thing*. We've been so distant lately. It's a distance I hate, but one we've grown accustomed to by now. The same way, maybe, prisoners get used to their cells.

But why does she have to seek closeness *now*? Couldn't it have been before? Or tomorrow? The timing is wrong. But then again, it often is.

Perhaps, I think as my feet pick up speed, this might be the beginning of... of *something,* with Cecilia. Something like the old days. Who knows? This is unexplored territory for me. Or territory faded and forgotten. Maybe we could go back to being a couple who talks and makes love and...

Has children?

Strange, here I am, fantasising about my own wife while I'm meant to go and meet another woman.

Alice, the image of her, drifts into my mind. Desire blazes up inside me. I want to be by her, close to her lips, her smiling teeth, her uncomplicated charm.

My mind in two places, I walk through the crowd until I see the river, the Founder's Arms, and the woman whom I married standing there, her smile a riddle I don't know how to solve.

15

The pub is warm and welcoming. Or it would have been, in different circumstances. A teenage waitress greets us as we step through the door. 'Where would you like to sit today?' she asks.

Before Cecilia can reply, I say, 'How about there, by the window?' I point towards an empty table with a decent view over the river—and of the bench where I'm meant to meet Alice.

My wife nods approvingly. 'Nice, yes.'

'Lovely,' says the waitress with a smile that looks as fake as mine feels.

The place is pleasantly quiet, but it's still early. Within half an hour or so, it will be flooded with office workers on their lunch breaks. I pull out my wife's chair, to let her sit down (and, I realise, to make sure I get the one that faces the window), then take my own seat.

'How was the meeting?' I ask, casually peering outside. The bench is empty, Alice isn't there yet. Who knows? She might not even turn up. I'm not sure if that would make me feel relieved or hurt.

'Oh, you know,' Cecilia says, swatting the question away with her hand. My wife has never been one for idle chat. Even in the early days, she was more comfortable with silence rather than empty words. I used to like that.

I struggle to think of something to say. There's another sort of nervousness creeping inside me. It's not only Alice: it's this strange feeling of being on a first date. Of having to impress the woman before me. Something occurs to me. 'Why were you calling from a private number?'

Cecilia frowns. 'What?'

'When you called me earlier, the number was set to private.'

'Oh, really?' she asks me, reaching for her purse. 'That's strange.' She fishes out the phone and unlocks it, running a hesitant finger across the screen. She frowns at the menus and options. She's never been comfortable with technology.

'Let me do it,' I offer, reaching out for it.

'Oh, no,' she says. And I somehow have the impression she said it too quickly. Cecilia stuffs the phone back inside the purse, shaking her head. 'It doesn't matter.'

She's very reserved, and I'm OK with that. It was part of her allure. Yet, the haste with which she put the phone away gives me pause. I'm about to say something, when the waitress shows up.

'Are you ready to order?' she asks.

'We are,' says Cecilia, although we haven't got round to looking at the menu yet.

She orders scampi from the chalkboard. I go for the pork pie. When the waitress leaves, I sneak another glance towards the bench. It's still empty.

'Nice, isn't it?' Cecilia asks, turning around on her seat to follow my gaze, misinterpreting it. 'This city would be nothing without the river.'

'Eh? Oh, yes, yes. True,' I say lamely.

She lets out a long sigh, then looks at me. I can stare any stranger in the eye, easy. With anyone I know, it suddenly becomes an anxiety-inducing experience. The better they know me, the harder it is. With my wife, it's almost unbearable.

The door of the pub opens, and a couple with a baby step in. The little one is screaming, and the two parents look utterly worn out. They're pushing the pram while carrying all sorts of parenthood paraphernalia. They somehow manage to reach a table, smiling embarrassed smiles at the other guests, bumping into tables, apologising, all while trying to calm the baby down. When they're finally seated, the two of them let out a sigh of relief and exchange a tired, happy look. I watch the dad lay a kiss on the child's bald little head.

I study him, as I often do with fathers, and feel a sharp prickle of pain in my chest. Ed once told me that, *Before you have kids, you just don't notice parents. They're sort of invisible. But once you do, you see them everywhere.*

I've learnt that, if you want children and don't have any, they're as visible as can be. Especially fathers. Proud, happy fathers. They're all over the place.

When I turn back, I notice Cecilia has been looking at them, too. She offers me a sad smile. I study her expression. She's warm, almost affectionate, in her tentative sort of way.

Just then, she lets her hand cross the table and holds mine.

I've hated my wife. She's condemned me to a life of sexless loneliness, of long, tortured silences. Of proximity without closeness.

But she's going through it too, isn't she? The loss of the child, it happened to her as well. It happened inside her own body. As intense as my pain has been, what could it ever be compared to hers?

I give her hand a little squeeze, brave a smile. She returns it. Her eyes, the same eyes that used to keep me up at night, restless with lust and longing, are fixed on mine. Studying me. I suddenly feel the unsettling, but oddly comforting, certainty that no one will ever know me as well as she does. How could they?

She tightens her hold on my hand, and I feel something quiver in my chest, a lump form in my throat.

Cecilia is the only person who can understand what I've been through. Of all the people on this blue-green rock, only she can. I feel like telling her that this suffering, it could bring us together rather than divide us. That we might still have a chance and should give it a try. It's worth it.

'Mark,' she begins, and there's a hesitation in her voice, a lack of control, of poise, that is so unlike her. 'I...'

I look away, unable to handle the storm of emotions erupting inside me.

And see Alice.

I catch her just as she arrives, out there by the river. She looks around, sits down. Despite it all, I can't help feeling a stab of arousal at the sight of her curves as her knees flex, the small of her back coming down on the bench.

Suddenly, it's like a speeding train has come to an abrupt halt. My mind heaves and struggles to regain its balance. I quickly turn back to Cecilia and realise with terror that I might have missed something she said. Has she spoken?

'Um,' I say. 'Sorry. What was that?' I give another little squeeze, but it comes out mechanical this time.

Cecilia's face turns cold. She withdraws her hand, looks away from me. And just like that, whatever just happened between us is gone.

I'm afraid she's about to peer out the window and spot Alice, but she doesn't. She picks up a fork and begins running the tines across the tablecloth, leaving deep marks in it.

'Nothing,' she says coldly. 'I... was just wondering if we

should be concerned about whoever it was in the garden last night.' It wasn't that at all, of course. 'The one you almost caught,' she then adds, drawing out the *almost*.

'Oh, no,' I say, shaking my head. 'Absolutely. Not at all.'

The waitress comes along, laying the steaming dishes before us. My appetite has evaporated. 'Smells delicious,' I say with a wide smile, and I force myself to eat.

We sit there for a while, eating in silence, as the crowds arrive, noisy and unwelcome. I throw casual glances at the window, pretending to be deep in thought. The sight of Alice makes me feel guilty. My body is drawn towards her, all alone out there. Her shoulders go up and down at one point. A sigh? I wonder what she thinks of me. I bet she hates me.

Ten minutes or so go by. Cecilia and I haven't said a word. I'm trying to come up with things to talk about, but it's difficult. Between Alice out there and the odd moment we just shared, I feel overwhelmed.

'So,' I begin, turning towards Cecilia, 'you—'

'I need to go to the toilet,' she says, interrupting me. She stands abruptly and goes off.

This is my chance.

I'm going to sneak out, run to Alice. Try to explain things, tell her why I can't stay. Or lie, rather. My heart beating fast, my eyes flick to Cecilia—she's still making her way through the crowded tables. She's walking slowly, as if lost in thought. I know I'll have to run out as soon as Cecilia enters the toilet. I'll have to be quick.

'Oh, come *on*,' I whisper. It's taking her ages.

Will Alice understand? I can't tell her about being here with my wife, although I'm not entirely sure why. She knows I'm married. And yet.

Finally, Cecilia closes the toilet door behind her. Here we go. I start to get up. But for some reason, I can't. I'm stuck there, palms pressed against the table, elbows up, ready to stand, but I can't.

Come on, she's been waiting long enough. Any minute now, she'll get up and leave. And then when will you see her again?

True. Except, something is holding me back. Maybe it's Cecilia, the closeness we just shared. That look in her eyes— thinking about it now, it was as if she were silently asking me *Can I trust you? If we give this another try, will I be able to trust you, Mark?*

But there is Alice, outside. With her beautiful, simple presence. There she is, a woman waiting for *me* to sit by her side. A happy, undemanding woman who wants nothing but to spend time with me.

What's wrong with that?

Despite this, I still can't get myself to move.

Go, go, go!

'Shit,' I curse, quietly bringing my fist down on the table.

If I don't rush, Cecilia might see me out there. See me with another woman. And she'll *know*. No doubt about it, she'll know immediately.

I start to move, but the two women in my life move too: Cecilia emerges from behind the toilet door, and Alice, outside, stands up, rubbing her hands together against the cold.

'Shit,' I whisper.

My chance has come and gone. As Cecilia walks to the table, I try to smile at her, but she seems to be avoiding my eyes. Alice, standing in front of the bench now, looks once about her, shakes her head, and leaves.

My heart sinks.

When my wife sits down opposite me, I can't help hating her. She doesn't speak. I don't speak. We end the meal in silence. Our usual silence.

16

A drunk homeless man stands on the street corner, swaying and mumbling to himself. He appears impossibly bulky, wrapped in layer upon layer of filthy clothing. A large brownish stain covers his chest.

I give him a wide berth, keep my eyes ahead of me, as does everyone else. As I walk past, he suddenly lashes out, pointing a finger at me, throwing sloshing words and spittle my way.

'*Pieth of sshith!*' he says, spittle flying, then bursts out laughing. His teeth look like horse's teeth.

I make sure none of his spit has reached me, then proceed to ignore him.

Cecilia and I parted five minutes ago. We exchanged a quick kiss on the cheek, a hollow *I love you*. They used to sting, these shallow farewells—I've always been one for pondered goodbyes, so to speak. But they don't hurt any more. I want them over with as quickly as possible. Especially today.

I notice I'm chewing the inside of my lip and force myself to stop.

Behind me, I hear the drunk call out again, *Pieth of sshith!* I wonder whether he's talking about me.

I'm close to the BeeCreative offices now, but I can't face it just yet. I wander aimlessly, and despite my resentment towards Cecilia, I tell myself again that I shouldn't be doing this. I *know* I shouldn't. It's childish, it's weak. As much as there's been nothing physical in my relationship with Alice, I know I shouldn't be doing it. It's intriguing and fun, but it's also perhaps time to draw a line under it all, now.

In front of me, an elderly lady is walking hand in hand with a little girl, her granddaughter maybe. At one point, the little girl points at a red car going by, and asks the old lady a question. I can't make out the words, but her voice is crystal-clear, musical. It's wonderful to see them walking there like that.

It ends here, I tell myself.

I decide to go back to BeeCreative, get some work done.

'Excuse me,' I say to the old lady and the little girl, as warmly as possible, as I step past them.

'Hello!' cries the girl, waving a hand in the air. She gives me a wonderful smile. I wave back, this childless man, and walk on.

And there she is.

Alice.

She's standing still, the flow of pedestrians drifting past her, insignificant. The way she's standing, I can see her profile. Her perfect profile. Then, with an absent-minded motion, she turns on her heel, and I'm left facing her shoulders. Some mighty force seems to want me to dash towards her and scoop her up in my arms. Give in to everything, to the weakness, just follow my desires.

I swallow, try to focus. It takes courage, this.

But my mind is made up.

Again, I wonder what could have been, consider life's

strange turns. I think of Cecilia, my wife. Of that moment in the pub earlier, with its glimpse of a happier life. My mind is set, but it's difficult. Yet, even as I make this decision, I feel taller, stronger. My back straightens, my shoulders relax, feel broader. I like being this confident man, whatever may come of my decision.

Before I have time to change my mind, before I even know if I should really be doing this, my hand is laying on Alice's shoulder, and I hear myself saying, 'Do you want to come to the sea with me?'

ALICE SLOWLY TURNS and looks me in the eyes. If I startled her, it doesn't show. The world fades into a blur around us. I feel like I've stepped onto a stage, playing a role I was born for.

She tilts her head to one side, then smiles. 'You know I will,' she says.

The perfect answer.

Then, unexpectedly, she adds, 'Do you like letters?'

'Letters?' Even my now-confident self is taken aback by this. I raise an eyebrow. 'What do you mean?'

She tugs at my coat, like a child. 'You know, *real* letters. On paper. I'd love to receive a letter.'

I've often thought that myself. Suddenly, all I want to do is sit down and pen an old-fashioned letter for the woman standing before me. 'Yes,' I say with a chuckle. 'I do like letters.'

She leans in, beautiful dark eyes peering into mine. 'Write me a letter, Mark,' she whispers. 'And I'll write you one. We'll plan our trip to—where is it again?'

'Blackwood Cove. Dorset.'

'Blackwood Cove,' she echoes. In her mouth, it sounds like a magical place. Her lips curl into a playful smile. 'We'll plan the trip in our letters,' she says excitedly. Her excitement, it's contagious.

'Yes,' I say, suddenly feeling sixteen again.

'Tape them to the bottom of our bench.' There's no hesitation in her words, and I think she must have been planning this. It's flattering, this thought is. Alice going about her days, plotting our clandestine correspondence.

'Our bench,' I say, loving the sound of it.

She nods. 'Yes.'

'I'm sorry I didn't make it, earlier. I was—'

Alice smiles the most tender of smiles. Shaking her head, she says, 'It doesn't matter. You're here now.'

An unexpected wave of gratitude washes over me. Her words are so easy, so powerful. So gentle.

'Feel like a coffee?' I offer.

She lets out a little sigh. Waving vaguely behind her, she says, 'I have to go now.'

It hurts, I want to be with her. I want it more than anything. But it's OK. There's a tether between us now. A link made of secret letters.

I nod. Her fingers caress mine. The white of her teeth. Her eyes. And she's off.

I stand still, watching her go. Just before the crowd conceals her from view, she turns around and mouths through those full, red lips, *Blackwood Cove*.

'Blackwood Cove,' I say, as if she could hear me.

Now, *that's* a goodbye.

17

There are two police officers standing at my front door.

I spot them before they do, walking home from the station. A man and a woman. They're speaking in slightly hushed tones, making it impossible for me to distinguish the words.

Keeping my eyes on them, I'm suddenly aware of the way I walk, my posture. I adjust to what is meant to look like a casual-stroll pace, just a man returning home after a day's work. But it feels ridiculously conspicuous, unnatural.

The woman shakes her head, dismissing something her colleague has just said. Are they talking about me? I watch as she rings the doorbell. The way she does it, with a hint of impatience, suggests it's not the first time they've rung.

Why isn't Cecilia opening? At first, I think she might be in the shower or something. Then I remember—she mentioned drinks with Gabbie this evening.

For an instant, I feel like turning on my heel and leaving quickly. But no, why should I? It's not like I've committed a crime, is it?

Except, you have.

It's unpleasant, having the police come knocking. I'm suddenly filled with the an-Englishman's-house-is-his-castle variety of indignation. Whatever they want, surely I needn't put up with it, right? Still, a conversation with them seems unavoidable at this point. My pace picks up speed. I decide to open the exchange, as if doing so might somehow grant me an odd head start, a vague dominant position.

'Evening, officers.' I allow an irritated question mark to echo through the words. *Why are you bothering me?*

She turns around first. Tall, curly brown hair, a slight forward slant to her posture, like a teacher addressing her young pupils. There's a spark in her eyes, a light that suggests sharp intelligence. Her partner is sturdy, bald on top with hair on the sides, with a repulsive little moustache sprouting above a surprisingly minute set of lips. He's a palm shorter than she is. I wonder idly what it must be like working alongside a woman who is that much taller than you.

'Mr Hamilton,' she says, stepping towards me and extending a hand. 'Mr Mark Hamilton?'

'Yes,' I say as we shake hands.

'I'm Inspector Angelina Lombardi, and this is my colleague, Sergeant Whitby.' Whitby nods without a word, eyes fixed on me.

'How can I help you, officers?' I say, pulling out the house keys and eyeing the front door. Polite, but clearly too busy, too *innocent*, to deal with them now.

'Oh, it won't take long,' she says. 'I'm sorry about turning up at your house like this. We tried to call ahead, but no one was in.'

'We work,' I say, a little coldly.

I wonder whether I should open the door. Being inside my home would make me feel safer. But that would mean inviting them in. What if they accept? So I'm left holding the keys in my hand, a little awkwardly.

'How can I help you?' I ask again, through tight lips.

She turns towards the house, then back to me, the hint of a quizzical look in her eyes. *Won't you let us in?* When she realises I'm not going to, she shakes her head with a smile, as if introducing a very minor matter, one that hardly deserves mention. But her eyes stay sharp, serious. Focused on me. 'Oh, we've received a report about someone behaving suspiciously here in your neighbourhood, and—'

'The intruder,' I interrupt her. So *that's* what they're here about. Relief floods my body.

She's frowning a little, tuning into my relief, analysing it. Perhaps wondering if it's sincere. 'The *intruder*?'

I wipe the smile from my face and try to resume my cold, slightly hostile body language. But it feels silly now. 'Yes. Um. As you say, there was a person hanging about the other night.' *Did* she say that?

'I see,' she says. 'Why do you call this person that, Mr Hamilton? *Intruder*, I mean. Did they try to enter your house?'

'Oh, no, it's just... I was in the garden, and I heard a noise. Coming from there.' I point towards the corner of the house, by the tree. 'So I went to check, and there he was. Inside my garden.'

'It was a man?' asks Lombardi.

Again, absurdly, the idea that it might have been Alice creeps into my mind. But no, no. *She's coming to Blackwood Cove with me*, I tell myself, the thought somehow definitely exonerating her from any possible wrongdoing.

'I suppose so,' I say, shrugging.

Lombardi shakes her head again, dismissing the topic. But why? Surely the gender of this 'intruder' matters. I expect her to follow the motion up with a question, but she just looks at me, smiling politely.

Whitby sniffs, twitches his nauseating moustache. 'Do you recall any details about this person? Something that may help identify them?' It's funny how he says it. Reciting the question rather than asking it. Like it doesn't really matter what I say. As if we are all having another, secret conversation, one lurking behind the words.

'Well,' I begin, 'it was raining. And it was the middle of the night, dark of course, so—'

'What were you doing in the garden, Mr Hamilton?' Lombardi asks, all of a sudden.

My mouth hangs open. She's caught me off guard. 'Hmm?' I say, pretending I somehow missed her question.

'You said you were in your garden, and that it was the middle of the night.' A dense pause. 'So I was just wondering what you were doing—'

'Hello?' a voice asks from behind me.

I turn around and watch Cecilia as she climbs the steps to the front door, to join us. She laces her arm around mine and lays a kiss on my cheek. This surprises me, given how we parted at lunch. I feel like pushing her gently away, but I don't. Somehow, it seems important to convey a happy family vibe to the coppers. 'Hello,' I say, with something of a smile. I detect a faint scent of alcohol on her breath, from her drink with Gabbie.

'Mrs Hamilton,' Lombardi says with a broad smile, shaking Cecilia's hand. There's a noticeable shift in her attitude. She'd somehow slipped into a vaguely accusatory tone, but it's now vanished. 'We were just talking to your husband about the... what was the word you used? *Intruder*, yes.'

'Yes, Mark chased him away,' Cecilia says. I can't help feeling a modest surge of pride in my chest. I'm *that* sort of man: the kind who springs into action, chases away the baddies.

'So you saw this individual too, Mrs Hamilton?' Lombardi asks.

Cecilia frowns. 'Well... no.' She looks at me hesitantly. 'But Mark said he heard someone, and—'

'Did *you* hear him?'

'No, but—' Cecilia begins.

Lombardi cuts her short. 'I'm just trying to make sure I've got this straight,' the inspector says with a reassuring motion of her hands, patting the air in front of her. 'You neither saw nor heard this person, but you're relying on your husband's account, correct?'

'Yes, true, but—'

'I understand,' Lombardi interrupts, with a warmth I can't help but find unsettling. When she turns to me, her smile is still intact, but that warmth seems to evaporate. I fear she's about to resume her previous question, ask me why I was in the garden. I don't want to discuss that, not in front of Cecilia. Luckily, she doesn't.

'Mr Hamilton,' she says, 'in pursuing this person, did you by any chance follow them onto someone else's property?'

'What?' I ask, dumbfounded. Then something occurs to me: is she implying that *I* am the person they're after? Does she think I made this whole story up, created an imaginary person, to point the blame elsewhere? 'No,' I say firmly. 'We ran along the road, just here. The intruder got away, so I went home. That's it.'

Lombardi nods. 'Hmm, I see.' She frowns slightly, like someone trying to wrap their mind around a complex mathematical formula. As if what I'm saying doesn't quite add up. Something inside me tells me it's an act, an expression she's perfected over the years, to throw off the people she's speaking to. But why use it on me?

'May I ask why you didn't call us, Mr Hamilton?'

It's a fair question, one I don't really know the answer to. Why didn't I call the police? Lots of little reasons, I suppose. I was soaked in rain and covered in mud. It was late. We were tired.

'I don't know,' I say. 'It just didn't seem important.'

Lombardi nods again, unconvinced.

'You said you're an inspector,' Cecilia says before Lombardi has the time to reply. 'Is that normal? Sending over an inspector for a simple case of someone loitering around at night? Wouldn't that be something for a... normal officer? You know, in a uniform?'

She's right, of course. It hadn't occurred to me. Again, I feel there's something else we're not aware of going on here.

Lombardi and Whitby exchange a quick glance. Then Lombardi runs her fingers along her cheeks, massages her chin. She looks at us, assessing. We just stand there, curious as to what she might be thinking. In the end, she lets out a sigh, gives Whitby a quick nod, then steps closer to us, lowering her voice.

'Mr and Mrs Hamilton,' she says, her eyes on the street, perhaps making sure no one is around to hear what she's about to say. She lowers her tone, just above a whisper now. 'There's been a murder in the area.'

We gasp. A coordinated intake of air that's almost comical. Cecilia's hands tighten around by arm. '*What?*' we both say, puzzled and horrified. Had I been chasing a *murderer* down our street? The thought makes me shudder.

'Not exactly close to here. A mile or so, in fact.' Her tone is grave, serious. Behind her, Whitby lets out a loud *tsk*, clearly not happy with her sharing this information with us.

'That's close enough,' I say.

She nods. 'True. But I'd like to stress that there's no immediate reason to panic. Likely a burglary gone south. Perpetrators usually avoid showing up in the same area when things like this happen.'

We're speechless. Cecilia looks at me, fear in her eyes. She seems so vulnerable now. Almost childlike. I draw her closer to me. I'm planning a secret weekend away with another woman, but I can't help feeling the need to protect my wife, to reassure her. It's funny how the mind works. The male mind, at least.

The man, Whitby, chuckles at our concern. 'There's no reason to panic,' he insists.

'*No reason!*' I say, raising my voice. 'Are you joking? Someone's been killed, *killed*, and you—'

Lombardi steps between us, holding her palms in the air, like some sort of traffic warden peacemaker. 'Please keep your voice down, Mr Hamilton.'

'I... OK, yes.' I shake my head, let out a bitchy little chuckle. Rage is bubbling inside me. I shoot Whitby a dirty look over Lombardi's shoulder. I wonder how *he* would feel if a murder had occurred close to his family home.

'I agree with my colleague,' Lombardi says. 'Your concern is perfectly understandable, but, as I say, there's very little reason to believe that the perpetrator will act again. Especially not in your area. The only reason we're here is because of the disturbance. We thought it might be worthwhile asking around, that's all.'

As she talks, I realise she's speaking to my wife rather than to both of us. These reassurances, they're for Cecilia, not for me. It makes sense, I suppose: my wife is quite shaken up. But there's something else going on here, as well. I sense it in the way her voice is colder when addressing me. In the way I catch her looking at me, studying me, and then quickly looking away when our eyes meet.

'Mr Hamilton, one more question—'

'A quick one, I hope.' I suddenly feel the urge to bring this whole thing to an end.

'Absolutely,' Lombardi says, flashing her smile again. Then, somewhat theatrically, that same smile falters. She seems to hesitate.

'What is it?' I ask impatiently.

'Please don't take this the wrong way, Mr Hamilton. Please understand, these are routine questions and, given the circumstances—'

'Go on.'

'Yes, sure.' Again, her voice is apologetic, but rings insincere. 'It's just... I was wondering whether you take medicines of any sort, drugs that might induce, um'—she clears her throat—'hallucinations.'

My heart is pounding in my chest now. I feel my fists tighten into quivering balls. '*Hallucinations?*' I ask, incredulous. 'Are you asking me whether I *dreamt* the whole thing? Do you think I'm *crazy* or something?'

'Mr Hamilton, please,' Lombardi says, once again raising her hands in the air, trying to defuse the tension. But even as she does that, I notice the look on her face: the keen analytic gaze of a researcher watching a lab rat squirm. 'It's a simple—'

'And anyway,' I add, interrupting her, aware that I'm almost shouting at this point, 'you said you've received reports, right? Someone else has seen the intruder, too. It's not just me, is it?'

'Calm down, Mark,' Cecilia whispers, stroking my shoulder. But I'm not going to.

'So if I'm a nutter,' I continue, 'I'm not the only one, am I? Must be others having *hallucinations* out there, too.'

There's a long, dense pause. And, just before Lombardi speaks, my heart sinks, because I suddenly *know* what she's about to say.

'The thing is, Mr Hamilton,' she almost whispers in an odd, slow voice, 'the calls we received, they were about *you*. People saw you in the street that night, no one else.'

Lombardi lets her words hang for a moment, like black butterflies fluttering between us.

'But...' I begin, trying to make sense of what she's just said. I feel Cecilia's concerned gaze on me.

'Please, Mr Hamilton,' the inspector says. 'There's no reason for concern. I'm sure there's a simple explanation for all this—you told us it was raining, so it was difficult to see anything clearly. You yourself caught little more than a glimpse of this person, whoever they were. It might just be that the people who called us happened to look out the window too late, after the... *intruder* got away. And all they saw was you.'

'Yes,' I say, nodding firmly. 'That's got to be it.' I don't like having to rely on her defence of my account of events, but I can't help it.

After that, Lombardi seems in a hurry to end our little conversation. She looks down at her watch, raises her eyebrows in what might be genuine surprise, and says, 'I'm sorry to have kept you. Thank you very much for your time.' She slips a hand into her coat and produces a card. 'If you think of anything, please ring me.'

Cecilia takes the card. Lombardi's name and contact details are printed on it.

'Will do,' I say.

The two police officers bid us farewell and head off. Cecilia and I are left standing there. Just before they disappear down the road, Lombardi shoots me a quick, sharp glance.

Cecilia turns the key in the door and steps inside the house. I follow her, without speaking. The silence in our home welcomes us with a thick embrace. There's an almost artificial quality to it, as if some sort of mysterious machine had drained any possibility of sound from the room. I shut the door behind us, and Cecilia still hasn't switched the lights on. We're in the dark. As my vision slowly adapts, the black contour of my wife's body emerges from the shadow. She stands a few feet away, but I'm not sure whether she's looking at me, or if I'm staring at the back of her head. For a few seconds, both possibilities appear equally true.

I'm afraid she doesn't believe me. That the inspector has planted a seed of doubt into her brain. Am I lying? Am I hallucinating?

But something else is troubling her.

I sense her question coming before it does, thick and hushed and horrifying.

'Do you think they know?'

I don't speak. The silence between us (the one I've grown so used to) pours into the greater silence of the house.

We're still in the dark.

18

On the night of the eleventh of August, 2010, a twenty-seven-year-old man called Michael Taylor broke into an isolated house on the outskirts of north-east London. Two people lived there: Amanda Richardson, a seventy-eight-year-old pensioner, and her paralysed and bed-ridden husband, Clark, two years her senior.

Taylor found Mrs Richardson in the kitchen, where she'd been preparing tea. Reports later explained that she suffered from insomnia, and camomile seemed to help her with it. Taylor produced a knife and threatened to kill her if she screamed. She didn't.

He proceeded to rape her while holding the blade to her throat. When he'd finished, he stabbed her seven times (three in the abdomen, three in the right thigh and once in the throat). Then, leaving the old woman in a pool of blood, he escaped the way he'd entered, through a window, into the garden and over the wall.

Mr Richardson, who couldn't move a muscle below his chin, awoke to the sounds of his wife moaning. The testimony he later gave to the police, the description of his utter helplessness and despair, is a difficult one to read. He was listening to his dying wife, mere metres away, incapable of doing anything at all.

But Mrs Richardson didn't die. After a stretch of time neither of them could later relate with certainty, she somehow mustered the strength to drag herself across the kitchen floor and into the living room. There, she grabbed the phone wire dangling off a small table beside the sofa, and pulled on it with feeble muscles until the phone dropped to the floor beside her. She then proceeded to call 999. When asked by the press how she found the strength of will to do that, she said that *hate* had fuelled her.

As fate had it, the victim survived, but the perpetrator did not.

According to the police's reconstruction, Taylor, who had so far led the life of a quiet, law-abiding citizen, climbed over the stone wall surrounding the property and dropped to the narrow strip of grass that separated it from the road. Something must have gone wrong, though, and Taylor is presumed to have struck the ground and fractured his ankle. The reconstruction states that the sheer momentum of the fall sent him rolling into the road just as a car was approaching. The car, which was moving at significant speed, struck him square in the right side of the head. Investigators told the press that the rapist and would-be murderer died instantly.

The investigators were wrong.

Taylor did indeed fall from the wall and roll into the road. A car did strike his head while travelling at speed. But he did not die instantly.

I know, because when I stepped out of that very car, in the dead of night, heart pounding and hands shaking, I found him on the ground, still breathing. The sound of this breathing was the stuff of nightmares. A choked rattle, the wet wheezing of things damaged beyond repair. Bruised and bloody and broken. He was there, this stranger, lying on his back in the white light of my headlights, one hand held upwards, clawlike and horrifyingly *rigid*. As if already dead.

It all happened so quickly, as people say. One second, I was driving through the silent night, slightly drunk after a party organised by Phil (Cecilia, who had caught the flu, had decided to stay home). The next, a blurry stain in my vision, the impossible flash of a man on hands and knees, just there to my left, looking my way. Then the thud, which came horrifyingly loud, the car swerving, spinning, tyres screaming.

Finally, the sudden stillness.

My first reaction was a noble one, I suppose. I leapt out of the car, my mind numb, but my instincts kicking in. There was someone in need of help, and I had to do something. But as soon as I saw the wretched mass on the ground, as soon as I heard that laboured breathing, I froze. I remember standing next to the car, incapable of moving. Letting out shaky little sobs, looking about, first hoping desperately that someone else would show up, direct me, take charge of things. Then hoping no one would.

The muttering engine. The sickening rattle in his throat. All else was silent.

Trembling, sobbing, I walked towards him. My shadow danced in the headlights, which shone like stage lights on the wounded man in the middle of the road.

The sight of his head, the angle at which it sat, almost sent me running. An ear, the left one, was pressed firmly against the shoulder, his neck unnaturally long and twisted to one side. A nauseating bulge loomed on its surface, like an egg grown just below the skin. I could almost sense the restricted pathways, the narrow, bleeding surfaces in the throat through which the air was desperately being pushed, on its way to the starving lungs. Half his face was a pulp of torn skin and shattered bone.

One terrified eye stared up at me.

I dropped to my knees, knowing there was nothing I could do to save this stranger, not really. I thought of holding his hand, but his fingers were broken, sticking out in odd directions like snapped twigs, and I couldn't bring myself to touch them.

'I-it's going to be OK,' I muttered. At least, I think I did.

They were going to throw me in jail for manslaughter, that was all I could think of. Me—a man with a good job, a beautiful wife, setting out to start a family. I'd lose all that, now. Cecilia, she might stick with me, but I'd go to prison. My life was over.

I trained my eyes along the man's body. In the low head-lights, he was a patchwork of reds and blues and purples. And between them, impenetrable black shadows, where bits of him seemed to have melted into the night.

I wanted to go, but couldn't. So I just stayed there, kneeling beside him, doing my best to ignore the sound of his breathing. This man was dying, he was dying because of me, and I simply had to do something to help him. I looked around, noticed what seemed to be the wall of a private prop-erty, the ghostly glare of what might have been lights coming from a home (Mrs Richardson's home, I later discovered). I considered running inside, asking for help. Too slow. I needed to act *now*. With trembling hands, I reached for the mobile phone inside my pocket. I'd just call emergency services, then get the hell out of there. I could place an anonymous call; no one would know I was here. That would work, right?

I stopped.

Would this place me at the scene of the crime? They had a thousand ways of tracking you, didn't they? If I called for an ambulance now, without giving my name, they could somehow later *triangulate* through the cell phone towers or something. They'd know I was here. They'd know I did it.

'Oh *shit*,' I sobbed. My eyes kept darting from the phone's screen to the man lying in front of me.

I shook my head clear. 'Fuck it.' I dialled the emergency number. Three taps, and then the green CALL button.

Just then, the man's crooked, tortured hand lay on mine, the one I kept on the road to steady myself. I shrieked, jumping back in fright and disgust.

His jaw, I noticed, was cracked. It shifted and wiggled, as if there were too many joints in it. He was whispering something.

I hastily hung up the call (had it gone through?) and brought my ear to his twisted lips. A humid heat rose from his open wounds, metallic and nauseating.

'What?' I asked.

'Y-*you*,' he rattled. A whisper, flowing unevenly through what sounded like bubbling porridge and shattered glass.

'Me?' I asked. The horror of a dying man addressing you.

I waited for him to continue. Long, I waited, until I realised the rasping breath had abated, and no more words would come.

The stranger was dead.

For a moment, an eternity, I just stared. Contemplating the fathomless mystery of a body without life. That eye: exactly how it had been but moments ago, same colour, same shape, even looking in the same direction. But somehow looking no more. Just pointing, like a *thing*.

I turned around, sat on the ground, my shoulders to the corpse. I buried my face in my hands like a child. Stammering thoughts, shaky fingers.

Something had to be done. Should I call an ambulance?

Or the police? Both, perhaps. They'd take us away, the corpse and the killer, one life ended, the other ruined.

I collected my phone, then stared gormlessly into the screen, squinting, cursing, unable to plot a way out of this nightmare.

The instant I called the police, my life would be over. The family we'd been planning, the stable career ahead of me, my whole life. Incredibly, my day-to-day existence was now in the past. Something old and gone, torn from me, full of unacknowledged innocence. This was me, now, the new me: meet Mark, drunk driver and killer.

What now?

My eyes drifted towards my car. The engine was still running. I could see a stain across one of the headlights, shining red. There were *bits* in it. The plastic casing had cracked, half of it missing.

I slowly, hesitantly, slipped my phone back inside my pocket, then stood, carefully, as if trying not to wake the dead man behind me. Without turning around, I made my way towards the car. Standing next to the headlight, just off to the side, to get the light out of my eyes, I noticed the damage was minimal. Besides the broken headlight, all I could find was a mark on the bumper. Might have already been there, too. The blood—I figured that would come off quite easily.

Somewhere, an owl hooted.

I opened the passenger door and rummaged through the glove compartment. As if in a dream, I pulled out a small pack of handkerchiefs, peeled back the sticky label, and extracted three of them.

The blood did come off easily. I pinched the paper in the middle, wiping in meticulous little circles, careful to avoid touching the surface of the headlight with my bare fingers. I kept going until all traces had vanished, at least in the dim moonlight. If I couldn't see anything from ten inches away, I doubted anyone else would, not at night. In the morning, I'd wake up early and wash it down properly with the hose.

When I'd finished, I looked around, trying to spot a safe place to get rid of the bloodstained tissues. Off the side of the road, maybe? There in the grass. Or I could tear them up, step on them, reduce them to tatters under my soles. But no—that wouldn't work, would it? Someone, the police, could come across them. I pictured a special forensic team in white overalls combing through every inch of this stretch of road, magically connecting the traces of paper to my shoes, to me. Was that likely? Did they dispatch forensic teams for hit-and-runs? Would they be wearing white overalls? My head was spinning.

I ended up tucking them back into the pack they'd come from, sealing it as best I could with the label. I'd flush them down the toilet, back at home.

Holding my breath, I opened the driver's door and got inside. The headlights were still shining on the body sprawled there in the road. I had to turn them off, to avoid looking at it. Carefully, I performed the strangest three-point turn in my life, flicked the headlights back on, and drove off. Just like that. A suffocating sense of incompleteness haunted me all the way. What had I forgotten? Had anyone seen me? Who had I become?

At home, I told Cecilia everything. It wasn't a conscious decision, more a necessity. It was simply too much to bear on my own. I talked and talked, choking back the tears, and she listened to every word.

When I finished, she simply sighed. She always looks flawless, even when awoken in the middle of the night. She laid her hand on mine, drew me into a hug. 'It could've happened to anyone,' she whispered. 'Let's forget this. Never talk about it again.'

I nodded, eyes closed, forehead resting against her shoulder damp with my tears.

THE CASE RECEIVED lots of coverage, with heroic Mrs Richardson appearing on all major news outlets. Her courage and charisma won the hearts of the public, and the authorities found themselves under pressure to wrap up the case as satisfyingly as possible. Alas, despite their best efforts, the driver of the car was never tracked down and identified, but the investigators' reconstructions were deemed timely and accurate.

Some of the tabloids hailed the driver a hero, some sort of ruthless, but ultimately fair, vigilante. A few of them believed the driver had somehow witnessed the event, was aware of Taylor's crime, and acted accordingly. In the King's Head one evening, I heard a table raise their pints of beer to the mystery driver. To me. 'Deserves a medal, that one does,' one of them said with a firm nod.

The fact Taylor was a monster made it easier, I suppose. It was a fact I tried to remind myself of every time my hands started shaking, the echo of his rattling breath haunting me.

There are two secrets in my life. One is I betrayed my pregnant wife. The other is that I killed Michael Taylor.

I replaced the headlight casing myself, two days after the accident. I found it online, at twelve pounds ninety-nine.

Cecilia and I never talked about it again.

19

I wake with pure white light pouring in from the window.

It's the morning after the police came knocking (sounds dramatic, doesn't it?), and I lie there for a moment, wondering whether Cecilia, somewhere behind me, is already awake. Without moving, I try to tune in to her breathing, decipher its rhythm. We used to awake in a tangle of legs and arms. Now, there's a cold, empty no-man's-land between us. Room enough for a child, perhaps.

But these thoughts don't fit the quality of the light. There's a crisp, happy hue to it. I realise all my fears from yesterday have evaporated. *Of course* the police don't know about Taylor and the accident. How could they? And even if they do, accidentally running a rapist over with the car isn't quite the same as breaking into a neighbourhood home and murdering someone, is it?

A neighbour saw me hanging around at night. So what?

Sorry, Inspector Lombardi, you'll have to look elsewhere.

Of course, there is the whole issue of the intruder: is this the same person Lombardi is after? Why would they be stalking our house? I try to think back to the other night, conjure up the glimpses I caught through the sheets of rain. They amount to little more than a dark blur, a shifting silhouette, vanishing into the night. There's *that* too—would a murderer flee? Flee from a man in his pyjamas, that is?

I set these thoughts aside and close my eyes, feel the light against my skin.

Work today, then the weekly beer with the lads. And, of course, my plans with Alice. Just thinking about it fills my heart with warmth and excitement. There's a touch of guilt, too, especially with my wife lying nearby. It's a touch I can ignore.

I roll over, ready to tiptoe out of bed, and I catch Cecilia peering at me just before she clasps her eyes shut, pretending to sleep. But it was there, the flash of her unreadable gaze, a question mark between her eyebrows. I suddenly wish I'd never told her about Taylor, never confessed to what happened. She's awake, wondering about me, her husband of many years. We've become a mystery to one another. Two books written in different tongues, covers shut, gathering dust in a forgotten place.

ON THE TRAIN, everyone looks like a corpse. Eyes down, backs rigid, swaying like puppets severed from their strings. I eye them with a strange sort of contempt, *knowing* no one else here is planning to write (love?) letters and share them in secret. Especially not with someone as beautiful as Alice.

I pull out a book, but my eyes won't stay on the words. They keep drifting up the page, then beyond it, to the rushing world outside. That's what I feel like now, a creature of speed and power and potential. Screw the intruder, screw the police, screw the sadness in my home. I'm elsewhere, savouring the sweet promise of Alice.

In the row opposite me, a couple of seats down, a man in a suit, unshaven, messy grey hair, lets out a long sigh, buries his face in his hands. I hadn't noticed him before. He emanates sadness. No one cares, or shows they care (which is the same thing, I suppose). For a very brief moment, I feel like saying something to him, offering some sort of reassurance, a degree of warmth. I don't, for fear his unhappiness might rub off on me. I don't need that now.

We ignore him. I sit straight; the others sway.

'IT'S GONE VIRAL.'

I grab the coffee from Bill's hands. His whole body is slack, mouth hanging open in disbelief. 'It's gone viral, Mark.'

'What are you talking about?'

We make our way through the corridor. As always, BeeCreative is buzzing with absolute boredom, barely concealed by the thin coat of Google-inspired colours on the walls.

'The video,' Bill says, almost to himself. 'The PimpPro *viral* video. It's... gone viral.' He actually scratches his head, bewildered.

'Wait a sec,' I say. 'The video? But we only came up with the idea—'

He scoffs. '*Idea.*'

'Yes, OK, you know what I mean. We only discussed it yesterday, how could—'

'That's the thing, the label was pressing us, wanted to know what we had for them. Before I could stop him, that muppet Sven replied to the email, mentioning a viral video.'

We've reached Meeting Room A. I push the door open, nod to Bill, inviting him to go first. 'And?'

'And,' he says, dropping into a chair, 'Mr PimpPro himself read the email. He was cc'd. Apparently, the painfully inept suggestion of a *viral video* was good enough for him. Went ahead and shot a video himself. On his phone.'

'What video is it?' I ask, powering up the laptop.

'Well... he's got this song, "Pop Yo' Ass", it's called.' He's about to continue, but can't let that one go. '"Pop Yo' Ass", Mark. Really? Is this what it's come to?'

'Go on.'

He sighs. 'Yes, so. Anyway, in the official video of this masterpiece, Mr PimpPro spends half of the time shouting into the camera, waving guns all over the place. *Guns*, Mark, left right and centre. That's the sort of gentleman we're dealing with here.'

I laugh. He doesn't.

'In his little home-made video,' Bill continues, 'PimpPro sings over the whole song. But instead of guns—which I'm sure he has lying about at home—he's holding vegetables.'

'Vegetables?'

'Yes. Vegetables.' Bill pinches the bridge of his nose. 'And some fruit. Cucumber, courgette. A banana.'

I laugh again. He still doesn't.

'Not sure what his point is, Mark, but people are loving it. *Loving* it.'

I've pulled up the video. One million views and counting since last night.

'No clickfarm?' I ask.

'No clickfarm. This is real.' Real is rare at BeeCreative.

The video is playing now: I watch as PimpPro smiles into the camera, right up close. We hear a click off-screen, the music begins. Bass thumping beneath high-pitched female backing vocals. The image shakes as he pumps his shoulders up and down, hints of dance moves. I notice he's sitting in a chair. A messy bed is just visible in the background (a super king-size bed). He filmed it in his bedroom.

When the chorus comes (*P-p-pop yo' ass, p-p-pop yo' ass*),

PimpPro produces a cucumber, points it mock-menacingly at the camera. He seems very proud of himself.

'Melody's catchy,' I say, winking at Bill.

He slowly rolls his eyes towards me, twitches his nose. No laughing matter to Bill, all this. 'Read the comments,' he groans.

'*No more gunz... Good job PimpPro... Veggies not guns...* They seem to have taken it as an anti-firearm stance.'

Bill sits up, eyes huge. 'Exactly! But *he* was the one waving guns about in the first place, in the official video!' he cries.

PimpPro has now produced a banana. I scan the comments. 'Yup, they're all hailing him as some sort of anti-gun hero.' I stop the video, and Bill lets out a sigh of relief. 'So he did our job for us. Makes us look bad,' I say.

'That's the other crazy thing,' Bill says, pulling out his phone. He taps around on the screen, then hands it to me. 'Here, look at this.' It's an email from the man himself. The message simply says: *U cunts r jeneuses.*

'By which,' Bill mutters, 'I s'pose he means *geniuses.*'

I frown. 'Hang on, he's giving us the credit?'

'Yup,' says Bill.

I stare at him in disbelief. 'Just because Sven mentioned a viral video in his email?'

'Yup.'

I chuckle. 'So, good news, really.'

He looks at me in shock. 'Good news? Really? Yes, wow, I'm so *proud* of this *jeneus* idea. Let me go add it to the CV.' His vast chest heaves in the thousandth sigh today. He checks his watch, starts getting up. 'Listen,' he says, 'I'll just pop—'

'*Pop yo' ass*?' I ask.

He pauses. 'Don't do this to me, Mark. Please.'

'Sorry. Couldn't help it.'

The muscles in his jaw quiver for a second. 'I'll pop over to my office. Call with Morino. Apparently, he was so impressed with your little stunt the other day, the whole *Don't just do it* slogan, that he might have something else for us.'

Bill's tone is cautious, but we both know this could be big. The image of Morino's sharp, minute features drifts into my mind—the way he'd smiled, impressed by my impromptu idea. I feel an irritating surge of childlike pride.

'Hm,' I say.

''Kay. Talk later.'

He heads off. I follow his waddling mass through the glass panels until he's safely out of view. When I'm sure he's gone, I pull out a plain white sheet of paper and a pen.

It's been a long, long time since I last wrote a letter.

FIFTEEN MINUTES IN, and the sheet is still painfully white. I haven't even dared to trace a single word. I tap the tip of the pen on the desk, bounce my knee, bite my lip. Had this been for Morino or any of the clients, I'd already have something decent to work with. But this is different—it's about Alice. It's not a sales pitch, nor a slogan.

What is it?

Words on paper, to a woman I hardly know.

Strange—the mere thought of Alice fills me with excitement, with a whirlwind of thoughts and glimpses of possibility. Yet it's hard to put them to paper.

What would I write if this were for my wife? I picture myself handing *her* a letter, meeting her perplexed, uninterested gaze. *A letter? Why in the world would you do that, Mark?*

A letter for Cecilia would be a bitter one. Or just thick, dark scribbles traced with an angry fist.

Guilt starts simmering in my chest again, but before it can boil over, I cast it aside. My mind is made up: whatever this leads to, I'm going to allow myself to enjoy a brief escape with Alice. I deserve it.

(*Do you?*)

Something outside catches my eye—it's Sven, approaching the meeting room. He has a chuffed smile on his face, clearly basking in the success of his incredible viral video non-idea. I sweep up pen and paper and thrust them into my pocket just as he's walking in.

'Mark, I—'

'Sorry, I'm in a bit of a hurry,' I say, pointing to my watch. 'Heading out for a while, OK?'

Before he has time to reply, I give him a patronising little pat on the shoulder, then dash through the door and towards the lifts.

I WALK TO THE BENCH, and all the way I'm desperately trying to come up with something decent to write in my letter. The words are still failing me. What tone to use? Witty? Warm? Seductive? Funny? Sexy? Formal?

A handful of people are queuing up at the coffee stand where we grabbed that first cup together. Not too busy now— the morning rush hour has gone by, and the lunch break is still a couple of hours away. I consider joining the queue, perhaps some extra caffeine in the bloodstream might help me come up with something to write. But I feel jittery enough as it is, so I just stroll past, eyeing the stand with a somewhat surprising feeling of affection. This small mobile establishment, the riverside bench I'm heading towards now, even the two square yards outside the house where we first met: landmarks on the map of this clandestine relationship of ours.

I like this image—a map that holds the coordinates of our budding affection. One you could produce to plot some tentative destination to all of this and measure the distance between where we are and where we thought we'd be.

I pull out the white sheet of paper, consider scribbling

something about this map that's now stuck in my mind. Would Alice like to read that? Would anybody? Even as I draw out the pen, it already sounds idiotic, far-fetched. A melancholic teenager's fancy.

And just as I'm standing here cursing myself, something catches my eye, under the bench. When I realise what it is, I smile. *Of course*, I think, shaking my head. *Of course she'd go first, wouldn't she?*

There it is, her letter. A sheet of paper folded again and again, into a neat little square. It's fastened with tape to one of the slats. After a quick furtive glance around me, I kneel down and carefully peel it off. Then, holding the letter as one would a butterfly, I sit down and take a deep breath. Why is this so intoxicatingly thrilling? Perhaps it's because my life has become so boring in all other respects.

I unfold the letter, pinching its corners between finger and thumb, until it's open and resting in my lap. Before reading the words, my eyes run along the lines where Alice folded the paper, small grooves of shadow across the white surface.

This is all the letter says:

When?

PS: BURN AFTER READING!

That's it. Five words (if you count *PS* as a word). One question and one exhortation. I scan the brief message slowly, meticulously, as I did with her first note. Funny, this 'letter' is even shorter than that original brief communication.

It doesn't matter. It's perfect.

There I was, dreaming up some long-winded nonsense, trying to find the right words to intrigue and enchant her. Five words from her, and here I am, intrigued and enchanted.

When? When are we going to Blackwood Cove together is what she's asking. Before considering an answer, I shift my gaze to the all-caps demand below. *Burn after reading!* There's something both funny and tender about this request. It's funny, because it really does feel like we're in some sort of spy story now. She must be feeling it too, and I like to find my silly emotions mirrored in hers. But it's tender, understanding, too. Some other woman might have demanded, or at least hoped, that I keep the letter safe, treasure it. But Alice knows I'm a married man. This is about protecting me from Cecilia, reminding me that, as much as all this is exciting and enjoyable, it's still illicit. We're partners in crime, and good criminals always cover their tracks.

I lean back against the bench, draw in a long breath filled with the damp riverside air. The river itself flows with unusual force, thick and filthy and nonetheless majestic.

When?

The truth is, I'd run off with her right now if she were here. It's hard to plan things, because my mind keeps feeding me images of the two of us walking barefoot along the Dorset coast, fingers entwined. Or treading through the woods, back towards the house, our pace measured but excited. And then her body, toned and smooth and electric, against mine.

When? This time, I picture her asking the question, a teasing smile on her face. *Come on, Mark, focus!*

I try to recall when the last BeeCreative retreat was. A company retreat might give me a decent reason for leaving the city for a couple of days. But chances are I never even went. The team activities leave us loathing each other more than ever, and the evening drinks are used by junior staff as occasions to kiss arse. It's unbearable for everyone involved. Bill once feigned a heart attack in order to get out of one.

Cecilia knows how much I hate the retreats. Perhaps I could tell her I've skipped so many, I can't possibly miss this one too. Except, what if she runs into one of my colleagues? It doesn't happen too often, but it does occasionally. Would she ask them why they aren't at the retreat? It's not the sort of thing she would do, but I can't dismiss the possibility entirely.

Something bobs up out of the river, for a second. A fish maybe. I catch a glimpse of what might be a mouth, a parting of eerily human lips, but dark and toothless. A ripple in the water, and the thing is gone. I watch the surface of the water, disgusted and intrigued, hoping it might emerge again. It doesn't.

This small occurrence leaves me with a sudden nausea, a feeling of unease. Clouds are gathering in the sky. It looks like rain.

Here I am, plotting a secret getaway with another woman. There's something in the air now, in the way the light has veered to a darker shade, that causes me to hesitate. Around me, the shadows appear to grow thicker. That unknown creature from the river, appearing out of the water like that, it feels like a bad omen, now. Like some sort of warning.

I look down at Alice's note, trying to draw comfort from it. It works. I close my eyes, let the images of Blackwood Cove flow back in, cleanse my mind of these eerie thoughts.

Senesi—that's it. I can tell Cecilia they've called us in for a two-day meeting at the Dublin office. Just me and Bill. There's no risk of her running into him, because Bill never leaves the office for lunch and heads straight home after work.

Why Dublin? Cecilia's voice, in my head.

Oh—the Dublin office handles Senesi's US marketing.

But BeeCreative has offices in the US. Why aren't they dealing with this?

Yeah, but the US offices are mostly for show. Just so we can add New York City to the list of places we operate in.

Do you have to go?

It's Senesi, Cecilia. Of course I have to go.

I start folding the note. Yes, I think with a smile, I can pull this off.

Cecilia knows Senesi is important, and wouldn't really question the likelihood of a meeting like this, or my need to attend it. Then it dawns upon me that she might not question any of it, at all. I realise she might not even care.

When? Alice again.

Next week, I think. Thursday through Saturday. Two working days, plus one to entertain the client.

I pull out my own sheet of paper and simply scribble down the dates, followed by:

Sound good?

I fold it carefully, just like she did, and use her strips of tape to fasten it beneath the bench, just like she did. I do all this while peering around inconspicuously, trying not to be seen.

Once it's done, I feel the urge to leave as fast as possible, as if this were some sort of crime scene. Then, just as I begin walking off, I remember Alice's request. I stop, search through my pockets and produce a lighter. Still looking around, I casually walk towards the embankment, and when I'm absolutely positive no one is looking, I unfold Alice's letter again and ignite the lighter. The flame quivers in the wind, but doesn't blow out.

With a small pang inside my chest, I bring the flame to a corner of the paper. At first, there's no fire. The corner simply turns black, the air around it suddenly visible, swirling with heat. Then the black becomes a flaky white, before vanishing altogether. The fire materialises, larger and hotter than I expected, and I almost drop the letter. But I hold on and watch as it's devoured by an almost perfect semicircle of black, white, then nothingness that spreads fast, growing in the flame's wake. In an instant, Alice's words vanish too, and I'm left holding a small triangle of burning paper. When I can't stand the pain any longer, I let go and watch it flutter through the air, on its way to the river. But it's gone before it can touch the water.

20

'Here you go, lads,' says Ed, fingers wrapped around four pints. He places them neatly at the centre of our table, not a drop spilled.

The King's Head is busy tonight, the room thick with bodies and chatter. It feels good. We're all here this time. Ed, Clyde, myself and even Phil's bothered to turn up.

'How's the little darling doing, Ed?' I ask, wiping a beer moustache from my lip.

'Oh, *God*.' He rolls his eyes in mock exhaustion. 'She's discovered Gabbie's make-up... here, check it out.' He pulls out his phone, starts thumbing through the pictures. Clyde and I lean in, already *ooh*ing and *aah*ing, while Phil inches forward, only just. He's allergic to children.

'There,' Ed says. 'This is her applying lipstick.' He raises the phone, showing it to each of us. In the image, Lilly is standing in the bathroom, her expression dead serious. The bottom half of her face, from the tip of her nose to the soft curve of her chin, is covered in a thick layer of strawberry-coloured lipstick, almost as if she were wearing a mask. She's frowning, clearly wondering what the adults find so amusing.

'It's like she's saying, "What's wrong? This looks *fan-tas-tic*,"' Clyde roars, slapping his leg and laughing a little too hard. He got here first, and I suspect he's already got a couple of pints in him.

I smile at Ed. 'She's a beauty, my friend.'

'Sure is,' he says proudly, turning the screen towards Phil, who glances at the image for less than a second, then twists his lips into some sort of smile and musters a frosty, 'Beautiful, beautiful. Yup.' His voice oozes boredom. I shoot him a dirty look, mouthing a quiet, *What's wrong with you?*

He shrugs—*What?*—then takes a long sip of beer. Phil, like most artists, is entirely devoid of empathy and sensitivity. He's also an arsehole.

Ed hasn't noticed. He's busy smiling at the screen, chuckling to himself as he puts the phone away.

'You're a great dad, mate,' Clyde says all of a sudden and slaps Ed on the shoulder with one of his big bear-hands. 'Truly are.'

Ed smiles modestly and then says, 'You would too, y'know? You'd be a fantastic dad.'

Clyde turns red, is about to say something, then bites his lip and reaches for his beer.

'Ed's right,' I say. 'You would.' I'm surprised to find out that it actually rings true tonight. Maybe it's just because I'm in a good mood, courtesy of Alice. 'You would, mate. Honest,' I insist. I notice Phil rolling his eyes, muttering a low *yeah right*, but I ignore him.

Clyde looks at me, his lips still on the glass. He meets my smile with a cold, intense stare. I frown, about to ask him what's up, but he looks away and downs his beer. As the others talk, I recall Ed telling me there was something up with Clyde, when we were at lunch at their place the other day. Something about him acting strange, I think. Maybe it's just because of how things turned out the last time we were at the King's Head, the whole thing with that woman. My stomach contracts in embarrassment at the mere memory of it.

Phil is looking around the pub, eyeing the women. He's wearing a pale blue shirt, which goes only too well with his ash-blond hair. Everything about him, his pose, the wave in his hair, all the way down to the folds in his clothing, seems both meticulously studied and effortlessly spontaneous. I notice lots of people glancing at him, both men and women. He has the sort of magnetic beauty you can't help observing. Phil's charm is exhausting.

I lean towards him. 'How's, er, what's her name? The girl you were with at the party the other night?' The night I met Alice.

Phil tears his eyes from a pretty young thing a few tables away, who proceeds to whisper something to a friend of hers. They both giggle. He stares at me blankly, his lips parted, as if I'd spoken in a foreign language.

'The girl you were with,' I say. 'At the party. The other night. Blonde, good looking.' I've just described at least ten of his latest flings.

He peers up, right eye squinting beneath a frown. He genuinely has no idea who I'm talking about.

As I watch him struggle to recall who his 'girlfriend' was, I ask myself what it must be like to live like Phil. To have no interest in a real relationship, no willingness to commit to anything stable, honest. To lack any sincere curiosity about other people, especially women. It must be horrifying.

Then something seems to click in his memory, but just as he's about to speak, his cell phone lights up. He glances down, then hurriedly picks it up.

He smiles at me awkwardly; then, twisting away and bringing the phone to his ear, he says, 'Can't talk now,' into the phone, in a hushed, tense voice. He's leaning so low his head is almost under the table. Then, in a whisper, he adds, *'Yes. He's here.'* At least, that's what it sounds like, although it might have been, *Yes. It's easier.* I'm not sure.

I turn to the others, wondering if they're seeing this too, and find Clyde sneaking another one of his suspicious looks my way. He quickly resumes a conversation with Ed about a TV series or something.

Phil whispers a few inaudible words, then straightens his back again. "Kay. 'Kay. Bye,' he says, louder now, but sort of mechanically, then hangs up.

What was all that about?

I consider asking him, because something tells me my question would make him squirm (and watching Phil squirm would be a thing of beauty), but the way he's acting, the way he doesn't know what to do with his hands—drumming on the table, clasping them, cracking his knuckles—stops me.

'I'll grab another round,' I say, getting up. And as I make my way to the bar, I'm struck by the inexplicable certainty that Phil was speaking to my wife.

That movement—the hasty way he fetched the phone off the table. It reminds me of how eager Cecilia was to keep her own phone from me the other day at the restaurant.

Phil and Cecilia. Could it be?

I've always been uncomfortable, jealous even, when Phil is around Cecilia. They both have that same sort of exceptional aura of beauty around them, the kind that sets them apart from everyone else. And they both work in the art world, of course. Phil as a creator, Cecilia as a curator. But, I think, other than that, they're quite different. Cecilia is quiet, caring (or used to be) and introspective. Phil is... well, he's a cunt.

Can't talk now. He's here.

Is that what Phil said?

'Hello...? What can I get you?' the bartender is asking me.

Not for the first time, judging by her tone. I stare at her for a second, bewildered. She's young, with pale skin and unnaturally dark hair cut short across the forehead. A student, I reckon. She's looking at me with a polite, mildly concerned smile on her lips.

'Oh, sorry,' I mutter. 'Work,' I add, by way of explanation.

'No worries.' She nods past me, towards our table. 'Four lagers?'

'Yes, thanks.'

While I wait, I look at my friends. Phil is sitting with his back towards me, stiff, shoulders drawn in. This definitely isn't his normal self. Ed and Clyde are chatting, with Clyde sneaking his occasional odd glances my way. What the hell is going on tonight? I try to fix my mind on Ed, his placid, reassuring smile.

The pub door opens. My eyes drift mechanically towards it just as a group of four or five pour in from the cold. One of them, a woman, looks familiar. I study her, try to remember where I've seen her. I watch her discreetly as she and her friends make their way towards an empty table, slipping out of their gloves and scarves and coats. Someone says something, and she laughs. It's a nice, genuine sound. One I've heard before. Suddenly, I know who it is. It's the woman from the other evening, the one Clyde tried to chat up.

I instinctively turn to him. He's seen her. He's watching her now, lips pursed, still as a statue, humiliation emanating from him in waves. Then his eyes turn to me. I really don't want him to know that I've seen her—that I've seen *him* see her—but he must've figured it out. He stares at me, chin tilted downwards, eyebrows drawn together. I whistle a soundless little tune and fix my attention on nothing in particular on the ceiling.

'Here you go,' the young lady says. Four pints are lined up on the bar. I thank her, pay, and grab the glasses.

As I make my way back to the table, I realise I don't want to be there. I really need a smoke.

'I'll just step outside for a sec,' I say, putting down the pints. 'Missed call from Cecilia. I'll just ring her to make sure everything's OK.' I don't bother grabbing my coat, and I walk fast towards the door. Then, halfway there, I remember the cigarettes and lighter tucked inside my coat pocket. I curse, spin on my heel, and head back to grab it.

Outside on the pavement, I let out a long sigh. A white plume of breath flows from my lips. I step away from the window, dig through my pocket for the cigarettes and finally, *finally*, light up.

The nicotine floods my bloodstream, and I feel the muscles in my shoulders unclench. Still, there's a nagging sense of unease, a restlessness that I can't shake. My friends, in the pub, these people I've known all my life—I wonder how healthy it is to cling on to our ties, to these semi-weekly gatherings. It used to be fun. Heck, even Phil used to make us laugh, with his stories about the artsy folks he knows. Now, tonight, it all feels like an enormous effort. I want to be away from them, even from Ed, with his serene family life. Pathetic Clyde, with his hostile attitude this evening. And Phil, who might have something going on with my wife.

I throw the cigarette stub in a puddle and grind it under the heel of my shoe until it turns into brownish muck. Wishing I'd brought the beer out with me, I light up another.

I turn around, walk towards one of the two windows of the King's Head that look out onto the street. Standing slightly to one side, half concealed by the wall, I peer in. Ed, Clyde and Phil are all craning their necks towards the centre of the table. Their eyes are wide, lips barely moving. They look like conspirators, planning some sort of dark deed.

They're talking about me, I think, for no particular reason. It sounds paranoid, but observing their intense gazes, the way the topic seems to have brought them all together, even indifferent Phil, makes me think I might be right.

Surprisingly, Clyde is doing most of the talking. He seems serious, focused, which is rare for him. Ed's brow is furrowed, while Phil seems to be listening intently.

I watch them for a second. Ed, whose face I can see clearly, shakes his head incredulously, perhaps dismissive of what Clyde is saying. Clyde gesticulates towards him, animated now, forcing his belly into the table. Ed shrugs, unconvinced.

What are they talking about? Why did they wait for me to leave?

Peering in from the dark, a strange sense of not really being there washes over me. I feel *out of focus*, as if the edges of my body have suddenly turned jagged.

I don't belong here anymore. Not tonight, anyway. I belong with Alice, along the coast, in the little clandestine world we're carving out for ourselves. That's where I want to be.

The image of that detective appears in my mind, unwarranted. What was her name? Something Italian... *Lombardi?* Yes, that's it. The thought of her makes me uncomfortable.

What would she make of my friends in there, talking behind my back? What would *she* deduct from their whispering and glaring and concealing?

For no apparent reason, I'm sure she'd tell me that I'm imagining things. That I'm summoning ghosts. That this, all of this, is just a twisted trick of my mind.

For some reason, this thought makes me shudder. I flick the cigarette far away and head back in.

'So?' Ed asks.

'So what?' I say. The words come out harsh, a rabid dog's

bark. I'm back at the table, and I want them to know that *I* know. That whatever they were discussing just a second ago, I know what they're up to.

Except, what if they're up to nothing at all? What if I *am* being paranoid about this whole thing?

Ed frowns. 'You said you were going to ring Cecilia,' he explains, stating the obvious. 'Was she OK?'

'Oh,' I say, with the creeping feeling of being an idiot ballooning in my gut. 'Yeah, all fine. She's fine. Thanks.'

I sit down and take a long, thirsty swig from my beer. The others might or might not be eyeing me with unease. Hard to tell at the moment.

'So...' I begin, having no idea about what I'm about to say.

'Mark, mate,' Phil says, relieving me from my impotent urge to speak. But, immediately, he seems to plunge into a similar hesitation.

'What is it?'

Phil clears his throat. 'Oh, nothing important. It's just, you mentioned Cecilia and reminded me of something.'

I don't like the sound of her name on his lips.

'Go on.'

He swallows. Is he nervous, or am I just seeing things?

'Well, I'm trying to arrange an exhibition at the Tate Modern. It's tricky, even with my connections. I reckon she'd be able to help out. Put in a good word, y'know? It's silly really, what with her work and what I do, we should be working together.' He smiles.

'Sure,' I say, as casually as I can.

Phil picks up his beer. 'Anyway, yeah, just that. Tell her I'll be in touch, maybe?'

Is he avoiding my eyes?

'Will do.'

I sense another lull in the conversation, and I don't think I can stand it. 'Listen, guys,' I say, 'I think I'd better head back.' I give no reason.

'Are you all right?' Ed asks me. His concern is genuine, as always.

'Course I am.' I smile.

'Hang on,' Clyde says, reaching into his pocket. 'It's my turn to buy you all a round.' He produces a bunch of scrunched-up fivers, a couple of coins slipping through his sausage fingers and rattling on the table. His evil eye is a little less evil, and I think perhaps whatever was said here earlier might not have been about me at all. 'Couple more pints?'

Perhaps I should stay a while longer, but Clyde has put me off. I *know* he's got something against me—*me*, the one who always stands up for him! I can hardly bear the sight of him. He's too fat, tonight, too alone. My eyes drift to the banknotes piled up in his hand, and I hate him for not having a proper job, a proper life. Not even a fucking wallet.

And Phil? How can I sit next to someone who is likely planning to sleep with my wife?

I flash them my warmest smile. 'Sorry, lads. Same time next week?'

Except, I won't be with them next week. I'll be with Alice.

21

Cecilia is in the kitchen.

She's sitting at the breakfast table, gazing outside, and although she is facing away from me, I know her eyes mirror the grey-blue morning sky. Her chin is resting against the back of her hand. Lost in thought. Lost to me.

I'm standing in the doorway, heart pounding in my chest, gathering the courage to tell her, ever so casually, about my days away. My supposed work engagement. As I step into the kitchen, I realise this is the first outright lie I've told her, with regard to Alice. The door to the kitchen has become my own personal Rubicon.

'Good morning,' I say. I don't make it sound too cheerful, because our *good mornings* haven't been cheerful for a long while. But I do feign a degree of energy, a spring in my step, as I hop-walk to the fridge. I grab a bottle of cold water, pop open the cap and ask her, 'Sleep well?' Not sure why, but I'm giving a just-got-back-from-a-jog sort of vibe, although all I've done is climb out of bed and walk down the stairs. It must be the nerves.

She casts her eyes upon me. And that's what she does, by the way: she doesn't just look at me. It's more like lifting something heavy and hurling it my way. There's an almost unbearable grace in my wife's movements. Perhaps because the guilt has sharpened my senses, but her turning around occurs in slow motion: the rise and fall of her shoulders as she breathes, the joining and parting of her eyelashes in a blink, the gentle sway of her hair and shoulders and, finally, her gaze on me.

I stand there, gazed-upon, bottle in hand, awaiting her answer to my inane question. *Sleep well?* It doesn't get more inane than that. Yet she doesn't answer. She just sits and stares for a minute, and her eyes are so fixed, so *intent*, it feels like they are drilling their own questions into my head, prodding, demanding answers.

Then comes a smile, and my muscles relax. The relief is so strong, I almost laugh out loud. 'Yes,' she says. 'How was it last night?'

'Oh, you know. The usual,' I say, putting the water back in the fridge. 'Phil said he might be in touch,' I add, just throwing the words out there, but immediately turning around to study her expression.

'Yes? Why?' Cecilia asks. Her usual sphinx self.

'He says he wants to try to organise an exhibition at the Tate. Thinks you might be able to help him.'

'Oh. OK, sure.' If something's up, it doesn't show. Her cell phone is on the island, sitting beside her arms, now crossed. It stands out among the cups and breakfast bowls, like a clue of some sort. I feel like grabbing it and scrolling through her call log, to find her call to Phil last night. Would it even be there? Surely not, right?

I walk to the island and reach out. My hand hovers above the phone for an instant. As it does, I watch Cecilia from the corner of my eye, eager to detect some sort of reaction. And perhaps there is—a slight stiffening of the spine, a tension in the air. But, again, it might all be in my head. I need a holiday. A holiday with Alice.

My hand drifts past the phone and grabs the coffee jug.

'Ah,' I say, pouring some into a mug. 'By the way, I might have to leave for a couple of days. Senesi. Bill and I are meeting them at the Dublin office.' I let out a I-wish-I-didn't-have-to-do-this sigh. 'We leave Thursday, back on Sunday.'

I've prepared my script. I have a reasonable answer ready for any objection she may put forth. I set my jaw, awaiting her response.

She reaches out and grabs a magazine from the messy stack on the chest of drawers, flicks distractedly through the pages. 'OK,' she says.

'OK...?' I ask, and immediately wonder if she's picked up on the disbelief in my voice. Disappointment too, perhaps.

She peers up from the magazine. 'It's Senesi, isn't it? It's important. Of course it's OK.'

And there it is: the go-ahead for my trip with Alice.

'Ah. Yes, great.'

Then suspicion hits me: *She's planning to see Phil while I'm away.*

I freeze, the mug halfway to my mouth. Is that really it? I'm off to spend time with Alice while she betrays me with Phil? Has it really come to this?

Our marriage was meant to be different, unique. It was meant to be *happy*. But then again, aren't they all? Suddenly, my brief escape with Alice appears entirely warranted.

I sip on the coffee, considering the possibility that I'm making all this up, a justification of sorts for my actions.

And yet, and yet.

Cecilia simply isn't that sort of woman, I tell myself. She

might be distant, cold, but she's not a cheater. She might not even love me anymore, but she wouldn't betray me, would she?

No, she wouldn't.

I watch as she distractedly draws up a sleeve, running her nails against an itchy spot on her arm.

'What's that?' I ask.

There's a dark bruise on her skin, just above the elbow. I put down the coffee and reach out, gently holding her arm in the cup of my hand.

'Oh, that,' she says, 'it's nothing, really.'

But it doesn't look like nothing. I push her sleeve farther up, gently, and see that the bruise is larger than I thought, spreading to just beneath the shoulder. Its purple-blue is a horrid sight against the white of her skin.

'Cecilia, what—?'

She pulls back, but I hold on. '*Really*,' she insists, 'I was carrying the shopping in, and I bumped against the cupboard drawer. That's all. It hurt a bit, yes, but it's fine now.' She's smiling.

And that smile, it unleashes a sudden complicated burst of affection that floods my system. Seeing her here, fragile and betrayed, hurts me. Odd details stand out: the faint wrinkles in the corners of her eyes (when did they first appear?). The dimple on her left cheek. The pressure of her slender wrist against my open palm. It feels like I could snap it, just like that.

'It's OK, Mark.' Her eyes are deep, beautiful.

I have to release her arm now, because I'm on the verge of telling her everything, confessing to my plans with Alice. Begging for forgiveness.

'OK.'

I pick up the coffee again and drink. Cecilia covers the bruise, returns to her magazine. We sit in silence.

But the image still lingers. There's something unsettling about that bruise, something sinister.

22

Monday.

Sitting on the tube, mind drifting. Cecilia's bruise. Alice's smile. Blackwood Cove. Inspector Lombardi. Phil's face. Work and Senesi. The intruder. The still and silent room that was meant for our son. Even, for an instant, Taylor's dead body lying on the road, motionless in the headlights.

I sit up, breathe in. My excitement at the prospect of leaving London with Alice is mingled with an ongoing unease, the sense that something is wrong. Not only wrong, but also blatantly obvious, except I'm the only one who can't see it. Like the rest of the world is in on a joke, while I'm left here wondering.

Someone, a few seats down, drops a coin. I spy the bare arm of a woman reaching for the ground to pick it up. The sound makes me think of Clyde the other evening. His fat hands holding the pile of scrunched-up banknotes, having clawed them out of his pockets. No wallet, just cash stuffed in his trousers. It had pissed me off, watching that, but it shouldn't have. It's not as if owning a wallet says anything about a man. Then again, perhaps it does.

I pull out my phone and scroll through my contacts until I find him. He's saved simply as 'Clyde'. I happen to know that my number appears on his phone under the name 'The Markmeister General'.

I stare at his name, that string of letters forever entwined with him, my childhood friend, the fat loser, the man he has become. This obese and graceless image inhabiting and obfuscating the memory of the kid I knew. Time can be cruel. In fact, that's all it is.

I tap the call button and bring the phone to my ear. I'm nervous, because there's always a sort of darkness surrounding Clyde, something you don't want rubbing off on you. I'm afraid this phone call might taint this day, somehow.

The phone rings, I hold my breath. Once, twice, then: 'I'm sorry. The number you have dialled…' I hang up on the little robot woman's voice with a sigh of relief. I can do this some other time. And, besides, whatever is bothering Clyde will probably fix itself.

'Go on, play it.' The voice of a spotty teenager in stained trousers and a worn hoodie. He's sitting next to a girl of similar age, wearing a bright white shirt and a red skirt held up by black braces. Heavy make-up, bubble gum. They're both staring into her phone. Everything they're wearing seems to be making a statement I can't quite grasp.

'Go on!' He leans his shoulder into hers.

She smiles, glassy eyes fixed on the smartphone's screen, her chin sinking into a second chin.

A second later, the carriage is treated to the thumping notes of the latest viral hit.

'P-p-p-pop yo' ass, pop yo' ass…'

The boy throws back his head and slaps his knee, letting out a gurgle. His teeth are coated in a thick layer of something the colour of peanut butter. He's loving it. The girl, still staring at the screen, nods approvingly, her thin lips parting in a cocky little smile.

'This is where he pulls out a banana,' the boy howls. 'Legend!'

Heads turn. Someone lets out a *tsk*. Most of us ignore them. A couple of people smile, I notice, and start humming the tune. I think of Bill, what he'd do if he were here now. I picture him losing it, freaking out, screaming at the two kids with his belly wobbling and spittle flying. The thought makes me smile.

I close my eyes.

In three days' time, I'll be setting off with Alice. How many hours is that? Seventy-two. How many seconds, how many slivers of time until I'm beside her? I can't tell.

As the wagon rumbles and hisses, I lean back and start counting. Happily, uselessly, I count.

One, two, three...

23

Alice:

> *Thursday, Friday, back Saturday?*
> *Will we sit in the sand and drink wine?*
> *Will you hold my hand?*
>
> *Am I asking too much of you, M.?*
>
> *P.S.: You know what to do.*

Me:

> *Yes. Yes. Yes!*
> *No.*
>
> *P.S.: I burnt.*

Alice:

> *I'll catch the 9:41 train from Victoria and be in Salisbury at*
> *11:20.*
> *Meet you there?*
>
> *P.S.: I burn in many ways.*

Me:

> *Meet you there, wine and glasses at the ready.*
> *I can't wait.*

There was no way to match her *I burn in many ways*, so I
simply told her the truth, in so many words. *I can't wait.*

And, just like that, a few notes concealed beneath a bench
lead us to our days in Blackwood Cove, to a home for our
budding love, to my betrayal of Cecilia.

24

I'm a confident, good-looking man in his late thirties cruising along the M3 in a rented open-top car. The sky is a flawless blue, the traffic obliging, and my destination is Alice.

In the boot are enough clothes for three days (and more, I wasn't quite sure what style I'd go for, so I grabbed a few extra shirts and sweaters), my toiletries, and a bottle of fine Chardonnay with two carefully wrapped crystal glasses. I play a thousand variations of Alice's reaction to them when I'll pull them out. Each one leaves me tingling with hope and expectation.

I bring my wrist to my nose, try to pick up the scent of my cologne (Green Irish Tweed, the same George Clooney favours, allegedly) against the wind. I like it. It's a manly-man smell, one Alice might think appropriate for the man she thinks I am. The man I *am*.

Salisbury is about an hour away now, the looming grey of London replaced by vast open skies and gentle green trees on either side of the motorway. I should get out of the city more often, I think, predictably. But it's true: the wider horizon seems to have relieved a pressure nestled in my head, one I wasn't aware of. It feels good to stare so far into the distance.

'OK, I'm off,' I said to Cecilia this morning. She was still in her pyjamas, warm and soft from the night's sleep. She stood by the door, golden hair slightly ruffled, and leaned forward for a kiss. Her lips were soft but ungiving, the kiss a quick one. 'Text me when you get there, OK?' she said, as if reading from a script.

We stood there for a second, me almost action-figure stiff in my suit and tie. Cecilia looked different this morning. The long, elegant strokes that make up her body appeared frail, hesitant, as if drawn by an insecure hand. As we assessed one another (guardedly and alert, the way you do with a possible, albeit minor, threat), I wondered if she could sense that I wasn't going to a Senesi meeting at all. That I was, in fact, off to meet another woman. But she couldn't. It hurt to think that, to know she was unaware, vulnerable, so I waved a little wave and went to meet the cab driver. She lingered by the door as I drove off.

I had the cab drop me off at Victoria, where I rented the car and bought the wine. The two glasses I'd taken from our rarely used dining set, late last night, rearranging it afterwards in orderly rows, as if untouched.

So here I am now, driving and daydreaming, when my phone starts buzzing. Keeping a hand on the steering wheel, I reach out to the passenger seat, where the annoying little machine sits, emitting its nagging tune.

It's Bill. What does he want?

I told him I'd need a few days off to attend a friend's wedding. 'Surprise announcement,' I told him. 'Sorry I couldn't warn you sooner.' It sounded sufficiently realistic. Plus, it's the sort of thing Bill's busy brain automatically filters out as uninteresting.

My eyes shooting from the screen to the road ahead, I

consider ignoring his call. But Bill isn't the sort of person you can ignore. What if he keeps calling and calling while I'm in Blackwood Cove with Alice?

I curse, hoping he might just give up. He doesn't. The ringtone has grown hysterical now, channelling Bill through its metallic notes.

I pick up. 'What's up?' I say casually. Before he can reply, I add, 'Bill, I'm driving; perhaps I should call you—'

'Pull over.' Firm, uncompromising.

I frown. 'Bill, listen, I'm in the middle of—'

'Pull over, Mark.'

Damn. What's got into him?

'OK, here's a petrol station coming up. Two secs and I'll pull up. Shall I call you back?'

'I can wait.'

Of course you can.

I let the phone drop into my lap, flick the indicator on and, cursing profusely under my breath, pull up next to the petrol station. Inside, the cashier eyes me through a gap in the shelves. He glances at me for a second, then looks away, uninterested.

I kill the engine and give it a few more seconds before grabbing the phone again. I do this gratuitously, just to piss Bill off a little more. I feel he deserves it.

'OK,' I say finally, 'what is it?'

'Where are you?'

I let out a frustrated little chuckle. 'Bill, I told you, I'm on my way to a wedding.'

'I know *that*,' he says. 'Where are you *now*?'

I'm about to tell him, but I hesitate. I don't want him (or anyone else, for that matter) knowing where I'm headed. I decide to ignore his question. 'What is it, Bill? What's going on?'

'You have to come back,' he says, his tone definitive.

I laugh, although I feel like shouting. 'Are you *joking*? I told you, I have to—'

'You have to come back, Mark. That's what you have to do.' Same stone-cold, unwavering tone. I can picture him: frown, wrinkled lip, sneer of cold command. All of a sudden, I'm speaking to Ozymandias. Before I can protest again, he adds, 'It's Senesi.'

Damn.

I push open the door and step outside to stretch my legs.

'Your idea, they want to run with it. But they want to run with it *now*. The big boss flew in from Milan yesterday, wants to meet us.'

'*What?*' I almost scream. 'Why didn't Morino warn us?'

Bill scoffs. 'Because he's an arsehole. It's some sort of psycho power play. You know him.'

I do.

'They want to discuss the whole *Do it Italiano* concept. And, if I recall correctly, there *is* no concept. It's just you winging it and somehow pulling it off.'

'But...' My mind is reeling. Why is this happening now? 'We were awaiting the formal go-ahead; we... Surely he can't expect...' I say lamely. I sound like a mumbling, trembling intern. I pinch the bridge of my nose and ask, 'What have we got?'

'A few sketches by Linda and Jayesh... a couple of layouts... that's it really.'

I swallow. 'What are they like? The sketches, I mean,' I ask tentatively. I already know the answer.

'What do you think they're like, Mark?' he growls indignantly. 'Do you really need me to spell it out for you? OK, all right. Sure, I'll tell you: they are a steaming pile of shit, Mark. That's what they're like. They're so bad I feel like gouging my eyes out, my friend. But that still wouldn't be enough, Mark, because the sight of them would still haunt my bloody dreams. So I'd end up having to put a gun to my head, Mark, that's what I'd need to do. And...'

I stretch my arm out, putting some air between the phone and my ear. Bill's voice rattles on, small and metallic, spewing disgust at our bright young minds' efforts. Eventually, he stops. When I bring the phone back to my ear, he's panting.

'Listen,' he says, his voice pleading now. 'I could really do with a helping hand here. There's no way I can sell this the way you did. Can you make it?' Then, like a stab in the heart, he adds, 'Please?'

My eyes drift beyond the petrol station, towards an open field, the rooftops of houses in the near distance. A small village whose name I do not know. I sigh.

For all his begging, I know Bill's desperate tones are due to the stress of the job rather than the prospect of me not being there when Senesi arrive. This pleading is a game of sorts, a pantomime for the benefit of nobody in particular. He knows I'll be there. Why? Because I always am. Because I'm reliable. Because: *Mark? You can count on him, no matter what.*

Clouds are gathering in the distance. It seems impossible; the sky was so clear just a minute ago.

'I can't, Bill.' And then again, because these words are so alien to me, at work: 'I can't.'

I have a sense of how unexpected this is for him, because it is for me, too. Letting a colleague down when a big project is at stake? This simply isn't me.

The dark clouds and the clear blue are pitted against one another now, like skies from different places. I wonder idly who will prevail.

'Are you serious?' he asks at last. The words come after a long, dense silence.

'Yes. I'm sorry.' I'm not sorry.

Bill is processing the information now, a grinding of worn

cogs in his mind. He's oscillating between fury and concern. How could I *do* this to him? *Why* would I do this to him?

I sit in the car again, slam the door beside me. Cars whiz passed on the motorway. Bill still hasn't spoken, but his silence is telling enough.

First I lie to Cecilia, now this professional betrayal. Again, it feels like a point of no return. As it turns out, there's more than one Rubicon to be crossed.

I'm mildly concerned, but as bad as this is, it's not like I'm going to be fired over it. I'm too valuable to the company, Bill and I both know it. We also both know I've never had to rely on that fact before.

'OK. I'll work it out somehow,' Bill says. He's too hurt, or worried, to be resentful, so the words come out strangely flat. But an instant later he spits out, 'What the *hell* is wrong with you, Mark?'

I have no idea how to answer his question, but there's no need to. Bill hangs up.

The man in the petrol station shop casts a look my way as I pull out. I wave a friendly wave his way. He frowns, confused.

The car seems to slide along the road, drifting frictionless towards our destination. Towards Alice.

Up above, the clouds have retreated.

25

I kill the engine in the Salisbury station parking lot. The air is brisk, the sun bright. I check my watch—ten past eleven. Ten minutes until the train, *her* train, pulls into the station. I don't know if that's too long or too short a wait. I can see the tracks from here and consider simply waiting in the car. But I can't sit still, I need to move, do something. Before getting out, I fix my hair in the rear-view mirror, smooth it out. I'm happy with my looks today. Nothing stuck in my teeth, eyebrows sharp and neat. I consider applying another puff of cologne, but I'm afraid it might be overbearing.

The station is quiet, a dozen or so people waiting, scattered across the platforms. There's a café, with a round wooden table in front of it. I order a cappuccino, then sit down, facing the tracks.

Without drinking the coffee (my stomach has currently shrunk to the size of a walnut), I realise that this is the perfect place for our encounter. The ideal spy setting: Alice and I, we meet in train stations, we write secret letters, we burn after reading. What is it about trains and mysteries, stations and mischief? Something to do perhaps with the blur of the world outside, a sense of momentary disorder, a place between places in which concealing one's tracks becomes easier. And then, the station itself: a passage, a non-location, with people stepping on and off the trains, coming and going, blending into transient crowds, then swiftly vanishing. Like someone abandoning the scene of a crime.

The scent of coffee is alluring despite my cramped stomach. I watch the lazy vapour spirals curl and loop and dissipate into the morning air. In the end, I give in and take a sip. The paper cup is hot in my hand and the coffee surprisingly good. I wonder if the taste of it will be too strong on my breath when I meet Alice. Would it be off-putting? What strange concerns to have at this point in my life.

Drifting back into our little spy-themed encounter, I think we should have established a secret dress code. Like they do in films. *I'll be wearing a hat, or a grey pocket square, or carrying a black umbrella.* It would have been fitting. Nonsensical, of course, because we already know what the other looks like, but fitting nonetheless.

Just as I'm thinking this, the voice from a loudspeaker announces the arrival of the train. I was lost in thought, so I miss the words, but a quick glance at my watch tells me it's time.

A loud hiss, the pressure of swirling air against my skin, and there it is, the train rolling in. I find myself standing, eyes darting from one carriage to the next. In my chest, my heart is both mute and beating too fast. I pause on one of the doors, *sensing* her presence beyond it. A concealed mechanism pushes it out and to the side, and people begin spilling out. There she is, magically (but also *obviously*) stepping out of the very exit I was eyeing.

I smile, then I laugh. Genuine, happy, slap-your-knee laughter. Because Alice is stepping off the train and, it would seem, into a Bond film: she's wearing a floppy, wide-brimmed hat that almost conceals her face. Beneath it, large impenetrable sunglasses and luscious red lipstick. Her clothing—an elegant yet nondescript grey dress flowing down to her ankles, white scarf, double-breasted trench coat, black gloves —is so *not* her, yet she looks stunning. She stops mid-platform, trolley case at her feet, and glances about. More than one man eyes her as they walk past. Before I can move, she lowers the sunglasses a little, revealing her deep, dark, mischievous eyes. She winks at me, then tilts her head towards the exit.

I nod knowingly. Of course—spies' encounters can't occur in the open. Smiling like a kid, I walk out, make my way to the car. She's following me at a distance, like a stranger. Like a co-conspirator. I hear footsteps behind me, try to tune into hers, pick them apart from the others.

When I reach the car, I stand by the door for a second, without turning around. The noise of the small crowd fades as people head off to their own further destinations, leaving the station behind. Just one set of footsteps remains, tap-tap-tapping towards me. Then it stops, and my nose is filled with the scent of Alice.

I turn around. She's not wearing the glasses now, and her pearl-white teeth are even whiter against the red lipstick. I feel like kissing her, but I don't. Not yet.

She looks down, hands flowing along her sides. 'Well?' she asks. 'How do I look?'

At this very moment, I can't think of anything more beautiful.

'You *know* how you look, Alice.'

I love the sound of her name in my mouth.

.   .   .

THE WIND WHIRLS through Alice's hair, capturing strands of it and making them dance like electric ribbons. She laughs, trying-but-not-trying to hold them down with the palm of her hand.

'Too windy?' I ask. 'Shall I raise the top?'

'No!' she cries. 'It's perfect.' She tilts her head back, eyes closed, arms stretched out. Gusts of air send waves through her clothes, embracing her, pressing against her skin, hiding and revealing the curves, the lines, the texture of Alice.

'Ah!' she says, suddenly sitting up again. '*Almost* perfect...' She unbuckles her seat belt and twists around to grab something in the back seat. Her shoulder brushes against mine, and I can't help glancing down, towards her waist, studying the way her back narrows there before widening gently at the hips, following some sort of secret geometry designed to drive me mad with desire.

'There,' she says, sitting down again. In her hands, a packet of cigarettes and a lighter. She pulls out two cigarettes, slips one between her lips, then turns towards me, placing the other one in mine. She wiggles the lighter in front of me until the flame has lit the tip to her satisfaction. She then lights her own, breathes in and says, '*Now* it's perfect.'

The road slips by; we've left Salisbury behind. Wiltshire gradually fades into Dorset, and everything is happening so smoothly, so easily, as if we were propelled by some benign force, shining down on us, approving of us. Whatever this is, it feels right.

There are silences between us, of course. Some long, some short. At first, I find them almost unbearable. My stomach contracts; I hold my breath, grit my teeth. But all it takes is a quick look at Alice, so comfortable in her skin. I relax. It's normal, isn't it? These silences, they're natural. We are, despite it all, almost perfect strangers.

But Alice's silence isn't that of a stranger. It's more like a comfortable absence of words. It sounds like... confidence, maybe. Confidence in her, in me, in our being together now.

While I'm thinking (*over*thinking) about these matters, she suddenly leans into me, presses her nose against my neck.

'What is *that*?' she asks, breathing in. She's so enthusiastic, so physical. I'm not used to this.

'Like it?' I say, embarrassed.

She nods silently, her cheek still resting on my shoulder. The skin on my neck tingles, as if drawn towards her lips. 'Hmm-hmm.'

I hold the steering wheel a little tighter, breathe the cool air in. It's confusing, all this. The novelty of a woman beside me. But that's unfair; it's not even true. I've had quite a few women beside me. I spend most of my time beside another woman, a beautiful woman—my wife. Yet this is entirely different for some reason. Cecilia, with her distance, her unwillingness to love me, *she* has made this different.

'Look!' Alice cries, once again tearing me from my spiralling thoughts. She's pointing up, towards the sky. 'Starlings!'

Hundreds of them, thousands perhaps. A murmuration, a living black cloud, swelling and flowing and coiling against the delicate winter-blue of the sky above. I slow down a little, as do the other two cars currently sharing this stretch of road with us. Their heads, grey silhouettes behind their windows, are turned towards the birds, too. Fingers point, mouths hang open in wonder.

We watch, all of us, the liquid motion of the starlings, as the cloud samples shape after shape, at times suggestive of familiar things (a cup, a duck, a cursive *E*), others, entirely alien. The rules behind their motion appear to be so simple. Closeness, distance, nothing else. *Get this close, but no closer. That far, no farther. Fly free, but don't leave.*

Alice turns towards me, and there's pink on her cheeks. Her eyes are wide and incredulous, her smile is that of a child. *Did you see that? Did that* really *happen?*

We both laugh, because it's all *too* perfect. Then the smile on her lips slowly fades, and her gaze is so deep, so pensive, I fear something might be wrong. I'm about to ask her, when she rests her head against my shoulder. I feel her hands wrap around my arm and give a little squeeze.

Something catches in my throat. It's ridiculous, but I'm so happy I could actually cry.

Bill's voice, low and raspy and furious: *What the hell is wrong with you, Mark?*

26

The sand whispers under our feet as we walk. We pick a spot to sit down, and before she does, I swing the rucksack off my shoulder, unzip it (careful not to show her the wine and two glasses tucked inside it—not yet) and pull out a blanket. I lay it carefully on the sand and the pebbles at her feet. Alice smiles, kneels down, tugging at the corners to smooth out the folds.

The cove itself is small, but stunning. It's off the beaten path, and tourists tend to go for the more easily accessible and better-known places along the Jurassic Coast—Durdle Door or Lulworth Cove to the west. But none of them beat Blackwood, to my eye. The small woods here creep up almost to the shore, with ancient ash, elm and oak trees leaning over the low cliffs that plunge into the dark sea. It's a place of rugged contrasts. White rock, grey sand, black waters. A grey-scale wonder that's at its best during a storm, when the wind screams its banshee screams across the frothing waves.

We decided to head to the cove before going to Lilac House. Neither of us was hungry, but agreed it might be a good idea to pick up a few things at the Cove Cafe, the small cafe-slash-mini-market near the beach. Plus, we both wanted to see the sea.

We left the car in the small gravel parking lot at the top of the slope that leads to the cove, with its handful of houses. Just two other vehicles shared the space with the rental—a battered and apparently abandoned white van and a Vauxhall belonging to the mini-market's owner, Mr Greene. I eyed it as we got out of the car, suddenly realising that he might raise an eyebrow if he saw me walking into the shop with a woman other than Cecilia. To be fair, he seemed to forget us entirely each time we left, but still, it made me feel uneasy.

I bit my lip as we walked down towards the beach, trying to figure out a way to keep Alice out of the shop.

But just as we reached the bungalow that houses the Cove Cafe, Alice stopped and said, 'Mind if I wait outside? I love this sea breeze.'

I hesitated, half wanting to stroll in holding Alice by the hand, have all this out in the open. But we weren't there yet. She sensed my hesitation. 'Mark?' she said, her eyes fixed on mine, chin slightly tilted down. *I know*, those eyes said. *I know, and you needn't worry.*

'Sure,' I said. Grateful, ashamed.

A bell hanging by the door chimed as I set foot inside. Mr. Greene was nowhere to be seen. I called out, got no response, then wandered through the sparse shelves of the shop, picking up a few snacks, trying to find something for dinner at Lilac House.

I heard a cough, then a groan, and the sound of something heavy being half-dropped onto the floor. 'Hello?' came Mr Greene's feeble voice, from somewhere beyond the shelves.

'Hello, Mr Greene,' I called back, stepping out for him to see me. A minute man in his late sixties, Mr Greene has eyes to match his name, shining behind thick glasses. He's always struck me more as an indoorsy, bookish type, somehow unsuited for the sea. He was standing beside the counter, a large box at his feet. He took me in with a small frown, which eventually relaxed. 'Oh, hello there,' he said. He never remembers my name. We used to find it irritating, Cecilia and I, the way he appeared to remove us completely from his memory every time we left Blackwood Cove. This time, it suits me just fine.

'Mind giving me a hand here, young man?' he asked, nodding towards the box. 'Bit heavy for me, this.'

'Of course,' I said, with a tingle of irritation. I wanted this to be over quickly, get back to Alice outside. As I made my way towards him, I threw a glance beyond the entrance. Alice wasn't there anymore. Perhaps she'd gone for a little stroll.

'Thank you,' Mr Greene said as I laid the box by the till. 'I'm getting old,' he added, more to himself than to me, looking at his open hands and shaking his head. I was unsure how to reply to that, so I gave him a non-committal half-smile.

He reached out for the few products I'd collected from the shelves. 'So, what do we have here...'

I stood fidgeting as he picked up a loaf of bread, stared at it from about two millimetres away, trying to find the price tag.

'I think that's one-fifty,' I offered. He nodded, but ignored me. He kept turning the packaging round and round and inspecting it, as if he'd never seen anything like it before.

'Ah,' he said finally, stabbing a bony finger into the plastic. 'There it is.' I watched him as he punched the price into the ancient till—1.50.

He then repeated the process for each of the purchases. Pick up. Inspect. Rotate. Frown. Inspect. Frown. Repeat. Locate. Tally up.

When he finally handed me the paper bag with the items,

I felt like punching him. 'Thank you, Mr Greene,' I said. I placed the shopping inside the rucksack, next to the beach blanket and the wine.

Alice was standing a few feet from the entrance, studying the faded postcards on a stand.

'Sorry about that,' I said. 'The owner, he's—'

'Is it really that pretty?' she asked, pointing towards one of the postcards, each one featuring the same setting, but in different times and from slightly different standpoints—the small cove that was mere yards from us now, concealed by a curve in the path.

'It's better,' I said with a smile. I offered her my elbow. 'Shall we?'

We walked side by side, the sound of the sea engulfing us.

A little old lady wearing an oddly elegant, but rather worn, pink coat was walking uphill, in the opposite direction. She might have been one of the locals, but I hadn't seen her before. Alice smiled at her, and the elderly woman stopped. Then she hobbled over to us and laid a pale, wrinkly hand on mine. Looking us both in the eyes, she said, 'You're such a beautiful couple, you know?' Alice and I both laughed.

'Thank you,' I said. 'That's very nice of you.'

'Oh, but you are.' She nodded with watery eyes, as if contemplating a fine work of art. We watched her as she went off. Alice looked at me and rolled her eyes. 'All *right*,' she said. 'This is getting silly.' Yes, simply *too* perfect.

I chuckled. 'Did you pay her to say that?'

Alice looked down, and I wondered for a second if my question had hurt her. Then, again, that quick affectionate squeeze, the full lips parting into a smile.

Our bodies close, we stepped into the cove.

· · ·

HERE WE ARE NOW, eyes on the waves, arms latched around our knees. 'You did it, Mark,' Alice says softly. 'You took me to the sea.'

Before I can say anything, she straightens up, wiggling her backside around on the blanket, getting comfortable. 'OK. Tell me something really embarrassing about yourself, Mark.'

'Right... and why would I do that?'

'Because we have to put a stop to all this... *perfection.* Or I'll stop believing it's happening, Mark.'

I nod, serious. I like how she keeps ending sentences with my name. Some sort of affectionate punctuation. It feels as if she's claiming ownership over me, somehow. Claim away, Alice.

'So? Go on.'

'OK. Hmm...' I'm trying to summon some story that might make her laugh.

What about that time I killed a rapist in a hit-and-run? Embarrassing, sure, but haha, good times.

A shiver runs down my spine. I banish the thought.

'Something really embarrassing. The *most* embarrassing,' she eggs me on.

'And you'll do the same?'

She raises a hand. 'Promise.'

'OK, OK. What about this,' I say. 'Oh *God...*'

'What is it?'

I shake my head. 'It's just... even just thinking about it makes me cringe.'

She claps her hands. 'Perfect! That's exactly the sort of thing I want to hear about.'

It's strange, but I enjoy feeling a little vulnerable in front of Alice. 'I don't think I've ever told anyone about it,' I say. 'Except maybe Ed.'

'Ed?'

'Oh, he's an old friend of mine. Close friend.' Mentioning Ed feels nice, too. It's like opening up a little bit of my world and inviting her in.

'OK. Go on.'

I inhale. 'Well, there was this girl I fancied. How long ago was this? Must be almost twenty years now, and still I cringe... anyway, I'd just got my driving license, and I was eager to show off. So I invite this girl out on a date. Heather, she was called. Amazingly, she accepted. The plan was to meet at the pub; then I'd take her for a drive. Nothing special, but it did seem so at the time. I borrowed my mum's car and got to the pub ridiculously early. One hour before we were set to meet sort of thing.'

'Nervous?'

'Too nervous. In fact, I thought having a pint might relax me a little. So I had one. And then another. And, maybe, a couple more after that.'

Alice laughs. 'I can see where this is going.'

'Oh, *believe* me, you can't.'

'Well, go on then. I want to know.'

'I tell you, it's painful... anyway, so by the time Heather shows up, I'm basically blind drunk. Not that I was aware of it, of course. In fact, I felt confident, charming. To me, everything was going fine, until we stepped outside.' I pause and shake my head.

'Come on!' Alice says, delighted.

'It must've been the cold night air, but as soon as I'm outside, it hits me—I'm drunk. I'm slurring my words. I'm walking weirdly. Smiling too stiffly. I mean, I was suddenly *aware* of it all. I start panicking—surely I can't drive in these conditions, can I? But I had to, that's why she was there, why I invited her out in the first place.'

I pick up a handful of sand, let it slip through my closed fist. 'By the way,' I continue, 'Heather, she'd noticed none of this. She hardly knew me, probably thought I was always this hyped up. A cool, fun guy. Which was what I was trying to project, right? And I wanted her to keep thinking that. Except, what I actually was, was a silly drunk kid trying too hard to impress her.'

'Oh, poor you!' Alice says.

'So we walk towards my mum's car. There's a row of trees along the street near the pub, that's where I'd parked. We get to the car, under one of these trees, in silence. She walks to the passenger door, and I'm opposite her. I remember fumbling for the keys, trying to find a way to somehow postpone this, tell her maybe we could do it another time. That's how drunk I was. But when I looked up, she was smiling, looking forward to the ride. I'm about to say something when she says, 'It's my first time in a car-date ever.' Is that even an expression? *Car-date?* Anyway, she couldn't wait.'

'Pressure!'

'Yes. I can't say anything at this point, so I decide to light a cigarette. I stick one in my mouth, you know, trying to act cool. But I realise she's looking at me funny. "You've got it—" she says, but I've already lit it and taken a deep puff. It tastes horrible. "You lit the filter," she tells me.'

Alice laughs.

'Now, that was embarrassing, yes. But nothing like what was about to happen. So I laugh, awkwardly, and get rid of the cig. Then I put the key in the lock and notice Mickey Mouse staring at me through the window.'

'Wait, what?'

'Yes, exactly. *What?* I thought. There he was, Mickey Mouse, sitting on the driver's seat. It takes me a second, but I realise it's a plush toy. Except—my mum doesn't have a Mickey Mouse doll in her car. Plus, the key isn't turning.'

'Oh my God,' Alice says, putting her face in her hands.

'Remember, I'm drunk and desperate to impress this girl.

So I look at the car. The model is right (an old FIAT), the colour is right, but... not quite. My mum's car was white. This was some sort of light cream colour. Plus, there's Mickey and an empty packet of crisps on the dashboard, crumbs all over. They weren't there before, either. I look up, heart pounding, and there it is, just past Heather's shoulder, a couple of cars down the road—my mum's car.'

'Oh, poor *you*,' Alice says, face still buried in her open palms.

'Hang on... the worst is yet to come. Heather is looking at me, wondering why the hell I'm taking so long. The thing is, a suaver bloke would have just laughed this off, but I *couldn't*, you see? I was too young, too nervous and too drunk. I was shitting myself.'

Alice lets out a choked little laugh.

'But this is the absolute worst bit—I have to tell her that I'd got the wrong car. So I open my mouth and... bloody hell, why am I telling you this?'

'Go *on*!' she says. 'You can't stop now!'

'So I start saying, "This isn't my ca—" and I swear, right at that *a*, a huge disgusting bug, a spider I think, just falls off the bloody tree above us and lands straight in my mouth.'

'NO!' Alice almost shouts. She looks at me, glistening tears in her eyes.

'Yes. I feel its horrid little legs on my lips, so I start spitting and sputtering, shrieking like a little girl. I stick my hand, my whole hand, into my mouth, to make sure it isn't there. I slap my face, shake my head like a wet dog.'

'Stop,' Alice says through a fit of laughter, 'please *stop*.'

'No, you have to be burdened with this too,' I say. 'So when I'm finally convinced I've got rid of the spider, I look up, and there's Heather staring at me with the most disgusted, perplexed look I've ever seen.'

'But what did you *say*?'

'Nothing. I just looked at her. She looked at me. Then she turned on her heel and left. This all happened in less than a minute.'

'Cigarette. Wrong car. Bug,' Alice says.

'Yup. Quite the crescendo.' I sigh. 'Heather never spoke to me again. I think it was more out of a sense of embarrassment for me, if you know what I mean. In any case, I can't blame her.'

Alice looks at me, mouth wide, eyes shining. She's beautiful. We sit in silence for a moment, absorbing my silly story.

'All right,' I say. 'Your turn now. Tell me your most embarrassing story.'

A sassy smile spreads on her lips. 'What?' she asks. 'Why would I ever do that?' Then, before I have time to protest, she leaps up and slips her boots off. I watch her tiptoeing towards the water, walking fast. When she reaches the dark, wet sand, she removes her socks, discards them carelessly beside her. I watch as she dips one foot in, tentatively, and shivers. She looks at me, both cold and excited. She then steps in with both feet. The water breaks at her ankles, sending little circles out in all directions, emanating from her.

Alice takes in the scene. Her hands are pressed against the small of her back, her expression satisfied. Like a general surveying a victory. 'Thank you, Mark,' she says.

'Hang on. I've got something for you.' I open the rucksack and produce the wine and two glasses.

'You remembered!' she says. Then, 'Are those crystal?'

I flick the glass. 'Not sure. Think so.' I plant the bottle in the sand and pull out a corkscrew.

Alice joins me on the blanket. Again, she's laughing. 'I can't believe it. This, it's just... perfect. Stupidly perfect.'

The cork comes out with a satisfying *pop*, and I pour the wine for us both. She takes the glass and wiggles close to me, so we're sitting hip to hip.

I raise my glass. 'What should we drink to?'

'To spies and love letters,' she says.

'Sounds good to me.'

Our glasses clink. We're about to drink, but Alice lays a hand on my arm, stopping me.

'Wait, wait.'

'Is everything OK?'

She rolls her eyes. 'Of course it's OK. I mean, look at *this*.' Her gaze encircles our glasses, the beach, the sea. 'But I don't want you to think it was because of the wine.'

I frown. 'What was because of the wine?'

'This,' she says and leans in to kiss me.

27

L ilac House. A small cottage nestled amidst the thick tangle of woodland called Blackwood, half a mile or so from the cove. Before becoming our secret getaway, it was the one I shared with Cecilia.

We bought it when our relationship still beamed with promise. It was meant to be a lovers' retreat first and a family escape soon after. But, as it turned out, our family stalled at two, and now Lilac House hosts another sad empty room to mirror the one in London. This one too is avoided, deserted. At least we didn't go and buy children's furniture for it, other than a bed.

From a place to celebrate our love (even physical, back then), Lilac House became a breeding ground for our resentment, a place of long silences and mindless occupation. We'd go there to tend to the garden, do a bit of robotic upkeep and, at times, walk along the beach. Especially Cecilia. She'd wander off on her own, her thoughts impenetrable to me. At first, in the months following the miscarriage, it hurt that she wouldn't invite me to join her. But with time, even the pain faded. I stopped caring because I had no choice. To care was to suffer.

Beautiful as it is, the cottage and its surroundings can change. At times, the light shifts, or my mood does, and all of a sudden, the woods appear too dark, filled with whispering shadows. And the comfortable isolation that Cecilia and I had loved, especially in the beginning, can quickly morph into a suffocating sense of eerie remoteness. Lilac House can be both stunning and unsettling.

Today, of course, it's wonderful. After the wine, Alice and I climbed the slope back up to the car, past the already-closed Cove Cafe, and drove here. We could have walked to the cottage, but it was easier to simply get our things over in the boot of the car. We held hands all the way.

The kiss: just the one, so far. I don't want to think about what it means, for me, for my marriage. But thoughts stir, bubbling away in a dark recess of my mind. It's surprisingly easy to ignore them, for the time being. I keep pursing my lips, as if to capture the feel of it again.

The gravel crunches under the tyres, and Lilac House welcomes us with soft green grass and solid stone walls, the evening's light reflecting pink off its ragged surfaces. I park the car in front of the cottage and collect our things. When we step inside, the air is musty but not unpleasant.

'Wait here. Get comfortable,' I tell Alice, nodding towards the sofa in front of the fireplace. 'I'll be right back.'

As soon as the door is closed behind me, I pull out my phone to text Cecilia. An alert tells me I have an unread message from Ed. He's asking me if I'll be at the King's Head tonight. I type out a quick apology, mentioning work, and send it off. Now, for Cecilia. I hesitate a second, then just go for it:

Sorry I didn't text you sooner. Got caught up. All good,
flight OK. Xxx.

There, that's it. Starting the message with 'sorry' angers me
a bit. I feel like I'm constantly apologising to my wife for one
reason or another. Why should I? Anyway, it's done. I mute the
phone and shove it into my pocket, shaking off the thought of
her. I walk around the edge of the house to the shed where we
keep the gardening tools and a stack of wood for the fire.
There are other things in here as well. Countless odds and
ends gathering dust. I pick up three large logs and a bunch of
smaller ones, piling them in the crook of my arm. They're dry
after months in the shed and should burn nicely. It takes me a
minute or two to find the firelighters (causing me a mild panic
—I doubt I'd ever manage to get the fire going without them).
They somehow ended up behind the lawnmower. I grab an
old paper, too, and tuck it under my arm. Balancing all this, I
kick the shed door shut and head back to the cottage.

But as soon as I step inside, I know I won't get to light the
fire. Not yet. Because Alice is standing there, where I left her,
but now her smile is gone, and her eyes are fixed on me. I
want to put the logs down, lay them on the floor, but they fall,
rattling against the stone tiles. We do not speak.

She holds my hand, pulls me towards the sofa. I follow,
my mind numb, silent. There are details. The sway of her
hips, the curve of her breasts, the fullness of her lips. Her
clean, textured scent.

I hold her, one hand in the thick coils of her hair, the
other on her buttocks, pulling, squeezing. Soft skin and firm
muscle. I feel them contract as she thrusts her pelvis forward,
rubbing against me. Her hands wander down my back, draw
me close, feeling my erection.

I kiss her neck, inebriated by her smell, pulling gently,

then not gently, at her hair. She lets out a trembling sigh, and I hold her tight until every inch of me is pressed against every inch of her. There's nothing else besides our bodies now. Not even love. Just unstoppable hunger for one another. We're animals.

'Fuck me,' she whispers. A glimmer of a thought—*Cecilia would never say that.*

Our clothes come off, hands tearing and tugging desperately. Alice lays her back against the sofa cushions; I'm kneeling in front of her. Her legs are wrapped around me, feet clasped behind my back. Drawing me in.

I can't remember the last time it was like this. I don't think it ever was.

WE MAKE LOVE, too. Many times. The sun sets on our bodies, and the night creeps in. There's tenderness, and there's primitive desire, and we get lost between the two.

Later, I finally do get to light the fire. We sit huddled close, on the carpet, wrapped in the makeshift cover of the sofa throw. Its warm folds are filled with small pools of shadow. The lights are off, and beyond the crackling, flickering light of the flames there is nothing but darkness.

We're naked, my bare skin warm where it touches Alice's. We're both silent, but I sense she wants to say something. Difficult words stirring behind her lips. A little sound, like a cough, then, 'I know... *it is what it is,*' she starts. What a considerate way of putting it. Like prodding delicately at an open wound, one we share. Cecilia, me, her. Wife, husband, lover. 'But,' she continues, 'if things were different, *this* is all I would want.'

This, right now, seems inevitable to me. How could I possibly give it up? How could there be anything else? Surely this is where I'm headed, and the current life I'm leading is just a temporary arrangement. A problem to be solved.

That's how it seems now, in the golden light of the fire. But, as appealing, as *obvious*, as it is, I feel a slight discomfort settling in.

I think of Cecilia. Then I think of Vanessa Wright. The thought makes me shudder.

Vanessa was a close friend of Cecilia's, a few years her junior. Another curator, fresh from the countryside, no contacts, no experience. But eager to learn the ropes. Cecilia mentored her, got her into the right circles. My wife genuinely loved her (at one point, I actually started to think she *loved*-loved her), and everything was always 'Vanessa this' and 'Vanessa that'.

Until, that is, she snagged an artist Cecilia had been eyeing for a while, one she'd been keen on introducing to a couple of the major galleries. Somehow, Vanessa got there first.

I remember the day she heard about it. Vanessa was so naive as to tell her about it. She thought Cecilia would be happy for her.

She was not.

I watched her stewing for days, her usual placid beauty twisted into a constant smirk. Deep frowns, teeth grinding. My wife can be vindictive.

She pulled strings, made calls. Until she got an old friend from uni, now arts editor at a major paper, to run a hit piece on the exhibition. Her friend wasn't particularly fond of the artist anyway, plus she owed Cecilia a favour of some sort. The piece was titled *A tasteless exhibition, a talentless artist* and was penned by some AA Gill wannabe. And, just like that, Vanessa's career was over. So too was the artist's, caught in the cyclone of Cecilia's wrath. I remember reading the article, sitting at the kitchen table, at breakfast. When I'd finished, I put down the paper and stared at her.

'Isn't this a bit much?'

She looked back at me, her eyes level. There was no trace of remorse in them. Just a secret smile, one only I could see, hidden behind her still features. Satisfaction.

'I don't think so,' she replied, a hint of a challenge in her voice.

The thought of Cecilia like that terrifies me now. Humili-ated, vindictive. She ruined a girl's career simply because she'd upset her. What would she do to me, the husband who abandoned her? Who betrayed her? What would happen if, say, I were to tell her I'm leaving her, to be with another?

She might understand. Agree, even. After all, we're both unhappy, aren't we? She must be suffering as much as I am. More, perhaps.

Except, she might not understand. She might not *care* to understand. And, of course, she knows something that could ruin me.

She knows I killed Michael Taylor.

The wood crackles in the fire. A pop and fizzle that drags me out of my thoughts. Alice is looking up at me. Her eyes are wide and loving and unthreatening.

'Is something wrong?' she asks.

Everything is the right answer. 'Nothing,' is what I say.

Then she says something that, I know, will haunt me for days. Forever.

'If things were different,' she whispers, 'we would have a family. Live in this pretty place. Me and you and our sweet children.'

Alice and I spend two days loving and eating and sleeping. Our lives are just this, here between the old walls of Lilac House.

Cecilia doesn't call. I text her a couple of times. I sneak out of the cottage to do this—not sure why, but I need to put distance between me and Alice when I do. I send hurried, scripted words I forget the instant I press the SEND button.

We venture into the woods in the late afternoon of our last day in Blackwood Cove. Hands in pockets and arms entwined, our words muffled by the scarves we wear high on our faces. The air is rich with the damp scent of earth and moss. Birds sing overhead. It is easy to forget, out here among the trees, that this isn't our life. It would be wonderful if it were.

Our shoes sink in the soil, and we laugh and smile with ease. Alice points to a fallen tree, and we sit on its trunk. We could walk all the way to the beach if we wanted to, but an unacknowledged agreement keeps us within range of Lilac House and the sofa in front of the fire. We haven't made love on the bed, and I don't think we will. An aura emanates from that room, one we don't wish to violate. Despite everything, that bedroom is still (for the time being) the one I share with Cecilia.

Alice pulls the scarf down, tucking it under her chin. She studies me, as if amused. 'You seem comfortable here,' she says. 'The busy city ad man, at home in the countryside.'

'Do I?' I ask. It's so flattering to hear oneself described.

She nods. 'Maybe this is the place for you.'

'I've never really thought of it like that,' I say, fishing around in my pocket for the cigarettes. I light two of them. We inhale, then blow out two bluish clouds of smoke. 'I grew up in the city, always worked in the city. This,' I say, tracing a circle with my finger in the air, to encapsulate our surroundings, 'was always meant to be a getaway, a place for weekends and holidays.' It was also somewhere Cecilia and I had sometimes thought of as a place to retire, but I don't say that.

Except, now it does seem like a place I could be happy in. I picture us (*us* being Alice and me) living here, in the comfort of Lilac House, exploring the woods and drinking wine on the beach. In this brief fancy, I think it would be easy for me to freelance, occasionally commuting to London to meet with clients. I could earn enough for a happy life. We'd have fewer needs and smaller expenses. In time, I could invite the old friends over. Ed, at least—he'd understand. Gabbie would be cold initially, but she'd eventually come to accept things. Then on weekends, Alice and I could tend to the garden, not in the solitary, brooding way we do with Cecilia, but laughing, chatting, helping one another. Building something together. In the evenings, I'd light the fire, and Alice could sit curled up on the sofa, wrapped in a woolly blanket. In her arms, perhaps, a child, sleeping peacefully. Our child.

I look at her now, in the velvet light of the evening. It's an odd experience, for a certain type of man, to look at a woman and think of her as the mother of their child. To *want* her to be the mother of his child. It's a deep, primordial feeling, a love more complete.

I nod. 'Yes. You're right, I would be happy here.' Then, hesitantly, 'Could you?'

Alice closes her eyes. She smiles, but it's a sad smile.

'Sorry,' I say hastily. 'It's a stupid question. I was just flattering myself, I suppose.'

She shakes her head. 'No. I don't think it's a stupid question,' she says. The branches sway in a sudden gust of cold wind. Shadows and light shift on Alice's face. 'You know the answer. But the real question is, what should we do about it?'

It's a loaded question, but she asks it lightly. There's no expectation in her voice. This upsets me. She deserves more than a weekend of passion. *We* deserve more.

And all of a sudden, I find myself telling her about Cecilia. About the child we never had, about everything that went wrong with our marriage. The words just spill out. I try to relate the distance that has set in between us, the sense of going nowhere, of being stuck in a sad place. I tell her that it used to hurt, that I wished we could fix it, somehow, but that's gone too, now. Because of her, Alice. At some point, she reaches out and holds my hand, but I only notice later on, during a pause in my restless talking. I even try to describe the ruthlessness with which my wife punished Vanessa Wright, wondering out loud how far her vindictiveness would stretch if I were to leave her for another woman.

When Alice speaks, it feels like her voice is emanating from the woods itself. 'We could cope with that. Whatever she throws at you, we could handle it.' A pause, then, 'Couldn't we?' she asks, but the way she says it suggests she's guessed there's more to my story. A crucial piece of information is missing, and I realise that without it, Alice could never understand.

Clouds have drifted across the low sun, and the shadows are thicker now. A veil covers her face, the woods stand silent. I can't help throwing a cautious glance about, to make sure no one is lurking among the trees. No one who could hear what I'm about to say, that is. And here, in the gathering darkness, I tell her about the accident and how I killed Michael Taylor.

WHEN I FINISH SPEAKING, we sit in silence for a while. It feels as if an icy wedge has lodged itself between us. Here we were, enjoying what actually felt like love, only to find it vanishing before our eyes. And it's not because she's horrified by what I did to Taylor. No—that, she immediately interprets as a tragedy, but one that has befallen me. This vanishing feeling, it's because of Cecilia.

Alice lights a cigarette. 'She could destroy you,' she says. Her words come out in puffs of smoke. She's not looking at me. 'You'd end up in jail.'

I nod. After all that talking, I find it hard to speak.

Sitting beside me, Alice assesses the situation silently. She hasn't run off or insulted me or called me a murderer. A warm wave of gratitude swells inside my chest. I turn to the woods, the grey silhouettes of the trees surrounding us. Small rustling noises come from every direction. I picture leaves yielding under padded paws, owls surveying the nightscape from the tangled branches overhead. The secret lives of animals coming out to claim the darkness for themselves.

Alice shuffles closer. She takes a quick breath, then asks, 'Have you ever cheated on her... before?'

'No,' I say immediately, mechanically. Why? I've told her how I accidentally killed someone, yet I can't bring myself to tell her about what happened in Scotland, with Claire. How I *have* cheated on my wife—my pregnant wife. It's both because of the shame and an absurd feeling that it would sound as if I had cheated on *her*, on Alice.

She nods silently, mulling over my words.

'You're sure,' she asks, eyes drifting upwards, towards the treetops and the darkness enveloping them. 'You're *absolutely* sure she'd do it? Tell the police about the accident?'

I swallow. 'Yes. I am.'

'So...' she begins, her voice lower now, more in tune with the surroundings. 'This cannot last. We cannot last.'

It hurts to hear her say so, but she's right. I suddenly think that this is where our weekend will end, that our making love in front of the fire earlier will be the last time we ever do it. I already miss it. This happiness, this fathomless joy, suddenly a thing of the past. Back to BeeCreative and London and the loneliness. Back to Cecilia. The idea of it all makes my heart race, a wild panic spreading inside me, depriving me of air.

But, just then, Alice turns towards me, and her eyes are glistening strangely. A speck of moon wallows in there, cold and beautiful.

I know what she's about to say, because I've caught myself considering it, too. A what-if fantasy, nothing more. But it's there.

'Unless... she were out of the picture,' she says. It sounds so simple. But she's not happy with that way of putting it. Maybe it's something to do with where we are, with our whispering, with the cover of darkness, but she's not happy with the lack of honesty in those words. She kisses me, then reformulates. 'Unless we kill her.'

HAD THE SUN BEEN SHINING, had we not spent two days in a dreamlike trance of love and lust, she would not have uttered those words, I know it. And I wouldn't be sitting here, actually contemplating the implications of what she's just said.

But we've tasted a happiness so rare, so intense, that the prospect of losing it is summoning dark, desperate thoughts. There's a wild animal element to her beauty now, the whites of her eyes too wide, her hair too black. Her beauty is so physical, so *present*, like a third person sitting here alongside us. I compare it to Cecilia's, with her high cheekbones and diaphanous skin, the unsettling remoteness of it. And considering Alice now, I'm reminded about how little I know of this woman sharing the silence of the woods with me. And once again, I'm reminded about how little it matters to me.

We dare not speak. Whatever we say next might lead down a path of no return, whether that means murdering Cecilia, or not doing so and continuing to live the sad life I lead now. So we just keep staring into each other's eyes, in this limbo of terrifying possibility, until finally she (not I) puts an end to it. 'Sorry,' she says, rising to her feet. She takes me by the hand and leads me back through the woods to Lilac House.

29

When we reach the station in Salisbury, I feel a slight nausea come over me. The real world seeping back in. The car stops, and we both stare ahead, towards the platforms. I'm not sure what to say. After our talk in the woods, we returned to the comfort of the fireplace and of our naked bodies. The sex had a new tint of desperation to it, as if we both knew it might be the last time.

'Thank you for taking me to the sea, Mark.' Her voice is soft, and there might be a vein of sadness in it.

I look down and see her hand reaching for mine. She rubs her thumb over my skin. Hers soft, mine not.

'I hope...' she says, '... I hope we can do it again.'

'We will,' I say. Something in the grey, cold air outside makes this sound like a lie.

I try to look her in the eyes, but it's suddenly difficult. Strange, it was so easy last night.

'I—' I begin, but nothing else comes out. Too much to say, I suppose.

'Hey, it's OK,' Alice says. She lays a finger under my chin, trains my face towards hers. Like a mother would do. That smile again.

I chuckle, or try to. 'I know.'

'Secret letters?' she asks.

I nod, the thought of them comforting. 'Secret letters.'

I start opening the door, but she stops me. 'No.' She slips the big sunglasses on, places the hat on her head, and just like that, she's a spy again.

The smile fades. She's nibbling on her lips, hesitant. Then she points those impenetrable lenses towards me and says, 'Mark, I'd do anything to be with you. Anything.'

Before I can speak, she leans in and kisses me.

The car door shuts with a metallic thud, and Alice is gone. A throbbing knot forms in my throat as I watch her walk away.

She stops, just before the entrance, and raises a hand. I wave back, but she's gone so fast. I don't know if she's seen me.

I DRIVE BACK to London in a daze. Roads, cars, petrol stations roll by in a colourless blur. The nausea now comes in thick green waves. I have the odd feeling that the world is somehow split, like two identical images superimposed but not quite aligned.

The time spent with Alice (those eager, passionate hours) seems oddly distant all of a sudden. I'm deflated, detached, the way you sometimes feel in the immediate aftermath of a tragedy.

There's a fast, rhythmic ticking sound coming from outside. I realise it's been going on for hours. Some unconscious reasoning process in my mind decides it's a pebble lodged in the tyre. Probably from Blackwood. I turn on the radio, try to drown it out with some music. But the sounds from the speakers rapidly turn into a meaningless drone. The pebble keeps tick-tick-ticking.

Perhaps I should call Alice. This distance I feel, it would vanish if only I could speak to her. Then I remember: I don't have her phone number. I never saw her pull out a phone during our time in Lilac House. No calls, no messages. How can she be so disconnected from the world while she's with me?

I don't know her number, and I know nothing about her past. Nor of her present, at that. She didn't tell me about it, and I didn't ask. It seemed comforting, these last few days— the knowledge that all that mattered was *now*. That whoever we were outside of Lilac House, those identities could wait.

Yet, as I drive towards London and my loveless home, I feel there's something perturbing about it all. Alice, I realise, is somewhat of an enigma. Incomplete, unaccountable, like a figment of my imagination. Like a spy.

THE KEY TURNS in the lock, and I step into our house. 'Hello?' I call out, slipping my coat off, in a warm but tired, just-got-back-from-the-airport sort of tone.

Cecilia appears at the top of the stairs. She's on the phone.

'It's Mark,' she says to whoever it is. 'He just got back.' She wiggles her fingers my way. 'Yes, I'll tell him. Great.' She sounds excited.

I fold my scarf neatly and drape it off the coat hanger. I massage my back, letting out a little groan. That's the kind of thing you do after a tiring journey, isn't it?

Cecilia hangs up and walks towards me. 'Bad flight?' she asks, kissing me on the cheek. I wonder, terrified, if she can smell Alice on my skin. I rinsed my face thoroughly in the gents' in Victoria after dropping the rental off. And yet.

'Oh, you know.'

'All OK with Senesi?' She doesn't really care. Why should she? Anything regarding BeeCreative bores me to tears, too. I also sense there's something else she wants to talk about.

'Who was that?' I ask, nodding towards the phone.

Cecilia lights up. 'Yes, I wanted to tell you about it.' She follows me as I head towards the kitchen, to pour myself a drink. I rarely drink at home, but I could do with a stiff one now.

'It was Phil,' she says. I'm pulling out a glass (must remember to replace the ones I took to Blackwood Cove), and her words make me uneasy. She's been talking to Phil while I was away.

While I was away with another woman. *Being jealous is hardly warranted, is it?*

I pour a finger of whisky into the glass. Then another one. 'Oh yeah?' I say. Casual.

Cecilia is sitting at the kitchen table now. 'Yes. We're organising an exhibition. His exhibition.'

'Really?' The alcohol burns my throat and soothes my nerves.

'Yes—I thought he'd mentioned it to you.' A pause. 'Are you OK?'

'Yes. Just tired.' I rub my eyes, mainly to avoid hers. 'You're right. He did tell me about it. At the King's Head.' I try to recall exactly what Phil said. All I remember is his hushed call, my suspicion he was whispering to my wife. 'But it sounded more like an idea than an actual plan,' I add.

'It was, but things are moving fast. Tate Modern had an opening, an artist's exhibition was cancelled. He said some awful things on social media, and they pulled his event.' I notice she's speaking a little faster than usual.

'What did he say?'

I've interrupted her. 'Who?' she asks, a little annoyed.

'The artist. On social media.'

Again, a frown. 'Why would you care?'

True, why would I? Stupid gossip. But I don't want to admit to my shallowness, so I just shrug.

'It was something about poor people smelling bad, but anyway—'

I'm tired, and for some reason I have to work hard not to laugh. I drink an imaginary sip from the now-empty glass, pressing my lips firmly against the edges. Still, I can't hold back a childish little snort. She doesn't notice.

'They asked me,' Cecilia continues, 'if I had anyone in mind who could fill the gap.'

I put the glass down. My head is spinning slightly. 'And you,' I say, 'thought of Phil.'

'Yes.' She pauses, then adds, 'It makes sense—he's quite well known. He has potential. Plus, he's a friend.'

A friend of *mine*, I almost say. 'Absolutely. Good job, it's nice of you.'

Cecilia tilts her head to the side and studies me. There's something unnaturally beautiful about my wife's skin. It glows with a soft milky-golden hue, as if a candle were forever shining its light on her.

IT'S LATER ON, when we're both in bed, that realisation strikes.

Cecilia is supposedly sleeping; I'm pretending to. Her, me and the gap between us. I stare through the shadows of our silent bedroom, out through the window and know, simply *know*, that I will never be as happy as I was with Alice again. Not while I'm with my wife.

I hold my body still, but I feel like stretching, squirming, going for a run. I realise I'm chewing the inside of my cheek and will myself to stop.

As sad, as inconsolable as my life is, at least it's familiar, isn't it? And who's to say things with Cecilia can't change? I remember the day at the pub, with Alice outside on the bench, waiting for me. I sat at the table with my wife, fidgeting nervously. Cecilia had been different, hadn't she? She was willing to give all this another go. For a second, I believed we could. And now, with my head on this pillow, I'm trying to fool myself we still can.

But we can't. Nothing can be the same after Lilac House.

As I've done so many times before, I tune into Cecilia's breathing, listen to it, waiting until it matches mine for a few instants. We breathe in, we breathe out. And then we're off on different rhythms once again.

This woman whom I once loved would be willing to ruin me if I left her for Alice. She would tell the world that I'm a murderer.

Murder. Murder. Murder.

The word floats round and round in my head, and I realise I'm finally drifting off into real sleep. The last thing my mind conjures up is Alice, there in Salisbury, wearing her spy outfit. But she's also right here, next to the bed, crouching in the thick shadows. She's whispering into my ear, telling me she would do anything, *anything* to be with me.

30

Bill greets me with a grunt. No coffee this time.

'Follow me,' he says, and I do.

Being back at the office is both soothing and utterly surreal. These appalling spaces are ones I can control. Here, I know exactly what is expected of me, and if someone had asked me, just a few months ago, to picture myself five years from now, I'd have felt able to predict my professional future with absolute accuracy. This is the secret appeal of every stable office job—its numbing apathy, its blissful predictability. Slip on a suit and tie (or a hideous hoodie) and ditch the guesswork.

'So? How was the wedding?' Bill asks, without turning towards me. Two young creatives are approaching him, but a single glare shot from beneath his bushy eyebrows is enough to send them running.

'Nice. Thank you.'

'Pff. I hope it was bloody worth it,' he snorts, shoving the meeting room door open.

The glass walls are covered with the remnants of Friday's meeting with Senesi—artwork for the *Don't just do it* campaign concept, printouts of the claim in a variety of fonts, mood boards, colour schemes, ad mock-ups. I wonder why they haven't been cleared out, but then realise Bill probably wanted me to see them. Remind me that I wasn't there.

'Surprisingly good work,' I say, taking a seat.

'Well, I had to give them *something* to talk about. We hired a couple of good freelancers, the stuff our people came up with was...' He massages his forehead. 'Well, you can imagine.'

'How did it go?' I ask, flipping open my laptop.

'Could have done with your help,' he mumbles, eyes averted. He wants me to feel the guilt. I don't.

'But,' he continues, 'it wasn't too bad. They liked the mock-ups. Morino asked where you were.'

'He did?'

'I told him you were busy with an emergency meeting for another client. Pissed him off no end. Not that he showed it, of course, he just pouted his creepy little lips and sat in silence. He did approve the work we did though.'

'You *must* have enjoyed that, Bill,' I say. 'Pissing Morino off?'

He can't conceal a mean smile, but he's still too angry to share it with me. 'Let's get to work,' he says, businesslike. Then he adds, 'Unless, of course, you've got better things to do, Mark.' Snidey.

I study him sitting there in the bright morning light. The admonishing frown, the tenseness in his jaw. His fists are fat balls, and his wedding ring, a vestige from a slimmer past, sinks into the meaty flesh of his ring finger. Bill, the loveable brute, the good family man. The few times I've met his wife, Lillian, it was her tenderness towards him that struck me: her holding his hand, casually, as she told me about his hatred of beach holidays, her warm laughter at his constant grumbling. I know why she loves him. With some couples, it's impossible

to figure it out (*How could* she *be with* him?), but with Bill and
Lillian it seems so obvious. Beneath all his mannerisms, his
pessimism, Bill is a solid, reliable man. You can fear Bill (and
if you're a junior employee of BeeCreative, you should), but
you can't dislike him. It's impossible. Watching him there,
annoyed and upset, I feel like rising and giving him a hug.

It surprises me how *easy* all this is. The Senesi project, the
prospect of today's meetings and decisions, even dealing with
an angry, ill-tempered Bill. Such mundane concerns. His
resentment is something I can handle. So much simpler, say,
than deciding whether to kill your wife.

I confuse him by smiling a genuinely affectionate smile.
'No, Bill. Nothing better to do.'

THE MORNING DRIFTS BY. I sit through meetings and conference calls, participating but somehow detached. When
lunchtime comes, I'm tempted to lock myself in a room somewhere and be alone. But I know I have to visit the bench, in
case Alice has left a note. I grab my coat and scarf and
head out.

Today, an elderly man is sitting on it, reading the *Times*.
Normally, I'd feel irritated by the violation of this space I've
come to regard as ours, but not today. I watch the almost
perfectly circular crown of snow-white hair, neatly cropped
around the balding top of his head, and wonder idly why he's
not wearing a cap. Heavy coat, woolly gloves, thick scarf, but
nothing on his head.

After standing around eyeing him, afraid of what I might
find under the bench, I decide to join him. I nod pleasantly in
his direction as I sit, mindful of keeping a polite distance. But
the old man was clearly enjoying his solitude. He peers at me
with something resembling horror, wide eyes and quivering
jowls, then makes a show of folding his paper, smacking it

over and over against his knees, until it won't fold any further. He tuts and shakes his head, then gets up to leave at excruciatingly slow speed. Slightly hurt, I watch him go in search of another bench.

I take a deep breath, eyes on the river ahead. Then, without looking down, I slip my fingers between the bars and feel around. An instant later, I pull away. Alice has not written.

It's hard to decide what this means. On the one hand, we only got back yesterday. She might not even have had the time to leave a note. Despite how it sometimes seems, she must have other things going on in her life. Or she doesn't want to write. I try to put myself in her shoes, imagine suggesting to someone that we should kill their spouse. Maybe the words she said, there in Blackwood, have filled her with shame. Except, I don't believe that. For some reason, it's hard for me to picture Alice ashamed.

In the distance, I spot the old man again. He is still wandering around in search of somewhere to sit in peace. I feel like waving him over, telling him I won't be here for long.

I could go and never come back to this bench. Never write a single word to Alice again. I could, conceivably, forget all about this whole thing and return to my life, such as it is.

Shivering from a sudden gust of icy wind, I close my eyes and examine what the prospect of that does to me, to my body. I picture myself leaving the bench now, never to return. The image of a letter from Alice fastened somewhere below me, rotting away in the rain, unread. The thought of never sleeping with her again.

It's like poison: my heart rate picks up, my airways constrict. I feel panic rising, a blind, mindless panic. A sudden longing for her.

Few people, I'm sure, walk about with Sellotape in their pockets. I do. Pen and paper, too. I press a white sheet against my lap, then hesitate. What to write? After a minute, I decide the simple truth is probably best.

I miss you.

I fold it carefully, making the edges meet, then tear two strips of tape and stick them to the note. When no one is looking, I slip it under the bench, pressing firmly against the metal bar to make sure it'll hold.

When I look up again, I notice the old man has found a place to sit. He's back to reading his paper, shaking his head disapprovingly at the way the world is going.

31

King's Head tonight? Not sure if Phil is coming, and I can't get hold of Clyde.

I read Ed's message with tired eyes. Clyde being hard to get hold of is a bit worrying, but I'm too exhausted to dwell on that now. I tap out my reply and send it off:

No, sorry mate. Caught a cold, would rather stay in.

It's Friday, early evening, and we're sitting in the kitchen, Cecilia and I. Me cradling a cup of warm tea (I really have caught a cold, and I hope the tea might help), her working at her laptop, opposite me. Silence, other than the clicking of the keyboard.

Alice hasn't replied to my note. I've thought, over the past few days, that if she died, I'd have no way of knowing. She'd just vanish. It would be a strange end to all of this. What would it have all meant? Just that I'm more than capable of cheating on my wife. Especially with someone beautiful. Cecilia herself has suggested this about me, at times. *You only love me for my beauty*, she'd say, back in the early days of our relationship, half smiling. Half not.

She lets out a frustrated little groan and clicks the mouse, then clicks it harder. 'Oh, come *on*,' she mouths. Something wrong with the computer, or, more likely, something wrong with her use of it. Another click, harder still. Her approach to technology irritates me, but I've learnt not to school her in that regard. Her interactions with computers are among the very few instances in which Cecilia doesn't appear in full control. It makes absolutely no sense, but I've often thought that she's too beautiful to use them.

Finally, the laptop whirs quietly, yielding to her demands. Now she's typing away again, absorbed in a way I've rarely seen her. There's normally an almost eerie *stillness* to my wife, the sort that is common among the brooding. But here she is, busy, almost jittery. I don't like it.

She leans down to pick up her handbag from the floor, then places it on the table, next to the laptop. I watch as she fishes around inside it and draws out her diary and a pen. Flipping rapidly through the pages, she finds a blank one and scribbles a note, then turns back to the screen.

It dawns upon me that she's likely busy working on Phil's exhibition at the Tate. Why all this drive?

'You're busy,' I say. I make it sound like an accusation, in a way that can only make sense to someone who is, or has been, married.

The typing stops. She takes me in with the hint of a frown. 'Yes,' she says, then returns to her work. The light from the monitor shines a dull tinge against her skin. She's wearing her hair in a casual bun, a pen holding it up. A few strands have escaped it and flow fair along her features. A hairdresser couldn't have done a better job. There are women who would kill to look like Cecilia.

'Phil, is it?' I say, taking a sip of tea. Again, an accusation, although I hadn't intended it to sound like that this time. Cecilia sighs, pushing the computer away. She closes her eyes and brings a hand to her slender neck, rocking her head slowly from side to side.

'You know, Mark,' she says, stretching her back, 'I thought you'd be happy about this.'

'What? I'm just asking.'

'I'm working, trying to help Phil. The exhibition is next week.'

'I know,' I say. 'It's just, I never see you so... *focused* on your work.'

This hurts her. It hurts her because it suggests I'm jealous, and jealousy is reserved to passionate couples, ones with a future. If she knew everything, my jealousy would appear even more obscene.

'All right,' she says, dismissing the matter with a wave of her hand. She has a way of making me feel stupid, childish. I watch as she pushes the computer away and gets up. But before she leaves the room, she can't help punishing me, at least a bit. She does this by staring at my forehead, a look of mild disgust on her face. I know why she's doing it—it's because, years back, I confessed that one of my fears is a receding hairline. She comforted me, at first, but she's often used it against me. A quick glance, pointed just above my eyes, is enough to flood me with self-doubt. But here's the thing: if I tell her I know what she's doing, she'd call me mad, she'd say I'm paranoid. She'd say that, even though she knows it's the truth. One of marriage's million insanities. Even now, I can't help ruffling the hair on my head (it's still there) and looking away.

Cecilia walks out of the kitchen in silence. I listen to her footfall on the stairs, followed by the bathroom door closing and, instants later, the water running in the bathtub.

My heart sinks.

Where is Alice?

I'm about to get up and empty the tea into the sink, when a faint, metallic note rings through the kitchen. It takes me a second to recognise it—it's a message. It's not my phone though, my alert sounds different.

Cecilia's bag is still sitting on the kitchen table. A greenish light is now shining inside it.

Then it happens again, another ring.

Not knowing exactly why, I quickly put the cup down and reach for Cecilia's handbag. The sounds were muffled, but the high-pitched notes from phones have a way of being heard, and Cecilia might soon be on her way down to fetch it. Unless, of course, she's heard it but thinks it can wait.

Regardless, I act swiftly. Ignoring a growing feeling of shame, I rummage through her bag (unlike the handbags of most women I know, Cecilia's is half-empty and extremely tidy) and pull out the phone. Sure enough, the screen reports two new messages. Holding my breath, I tap on the alert. No sound yet from upstairs.

The phone brings up the SMS app. The messages are from someone labelled simply as 'P'. The first one is an image, the second a question. But my attention (my horror, my disbelief) is focused on the image.

It's a penis. Large, half-erect, jutting downwards from a tuft of reddish pubic hairs. The image is slightly blurry, and my ad man mind can't help judging it as amateurish. Wrong angle, bad framing. But it does the job.

Beneath the image, a single, illiterate line:

U like?

For a second, my mind can't process what I'm looking at. My immediate thought is that this message simply can't be addressed to Cecilia. Everything about it, the vulgarity, the bluntness of it, is entirely alien to my wife. This, this *cock*, is far too earthly, too obvious, to have anything to do with her, right? I stare at it uncomprehendingly, the vision of it negating my understanding of reality.

I scroll up, in search of previous messages from 'P', but there are none. Could this be the beginning of their correspondence? A dick pic and *U like*? I decide she must have deleted them, the same way she'll delete these. For a second, I consider the possibility that this might be an intrusion, an unwanted communication from a stranger. But it can't be— this number is saved among her contacts.

Upstairs, the bathroom door opens. A sharp, quick sound, followed by Cecilia's footsteps coming downstairs. Fast.

I panic, consider whether I should forward the messages to my number. I could do it, but she'd know, unless I deleted the outgoing messages. No time. I snatch my own phone from the table, position hers in front of the lens, and snap a picture of the screen. Then I shove the phone back into the handbag and almost leap back into my chair.

Cecilia's footsteps are still coming, but slightly slower now, more controlled. She ambles into the kitchen in her bathrobe. Her posture is relaxed, but there's a keen alertness in her eyes. I feel her gaze on me while I sit still, pretending to scroll idly through a newsfeed on my phone.

'I forgot something,' she says, collecting her handbag. She picks up her notebook, too. Then, without a word, heads back upstairs.

My hand trembles slightly, and I find it strange, because the rest of my body has turned to stone.

32

I'm sitting in the dark. Hunched over my phone, on the sofa in our living room. It feels hot, I'm sweating, but I can't get myself to go and turn off the heating. Upstairs, Cecilia is likely sleeping, but I'm not ready to. Nor am I quite ready to climb into the bed beside her.

Here I am, a man staring at a penis, trying to figure out who it might belong to.

P.

Who is 'P'? Of course, in my heart of hearts, I know it must be Phil. But I'd rather ponder other possibilities before delving into the consequences of the more likely one. Who else could this person be? I ask myself. Perhaps it's just that— P for *Person*, the one who might very well be sleeping with my wife. Or P for *Placeholder*, reserved for anyone wanting to. Still, I think, aware of a growing pain in my neck from sitting too still for too long, it might all be some sort of joke, something Cecilia isn't involved in at all. P for *Prankster*, *Pretender*. P for the *Plotter* who seeks to take my wife from me.

P for *Penis*?

Insanely, I try to think back to the last time I clearly saw

Philip's manhood. It must have been years ago, as teens, some stupid summer stunt, swimming naked in a friend's pool. I recall the discomfort at witnessing his confidence, his willingness to simply strip himself of his clothes in front of the girls who were with us at the time. I've never able to do that sort of thing. I still remember their giggles and how their eyes, albeit shyly, kept wandering back to my friend's faultless body. It hurt, that strange feeling that his confidence somehow detracted from mine, his charisma overshadowing me. Always the second-best looking. When in a foul mood, I'd say to myself, *At least I'm not Clyde.* I still do.

I think back to the last time we pissed together in the gents' in the King's Head, but I can't remember. The truth is, most men don't spend a lot of time studying their male friends' genitalia.

Letting out a frustrated sigh, I study the intricate pubic hairs for the hundredth time, trying to pair their hue to that of Phil's hair. One second, it seems like they could be a match. The next, I ask myself what the fuck it is I'm doing.

Another vacuous thought, but one I can't quite silence: this penis is larger than mine. Not by much, but enough to make me feel a stinging, childish discomfort I haven't felt since school, when boys are first confronted with the issue of size.

I finally press the lock button on my phone, and the image is wiped away, replaced by a black screen. I sit back, letting the phone drop between my legs, trying to relax the muscles in my neck. A part of me says I shouldn't rush to conclusions, that this could easily mean nothing at all. It might be a mistake of some sort, although it's hard to imagine how, at the moment.

But another part of me sees these arguments as weak, the pathetic defences of the unwitting cuckold, too cowardly to confront the obvious facts.

Someone is sending dick pics to your wife. What else could it mean?

I press the palms of my hands against my eyes. I'm tired, but sleepless.

P.

If it is Phil, why didn't she conceal it better? Had I been receiving messages from a lover, I'd use a full name, a false one, possibly a man's. Tom, Francis, Chris. I'd make sure the phone wasn't lying around, ever, not even for a minute. I'd activate the screen-lock and create a strong password. And I'd definitely instruct the other person (Alice, if I had her number) not to send me intimate pictures like that.

I'm fuming. Also, there's this odd irritation mounting, an insane frustration at how inept my wife is with technology.

Then, the shame: all I'm saying is that I'd have handled the betrayal better than she has. Is that the kind of man I am?

No, worse. You're the kind of man who discusses the possibility of murdering his wife with his lover.

Maybe she simply never expected me to go nosing around through her messages, because she actually has nothing to hide, and this is all a misunderstanding.

But it isn't, is it? How could it be?

I shift around, try to find a comfortable position, but there isn't one. I frown, twitch, chew my lip. It's not just the nauseating idea that my wife might have a sex life outside of our marriage, it's the fact that she's deprived us of one. And with it, the prospect of finally having a family. A child.

Those initial weeks, after the miscarriage, in which I pathetically begged her to sleep with me. My hand sliding over to her through the covers, only for her to retract, turn away. Cold and distant, lost in thoughts I could only partially understand. She had carried the life we lost. It's something, that feeling, no man can ever fathom. In the end, I gave up, accepting this life of sexless cohabitation, always secretly thinking of it as a temporary arrangement, but one we got caught up in and couldn't free ourselves of.

Now, Cecilia is likely sleeping with another. Now, I shall never be the father of her child, but someone else might. The thought makes my head spin.

I picture Alice, her smile. I know what she'd say if she were here. She'd say that this is *good*. That there's a silver lining to this obscene story.

If she's betrayed you, surely you can just leave her. Be with me.

But.

But.

Alice doesn't know Cecilia. Regardless of her actions, Cecilia would still see me as guilty of betrayal. Her cheating on me, if indeed she is, wouldn't justify mine. It would simply be another source of humiliation, a tool in her repertoire of punishments to inflict upon me. A minor one, if compared to the Michael Taylor revelation.

In my mind, Alice sighs sadly and looks down, the way she did in Blackwood. Then she fades, swallowed by the shadows in the living room. In her place, impossibly, is my father. I can't visualise him, not exactly. Rather, I sense his presence. He's silent, sleeping perhaps, the way he sometimes would, sprawled out, belly showing, on the sofa. I consider him, his barbaric, unsophisticated ways. The stench on his breath. His hatred of my mother. The endless supply of resentment. I wonder, here in the dark, if he's the secret reason for this desire of mine to become a father. Become the man he never was. Be the loving, dependable, understanding father he wouldn't, or couldn't, be. Then he too fades, and I'm left here alone in the dark. Two things I feel: a sudden, desperate longing for Alice, and an unspeakable hatred for my wife.

. . .

A GASP, and I'm awake. Sitting up, disoriented. This isn't my bedroom, it isn't the space in front of the fire in Lilac House. It's pitch black, and I'm covered in sweat.

My eyes adjust, and I realise I'm still on the sofa, in our living room. An echo of unease, of discomfort, simmers in my gut.

The phone is lying on the floor, a rectangle of thicker black. I scoop it up to check the time, but the battery is dead. Flipping thing. I toss it against the cushions.

I feel like I'm missing something. Then I realise it's two things: one I can't put my finger on, a lurking suspicion that there is something so obviously *wrong* about this whole story, something that, once revealed, would change everything.

The other is the reason I woke up. It's a noise, a voice, coming from outside.

The intruder.

Before I know it, I'm scrambling to my feet. I knock the phone to the floor and step on it. It makes an awful sound, and I think I might have cracked the glass screen. It doesn't matter. I'm rushing towards the front door, holding my breath, stopping only to try to find my shoes by the entrance. They were here, damn it. But all I can half-see, half-feel are pairs of Cecilia's countless evening shoes, slippers, boots and God knows what else.

Come on, come on, come on.

I finally find one of mine, a dress shoe. Not ideal, but it's something. Where's the other?

Outside, the intruder has gone silent.

Cursing, I throw the shoe to the ground, decide I'll have to do this in my socks, and grab the door handle, pushing with my shoulder to fling it open. It's locked. Cursing louder now, I fish the keys from the porcelain dish by the entrance and shove them in the keyhole.

My hands are shaking, all my anger, outrage, and thirst

for revenge are surging now, hungry for someone to blame. The intruder, as it so happens, would be perfect.

I shove the door open, and it hits the wall outside, rebounding. I feel it strike my shoulder, hard, but I'm already on the steps, in my socks, and as soon as I step out onto the street, I walk straight into a puddle, soaking them through. It's raining.

The air is glacial, and the sweat on my skin turns ice cold. I realise I'm still holding my breath.

And there he is—the intruder.

He (or she) is standing in the middle of the road. Exactly in the middle, in fact, one foot on either side of the white line. At first, the intruder appears to be lacking a head. His torso tapers towards the top, ending with a protruding shoulder and a single arm. A headless, demonic creature in an urban tracksuit.

But then the figure shifts, and I realise he was simply twisted, turned to one side, fiddling with something in his pocket. Almost definitely a *he*, despite the hood pulled up covering his face in shadow.

I throw myself at him with a roar. I run, awkwardly, on the tips of my toes, but without hesitation, plunging into puddles, smashing through a wall of thin needles of rain. I'm gathering speed and momentum, and I couldn't stop even if I wanted to. The figure is suddenly inches from me. I register the flash of a pale white face, a mouth open in horror.

My full weight crashes against him, and I'm surprised by how light, almost insubstantial, his body is. We're on the ground, my body lying on top of his. In a second, I sit up, straddling him, and start pummelling the hood, the head inside it, with slaps.

'*Fucking intruder*,' I snarl. This name I've given him, the one I use in my own thoughts, sounds ridiculous spoken out loud. 'How fucking *dare* you?' *Smack.* 'Eh?' *Smack.* 'What do you want from us?' *Smack*. 'What the *fuck* do you *want* from us?'

The intruder has brought his hands to his face, palms out, trying to parry my blows. I notice they are long, bony, sickly white. Something is wrapped around one of his wrists, some sort of black tape.

'*Stop... stop,*' he begs, but I have no intention to. In fact, I decide he deserves something more than a few meagre slaps. I raise a fist in the air, elbow pulled all the way back, trembling with rage—a rage that might actually have very little to do with this person and a lot to do with my wife. Then I hear the crystal-clear ring of a bell.

What?

It's so nonsensical, such a non sequitur, that I freeze. It's a minute sound and a happy one. As if Tinker Bell had suddenly decided to fly over and join us, out here in the night.

I turn around and spot a dog. There it is, a yard away and impossibly tiny. Fluffy white fur, eyes like black marbles, plush-toy lips pulled back to reveal minuscule pointy teeth. It's growling at me, if you can call the low purring sound in its throat a growl. Around its neck, a collar with the little bell hanging from it.

'Mr *Hamilton*?'

My eyes go from the dog to the man I'm sitting on. He's pushed back the hood to get a proper look at me, and his face is filled with a mix of fear and utter disbelief.

As I sit there in the rain, arm still raised, I realise that I know him. It's Mr Banks, from a few houses down the road.

Why would Mr Banks be spying on us? is the spontaneous, idiotic question that arises. I hesitate, and he senses it. He shoves me off him, indignant. I let him.

'What the *hell* are you doing?' he says, as we both get to our feet. He dusts himself off with trembling hands. Except there's no dust, just mud and rain, so all he succeeds in doing is smudging it around a bit. I notice that the thing wrapped around his wrist is simply a dog's leash. '*Intruder?*' he shrieks, furious and quizzical. 'What the *hell* are you on about?' The dog echoes his owner's feelings with a burst of quick, squeaky barks.

I try to speak, but nothing comes out.

'Are you *mad?*' he insists. 'Are you out of your bloody *mind?* You just *assaulted* me, is what you did. You *assaulted* me. Why? Because I'm walking my blimming dog around at night!'

'Why at night?' I ask, unthinking. Given the current situation, it sounds absolutely insane.

'*Why at night?*' he echoes, looking around, as if for the benefit of an audience. Then, oddly, he says, 'Because it's *Friday!*'

This answer baffles me, and I'm about to ask him to clarify, but I catch myself before doing so.

As the realisation of what has just happened begins to sink in, I sigh, hang my head in shame. 'Mr Banks...' I start, palms towards him. 'I'm so, *so*—'

'You're *insane!* That's what you are.' The dog, emboldened by his owner's anger, is getting so worked up that it actually lifts a couple of inches in the air every time it barks.

'It's just, we've had someone in our garden...' I start, but it feels pointless. I shake my head. 'Listen, Mr Banks, please let me call you an ambulance.'

He scoffs. 'An ambulance! The police, more likely!'

'Don't call the police,' I blurt out before I know it. In the instant that follows, I have time to hope it sounded like, *There's no need for that, really, Mr Banks. I'm genuinely sorry, and we can solve this in a civilised manner.* But it doesn't. Maybe it's because of the secret thoughts of murder, or Taylor's ghost still haunting me, but it just sounds like the desperate plea of a cornered criminal.

Banks picks up on it. He seems surprised by my reaction, his eyes narrowing as he studies me.

I clear my voice. 'Really, Mr Banks,' I add hurriedly, eager to interrupt his train of thought. 'Let me call an ambulance. Or drive you to A&E.'

He tugs on the leash, and the little dog is lifted clear off the ground again, landing by his side. 'You overestimate your strength, Mr Hamilton. I fought in the Falklands, sir,' he says, squaring his narrow shoulders, bony chest jutting out.

I look to the ground and sigh. 'I don't know how to apologise, Mr Banks. I—'

'Never mind all that,' he says. Then, to the dog, 'Come on, Cicero.'

He walks off, a little unsteadily, towards his house. Cicero is throwing quivering glances at his owner, then back at me, as if disappointed that the excitement is over so soon. To my dismay, I notice a couple of people standing at their doors. In other homes, curtains twitch discreetly.

'Oh, Mr Hamilton?'

Banks is standing at his front door, one foot inside the house. 'The police are going to hear about this.'

33

I follow Cecilia into the gaping mouth of Tate Modern's Turbine Hall. The sky disappears, replaced by the dark distant glass ceiling, as the vastness of the building swallows us all.

We're a group of about fifty people, perhaps more. Some are friends of Cecilia's or Phil's, but most of the others are from the media. Arts editors, columnists, even bloggers, all invited to this 'soft launch' of Phil's exhibition. They're a noisy bunch, all of them, greeting each other with high-pitched laughter and floating cheek kisses. Their hairdos are extravagant, and their clothing as flamboyant as it is predictable.

Ed and Gabbie are here, too. Clyde isn't, and I don't know whether that's because Phil didn't invite him, or because he turned down the invitation. I stick by them, basking in Ed's absolute normality, his being completely out of place among the crowd of aesthetes.

'What's that, Dada?' Lilly asks Ed, pointing towards the floor with her podgy gloved hand. The babysitter cancelled last minute, so they've had to bring her along too. Her face is a small oval, almost entirely concealed by the layers of scarf, hat and hood Gabbie has wrapped her in against the cold.

'What's *that*, Dada?' she insists, irritated by her father's lack of attention. Ed peers down. 'It's your feet, darling,' he says, as if it were a perfectly normal answer to a perfectly normal question. I chuckle, but Lilly nods thoughtfully, quietly studying her shoes as she walks hand in hand with her parents, one at either side of her.

The Turbine Hall is almost completely dark, due to an art installation unrelated to Phil's exhibition. 'Quite interesting,' Ed says, nodding towards the walls. And it is: the sheer surfaces of the hall are covered in human-sized glow worms, each emitting pools of surreal green light in the shadows surrounding us. They cling to the cold surfaces of the hall, their swollen, larvae-like bodies only just visible in the half-light. A placard states that the artwork, by someone calling themselves Anabolic Anonymous, is titled *The Temptations of Cassandra*.

Up ahead, Cecilia and Phil are slowly leading the crowd towards the entrance. My wife is in PR mode, charming and talkative, enthusiastically introducing her invitees to Phil. Her eyes are wide and her smile ready. I hardly recognise her. Standing beside her, Phil is projecting a sort of bored confidence, as if all this—the visitors, the exhibition, the recognition—were simply owed to him. But I spy his nervousness beneath the posturing. He's fidgety, running a hand through his hair, twitching his nose, throwing rapid glances about him. Is this because he knows his career depends on the reviews these people will be penning tomorrow? Or maybe it's because he's having an affair with my wife, and us both being here is taxing on him?

The crowd is now pooling in front of the entrance. Posters hanging at either side of the wide glass doors announce the name of the exhibition:

Sightings of the Übermensch.

Phil's own face features prominently below the words (of course), in a low-fi selfie depicting my childhood friend with the words *SUCK ME* scrawled across his forehead in red lipstick. Ed sees the posters, then shoots me a little look that would normally have had me burst out laughing. But I'm not exactly in the mood, with the dick pic still very much at the forefront of my thoughts. I manage a mocking smile, but that's all.

At one point, a woman approaches the star of the evening with the same congratulatory two-tone call of '*Phi-iilll!*' I've heard at least ten times since we got here. As she throws her arms around him, I realise I've seen her before. I know her from somewhere, but where? It's only when I hear Phil reply in the same notes (first one high, second lower and stretched out), '*Jack*-kieee,' that I'm able to place her—she was the host of *that* party, the one where I met Alice. I wonder, with a sudden breathless pang, if this means she might show up tonight.

Cecilia, standing by the entrance, claps her hands twice, and the crowd's chatter fades out. She's wearing a long, flowing dress, simple but stunning.

'Well,' she says, 'thank you all for coming.' This elicits a nonsensical giggle from the crowd. 'We have the entire museum to ourselves tonight, but please don't wander off. I doubt you would, anyway—Phil's art is so unique, so *captivating*, we'll end up having to drag you out of the gallery ourselves when the evening is over.' More giggles. Someone cheers. For all his show of confidence, Phil is nervously nibbling at his lip. Cecilia lays a hand on his shoulder—a small gesture, but one that makes my stomach squirm—and adds in a soft, affectionate voice, 'It genuinely is. I've known him for years now, but I've only *really* got to know him and his beautiful creations over the past few weeks.' She pauses here, all eyes on her, and I'm left pondering the meaning of that '*really*', that '*know*'. Also, Cecilia met him through me, but there's no mention of me, her husband, or of any of the others.

A pause, during which she smiles and shakes her head imperceptibly, as if there were things she could add, but which would be lost to us. Turning back to the crowd, she says, 'You're in for a treat, ladies and gentlemen. We all know it is rare to witness talent, *true* talent, to be there in the early stages of a great artist's career. But that's exactly where you are tonight.'

The crowd claps enthusiastically. To my right, Gabbie leans towards Ed and myself and whispers sceptically, 'Crikey, she's bigging him up, isn't she? *Great artist* and all that.'

'She's a good marketer,' Ed says with a shrug.

I nod. Perhaps that's all this is. Marketing.

Yeah, right.

When the clapping dies down, Cecilia says, 'We've set up a little interview corner in the gallery, so all you members of the press will get a chance to sit down with Phil.' She turns towards him. 'Is there anything you wanted to add now, before we enter?'

Phil appears to be caught off guard, his eyes widening slightly, a sudden stiffness in his shoulders. But it doesn't last long. This is Phil, after all. 'What can I say?' he says. 'I hope you like it.' A brief pause, punctuated by his bad-boy smile creeping across his face. Chin raised, eyes glittering, he adds, 'Or not. I don't really care.'

This absolute platitude is greeted with raucous laughter and applause.

Cecilia smiles. 'Let's go.'

. . .

WE'RE ONE FLOOR UP, where a large room houses Phil's art. It's scattered all around us, paintings, sculptures, installations. The *Sightings of the Übermensch* banners hang by the two entrances, Phil's vain expression hovering above us.

The visitors chat and mingle, champagne flutes taken from the richly assorted snack table pinched between their fingers. Photographers' flashes go off all over the place, like silent explosions. Critics study Phil's work, nodding pensively and stroking their chins. A loose queue has formed in the north-east corner of the room, where Phil is sitting in a chair, taking questions from interviewers. Cecilia stands beside him, stepping away only when photos of the *artiste* are taken. I spy them out of the corner of my eye as I wander about, nibbling on a sandwich I have no appetite for.

'What's *this* all about?' Gabbie asks Ed, a few feet away. She's staring at one of Phil's installations: a washing machine, its round door open, with a glossy mass of porn mags spilling out of it. The words *VINTAGE SINS* have been scrawled across one side of the washing machine in thick brown letters.

Ed is busy unbuttoning Lilly's winter coat. He throws a quick glance at the appliance. 'Pff. No idea.'

Gabbie shakes her head. 'Not sure I like his stuff, to be honest.'

Ed nods towards the growing queue of people waiting to interview Phil. 'They seem to like it though. I s'pose that's all that matters, really.'

She raises an eyebrow, unimpressed. Speaking a little lower, she says, 'It's still rubbish though, no matter what this lot say.'

For once, I think I can agree with Gabbie.

I amble casually towards the interview corner, pretending to admire the abstract paintings, the erotic sculptures along the way. I stop about six yards from where Phil is sitting, within hearing distance of what they're saying. I find myself standing in front of a large canvas depicting a woman's buttocks and legs, lying on what appears to be an unmade bed. Only half of her body is portrayed, from the waist down, her skin pale against a dark background of silk sheets and impenetrable shadows. Annoyingly, I have to admit that this one is good—the chiaroscuro dramatic but realistic, the composition original. For a minute, I'm genuinely interested in it and forget about my intention of studying Cecilia's interactions with Phil, nearby.

Cecilia... are these her legs? Am I staring at an erotic depiction of my wife?

I shift my gaze to the placard to the right. The small plastic rectangle tells me the painting is called *Confession*.

A confession by whom? About what? Cecilia confessing her love for him? The other way round? Or, perhaps, Phil's confession to me—*I've been sleeping with your wife, mate.*

I turn towards him. He's leaning back in his chair, long legs crossed, one hand absent-mindedly running through the hair on his nape, as he answers a question from the journalist sitting before him. Standing close by, Cecilia smiles quietly, hands crossed in front of her like a diligent schoolgirl, nodding from time to time.

'It's not about life,' Phil is saying. 'Life is tedium, inauthenticity. Fuck, you know... art, if it is to be anything at all, has to be the opposite of that. The *polar* opposite. Take Heidegger...'

He's wearing a faded grey hoodie and worn jeans. Everything about him, his posture, signals a barely contained indifference. As if none of this really matters to him at all.

For some reason, my gaze is captured by his shoes—a pair of Converse All Stars (of course). Right ankle resting on his left knee, his nervous wiggling foot suggests again that he might not be so indifferent after all.

I step away from the painting (it might be art, but it still feels slightly wrong to be staring at a woman's bottom for too long). Yet I can't get my eyes off Phil's shoe. The diamond-shaped pattern on the sole, the neat circle in the centre, enclosing the size—a *ten*, like mine. There's something there, in that number, in that shape, like the hint of an elusive answer.

Just then, the journalist's chair scrapes backwards as she rises. I watch her extend a hand towards Phil—who stays seated—and thank him. 'Let me tell you,' she says, with a mock-conspiratorial tone. 'Spoiler warning: the *Guardian*'s review is going to be an *excellent* one.'

Phil can't conceal his smile at this and turns towards Cecilia. She leans a hand on his shoulder and gives a little squeeze. I realise that there's no twenty-something blonde beauty accompanying him tonight. Interesting.

Another journalist steps forward, eager to take his seat in front of Phil. 'Hi,' he says. 'I'm Ben, from ArtOrDie dot com, and I *have* to say—'

Whatever Ben from ArtOrDie dot com *has* to say, he doesn't, because a loud shriek tears through the room, interrupting him and everyone else. Heads jolt and turn, trying to find the source of the disturbance. And there it is: little Lilly, charging forwards, unsteady yet fast, pounding the floor with her small, bun-shaped feet. Her eyes are wide with excitement, an open-mouthed smile gleaming on her face. She's running straight towards me, and something tugs at my heart, watching her bumblebee frame dashing in my direction, so innocent, so *real* against the backdrop of all these chattering, posturing adults. I feel the impulse to open my arms wide and sweep her off the floor into a hug.

But she stops a few feet away and points at the painting behind me. 'BOTTOOMMM!' she shouts, delighted. 'BUM! BUM! BOTTOM!' The silent room is filled with her gurgling laughter as she stares unbelievingly at the image. She looks at me and says, by way of explanation, 'That's a bum!' In her mouth, the *th* comes out as a *d*. *Dat's a bum.*

A red-faced Gabbie comes shooting out of the crowd, half crouching, eyes darting left and right, trying to spot her daughter. Around her, some people giggle, others tut. Ed strolls out a second later, his smiling eyes fixed on Lilly.

'*Shush*,' Gabbie hisses, yanking the child's arm and eyeing the crowd with embarrassment. 'You can't say that, it's rude.'

Lilly frowns, upset. Her lip quivers, and an instant later she's crying. Loud, desperate wails that reverberate through the room. Gabbie rolls her eyes as Ed kneels down beside Lilly. 'Don't cry, my darling,' he says in a soft, soothing voice. Lilly leans into his shoulder and wraps her short arms around his neck.

Phil is staring at them with protruding eyeballs, lower jaw jutting forwards. He's fuming. '*Oi!*' he calls out to Ed and Gabbie, in a hushed, menacing voice. He jerks his head to the side, saying, '*Get that brat out. Now.*'

Ed lets out a long sigh and picks Lilly up. As they make their way outside, Gabbie throws a venomous glance towards Phil. '*Cunt*,' she mutters, loud enough for him to hear her.

There's a brief silence, then the chatter picks up again.

The blogger hesitantly extends his hand to Phil again. 'Kids, eh?' he offers with a half-smile as he lowers his considerable weight upon the chair.

Phil scoffs and shakes his head. 'Yeah, sorry about that.'

I study Cecilia. There she is, by his side, standing stiffly now. I ask myself why she hasn't told him that was too harsh, that one simply doesn't speak to parents like that. It angers me, to watch her accept his behaviour so passively. Gabbie's her friend too, after all, isn't she? And she loves Lilly, I know she does.

This place is starting to feel too crowded. I watch the

guests, with their intellectual air, their restless hand-waving, the bright colours of their glasses' frames. Snippets of conversations waft my way: bland insights into art, crass sexual puns delivered in middle-class mockney accents, incessant maligning of absent individuals. My dad, ever the working-class victim, would fucking hate them all.

I stare at my wife, willing her to turn around and meet my eye. Not for her to smile at me, or stare at me with her maddening sphinx expression, but simply to acknowledge me. *Me*—the man she married.

I call her in my mind, again and again, until I can almost feel her name pressing against my forehead. *Cecilia. Cecilia. Cecilia.*

What am I doing?

Whatever it is, it isn't working.

With a last glance at the buttocks in the painting, I leave the room in search of Ed and Gabbie.

34

The Tate at night is a labyrinth of cordoned-off corridors and closed doors. I walk alone, savouring the silence, following the route imposed by these barriers. The air is fresh and still. I can't find Ed and Gabbie, but I do run into a member of the museum staff: a tall, skinny man in a white shirt, lurking ghostlike in one of the corners. His hair is black and his skin mottled with acne scars. 'You're a guest at the Philip Jones exhibition,' he says. It's not a question. I nod.

'Can I help you?'

'I'm just going for a smoke,' I say.

He nods thoughtfully, as if I've just said something profound. Then he turns around quietly and opens a door I hadn't noticed, summoning it out of nothingness. 'Down these stairs and to the right. It'll take you outside. You can come back the same way, as long as you close the doors behind you again on your way up, sir.'

I thank him and make my way down the stairs. His presence looms behind me as I descend, silent, like that of some

Dante character pointing me towards my own personal circle of hell.

LONDON'S NIGHT sky is a bulging vault of bloated brown clouds. I smoke two cigarettes (lighting the second with the glowing tip of the first), the nicotine silencing my thoughts of Phil, of Cecilia, even of Mr Banks—the non-intruder, who apparently hasn't pressed charges. After my attack on him, I spent the following day expecting a visit from Inspector Lombardi, conjuring explanations and apologies. But Banks must have reconsidered, or perhaps the police are simply too busy to deal with it.

The chimney of the museum towers above me, brick after brick of industrial grandeur. I stare at it, head thrown backwards, until its titanic proportions make me uneasy on my feet.

As London buzzes around me, I feel like this should be a time for decisions. Yet I'm overwhelmed, uncomfortable, incapable of action. There are two paths ahead: accepting the status quo (unbearable), or murdering my cheating, unloving wife (inconceivable).

Where are you, Alice?

And just as her name drifts through my thoughts, the door behind me, the same one I exited from five minutes ago, creaks open. I turn, almost certain to see her there, like a gift, like a solution to all of this.

But it's not her.

'Fuck,' someone says, tripping in the lower door frame. Tall, slender, broad-shouldered, his hair almost the exact same golden shade as Cecilia's.

'Phil,' I say.

He looks up at me, startled. He squints, his eyes adapting to the darkness outside. 'Mark? Is that you?'

'Yes.'

Phil half-turns towards the door, as if he were reconsidering. Then he squares his shoulders, shrugging off his hesitation, and walks towards me.

'What are you doing out here?' I ask. I study him closely, trying to read him, to drill into his thoughts.

'Needed a breather,' he says. 'It's mental in there. Fucking journos, asking the same stupid questions again and again.' He shakes his head.

We're standing in a long blade of shadow, and to anyone watching from one of the windows, we'd just be two black silhouettes.

'It's good though, isn't it?' I offer. 'Means they're interested.'

'Oh, yeah, sure. Cissy says that—'

'Cissy?'

He bites his lip, averts his eyes. 'Cecilia... don't you call her that? I thought I got it from you.'

I take a deep, slow breath. It dissipates between us, a white cloud caught by the wind. 'No. I don't.'

Phil rubs his hands on his jeans, trembling in the cold. 'I was so eager to get out of there, I didn't even bother grabbing my coat.' He flashes a hesitant smile.

We stand there for a bit, in silence. The traffic is suddenly still, and all we hear is the black mass of the river flowing nearby.

'I'd kill for a cigarette,' Phil says, thinking out loud.

I slip my hand in my pocket and offer him my packet. 'Here. Have one of mine.'

'Oh, cheers,' he says, genuinely relieved. He lights it, then looks at me, an eyebrow raised. 'Hang on—I didn't know you smoked.'

'I didn't know *you* smoked.'

'Oh well. You know, one every now and then. I don't buy them or anything.'

'Yeah. Same here,' I say, nonsensically.

He nods, then shoots me a conspiratorial glance. 'I won't tell the missus.'

Here he is, trying to establish some sort of bond between us. The cunt.

'Yes.' I smile. 'Please don't tell *Cissy*.'

He takes me in, then nods quickly.

We smoke. Inhale, exhale, silence.

'Come on, mate,' I say, my voice suddenly jolly. It echoes, too loud, against the vast walls that surround us. I'm fucking with him. 'This must be exciting, right? Your own show at Tate Modern! How's it going?'

He's taken aback, unsure how to interpret my tone. But it's a safe topic, and I think I spy something like relief on his face. Of course, I might simply be seeing things.

'I suppose it is exciting, yes. It's just, they're stressing me out with all their questions. *Where do you draw your inspiration from?* I got that about ten times. *Who are your influences?* that's another one. And some of them, especially the bloggers, they're after some sort of controversial statement. They keep...'

Phil moans and whines, and I just zone out. Here he is, a man offered the unique opportunity of being a popular artist, and all he can do is bitch about the questions he's getting.

My gaze drifts downwards, towards his crotch. I try to picture the penis from the message tucked in there. If he is actually sleeping with Cecilia (*Cissy*), could he really be standing out here, having a smoke and talking to me—the friend he betrayed?

I read his expressions, the gesticulations of his hands. How does a guilty man behave? Is there a secret body language that can betray them?

There's a pause in his monologue, and I realise he's asked me a question, or said something that demands a reaction from me. There's an echo of complaint in the air: he was probably just criticising someone or something. I simply shake my head, then nod in a generic yeah-man-fuck-that-shit sort of way. It seems to work, and Phil starts droning on again.

The moon blinks through a gap in the clouds. A slither of a moonbeam washes over his shoulder for a second. Caught in the light, a strand of his golden, wavy hair resting there.

And as I stare at it, entranced, something in the back of my mind seems to quietly slide into place. Like a secret whispered into my ear by a Muse. Something so small, so obvious, it could easily have been missed. The hidden path that leads out of the woods.

I raise my arm, moving my hand towards the strand of hair. Slowly, carefully, as if fearing it might fly away. I pluck it between index and thumb, the way you'd do with something unimaginably precious.

Phil's head snaps towards me. 'What you doing?'

'You had something on your shoulder.' I smile reassuringly. 'Can't look shabby tonight, my friend.'

'Right, OK.' He looks at me suspiciously. Then sniffs and flicks his cigarette to the ground. 'OK, better get back... You coming?'

I turn towards the river, watch the headlights creeping behind Blackfriars Pier. 'I think I'll stay here a while longer.'

There's a serene, zen-like quality to my voice now, I'm aware of it. It's disturbing Phil, who stares at me like you'd do with a wild creature who might just be about to lash out. 'All right,' he says in the end. 'Catch you later.'

He hurries towards the door. Six swift eager strides, the door creaking, and he's gone.

I pull my hand out of my pocket. There it is, still safely

lodged between my fingers—the golden strand of Phil's hair. I study it in the murky light, this minute, almost insubstantial tendril of possibility. Holding it still, I slip the plastic wrap off the packet of cigarettes and gently tuck it in there. Then I twist the open end of the wrap until I've got a neat little package. I hold it up, like a researcher studying some rare specimen in a vial, and watch it flutter in the wind. After making sure it's closed safely, I push it deep into my pocket so it won't somehow slip out.

I'm about to leave, when something guides my eye towards Phil's discarded dog-end lying on the ground. Inspiration strikes again.

It just keeps getting better and better.

I kneel down, about to pick it up—but I freeze, my hand hovering an inch away.

Not with your bare hands.

Right.

I scoop it up in a tissue, then fold the paper carefully, like I did with the plastic wrap, until it's sealed. Standing there in the shadows, I close my eyes and fill my ears with the murmuring whispers of the river.

ON MY WAY BACK, I bump into Gabbie. She's standing in a corridor, not far from the room that hosts the exhibition, holding a sleeping Lilly in her arms.

'Mark!' she says. 'Thank God. Listen, do you mind holding her for a sec? Ed's gone to fetch the car, and I desperately need to pee.'

'Of course. You leaving?'

'Yeah. It's late, Lilly needs to get to bed. Plus, Phil's being a cunt. He walked right past me a few minutes ago and just ignored me.'

I chuckle at that.

'We were trying to find you, to say goodbye. Ed says he'll ring you tomorrow. Here,' she says, placing Lilly in my arms. 'I'll be right back.'

Gabbie scuttles off in search of the toilets. I'm left alone, with the sleeping child in my arms. The voices from the exhibition room are faint and strangely unreal, a dull drama playing on a radio far away.

Lilly's cheek is resting against my shoulder, like a soft pink pillow. I study her miniature rosebud lips, parted now, and listen to the gentle, steady sound of her breathing. She's snoring slightly, the air occasionally catching somewhere in the back of her mouth. Her breath is warm and clean. I begin a slow walk up and down the corridor, rocking her gently as I move. Her weight feels good in my arms, and my arms feel like they were meant to bear it. She sleeps so deeply, so peacefully, and I wonder when, at what age, it is that we stop sleeping like this. Lilly's sleep is absolute, something done with complete abandon, in the knowledge that the world is a safe, loving place. One that revolves around her. Ed and Gabbie have filled her with this belief. They are good parents, loving parents.

My mind wanders to our home, to that empty room, the promise it had held.

'*Shh, sleep,*' I whisper. '*Sleep.*' I realise a tear is running down my face. It tickles, but I don't want to wipe it away because it would mean having to shift Lilly.

I want this.

This is all I want.

I tighten my hold on her ever so slightly, a sort of one-way hug, because I feel I have to thank her for something, although it wouldn't be easy to explain exactly what.

Footsteps gradually fade in from the corridor, and Gabbie appears. It feels too soon. She's speaking into a phone. '... five minutes. Yup, on our way.'

I quickly wipe my face against my shoulder to get rid of the tears.

'Mark's here,' she's saying, now standing beside me, still speaking into the phone. 'He's got her... yes... yes, I'll tell him.' She turns towards me. 'Ed says he'll catch you at the office... OK, be there in five. Love you.'

She slips the phone into her handbag, then extends her arms towards me. 'Thanks for that,' Gabbie says. She scoops Lilly up in a way that feels too rough, too hurried. But they're simply the practised motions of a parent. Lilly hardly notices. She lets out a little sigh and keeps on sleeping.

Someone over in the exhibition hall bursts out laughing. It's an unpleasant, artificial sound. 'Listen,' Gabbie says. 'Tell Cecilia I said goodbye. I'd go in myself, but Ed's waiting outside. Plus, I might end up punching Phil.'

I tell her I will. She walks off, Lilly's little feet bouncing gently at her sides with every step.

In the hall, people are still hanging around, the buzz gradually fading. A handful of journalists are left standing in line, awaiting their chance to interview the *artiste*. I stand by the entrance, neither inside nor out, watching my wife and not knowing who she is.

The ghost of Lilly's pressure still weighs against my chest. I don't want to forget what that felt like. Whoever Cecilia is, I'm a man who wants a woman to love and children to hold.

A few yards away and oblivious of me, Cecilia leans forwards and says something in Phil's ear. As she does so, she holds back her hair so it doesn't get in the way. Her movements used to enchant me.

Something needs doing.

35

What you said in the woods.
We should do it.
I'll be here every day at 1.
Please come.

I love you.

36

A thick silence has set in between me and Cecilia. We wade through it, like ghosts in a haunted house, eyeing each other with suspicion.

But I might be wrong. Perhaps there's nothing new about this silence. Maybe it's the same one that has filled our home since the loss of our unborn child. And Cecilia's looks (in those rare occasions when she does look at me) might not be suspicious at all. Just indifferent.

I study her quietly from the sofa, pretending to read a book, or sipping a coffee at the kitchen table. She's busier than usual. The exhibition was hailed as a success, and there's been an endless string of phone calls and emails she's had to attend to. It could be, I know, that she's simply too busy to talk to me. Or that she senses I'm upset about something, and has decided (as she so often does) to ignore the issue away. But at times, it feels as if her affair with Phil is now out in the open, albeit unacknowledged. The proverbial elephant sending dick pics in the room.

It took me two days to track down the exact model of Phil's All Stars. They've been out of production for a couple of years, and only a single shop in London seemed to have them in stock. I didn't want to search for them on my computer, nor from the office, for fear of leaving traces online. So I did it all by phone. Standing in phone boxes for the first time in years, amid cracked glass, stained paper wrappers and the stench of piss. Speaking to shoe shop after shoe shop until I found them.

'Don't you want to try them on first, sir?' the shop owner had asked me, a quizzical look on his face.

There I was, holding out the cash, so eager to grab the shoes and get out of there that I forgot about that.

'Oh,' I said, fumbling for a reason not to try them on. 'I have the same exact pair. I'm sure they'll fit.' I was wearing sunglasses. It was raining outside.

'OK, sir.' He took my money and nodded a stiff goodbye as I hurried out.

The shoes are now tucked away in the back of one of my drawers. Inside the right one, in two separate Ziploc bags, Phil's cigarette and his pale blond strand of hair.

37

Alice appears three days later.

I'm sitting on the bench, staring mindlessly at the river, and suddenly she's beside me. A shifting in the periphery of my vision, a new pressure in the air. I turn, and there she is. Smiling under apologetic eyes, entertained perhaps by the idiocy of my surprised expression.

'Sorry I had you wait,' she says. She looks down, kneading her hands. 'I needed time to think.' Her profile is almost painfully perfect.

I've been waiting so long for her to join me, on this bench, that I'm at a loss now. I had words ready, speeches drafted and recited over and over, mumbled to myself here by the river. Soothing, comforting, loving words, meant to win her over, to bring her mind back to Lilac House and what we'd felt there. Now that she's actually here, sitting beside me, those words are gone, replaced by a strange mixture of panic and relief.

'Please don't apologise,' I say.

Then I remember why we're here. The purpose of this meeting.

What you said in the woods.

'Listen,' I say, swallowing. I still haven't dared reach out to touch her. 'If you don't want to... you know. *Go ahead* with this... I'll understand, Alice.' I nod sympathetically. 'I really do. You can get up, walk off, and I'll understand.'

She looks away, towards the waters. I'm losing her, I think. I suddenly realise how different this is for her. It must be. I'm the one stuck in the dead-end marriage, the one sizzling with resentment, going about Tate Modern plotting murders. From the outside, from her point of view, this is simply about being together. Being with me. How could that possibly be reason enough to kill someone?

The spell from Lilac House has faded, for her. That's clear now. She returned to her normal life, away from there, from me and from talk of killing. A few days of normality, and the prospect of murder now seems absurd to her, of course. Of course.

How could I have believed that this story would have a happy ending? One with Alice, a sleeping infant, and me huddled together in the cottage, rocked to sleep by the sound of wind on the waves?

I'm chewing desperately at the inside of my cheek. I will myself to stop. 'Alice—' My voice is trembling.

'I do, Mark.'

I'd gone so far down the tunnel of self-doubt that I couldn't decipher her words. 'What?' I ask idiotically.

She kisses me. Then, her breath warm and sweet against my skin, she whispers, 'I want to do this. I love you, Mark, and I want to do this.'

WE POP over to the stand and grab two coffees before returning to the bench to plot my wife's murder.

I'd be lying if I said there isn't a sort of playfulness about this, a childlike excitement. It wears off somewhat as we go into the detail of it, but it's there.

'This is how we do it,' I say, lowering my voice. 'We fake a break-in.'

There are people passing by, but their presence isn't alarming, for some reason. I feel safe here, conspirators hiding in plain sight.

Alice raises an eyebrow. 'A break-in?'

'Yes. In our house. I haven't mentioned this, but we've had some weirdo hanging about at night in the last few weeks.'

'*What?*'

'Nothing to worry about, really,' I say. 'Quite the opposite. Whoever it is, this plays straight into our hands.'

I explain to Alice that we can stage it, make it appear as if the intruder had been obsessed with Cecilia. He's been stalking her, peeping in through our windows, finally giving in to his sick urges and murdering her. The words flow easily —I've been playing this through my head endlessly in the last few days, adjusting the detail, fine-tuning the story, like a screenwriter ironing out the specifics of a film script.

'It's perfect,' I say to Alice, taking a sip from my coffee. 'The police are also aware of it.'

'You called the police?'

'No, not exactly.' For some reason, the thought of Inspector Lombardi makes me shudder. Yet her visit, which had so unsettled me at the time, might turn out to be a blessing. If the possibility of a stalker is already planted in the inspector's mind, she might more readily accept the version of events I'm fabricating.

Alice's eyes are focused somewhere in the middle distance, her fingers brushing against the cup in her hand, making it revolve against her palms. Thinking. Then, reaching some conclusion in her reasoning, she shakes her head, unconvinced. 'No,' she says. 'This doesn't make sense.

What about motive? OK, this guy is crazy, and he loves your wife. So he kills her? Then he just vanishes into the night, and that's that? Hmm. No one to point to, other than this somebody who hangs about your house.' She shakes her head again. 'No. Too weak.'

'But we *do* have someone to point to. And he *does* have a motive,' I say, realising that I'm taking pleasure in creating anticipation.

'Who?' Alice asks, with a nudge.

'A friend of mine. He was at the party, actually. The one where we met.'

Alice frowns. 'Can't be much of a friend,' she says.

I chuckle at that. What sort of friend does one have to be for you to want to pin a murder on him? 'No, not much of a friend.'

'Who is he?'

'An artist. She's working with him.' I hesitate, before adding, 'There might be more going on, I don't know.'

For a second, I fear Alice might think that *this* is what it's all about—me getting back at Cecilia. Honour besmirched. The cuckold's revenge. I sneak a sideways glance at her, but she's not looking at me, she's busy following her train of thought.

'Good,' she says, to my surprise. 'If there's a chance they're involved, it can help provide some sort of motive.' She pauses, reaches out for my hand. 'Listen to me,' she says incredulously. '*Provide some sort of motive.* I sound like something out of TV.'

I give her hand a little squeeze. 'Motive. Exactly. He's in love with my wife, they're having an affair, but she doesn't want to put an end to our marriage. Jealousy eats away at him. He's increasingly unstable, stalking her. Hanging about our house at night. Until, finally, it's too much, and he kills her.'

'A crime of passion.'

I nod. 'What do you think so far?'

She considers. 'But why would the police suspect him... your friend—what's his name?'

'Philip,' I say. Mentioning his name in front of Alice makes me feel uncomfortable.

'Why would they suspect him?' she asks again, then adds, 'I suppose you could mention it to your other friends. Say you think your wife might be cheating on you with him. But surely that wouldn't be enough, would it?'

I smile. 'It's a start. I can do that. But there's something better.'

I don't know why I've been carrying them around with me. I just couldn't stop thinking about how impressed Alice would be once I revealed my stroke of genius. Like a prop that makes the audience gasp. I slip my hand into the rucksack I've been carrying along with me to the bench in the last few days, and produce the two Ziploc bags. 'Careful,' I say, 'don't open them.'

Alice holds them up, against the sky. She takes in the cigarette end, twisted and stained. Studies it carefully. Next, the strand of hair, almost insubstantial in the sunlight.

She hands them back to me. 'They're his,' she says, a hint of incredulity in her voice.

'Yes.'

She nods. 'That's better,' she says after a pause.

I make sure the two transparent bags are still sealed, then slip them back into the rucksack.

'I have his exact same shoes, too,' I say. 'I'll walk about the garden, leave prints. Plant the cigarette.'

'And the hair?'

I clear my throat. 'On the body.' It comes out in a croaky whisper.

Alice takes a deep breath. She leans forward, resting the

cup of her now-cold coffee on the pavement below. She stays like that, so, when she speaks, all I can see is her shoulder, her thick dark hair.

'What about me?'

'What do you mean?' I ask.

'You do... *it*. You plant the hair and everything. You deal with the whole thing.' She pauses, then, shaking her head slightly, 'What about me? What do I do?'

I frown. 'I don't *want* you to do anything. I can handle it. You stay safe.'

Alice lets out a little frustrated sigh.

'Alice, it's better like this. So, if anything goes wrong, it's on me. I don't want you to be connected to this in any way. In any *obvious* way.'

She finally turns towards me, a lock of hair caught in the breeze. 'You don't understand,' she says. 'Your plan... it can't work like this.'

'Why?' I ask, with a hint of irritation. I think it might show, because she rests a reassuring hand on my knee.

'Mark, if you plan to do it yourself, it means you'll be in the house, right?'

'Of course.' I raise a hand to silence her momentarily. 'But it makes sense. I have to be there. It has to be a normal evening. We're in the house, sleeping, the murderer slips in at night and kills her in her sleep.'

'But, Mark,' she says, 'put yourself in the police's shoes. On the one hand, you have a cigarette and a strand of hair. Some vague talk about a lover. On the other, a husband, the only person to certainly be in the house at the time of the murder. A husband who, by the way, might be feeling vindictive, given the aforementioned talk of a lover.' She sounds like a teacher explaining a very simple concept to a rather dim pupil. 'The police are busy, Mark. They might consider alternatives, sure, but you'll be suspect number one. Right from the start.'

I'm about to remind her about the shoes and the foot-prints, but I realise how weak it sounds, now. I sigh, thinking about what she's just said.

'What if your friend has an alibi for that night, by the way?' Alice adds. 'A solid alibi that puts him somewhere else, with someone else, perhaps. What then?'

'We can find a way around that,' I offer feebly. I feel deflated. My plan (Phil breaking in, stabbing her in her sleep, vanishing into the night) had seemed so simple, so *efficient*, only a handful of hours ago.

'I *need* to be involved, Mark,' she continues. 'Don't you understand? I need this to work. For us. But for it to work, we have to plan it carefully.' She pauses, peering deep into my eyes. 'We have to do this together.'

I seek out her hand, hold it tight. Finally, I nod. She's right.

'Mark,' she continues, her eyes gentle, 'listen. This is great, really. No—I mean it. It's a great starting point. We can work with this.' She runs a hand through my hair, just above the ear. She's staring straight at me, from inches away, but her expression is that of someone taking in a vast, moving land-scape. 'You're so handsome,' she says, as if to herself.

How can she make me feel like this?

'Listen,' she says, straightening her back, 'you're too wrapped up in this. How could you *not* be? You're her husband, there's no way you can see things objectively. Give me a bit of time to think about it. Maybe I can come up with something.' She says it so confidently, I immediately feel warm relief flooding my veins. I know, instinctively, that Alice can take my plan and make it viable, somehow. It's as if I've just handed something extremely delicate to her—something extremely burdensome and delicate, in the mutual under-standing that she will take care of it.

We peer into one another's eyes, and if there's any hesita-tion, the hint of an afterthought, it is one I cannot see.

At that instant, my phone rings. It shatters this strange moment, thrusting us back into the world. I peer down. It's a text from Bill:

Where the hell are you? Meeting started 10 mins ago!

'I have to go,' I say to Alice. 'I don't want to, but I have to.'

She kisses me. 'Yes, go,' she says. 'We'll meet here in two days' time. And I'll have a plan for us.'

THAT EVENING, at home, Cecilia appears to be very busy. She's texting a lot, at times serious, at times giggling. I'm on the sofa, opposite her, trying to read a book. It's proving rather difficult. My mind keeps wandering back to Alice, to our plan. Occasionally, it strikes me that that very plan entails murdering the woman sitting over there, in the armchair. The emotions that blossom in my chest, in these instances, are complex. Sometimes, I feel a swell of affection, almost of love, for Cecilia. Other times (especially if she happens to be smiling into her phone), it is more like a glacial breeze, a hardening of feelings.

A poster of the exhibition has gone up in her study, upstairs. I noticed it earlier, but haven't commented. It's the first time she's done that sort of thing.

At one point, in reading something on the phone, she laughs out loud. I spy her as she brings her nymph-like hand to her mouth, resting it against her lips, eyes beaming. This coquettish bearing, it's so unfamiliar. It makes me uncom-fortable.

I don't ask her what she finds so funny. All I manage is a low, bitchy grunt. I frown, trying to convey the notion that I'm trying to read my book over here, thank you very much. Cecilia seems not to notice. After a while, she heads off to bed ('Night,' she says casually, almost as an afterthought), and I'm left here alone. It's at least a couple of hours before I join her in bed. I want to make sure she's asleep, as I can't bear the idea of lying beside a conscious Cecilia now, for some reason.

The sheets are cool and soothing, her breathing steady. Holding my breath, I reach out and run my fingers along her arm, feeling the smooth, warm skin. Then, gently, I wrap my thumb and index finger around her wrist, their tips touching. I'm surprised, as I always am, at quite how narrow it is. Cecilia lies still, a milky silhouette bathed in shadow. I watch her, afraid that she'll wake.

There, sheathed in that thin layer of skin, I feel the bone. It shifts gently beneath my thumb, so impossibly close to the surface, yet so alien, so inanimate. Hard, dull, soulless. And for a fleeting instant, I can picture it clearly: my wife no longer a person, but a still and lifeless body.

38

T wo days later, and we're here again. Two freshly
brewed coffees in our laps, sitting close. It's as if
we've never left.

'So?' I ask rather nervously. I want Alice to have come up
with something.

'So...' she says, and for a second I fear she's come up
empty, that we've hit another roadblock. We'll just keep post-
poning, devising then scrapping plans, until we simply give
up. But then a slow, sly smile spreads on her lips. 'I think I
have it,' she says.

Cradling the cup in my hands, I motion for her to
continue. She dips her chin, eyes focused, collecting her
thoughts. Then she starts talking.

'This is what we're going to do.

'First of all, yes, we're going to frame your friend. The
artist you mentioned. The hair, the cigarette—they're good.
You must tell one of your other friends that you think your
wife is having an affair with him. I assume you have friends
in common, right? Perfect. Take the common friend who

trusts you the most, and tell him. No need to go heavy-handed, it's just a suspicion. But mention it. It'll be useful later, when the police start asking questions. Because they will. We both understand that, don't we? Good.

'Second. I've thought about it, and it doesn't make sense to do this in your house. Too much could go wrong. Snooping neighbours, bad logistics, the police likely only minutes away. All this is dangerous enough as it is. No need to make things easier for the investigators. *Husband murders wife in their own house, tries to cover it up.* It's just too tempting for them. We want to avoid that sort of thing.

'So no, not at your house. We're going to do it somewhere else: at Blackwood Cove.

'Think about it. The cottage is isolated, which means we won't need to worry about sounds. I doubt you could even hear anyone scream from the closest houses, the ones by the cove. Those are the closest ones, aren't they? Good.

'And say someone does hear something and they call the police, it would probably take them a while to find the place. I've checked: the closest police station is six miles away. It might not be ideal, but it's pretty good. A whole lot better than a house in the suburbs, in any case.

'So we time this. We time it to perfection. You and your wife head out to Lilac House for a weekend. I won't suggest how you get her there, you're better placed to figure that out. I'm sure you can do it. Anyway... in the evening, you leave the house. You'll need an excuse. Maybe you've had a fight and storm out. Maybe you tell her you need to pop out to get something. The point is, you go to a pub two towns over. I've found the perfect one: it's busy all the time. You order a few drinks, have a chat with the other punters. You want them to remember you. We're establishing your alibi.

'As it so happens, Philip will be there too—no, not at the

pub. Not at Lilac House. But he'll be in the area, to attend a rather glamorous garden party organised by a rich, extravagant collector who is interested in purchasing his art. Or so he thinks.

'Truth is, of course, there is no collector. We're just luring him to the area. Also, we don't want him rocking up with a date, so we'll make sure the invitation is strictly for one. Our collector is very secretive and selective with whom he invites to his estate, you see. This should also flatter Philip. Don't worry, I'll deal with that. It's just a matter of sending a couple of emails and maybe making a call. He's never heard my voice. He'll know me only as the collector's assistant.

'By the time he gives up trying to find the place, his presence in the area at the time of the... the *you-know-what* will have been established. Any investigator will be able to trace his movements via traffic cameras, all the way from London to Wiltshire.

'And while he's wandering aimlessly between dead-end dirt roads and countryside paths, wondering where the hell his would-be benefactor lives, you will be sitting in the pub, getting noticed and no doubt admired by the locals.

'Where does this leave me? In the cottage, with your wife.

'Not initially, of course. I'll get there on my own. When you've left—which will coincide with the time Philip is in the area—I will sneak in and... you know. *Do it.* Wait, wait. Listen.

'I will not fail. I can promise you that. In fact, it's going to be the simplest step in our plan. Once it's done, I'll pick up her phone and call you. At the pub. You will answer, you will listen, and mention your friend's name. "*Phil? What's he doing there?*" something like that. Then you'll jump up and rush out, saying, "*Don't worry, don't open the door, I'm coming.*" You'll make it sound like an emergency, loud enough for everyone in the pub to notice.

'After that, I'll plant the hair and the cigarette and vanish into the night. Which means I'll have to take them. It might be tricky for me to actually wear the shoes, but I could use them to fake his footprints there. Do you have them on you now? OK, next time we meet. Don't worry, I'll keep them safe. I'll have to.

'Once it's all done, we won't communicate for a couple of months. At *least*. There will be an investigation, and they will look into you. You will have to be strong, put up with all sorts of questions. The press might come after you, too. But your alibi will be rock solid. While your friend—I read about him, he's been in the papers recently, hasn't he? A known artist, a beautiful woman, a murder. And no alibi. I'm betting the police and the paparazzi will be all over him as soon as you've been cleared. It writes itself: your wife tells him she's heading out to the country with you. She wants to fix her marriage, end their affair. But he won't take it. He follows you, finds her home alone, and kills her.

'Then, Mark... one day, when that's all over with, you'll just happen to meet a stunning young woman called Alice... you'll mention her to your friends... saying you *know* it's a bit soon, but... but you are happy with her, so happy... and you think you might give it a go. No point in dwelling in the painful past, right? "*Of course not,*" your friends will say. "*You need to move on. Go for it, Mark. You deserve this.*"

'And from then on, Mark, it will just be *us*.

'Finally, just me and you.'

I HADN'T BEEN LISTENING to Alice as much as I'd been visualising, *inhabiting* even, the tableaux she was describing: Lilac House, dark and silent, Alice moving like a shadow towards an unsuspecting Cecilia. Me in the pub, elbow-to-elbow with strangers who would later serve as witnesses to my innocence. Even Phil, in his car, cursing and swearing at the satnav on his phone, trying to figure out how the *fuck* to get to this rich bloke's house, peering out towards the narrow road ahead, the tall hedges at his sides, so similar to the road he's been down a minute ago...

'I think it can work, Alice,' I say, suddenly back on the bench again. 'I think it really could.'

'I think so, too. I mean, it's far from perfect. This all depends upon your friend accepting the invitation, for one. But if he's the artsy-fartsy type he seems to be, I'm willing to wager he's vain enough to accept an exclusive invitation from a wealthy collector.'

I can't help laughing. 'Yes, *vain* describes him quite well.' I think it over again, trying to actually consider the unfolding of events. It's complicated, trying to predict the outcome of this story. 'Wait,' I say. 'What if he tells people about the invitation ahead of time? Say he mentions it to a girlfriend? It would undermine our story that he's heard Cecilia and I were going to Lilac House, so he decides to follow us and kills her, right?'

'Not really. It would just sound like him establishing an alibi. A weak one: he's off to meet a mysterious collector no one else has met, on his own, on the very same night your wife...' She lets that hang, then adds, 'Too convenient for him, right?'

'OK, but what if—'

'Listen, don't worry. I've thought this through. Plus, if everything goes to plan, there'll be no one to contradict your version of events, except perhaps a girlfriend of his, but she would hardly be considered a reliable witness.'

I open my mouth to interject, to say that Cecilia could very well contradict our story, but I close it again. Of course, if everything *does* go to plan, Cecilia will be quite unable to do anything at all. Again, I think of her there, in the house with Alice. Two women in the shadows.

'Alice, are you sure you can—'

'I've told you,' she interrupts me. '*That's* going to be the simplest part. Not *easy*, of course, but it's the one with the least to it. And,' she adds, brushing her fingers against my cheek, 'you're the one who's going to have to deal with everything else. Don't underestimate the police, Mark. They'll try to break you, and they'll do so until your artist friend will start looking like the easiest option. But they'll start with you.'

'Yes. I know,' I say. 'But I can handle it.'

Alice sighs and looks at me with a hint of concern, as if anticipating the pressure I'll be under. Questioned by the police for the murder of my wife. Who would have thought?

'One thing,' I say. 'Will we meet at the house? When I get there from the pub, I mean.'

'No,' she says. 'I'll be gone.'

I don't like the sound of that, for some reason. It rings like a bad omen. 'Where will you go?' I ask her.

She shakes her head. 'I can't tell you, Mark. I don't want to. The less you know about me, my whereabouts, the detail of my part in this, the better. Plausible deniability, it's called.'

I feel like protesting, but I don't. Again, she's right.

Alice turns her face to the sky. It's a clear day, albeit a cold one, and the sun appears to be shining down on her like a spotlight. She speaks with her eyes closed. 'There are a couple of other things. We should make sure it's a grey, rainy day.'

'Why?'

'The messier it is, the harder it will be for the police to piece things together. Mud, rain, dirt—I'll be less likely to leave a clear trail behind me. It will also mean there will be some sound to cover my movements in your house.' She nods to herself. 'Yes, a stormy night is what we want. We just need to keep an eye on the weather forecasts. A couple of weeks in advance should give us enough time to organise things.'

'OK,' I say. It makes sense. And there's no shortage of storms in England, after all. Especially at this time of year.

'Also,' she continues, 'we must make sure there is nothing, absolutely *nothing*, linking the two of us.'

I think about this for a second. To be honest, there's little linking us already. No phone calls, no meeting in front of people we know. No trace of our messages, which we diligently burn. In fact, I'd be hard-pressed to prove Alice's existence, if asked to do so.

'This,' she says, her gaze fixed, 'me and you being together, all depends on us doing things properly. If we make a mistake, if they link the two of us, and me to the crime scene... well, it's all over, isn't it? It would have all been for nothing.'

'I know.'

'We will meet once more before you go to Lilac House with your wife. And after that, nothing until the time is right.' She pauses, as if scanning my eyes for weakness, for hesitation. 'If you're sure we want to go ahead with this, I mean.'

Is there uncertainty in me? Perhaps. But it's a spectre, something distant and inconsequential. A shimmering ghost up against the utter reality, the *fullness* of Alice here beside me.

By way of answer, I lean in and kiss her. A slow, deliberate kiss. 'Nothing until then,' I whisper in her ear. 'And yes, I am sure.'

We part soon after. Our next meeting is to be our last one before the murder.

Alice vanishes into the crowd, and I head back towards the office. I'm in no hurry, having cancelled all the meetings scheduled for today—I told Bill I needed time to think about a new pitch for Senesi. Begrudgingly, he accepted. There's no rush, yet my steps are swift, nervous. Time has accelerated, hurling us towards a stormy night in Blackwood Cove and my wife's body on the cottage floor.

I shudder, shaking my head.

That's when I look up and see Cecilia.

39

I freeze.

All exterior sounds are muted: I hear nothing but the loud, cavernous pounding of my heart filling my ears.

She's been following me. She's seen Alice. What's worse, she's aware of our plans. She's going to ruin me, blackmail me, destroy me. There will be no future with Alice, not anymore. How could I ever have believed I could outwit my wife, her cool, vindictive mind?

She's looking straight at me.

But it's only an instant, I realise, a fraction of a movement that progresses past me, landing her gaze elsewhere, to rest on the traffic light nearby.

Cecilia is standing less than twenty yards from me, a band holding her hair back, trench coat fastened at the waist, a bulbous pair of sunglasses resting on her head. Her arms are wrapped about her, against the cold. For a second, she reminds me of Alice in her spy outfit, emerging on the platform at the station in Salisbury.

No, she isn't looking at me. In fact, she doesn't appear to have noticed me at all.

Cecilia is waiting to cross the road, just another person among dozens. Beside her, a woman wrestling the toddler in her arms into compliance, a suited businessman, a hooded youth. I unclench the muscles in my abdomen and duck behind a signpost, eyes locked on her. From here, I read the minute, telltale signs of her being nervous. That certain rigidity in the neck, her chin held higher than usual. The half-frown in her eyebrows, lips lightly pursed. It's odd, seeing her like this.

The light switches to green, and Cecilia is swept in the general forward motion of the other pedestrians. After a second's hesitation, I follow.

I don't know why I didn't just wave, grab her attention, as I would normally have done. As, in fact, my pretence of absolute normality would dictate me to do. Yet there's *something* in her posture, in her motions, in the way she is now lowering those sunglasses to conceal her eyes, that makes me suspicious. That propels me to follow her, unseen.

I keep what I think should be a safe distance, my pace matching hers, some fifteen yards behind her. The midday throng offers concealment, and, when I happen to lose sight of her for an instant, it surprises me just how easy it is to pinpoint her again. Her graceful, swaying figure so unmistakable amidst the grey crowds.

Without thinking, I dig the phone out of my pocket, quickly unlock the screen, and tap Cecilia's name among my contacts. I bring the phone to my ear and, a second later, hear the ring.

The rhythm of Cecilia's walking falters as she glances down towards her handbag. Still moving, she pulls out her phone. Then stops. I watch her as she studies the flashing screen. She hesitates, calculating.

Go on. Pick up now.

She takes a breath and answers.

'Mark,' she says, and starts walking again.

'Hi, is this a good time?' I ask, tracking her closely.

'Well... not really. I'm...' The briefest of hesitations, then, 'I'm just walking into Tate Modern. For a meeting.'

'Right.' She lies so naturally, so *fluently*.

'Was it important?'

'No, no. Not at all. Just wondering whether you felt like Indian tonight. Takeaway. I can grab it on the way back.'

'Hmm. Not sure. But you get it if you feel like it—oh, here they are. I have to go.'

'Alright, bye,' I say, but she's already hung up.

I watch as she slips the phone back into her bag, so casually it almost hurts. Cecilia lying to me as if it were nothing. I feel anger brewing in the pit of my stomach. And yet, undeniably, there's a hint of voyeuristic excitement, too.

We're heading north, leaving the river behind us. A street performer, off to our side, is staging a rather impressive spectacle, with flashing flames and rotating blades. A group of people have gathered, cheering him on. At one point, the performer feigns a mistake—a torch has set fire to his hair! People gasp, but he slips his hands below his hairline and swiftly removes what turns out to be a wig. He flings it safely into a bucket filled with water nearby. The crowd bursts out laughing.

Cecilia walks past as if they weren't even there. Fast-paced, indifferent to our surroundings. Her eyes are pointed straight ahead, and only once does she turn around. A casual glance over the shoulder that almost causes me to experience a panic attack, as it seems, again, that she's looking straight at me. But she can't have been, because she just keeps going, averting her gaze.

There is a sense, now, that I'm moving through the frames

of an action film. The pursuit through the bustling streets, the unknowing, beautiful woman ahead.

At one point, she turns a corner, disappearing from view. I hurry, bumping into passers-by and issuing unfelt apologies as I try to reach the street corner, fearful she might have vanished.

But she hasn't. In fact, I have to stop abruptly, duck awkwardly backwards, as I emerge on the other side, because Cecilia is close by, motionless now, her back still turned, standing before an outdoor table, in front of a café. Her head is tilted downwards, addressing someone sitting down before her. I can't see who it is from where I am, because her body is in the way.

Who do you think it is?

I watch as she leans forward, for a kiss. It's a quick peck on the cheek, a social greeting, nothing more. Then she sits down, finally revealing the person sitting opposite her.

It isn't Phil.

I gasp, actually bringing my hand to my mouth.

Sitting at the café table with my wife, bulging belly and balding head, is Clyde.

EVEN IN NORMAL CIRCUMSTANCES, this would have surprised me. While Cecilia is friendly with Clyde, always has been, they've never been close enough to go out for a coffee together. It's simply not that kind of a relationship. Or so I thought.

Clyde raises a beefy arm to attract the waiter's attention. As he approaches, Clyde turns to Cecilia, asks her something (*What are you having?*). She gives a little non-committal raise of the shoulders. He exchanges a few quick words with the waiter, who nods and departs.

A few seconds of tense silence follow. Cecilia's eyes, still hiding behind the sunglasses, are downcast. Clyde studies her nervously, then produces a packet of cigarettes and lights up. He's about to say something, but the waiter arrives, balancing a tray on one hand. They watch in silence as he elegantly positions two cappuccinos on the table before them, then, with a smile, glides off again.

Cecilia reaches out, takes a hesitant sip. Clyde just sits there, elbows on the table, smoking restlessly.

What the hell is going on?

Finally, he seems to gather enough courage to say something. With beautiful women, Clyde will often default to impersonating the buffoon, the self-deprecating sort. I've never seen him pull it off though, as he lacks the charm. With those who know him, such as Cecilia, he'll manifest an uncomfortable, red-faced politeness, all rigid smiles and clumsy courtesy. But there's none of that, here. He's nervous, yes, but he's also focused, sombre.

I watch his lips move, study the effect his words are having on Cecilia. He talks for quite some time, three minutes straight perhaps, with little hesitation. I'd say this is some sort of speech he's practised. A declaration of love? That is what I suspect in the beginning... but no. His expression is too *driven*, too confident, for that. At one point, he plants his index finger on the table, a meaty fencepost, then brings it down again and again, stressing his words. He reminds me of some incensed preacher.

To my surprise, Cecilia lowers her forehead and starts crying. Her shoulders make minute shuddering movements, girl-like, as she buries her face in her hands.

If Clyde's conduct is surprising, Cecilia's is simply staggering. I have never once seen my wife like this.

Rather than interrupting his speech, he keeps going. Softer now, perhaps, his eyebrows slightly raised, torso leaning forward, suggesting he might be speaking more gently. But whatever he said that elicited the tears in my wife, he's still saying it. It strikes me that he's *explaining* something to Cecilia, something he's aware of, which he's trying to convince her about.

She reaches out for another sip of coffee, but then retracts her hand, bringing it to her lips to conceal another fit of sobbing. Clyde doubles down, making his point, putting forward his argument, and, slowly, gradually, Cecilia seems to yield. She nods, first to herself, the half-conscious movements of someone who is coming to a gradual realisation. Then she looks up, towards Clyde, and nods more forcefully.

I stand spying on my wife and my friend, but the meaning of their conversation is frustratingly enigmatic: the lack of symmetry between the apparent simplicity of this whole thing (two people sitting at a table, talking, one of them crying), and the riddle of what brought them here, what they might be saying. It feels like trying to read a language ever so similar to one's own, but yet different. The meaning was there, obvious perhaps, but not to me.

Clyde knows about the affair.

Could it be? Could he know about Cecilia and Phil? Has he summoned her here to try to dissuade her, talk her out of it? Would this explain the peculiar behaviour he's shown towards me as of late? Perhaps what I thought of as irritation, hostility even, was simply some sort of conflicted guilt— Clyde knew about the affair, but didn't know how to broach the subject with me. He somehow found out about it and was trying to figure out the best way to address the issue. But, having a crush on Cecilia, he decides to play the confidant, rather than come to me.

If this is true, it would also prove beyond doubt that Cecilia is having an affair with Phil.

I'd say the dick pic was proof enough, wouldn't you?

I also realise that this is good news. If Clyde is indeed

aware of this, if he's trying to talk her out of the affair, to stop her cheating on me, and she agrees, this fits perfectly with our narrative of the jealous lover. Phil, abandoned but incapable of accepting the fact, murders Cecilia in a fit of rage. Alice will be happy to hear about this.

Cecilia is standing up now. She's saying something to Clyde, and he nods uneasily. I try to interpret his expression, but it's impossible to pinpoint what he's thinking. He's serious, and there's something about him that suggests relief. She leans towards him and gives him a hug. It's a tight one, and I can almost hear her thanking him. He's shaking his head, whispering something (*It's nothing, really*), but I can tell the embrace is disconcerting to him. He's always been infatuated with Cecilia. Many people are.

An instant later, she's fetching her handbag from the chair. I retreat into the crowd, chin down, heading back towards the office.

40

A t work. Can't get anything done.

I'm meant to be writing a case study for the BeeCreative internal newsletter (which goes by the bewildering name of *BuzzNews*), telling our readers about the Senesi account, how work is progressing. I doubt anyone actually reads the bloody thing, yet it pops up in our inboxes once a week, punctual as death, every new issue featuring the torturous contributions from five or six staff members from across the company branches.

The last time I did actually open it was last year, and not because I was interested in the content itself. I just happened to be scrolling through my inbox, when I noticed, among the names of the unfortunate contributors, one that stood out. My finger hovered above the email for a second, hesitant, then tapped.

I scrolled down to the entry that had caught my eye:

Revving up Christmas click-through: Effective CTAs for the festive season.

And there, just below the title, the author's name—*Claire Anderson*. The piece also featured a small icon-sized image of her. I sat there, vaguely nauseated by the topic of her article, as well as by her features. I studied her full, round face, the voluptuous lips, the suggestive eyes, still very striking despite the rather impersonal, washed-out style of the corporate headshot. Claire. The woman with whom I'd cheated on my pregnant wife. So strange to think of her, up there in Scotland, penning articles about what words to use in a call to action.

Click here now... Sign up for your FREE copy... Betray your wife with a luscious Scottish lass.

I cast these thoughts away and find myself peering out the window, into a grey, sprawling London.

Whatever happened with Cecilia, whatever I did wrong, I won't let it happen again with Alice.

After five more fruitless minutes spent staring at the screen, trying to conjure up something vaguely entertaining to say about Senesi, I pull up the chat box and send a message to Ed.

Fancy a beer this evening?

He gets back to me almost immediately:

Not Friday? Gab might disapprove.

It's not our usual night out (although we hardly seem to bother at all, lately). But that plays to my advantage. I want Ed to sense this is an unusual request.

I reply:

As you like, mate.

Then I wait a second and add:

Sure you can't?

Ed:

Is everything ok?

Me:

Yes. Sort of. Would appreciate a chat.

Ed, without hesitation:

Absolutely, mate. Half nine at the KH?

My heart warms at this. Good ol' Ed. A hint of unease too: I'm planning to deceive him.
Me:

Super. Cheers. I appreciate it.

Ed:

No worries!

I check my watch. Almost five hours before I meet him. Uxoricide is a restless affair.

I'M on my second pint when Ed pushes open the door and enters the King's Head. I've counted eleven people doing so since I got here, raising my eyes expectantly every time someone has appeared at the entrance.

He's flustered, tired, with dark bags under his eyes. I can picture him going through his parental bedtime duties with Lilly, negotiating his leave with Gabbie, then finally heading out to meet me. Despite it all, the smile he flashes is a sincere, affectionate one.

'Hey, buddy,' he says, with a quick hug. 'All good?' There's a note of concern in his voice.

I give a non-committal shrug and deflect the question. 'What you drinking?' I ask, standing to make my way to the bar. It's hard to meet his eye.

'Just a pint.' He takes off his scarf and coat, folds them meticulously and drapes them off the back of his chair.

Waiting for our drinks, I try to steady myself. I casually bring my fingers to my neck, feel the blood pumping through the artery there. Will it to slow down.

Back at the table, I ask Ed how his day has been, eager to delay his questions.

'Oh, you know,' he says before relaying the usual: uneventful day at work, Gabbie, Lilly. I've heard it all before, the repetitive recital of someone who doesn't like to complain, nor feels he has the right, or the need, to. Except he rattles it off almost in a hurry this time, and I sense the urgency he has to discuss the reason we're here. He's concerned.

I throw him a couple more questions, buying time, but he's not having it. 'Mark,' he says, eyebrows steepled, 'tell me what's happening. Why did you want to meet up?'

I swallow. 'There's no nice way of putting this, Ed.' My voice has a rather theatrical quiver to it. 'I think Cecilia is cheating on me.' Dramatic pause, then, 'With Phil.'

I study him intently, assessing his reaction. I'm not exactly lying to him, because I actually do believe what I'm saying.

But I'm manipulating him, my childhood friend, getting him to support my story, my version of events, although he still doesn't know it. Making him play a role in all of this.

'Mark...' he begins, stunned, lowering his glass to the table. He believes me, I know that immediately. And he's on my side, I know that too. 'That's... my God. Are you sure?'

I nod. I can't quite get myself to add anything else, for a second. I realise my hesitation is coming across as shame, embarrassment. And it is, although for reasons not immediately obvious to him.

'It's OK, mate. Speak to me,' he says.

I take a long, thirsty swig of beer. 'I... I found messages on her phone...'

'From him? You sure?'

'Yes.' *Am I?*

'Shit.' He looks around the pub incredulously. This has hit him hard. '*Shit*. When? I mean—how long has this been going on for?'

'Hard to tell. Definitely since the exhibition. I had noticed she was more... *distracted*, you know? Distant. But I would never have thought...' I let silence fill the gap.

Ed is absolutely at a loss. It's like watching him flounder in a pool. These things simply don't happen in his orderly world. Betrayal, affairs: they are entirely alien to him. 'Gabbie did *say* it was a pile of crap, that exhibition,' he blurts out, as if to comfort me. He blushes. 'Sorry,' he says, shaking his head, 'how is that of any help?'

'It's tough, Ed,' I say.

'You know...' he says cautiously. 'Clyde had mentioned something about there being problems between the two of you.'

My ears perk up at this. 'What?'

He reaches out for his beer, sneaking a glance my way. 'Oh, it's probably nothing... but, when was it? Last time we were here, I think. You'd popped out to make a phone call, and he told us he thought there was something up between you and Cecilia.'

I remember now. I made some excuse and headed out for a smoke. I spied them from the window and felt, somehow, that they were talking about me. Apparently, I was right.

'What did he say?'

'Oh, not much. He just said that he had suspicions. Thought the two of you were fighting or something. But just as he was about to say more, you got back.' Ed sighs. 'He never brought it up again. But, come to think of it, he's been strange ever since, hasn't he?'

I nod, thinking about him and Cecilia yesterday.

Ed frowns. 'Hang on though... Phil was there that evening. At the table with us. Why would he raise the issue in front of him?'

True. Why would he?

'Maybe it was some sort of veiled threat aimed at him?' I say, thinking out loud. 'He's not too fond of Phil, is he?'

'Maybe,' says Ed, unconvinced. 'Anyway, it doesn't matter really, does it?'

'I suppose not.'

A quiet beat.

'What are you going to do?' His voice is soft, full of understanding.

'I don't know,' I say. I want to leave it at that, but then words start flowing. 'It's hard to talk to her, you know? It always is, since we... lost the baby. Before I met Cecilia, I'd never been in love, not really. She's taught me what real love, *adult* love is. I knew I wanted to be with her, Ed, I knew it from the start. I couldn't stop talking about her, remember? And I couldn't believe it, not quite, when she accepted my offer of a date. Even later, when we were an item, I kept doubting my luck. Had to pinch myself. It's also because of how she is, you know? The ethereal sphinx. So beautiful, isn't she? Never speaks much, not even to me. So you never know quite where you stand with her.' I pause, surprised by the sincerity of my words. 'But it poisoned us, the miscarriage did. Everything changed. We were in a different world suddenly, one we weren't equipped for. We somehow drifted apart, an inch at a time, day after day. Sad, that.'

'Mark, mate...'

'I should have done something sooner, you know? Acted. But it was hard, everything was hard. Talking most of all. Talking sincerely is an impossibility. I thought I'd be a dad, Ed. I thought I'd be a good one, too. We had it all ready, the room and everything. You know that. I'd fall asleep on her tummy, whispering stories to the baby in there. They can hear at six months, did you know that? Incredible, right? That's when we lost him, six months. It's not fair, is it? It's not fair, Ed.'

My eyes are welling up, and I have to stop. What am I doing? This wasn't meant to be a confession. Quite the opposite.

His eyes are red too. He's looking down, at the table, contemplating this sadness I'm burdening him with.

Then I have an idea. There's no time to weigh its consequences, but it seems to make sense. Clearing my throat, I say, 'I might take her to the cottage. You know, over in Blackwood Cove. Try to mend things.'

He eyes me cautiously. 'You can forgive her?' he asks me, and I sense from the tone in his voice that he *wants* me to forgive her. Go back to how it was before. Restore the equilibrium.

Never.

'Yes,' I say. 'Of course I can forgive her, Ed. I love her.'

. . .

WHEN I GET HOME, the lights are out. Cecilia is upstairs, supposedly asleep. Despite the silence and the dark, there's a restlessness to this night, something that makes it impossible for me to slip into bed now. I stand in the darkness of the living room, eyes shut, and realise I might be slightly drunk. The floor beneath me is rocking gently, my breathing is somewhat laboured, uneven and too loud.

There's no chance of sleep, not yet. I make tight fists with my hands, then release them. Fist, release. Fist, release.

The shoes.

Yes, that's it. I almost run to the wardrobe in the kitchen, the one where all the unused bits and bobs end up. Here, on my knees, I dig out an unremarkable plastic bag, worn with age, from beneath a box containing a mixer whose blades have long been lost. I pause for a second, listening out for Cecilia. Then, satisfied that she's nowhere near, I carefully pull out the Converse All Stars.

Sitting on a kitchen chair, I slip off my office shoes and put the All Stars on. They feel so light, almost insubstantial, other than the rather thick sole.

Shoes for twats, I think, twisting my right foot left and right and eyeing them with distaste. *Shoes for man-boys and artist-wannabe cunts.*

Fuelled by my new-found stylistic snobbery, I stumble back towards the front door, mouthing obscenities while trying to keep it quiet. Yes, I probably have had too much to drink.

It's winter, but there's a summer-like quality to this night, a sense of expectation. I sniff the air and detect an impossible trace of jasmine.

I peer towards old Mr Banks's house. Lights off there, too. I hope he isn't hanging about walking his dog tonight. Wouldn't really want to bump into him and that barking shit sausage again.

I hop down the steps and walk along the front of the house, to the garden on the side. I could do with another beer, come to think about it. I stare down at my Converse-clad feet, standing on the line between the pavement and the lawn, as if frozen before a boundary of some importance. Oscillating ever so slightly, I step onto the grass and start walking about my lawn, the mud there, in a strange determined fashion. I press my feet down hard, wanting to leave the marks behind. Planting footprints (Phil's footprints) for the police to find. It seems to be working; there's one clearly visible in a grassless patch. I can even make out the shoe size, stamped in the dirt, mirrored back to me in a reversed '01'.

'I'm numba one,' I say, amused.

It occurs to me that the intruder would be standing beneath our window, were he here. The Phil-intruder of our narrative, consumed by his passion for Cecilia, haunting our garden and eyeing our bedroom.

So there I stand, looking up at the room I share with my wife, and I think that it's odd, this whole affair, my standing unsteadily here, plotting my way out of wedlock.

It strikes me that it would be interesting, after all, if Phil really *were* the intruder. And why not? It would make sense, wouldn't it?

I feel a thin wave of unease, almost fear, drift through me. I turn around, half-expecting to find someone there, staring at me. Someone, maybe, not entirely human, come to punish me for my sins. To bring a bit of justice.

'*Mark?*'

I shudder and let out a little terrified squeak. Someone is calling my name. Whispering it.

'*Mark, what are you doing there?*'

I look up and find Cecilia, beautiful in the moonlight, staring down at me. She seems perplexed, yes, but there's also a hint of disgust in her expression. A why-do-I-still-have-to-deal-with-this-pathetic-man sort of look.

I peer back up at her, wondering whether she can see the shoes. I don't think so.

'*Nothing*,' I whisper back.

She looks at me for a beat, wavering here in the grass, then shuts the window.

41

Invitation for one enthusiastically accepted.
Weather suitable this weekend.
We meet this Wed at one. Bring all things.
Speak to her.

I love you,
A.

42

'For *Chrisssake*, Mark, are *you* listening, at least?'

I blink, suddenly aware of Bill's round, red, sweaty bearded face staring at me from across the chaotic expanse of the meeting table. His expression oozes such levels of *et tu, Brute*, back-stabbed dismay that I don't know whether to laugh or beg for forgiveness.

It's Monday afternoon, I've just read Alice's note, and my mind is wandering. Understandable, given the circumstances. But Bill, who is intent on trying to wrap up a presentation we're preparing for Senesi, would not understand. How could he? I consider that for an instant: the possibility of sitting him down somewhere and uncoiling this whole ugly affair before him, picking apart its knots, like untangling the bony, angular legs of some monstrous insect. I picture the two of us, in white generic-scientist overalls, peering over its repulsive body, Bill horrified, me pointing and explaining. *I plan on murdering my wife, Bill. And this is how...*

'I wasn't listening, Bill. I'm sorry.'

My response elicits a snort from one of the young marketing prodigies attending this meeting. But it's a brief one, awkwardly swallowed back the instant it was let out, leaving a terrified silence in its wake. It's Jayesh. Sven is sitting beside him, already shaking his head and pointing towards his friend, protesting his own innocence. Bill lets out a low grumble, causing Jayesh to shiver and shrink small— impressively so—but his anger is primarily aimed at me now.

'Mark, come *on*.' He holds his arms wide, a supplicant. Behind him, on the screen, the slides we've designed for Senesi. Muted colour tones, an elegant serif font for the copy and captions. They've asked us to develop the *Don't just do it* concept, expand it to encompass their entire catalogue. This is our stab at it.

I stare at the images, the text on the screen, and wonder how I possibly can fit all *this* into my mind, when the space there is now so full of Alice, Cecilia and murder.

'Next Tuesday, Mark,' Bill says, then turns to the others, the panic-stricken audience. 'All of us. Next bloody Tuesday we present this to Morino. And he'd better like it.'

I nod, along with the others, and it occurs to me that if all goes as planned, next Tuesday I'll be a widower. One at the centre of a murder investigation, at that. Stranded in Blackwood Cove, at the mercy of the police. Which of course means that I'll have to let Bill down again. This causes some degree of guilt in me. Here he is, eyes wide and sweat-stained armpits, giving it his all for the client. I wonder if management will call off the meeting when the news breaks. They will undoubtedly have another, more discreet one, to discuss what the company line will be, should it have to express itself on my case. Will they stand by me? Will they suspend me, or fire me immediately? Will they wonder how to play this to their advantage?

'Next Tuesday,' I say, giving him a confident nod. He's about to continue his rehearsal, turning towards the screen again, but lingers on me for a second, a cloud of suspicion and mistrust darkening his face.

CECILIA IS IN HER STUDY. I am at the bottom of the stairs, two cups of tea in hand, looking up. I've practised the words, the tone and expressions all day long. Yet now I falter.

The house is silent, except for what might be her typing up there. Our (as in mine and Alice's) whole plan now depends upon her accepting this invitation. Her, my wife. The woman in the study.

I close my eyes, take a slow, deep breath. I feel the weight of the cups in my hands. Focus on that, trying to silence the thoughts.

Here we go.

My footsteps on the stairs sound too hesitant at first, so I try to give them a more casual rhythm. The tea sloshes in the cups as I ascend, and I'm almost tempted to affect a distracted whistling, but that would be a bit much. All too soon, here I am, in front of her door. I lean in for an instant, and I realise she isn't typing, that the sound I heard is the rain, outside. A first hint of bad weather that will sweep through the country in the coming days. Just as the forecast has predicted.

I knock, spilling a drop of scalding-hot tea on my hand. And this small setback is almost enough to call the whole thing off, the pain and shock of it amplified by my nerves.

'Come in,' says Cecilia. I push the door open, and there she is, sitting under the photo of the American diner, as composed in her armchair as I am clumsy, edging slightly hunched through the doorway while trying to balance the liquid in the cups.

The computer screen in front of her is off. She is not holding a pen or typing something into her phone. Everything around her is motionless. It seems she might have simply been sitting here in silence. With Cecilia, simply *being there* becomes an activity in itself.

She eyes me at first, an eyebrow ever-so-slightly raised, and I can't help but feel I'm intruding on this silence of hers. Then, noticing the tea, she says, 'Oh, thank you.' I walk towards the desk, each step a herculean task, and offer a cup. She reaches out, still studying me.

'To what do I owe this?' she says, bringing her lips to the rim of the cup and blowing gently. The spirals of steam quiver frantically and dissipate.

I smile. 'Oh, you know. Nothing.' I fish for my script, but it's gone.

Cecilia takes a small sip. Testing the heat. Then, both hands wrapped around the cup, she brings it to her chest, as if in need of warmth. There might be some intricate message in this gesture. There might not.

I scan her expression, seeking some acknowledgement of her affair, perhaps, a silent confession, but there's nothing I can decipher. She's still peering at me, as if to say, *Anything else, Mark?*

'You know,' I start lamely. 'I was thinking…'

This is it. This is where I lay the trap, coax her towards it. It's strange: even now, I have to ignore the hint of hesitation in me, my natural aversion to conflict. I somehow have to keep my feelings focused on the anger at her abandonment of our project of starting a family. Her distance. Her betrayal with my friend. I have to follow the compass of my resentment, stay on track.

Cecilia looks up at me with that stillness of hers, that unsettling depth of expression I've never quite found in anyone else.

'I was thinking we could go to Lilac House this weekend. Leave Friday evening, spend a couple of nights there.' I'm staring into my cup. 'It would be nice.'

Cecilia says nothing. For a long time, she says nothing.

When I look up, incapable of standing the silence any longer, she turns away, towards the woman in the diner, as if picking up some confidential conversation they were having between them.

I'm about to speak, although I'm not sure what I'm going to say, when she looks back at me and smiles her inscrutable smile.

'Yes, it would be nice.' She brings the cup to her lips and takes a longer sip this time. 'Let's go, Mark.'

'Great,' I say stiffly, with an odd little bounce off my heels. I walk backwards towards the door, and it feels like I'm vanishing into a long, dark tunnel stretching out behind me, her searching lighthouse gaze almost tactile against my skin. For a brief instant, it feels as if she knows everything. As if she's giving me a chance to confess.

'Great,' I say again, then close the door behind me, like a treacherous footman, and scuttle down the stairs.

It's night. I'm in bed, Cecilia isn't. She had a shower, a while ago, and the water ran and ran. It's stopped now, but she's still in there despite it being past midnight. I'm dozing off, exhausted by the endless, half-aware thoughts and machinations going on in my mind. It keeps creeping back to my wife, my mind does, sensing her presence beyond the walls, absent but threatening, like a dark heart pulsing there.

I close my eyes and try to sleep. Steering my thoughts away from Cecilia, I think of Alice. And I whisper her name, again and again: the brief exhalation, the quick touch of the tongue, the sweet release of the *s*. I repeat it like a mantra, like a prayer, over and over and over, until the night itself is wrapped in her and my thoughts at last sit still.

43

Cecilia sits beside me, silent, peering out through the rain. The engine hums along, and at times the tyres tear fast through puddles on the road and make a sound like shredding paper.

We had a light breakfast at home, then left so as to fit in lunch somewhere along the way. At the kitchen table, I had to look away most of the time, aware of the fact that I was witnessing my wife's last breakfast. She sat there, leafing through the paper absent-mindedly, a crumbly nibble of toast pinched between her fingers. 'More toast?' I asked her, nodding towards it guiltily, suddenly terrified by the prospect that she might never eat any again. When we stepped outside, luggage in hand, the clouds were thick and threatening.

We drive out of London, and I try to act casually, but 'casual' is a very odd thing to be around one's spouse. I drum my fingers to the tune playing on the radio, half-humming along. I clear my throat. I shuffle around in my seat. I wonder what a casual me would look like to her.

'I don't mind it when it rains at the cove,' Cecilia says, still peering outside.

'True,' I say. 'It's cosier, isn't it?' Her eyes track something I can't see. A bird perhaps. I'm not sure whether she's heard me.

At twelve thirty, we exit the motorway and drive around a bit until we find a small pub sitting along the banks of a pretty stream, today's specials chalked up on a blackboard in neat handwriting. 'Shall we check the reviews online?' I ask her, pulling up in front of it and killing the engine.

Cecilia turns to me as she's leaning forward to fetch her handbag. Her eyes, it seems for a second, carry accusations she might not even be aware of. 'Let's live dangerously and just try it ourselves, shall we?' she says, with half a smile.

The woman who is fucking one of my best friends, the woman I married, walks ahead of me as we make our way to the black wooden door of the pub, pebbles crunching under our feet. It's drizzling now, but neither of us has bothered to grab the umbrella from the car. There's something unsettling in how vulnerable she appears from behind. How narrow her shoulders, how tender her nape.

Cecilia stops by the door, and I reach out to open it for her. The warmth of a crackling fire washes over us as soon as I do. I nod towards the interior of the pub. *Please, you first.*

'Why, thank you, Mark.'

44

On the last day of her life, my wife orders shepherd's pie and half a pint of ale for lunch. It's unlike her, this. She usually goes for more delicate tastes and textures when we eat out—fish, mostly. A light salad. French wine. What I know of fine dining, I learnt from her.

'I'll have the same, thank you. Full pint, please,' I tell the sixty-something pot-bellied man who is taking our orders. He nods along, but hardly bothers to look at us. There's something dishevelled about him that contrasts with the cosy cleanliness of the place: dragging gait, untucked shirt. The brown-scale colour scheme of his clothing. His are caveman hands topped by surprisingly neat and spotless nails. When he finishes scribbling down our orders, he plonks down a bottle of water, then shrugs an acknowledgement and drags himself off towards the kitchen.

I turn towards Cecilia, to share a puzzled-yet-entertained look with her, but she's scrolling through her phone. Twisting my head, I can just make out some of the words sliding up the screen:

*Exhibition. Breakthrough. Success. Philip Jones. Philip
Jones. Philip Jones.*

I reach out for the water, hold the glass tight in my hand,
and drink. I'm very thirsty all of a sudden.

ALICE HAD me repeat the plan to her five times straight
yesterday on the bench. Every detail of it. And after I'd
handed Phil's hair and the cigarette end to her (which she'll
plant tonight), as well as the shoes, she had me go through it
one more time.

And since then, the steps of our plan have been playing in
the back of my mind, a low, repetitive hum I seem to have
little control over. Each phase boiled down to a single
sentence:

1) Get to Lilac House with Cecilia.
2) Leave alone.
3) Head to the pub.
4) Make myself seen.
5) Answer the call from 'Cecilia'.
6) Look concerned, speak loudly and remember to say
Phil's name clearly. (*Phil? What's he doing there...? OK,
lock yourself inside. I'm coming right now!*).
7) Rush out.
8) Get back, find my wife's dead body and immediately call the police.

Sometimes, I catch myself mouthing them, these eight
steps. Last night, as I lay in bed (and sleep came surprisingly
easy), I wondered drowsily how BeeCreative would market
them. Something old school, perhaps: *How to kill your wife in
8 simple steps—and get away with it!*

After handing over the hair, the fag, and the shoes, and going through them once more, Alice and I sat in silence for a while, hand in hand and eyes on the river. This was going to be our last moment together for quite some time; we both knew that. I brushed my thumb across the soft skin of her palm, trying to read her thoughts in the minute troughs and crests there, like a Braille-reading fortune teller.

And sitting there, a couple like any other, I realised there was no fear in me. Trepidation, yes, but not a single trace of fear. What we're planning is what I truly want.

I leant closer to Alice, inhaled her scent. And there it was again, that giddy mixture of arousal and promise, the image of my being inside her.

The child we would have. The father I would be, so unlike my own. My own miserable, resentful, unloving father. And yet, in that elated state, I was ready to forgive him too, forgive him for everything, because parenthood (I imagine) is complex.

What kind of parent are you? *Are* you a parent? A loving father who kneels beside his child's cot to whisper made-up stories? And does so until he hears the even breathing of sleep? Until his knees and back are killing him, and beyond? Are you short-tempered, cold? Do you raise your voice? Has parenthood improved you? Do you miss the freedom? Do you love having something (something beautiful) to commit to? Has it given meaning to your life? Is it a drag, really? Are you terrified by what life may hold for your child? Are you relaxed, optimistic about the future? Would you want to slap your son at times? Or would you never harm your child? Would you murder anyone who does?

What about me? Am I a good father?

Well, you see, that's the issue. I've had no way of knowing. I like to think I'd be. That father, the one kneeling beside his daughter's cot, whispering tales of dragons and princesses and castles, I think that's me. But I don't know, do I? I'm child-less. A lesser man.

But not for long.

'Let's walk,' I said to Alice. She looked at me, surprised, taken aback maybe.

'Walk?'

I stood up, held out my hand. 'Yes, let's.'

She considered this for a second, then said, 'OK. Follow me.'

I did. Alice tends to lead when we walk. In the few instances when we've walked together through London, her steps are never wandering. Even when, like yesterday, there was no clear destination, her directions were pondered, following a map I was not privy to. I think it's caution. There might be people whom she doesn't want seeing us. Especially not at this stage in our plotting.

We walked along her cryptic route for a bit until finally we stopped, hugged and parted.

Before letting go of me, she whispered, 'Remember: we are doing this for love.'

I SNAP out of my mind, look across the table, and realise Cecilia isn't there. I sift through the moments that have just gone by, and recall her saying something about going to the loo. How long ago was that? Her meal is sitting on the table, getting cold. It feels like quite some time.

I exchange a nod and a smile with the only other diners, sitting across the room from us (a quiet party of three—an elderly couple and their middle-aged daughter, perhaps) then fiddle around with my phone for a minute.

Where is she?

I turn around in my chair, trying to spot the toilets, but

there are no doors opening onto the dining room, other than the kitchen and the entrance. Strange. Then I notice, half-hidden behind an unplugged fruit machine, a small corridor leading out of the room. Must be down there. But I don't recall Cecilia walking out that way, even in my distracted state.

I count to ten (still no sign of her), then stand and make my way towards the corridor. I feel my heart beating against the collar of my shirt. The fruit machine, its buttons dull and faded, sports an eerie cartoonish depiction of a smiling man, his balloon face set above the words JACKPOT JOE. The machine promises all sorts of wins and rewards, laid out in a once-dazzling array of pound symbols and graphics and exclamation marks. I step past it like I would an unpleasant stranger.

The corridor beyond is dark, but I don't wait for my eyes to adjust. I can't. Something isn't right, I feel it, and I need to hurry.

'Cecilia?' I call out. It comes out broken, almost a squeak. I'm about to say her name again, when I find myself standing in front of a door. Without knocking, I wrap my hand around the knob and shove it open. It's a toilet, clean and quite large, two sinks beneath a broad mirror, cubicles off to the side.

'Cecilia?' I ask again, louder this time. There is a loud mechanical droning noise here. Kitchen vents, maybe, or the heating.

I walk in. 'Hello?'

No reply.

Two cubicle doors are open, revealing the unoccupied spaces within, but I notice another one beside them, on the far end of the room. This one is closed.

I walk towards it, and suddenly my legs are stiff. Time is both flying and frozen. Where is Cecilia? This is not supposed to be happening. I have a plan to stick to. Steps to follow.

I knock, loudly. 'Hello?' I might be shouting. No answer. I try the door. It opens, and beyond it is nothing—beige tiles. A toilet seat, with a white pubic hair resting on the edge.

I retrace my steps, heading back towards the dining room. There's sweat on my forehead. By the way the diners look at me when I enter the room, I realise anxiety is beaming off me, but I don't care.

'*Cecilia?*'

I cross the dining room, and then I'm out of the pub, standing in the rain. I look towards the stream, the small beer garden. Two benches, equally empty. I hesitate, then make my way towards the water, although I can see there's no one there. I call out my wife's name, two, three times, turning on my heel, trying to take it all in, find her lurking behind a tree, a hill, a detail of the painting-like scenery surrounding us. Peering at me like a devilish illustration in some medieval manuscript.

The world is spiralling around me, in a whirl of infuriatingly gentle countryside colours, a million hues of green and grey, a touch of white and blue. *Cecilia knows*, my mind is telling me. *Cecilia knows, and the plan has failed. Forget Alice. Forget fatherhood. Forget it all.*

I'm panicking. Then something strikes me, something I missed, and I rush back towards the pub's entrance, flinging it open. The pot-bellied owner stares at me, open-mouthed, almost dropping the warm dish he's carrying (fish pie, I think).

I'm back in the corridor, and there it is, something my mind had picked up, but which hadn't quite registered: another door, in deeper shadow, just farther down from the one I'd opened minutes before. I lean on the handle, breathless, suddenly half blinded by the light of the spotless women's toilet I've burst into, and Cecilia is standing there, looking at me through her reflection in the mirror, a lipstick hovering by her lips, and saying nothing at all.

45

I 'm kneeling in front of the fireplace in Lilac House, an icy draft blowing down from the flue, making me shiver. We got here at 4pm and dropped by the Cove Cafe to fetch a couple of things. Last time I was there, Alice was with me, waiting outside, in the sunshine. This time, Cecilia and I entered the shop together, our coats dotted with rain. Mr Greene saw me first and, as usual, returned my greeting with a puzzled arched eyebrow: *Who are you?* Funnily enough, he seemed to recognise Cecilia this time. He smiled and shook her hand and then nodded towards the window. 'Foul weather over the cove,' he said.

We didn't stop by the beach. It had started to pour down, so we just sort of paused in front of Mr Greene's, bags in hand, craning our necks to try to catch a glimpse of it. All we could see was the thin grey line of the sea at the horizon and the swirling black clouds above. It struck me that Cecilia would never see Blackwood Cove again.

The cottage greeted us kindly, as it often has. Beautiful, welcoming and comfortable. Except the cold had seeped through the walls and the old narrow windows. It had never quite felt like this before. 'Fetch the wood, will you?' Cecilia asked as she emptied the shopping bags in the kitchen.

In the shed, the air was thick and damp. I couldn't carry both an umbrella and the logs, so I got soaked, running from door to door.

As I lay the wood in the fireplace, Cecilia takes her things to the bedroom. I draw out a match, and I'm about to strike it when, out of the corner of my eye, I notice she's stopped in the corridor. I make noise, shifting the logs around, pretending to be busy, and study her secretly. I know what she's about to do (I've so often done it myself), but I can't help spying.

She's halfway down the corridor, her left arm lagging behind, fingers looped around the suitcase's handle. She's paused, head low and slightly to the side, like someone expecting a loud bang. Then, slowly, she raises her free hand and rests it against the wood of the door to her right. For an instant, the illusion of feeling it through her fingers: the flakes of paint, the ruggedness of it, its painful familiarity.

I cough, loud, to break her trance, because I can't stand to watch her there, in front of what was meant to be our child's room. Her slender fingers on the door. The sigh in her shoulders. It all fills me with bile and resentment. Appallingly perhaps, it also awakes a hint of love for her.

I cough. She moves. I get on with lighting the fire.

Hardly a fire. A hint of a flame and lots of smoke. A sad, hissing, spitting fire with no heat to give. Cecilia has taken a cover off the bed and wrapped herself in it. I sense her eyes against my nape as I poke at the wood, cursing quietly. The rain outside falls fast and steady. She puts something on to cook, then goes for a shower and disappears for what feels like hours.

Then, her voice behind me. 'It's ready,' she calls out, laying a dish on the table.

I'm so busy hurling mental insults at the fireplace that I only notice the contents of the bowl when I'm sitting right in front of it. Cecilia has made tomato soup. This gives me pause, because *tomato soup* was once an entry in our own private couple's dictionary. One that came out of Lilac House.

When we first bought the place, perhaps the very first time we spent the night here, we accidentally locked all our belongings inside the car, along with the keys. I still remember the spark in Cecilia's eye and her sharp little smile (yet even then, so controlled) when we realised what had happened, peering incredulously at each other over the roof of the car.

We would laugh about that sort of thing back then. And we did. We laughed, noticed with some relief that Cecilia at least had the keys to the cottage on her, and I had a few quid in my pocket. Enough, as it turned out, for a cheap bottle of wine and a tin of tomato soup from Mr Greene's.

I peer down at the thick red soup. Is this some coded message I'm meant to decipher? A hand reaching out across the void? A last-ditch attempt at saving our marriage?

There's no telling, of course. Cecilia picks up a slice of bread, tears a corner off delicately, reaches out for the spoon, and all her movements are detached, unreadable.

'Thank you,' I say, bringing a spoon to my lips and blowing. In the fireplace, the logs hiss like furious cats. For a few minutes, that seems to be the only sound. That, and the hushed clinking of our spoons against the bowls. I'm trying to think of something to say, but my mind is buzzing with what-comes-next. I'm meant to head out to the pub at eight. It's only six thirty. How is time going to pass? I almost sprain my wrist, checking the watch. 6:32... 6:35... Then, after five minutes: 6:37. I could have sworn.

'So what's the plan?' Cecilia asks, and all of a sudden

everything is frozen, and her eyes are tunnelling blades. *The plan. She knows. She knows, and I am caught.*

She frowns lightly, almost smiles. Her face says, *You didn't possibly think you'd get away with this, Mark, did you? That you could fool me? Tell me you aren't so stupid, Mark, please.*

I look at her through the rising vapours of our meals, and I know, I simply *know*, that I have GUILTY stamped all over my face now. My cheeks are flushed, my collar feels tight, and a wave of glacial heat scurries across my shoulders and burrows its way down to my stomach. I stare at her, desperately fishing for something to say and finding nothing but horror.

Her smile vanishes. The frown doesn't.

'Mark...' she says. 'The Senesi project you were working on. It seemed to be going well. Just wondering what the next steps were.' She takes a sip of wine, studying me closely. 'Are you OK?'

'Oh,' I say, and I feel like a bad actor impersonating myself. Reaching out for the wine (hadn't even noticed it), I shrug carelessly, as if it were a matter of no importance whatsoever. Which, given the circumstances, is quite true. 'Yes, um... they liked our ideas, seem to want to run with this tagline I came up with, but make it the slogan for the whole brand, you know.' How did I end up in such a dull line of work? Even now, I wonder.

I bumble on for a while, averting my eyes, chuckling too loudly at my own snidey remarks about our people or Senesi's. Then, desperate to fill the silence I feel is coming, I say, 'And what about the exhibition? It went well, right?'

Her gaze lingers on me for a second, then she focuses on the soup again. 'Oh, you know,' she says. And leaves it at that.

I do know, I think. *I know everything. You think you're clever, Cecilia dear, but you'd be surprised at just how clever your husband can be.*

She puts her spoon down, then takes in the room. She pauses on corners and spaces and things, the way I've only ever seen Cecilia do. With eyes that make you want to be *looked at* by her. Studied, considered, by her. Wondering at the kinds of thoughts she reserves for you, as if you could only truly be *someone* (someone worthwhile, maybe even your true self) if she were thinking about you.

I still remember that desperate feeling, in the early days. The need, almost, to be in her thoughts. The panic at the idea of someone else inhabiting them. Of drawing her bewitching eyes, her mind, upon them, and away from me.

And while there is much more to all this than just that, it is still an element, even now, isn't it? Phil is in her mind. I am not.

'I've always loved this place, you know?' she says. And there's something in the way she says it, something in the truth of it, that makes my eyes well up, my throat choke. I bring the napkin to my face, cough into it, trying to clear my mind. We've been through a lot, us two.

I'm almost hesitating, filled with doubt, and I simply can't be, so when again she asks, 'Are you OK, Mark?' I grasp this chance with all I have and say, 'I just feel like a walk. A pint, maybe. I might head out soon, if that's OK.'

She nods faintly and, with that, the plan is back on track.

TIME DOES PASS. Slowly, especially after dinner, especially that last half an hour. But it does. After the dishes are washed and left by the sink to dry, there's a moment I wish we had a TV here, to pop something on and drown out the silence. But we had never thought of this as a 'place with a TV'. And we hadn't been people who needed silence drowned out before. For a second, I consider playing something off my phone, but it feels obscene to have that little rectangle spouting out nonsense on the evening of my wife's murder. So I poke about in the fireplace (the fire magically improved at some point during dinner, and now the flames are dancing wild), pretend to rummage through my suitcase, beg my watch to speed up.

Until, now too sudden, it's 8pm.

Cecilia, wrapped again in the bed cover, is on the sofa. She's holding a paperback to her chest, but her eyes are on the ceiling, mind elsewhere. Part of me wants to keep looking at her, impress the image of Cecilia in my memory, but she would notice. She would notice, and I don't know if this image is the one I want to keep. I hadn't thought about this sort of thing—one can hardly plan for them. Besides, there's no time.

I stand, flatten out my trousers at the knee. Say, 'All right then,' with a little inhalation through the teeth, as if my trip outside is somewhat of a chore rather than something I myself have decided to do. I move to grab my raincoat from the hanger by the door, and just as my fingers touch the fabric, lightning flashes outside the window.

'Are you sure?'

I know she means *Are you sure you want to head out in this weather?* But, to me, it sounds exactly like *Are you sure you want to go ahead with this? Are you sure, Mark, that you want to kill me?*

'Yes,' I say. And just as I do, the air is filled with the low, drawn-out rumble of thunder. 'Maybe I can pick up another bottle of wine,' I add.

'Goodbye then,' she says.

As I open the door, I can't help turning to look at her, steal that last glance of my wife. And *this* image, perhaps, is appropriate: she is sitting straight, her skin as fair as ever, the gold of the fire in her hair. Her expression, as always now, calculating, silently accusatory. Her thoughts unreadable. Her beauty undeniable. My wife. My first true love. The would-be mother of our child. The one who lost our child. The cheater. The enigma. The sphinx.

'Goodbye.'

OUTSIDE LILAC HOUSE, the sky is so dark it might as well be the middle of the night. My ears are filled with the roar of rain hitting the ground, and the sudden cold feels like a current under my skin.

I look out, towards the thick woods. Nothing but blackness there, beneath a dancing crest of silver leaves. I picture Alice, somewhere out there, moving quietly among the shadows. Is she there now? If she is, how did she get here? Can she see me? Elsewhere, under this same sky, I imagine Phil driving about in his car, wheels skidding in the mud, squinting through the sheets of rain.

I get into my own car and do not look at the cottage before backing out, half-blind, and driving off.

46

The pub is called the Queen Elizabeth. It sits squat on the corner of the road, and although it has the fixtures of a charming countryside pub (thatched roof, ancient stone walls), it somehow lacks the charm.

I park the car, take a deep breath, then pull the collar of my raincoat up above my head and dash out, through the rain. I have to leap over a torrent of filthy rainwater to get to the door, and as I push it open, I know instantly that this isn't going to go as I'd pictured it. Listening to Alice, back on the bench, it all sounded quite doable. I thought I'd be sitting here, nervous, yes, but composed. Chatting with the locals, doing my best to charm them into remembering me. Revealing nothing. Establishing my alibi. Acting cool until her call came.

I step into the pub, and I'm a wreck. Despite the cold, I feel sweat flowing out of every pore. I'm walking unsteadily, chin against my chest, shoulders high. How the hell am I going to get through this?

I spot a free stool at the bar and almost run for it.

The storm seems to have kept most punters away. Slipping my coat off, I sneak a look around and count eight patrons. They are eyeing me, more with mistrust than with interest. One of them (an elderly man with a snow-white beard and a stern frown) is studying me quite insistently, so I give him a nod. He looks away, towards a muted TV hanging off a corner of the wall. Footballers chasing a ball. Not the jolliest of places, the Queen Elizabeth.

'What can I get you?' The publican stands before me, behind the bar. Big belly, broad shoulders, bald head. What might be suspicion in his eyes.

Stop it, they've never seen you before, they're just curious, you idiot.

'Pint of lager, please.'

'Huh,' he says by way of reply, as if I'd surprised him with some mildly amusing fact. He holds my gaze a second too long, then grabs a glass and brings it to the tap.

Calm down. Calm down now.

I pull out the phone, check the signal. Alice told me she'd checked that the phone would work here, and she's right. But it doesn't hurt to check again, plus I need something to do with my hands. *How did she even know it would work here?* I wonder. Maybe there's some way of finding out online. Maybe she even came out here to test it. She's thorough.

My fingers leave long wet streaks of sweat on the screen. I press the lock button and rest it, face-down, on the bar just as the publican is placing my pint in front of me. 'Cheers,' I say, and I think perhaps my voice sounded quite calm this time. I even try out a smile, which feels almost normal.

There are two other people sitting at the bar, a couple of stools away. After serving me my beer, the publican gravitates towards them, and there's something in his movements that suggests relief. Or maybe it's just the way I see it.

The beer is cool and sparkling, and I realise I'm desperately thirsty. I down half of it in one go, then force myself to stop. My hands are trembling lightly.

Someone lets out a groan. I turn around and realise it's a reaction to something happening on the TV screen. I rotate a little, angle myself towards it and try to focus on the match. But the teams are unfamiliar, and I don't recognise any of the players. A muscle seems to have contracted in my throat, and I can't relax it. Swallowing is uncomfortable.

What is Alice doing right now? Is she slipping into Lilac House, black-clad and unwavering? Is she holding a knife? Or a gun, perhaps. I think of the ways she might have decided to do the deed, and it feels like I'm watching an old Hitchcock: the victim beautiful and unsuspecting, going about her business. The house quiet. The shadows long. Me, the viewer, squirming in the knowledge of what is about to happen.

I take another swig. We said nothing about time, so I'm not sure how long I'm going to have to sit here. I'm desperate for another beer, but I don't want to come across as too eager to drink.

Establish your alibi. Wait for the call. Say Phil's name, say it loud, then get up and leave.

This, in my mind. Again and again. But I can't be sure I'm 'establishing my alibi'. Is this enough, sitting here with a beer, looking weird? I eye the publican, who is listening to the two blokes on their stools. Maybe I should contribute something, say something, so they can remember me more clearly. And not as a weirdo.

Before I know it, I'm saying, 'Rubbish weather, isn't it?' but halfway through it seems so pointless, so inane, that I stumble upon my words. They kind of peter out into a whisper. The publican turns towards me, confused, and asks, 'What was that?'

I try to swallow, then point to my glass. 'Another one, please.'

Something happens on the TV screen, and the man with snow-white hair lets out a sickened sigh and shakes his head at the injustice of it all.

I'M HALFWAY through my second beer and still no sign of Alice.

I've been practising my lines for when she does call. The way I'm going to pick up the phone after a ring or two, mildly surprised. *Cecilia?* Pause. *Is everything OK?* Concern rising in my voice. My first *What?* loud enough for the people here to notice, to wonder what is going on. Then—*Phil? What's he doing there?*

I wonder how loud I should say his name. Whether I should stress it or that *he* more. I practice it on my lips for a while, then realise I'm whispering quite loudly. No one seems to have noticed, but I'm rattled enough to stop. When the time comes, I'll just have to improvise.

I force my thoughts away from the call and gradually tune into the conversation at the bar.

'... I've tried it all, you know?' one of the men is saying. I can only see his shoulders, hunched. 'But she won't talk to me. She just won't. I—' He's about to add something, but shakes his head and goes for his beer.

'You can't be hard on yourself, mate,' his companion says. This man, I can see. Short but well-built, thick red moustache, piercing black eyes under a woolly hat. There's something of the woodsman about him. Or a sailor on a whaling ship. He's soothing, this man, reassuring. A true *mensch*. I could do with some of his talk, I think. Opposite them, behind the bar, the publican nods quietly.

'What she's been through, no wonder she doesn't want to talk,' the man with the moustache adds.

'He's right,' says the publican. Then again: 'He's right.'

The one with the hunched shoulders scoffs, but not in an arrogant way. Sad, rather. He holds his glass in his lap and peers into it as he speaks. 'I remember her when she was five, coming out of... you both remember her, right? Her smiles. Always jolly, she was. I never even wanted her in the beginning, you know? It was Jane; she was pushy. Americans can be. She went on and on about having a kid. I sort of just gave in, in the end. Same old story, I s'pose. Light of my life, she was, from day one. Couldn't believe it. She's so beautiful, isn't she? She is to me, anyway... She was five, coming out of school, and they'd stand there with the teacher, us parents waiting about just outside the gate, until each kid would point out their mum or dad. Then the teacher would let them go. And I tell you, every time it came to her, she'd point her little finger at me and tug on the teacher's coat, and she'd say, "There's my daddy," and each time my heart would stop for a second, you know? My little girl, her smile, her little finger pointing right at *me*. It was an honour, that. Fill me with pride, it would. You know what I mean?'

The others nod.

'When was the last time you spoke?' asks the one with the moustache. His eyes are fixed on his downbeat friend, and he holds his beer with a firm hand, his elbow at a perfect ninety-degree angle. There's genuine concern in his face, and I feel drawn to him, to this stranger.

'Oh,' the other one says, waving a vague hand in the air. 'Last week, it was. But only for a few minutes. She says she still has to get used to the time difference in New York. Still jet-lagged. I said I understand, kept it short, but it's been almost two weeks now that she's got there, so it's more of a case of wanting to avoid me, I think. I told her to call me on Monday if she felt up to it, because I know she's free Monday mornings. She said she would, but she hasn't.'

The publican produces a rag and starts wiping down the

surface of the bar, absent-minded but meticulous. He shakes his head in a that's-life-isn't-it? sort of way.

I realise I've been slowly drawn into this exchange, the lull of these men's voices. And while half of my brain is shrieking and having a nervous breakdown, trying to bring my attention to Cecilia and Alice and what awaits me later tonight, the other half is fascinated by this quiet talk among friends.

I wonder who they are, the people in his story. Jane, the wife who wanted a child. Did he say she was American? I picture a painter, an artist of sorts, visiting the UK and falling in love with the English countryside, and perhaps with this man too. She stays, and they start a family. But this is all in the past. The girl is in New York now—with her mother?

'Mate,' moustache man begins, his voice vigorous. 'We were all fond of Andy, weren't we? Everyone loved him. Remember how suspicious we was, at first? This strange bloke rocking up here from the city, always wearing a smile, helping out old ladies with the shopping, lending a hand to anyone who needed it? Remember Penny's cottage, how he sorted all that mess out? He won us over in no time. Because he was a good lad. Better than that. He was a fine human being, Andy was, as good as they come.'

So another character is introduced: Andy. I picture a tall, lanky twenty-something with a gentle face, stalking across these green fields.

'We were all distraught when it happened, weren't we? Imagine what it did to your girl. And, you know... It's tricky, hearing these things as a dad, I know that, but those two were *made* for each other, mate. Filled your heart with joy, seeing them together, hand in hand, walking through the woods or down by the cove. I once got off the boat, hear this, and he was there, knees deep in the water, playing a guitar. Thing is, he couldn't play the guitar, could he? He was just strumming those strings and howling a song he'd made up for your girl. She was sitting on the beach, looking up at him and shaking her head with such a smile, mate. Such a smile.'

The other two are deep in thought now, and I can sense there is a great sadness hanging between them.

The first man empties his beer, then lays it carefully on the bar. 'I know, I know,' he says. 'I was fond of him, too, believe me. But it's been a whole year now, y'know? And now she's gone and left for God knows how long, and I miss her. That's all, really. I miss my girl.'

The man with the moustache reaches out and rests a hand on his shoulder, holds it tight. He's about to say something, I think, and I lean in a little, because I don't want to miss any of it. But I do. Because, just then, my phone's ring tears through the silence, and when I pick it up with shaking hands, I realise it is Cecilia who is calling.

47

I stare at my wife's name, there on the screen.

CECILIA

The phone vibrates in my hand, nudging me to pick up, but I can't. It's ringing too loud, and I realise everyone is staring, so I mute it with my thumb.

Why is she calling? What has happened? Where is Alice?

There are so many ways this could have all gone wrong, that my imagination panics, flooding my mind with a tsunami of terrifying possibilities.

Don't be an idiot. It is Alice. She's calling from Cecilia's phone, remember? She has to pretend to be her. Pull yourself together, for fuck's sake. This is where you play your part, so you'd better play it well.

Of course, how could I have forgotten? I fumble with the phone and force myself to relax. *You know what to do*, I tell myself. *You've got this: ask if everything's OK. Sound worried. Mention Phil. That's it. You've practised it. Go on now.*

I've got everyone's attention. I frown theatrically at the phone, then slide my finger across the screen and bring it to my ear. I recite my first line, careful to channel the right amount of concern. 'Cecilia? Is everything O—'

That's as far as I get.

'Mark, something's gone wrong.' Alice's voice, the sickening note of panic in it.

I glance at my audience, and most of them are peering back at me, wondering what all the fuss is about. Suddenly, I don't want them listening in anymore. I cup a hand over my mouth, sink my head between my shoulders. '*Alice*,' I whisper, turning away from them. 'What's wrong? What happened?'

'It's... it's that...' I can hear the rain in the background. Or is it static? She sounds so far away.

'What is it...? Did you not—'

'Yes,' she says, and I can picture her shaking her head, frustrated by my lack of faith. 'It's done. It's done.' At this news, a momentary flash of relief. Then a wave of guilt, of fear.

'It's just that...' she continues, and I feel like screaming. Why won't she just say? 'Oh, Mark,' she says, 'please come here, will you? Just come here. I need you.'

'On my way,' I say. And despite the fear, it feels comforting to have something to do. I stand, grabbing my raincoat with my free hand.

'Oh, and Mark?' she says.

'Yes?'

'Don't mention Phil's name.'

This, for some reason, terrifies me. I'd like to ask her why, but I know there is no time. She must detect my hesitation, because she says, 'Mark, don't worry. It's done, we'll be OK. I just... I just need your help with something, OK?'

'Of course, yes.'

'OK. Come back. Come here now.'
'Yes,' I say. Then, 'I love you.' But she's gone.

48

I n the car, hunched forward, gripping the steering wheel so tight it hurts. But I can't loosen my hold on it. Outside, the furious battering of the rain against the windscreen, relentless, a swirling white storm of feverish particles, the night impenetrable beyond.

I keep my eyes low, on the road, because all I can make out is a stretch of about three yards of asphalt ahead, dull grey in the headlights. The curves come fast and unexpected. From time to time, lightning flashes, revealing the silhouettes of twisted trees to my left and right, the shapes of unknown places. The thunder is lost in the tumult.

I wipe the rain, the sweat from my eyes, and try to focus, but it's close to impossible, because all the time my mind is whispering thoughts about Alice, about what has happened at Lilac House, about my wife, her lifeless body—the horror of it. The horror of her alive.

And the questions. Too many of them. Is Alice wounded? Will I get there in time? Is this something to do with the intruder? For some reason, I think it might be. That figure I'd almost forgotten. Has he—or she—got anything to do with all this? And why, why did Alice ask me not to mention Phil's name in the pub, when that was such an important element in our plan?

Our plan—is it still going to work? Will Alice and I be together when all of this is over?

She said it's going to be OK. She just needs my help with something, that's what she said. Focus now, focus on driving.

I don't want to, but I keep digging in the well of my memories, my hands coming back up filthy with images of Michael Taylor lying dying in the road (a road quite like this one, in fact). His warped, bloodstained body, the rattle in his chest. Then, nonsensically, my first meeting with Alice, at the party. The sound of her voice. The small explosion of sparkles when she flicked her cigarette and it hit the road. Then she's gone, and it's Phil, his manhood on my wife's phone. Ed, Gabbie and little Lilly. Clyde, so alone. Bill at work. That inspector, Lombardi. And Cecilia, of course, my treacherous wife. They gather in my thoughts, this small crowd, unwelcome all of them. And yet, I feel someone is missing, a space there among them, wide enough for someone else, someone important.

Stop it. Stop it. STOP IT.

I punch the steering wheel and let out a scream, casting away the thoughts, the people. I tell myself it'll all be all right, that I have to be strong. This was never going to be easy, was it? Murder. And, again, I remind myself about what Alice said on the phone but minutes ago—it's done. It'll all be fine. It'll all be *fine*.

The car skids across a puddle, raising a frothy wave of mud and water. I curse and struggle to keep it on the road. Where am I? I must be close now.

Keep your eye on the prize, I tell myself. And the prize is Alice and fatherhood and a happy life. This is all worth it. Whatever awaits me at Lilac House, I know this is worth it.

And just as I think that, I recognise the turn towards the cove. I shift into a lower gear, and the engine roars, rocking me forward. The tyres somehow negotiate the water on the road, and we make the turn. Lightning explodes in the skies as I speed along, past the gravel parking lot at the top of the slope, Mr Greene's place farther down to my right. I yank the steering wheel and make a left, entering our road. Potholes everywhere, the car bouncing, hard things striking the under-carriage too loudly. Grating, scratching. The woods closing in around me. Then, finally, the second left turn and I'm on our driveway, and there is Lilac House, dark and colourless in the storm, and there is our front door, open a crack and dark beyond, and there, in front of it, is Alice, her face a blur, holding something in her hands.

49

For an instant, I just sit here, staring at the watery figure of Alice outside. There's a silence inside me now, an utter, breathless silence. I savour it, aware that it is time, that I have to get out and run towards her right *now*, but holding on to this moment for a moment longer. Then I kill the engine, turn off the headlights, and the whole world vanishes into darkness. Next thing I know, I'm running through that wet, windy darkness, towards her, towards Alice.

I can barely see her, barely see anything, but there I am, standing beside her, then wrapping my arms tight around her body. 'Oh, Alice,' I say, my voice quivering. I can't help it. 'Oh, *Alice.*'

'It's OK,' she says, so much braver than me. 'It's OK, Mark.' She pushes me away, gently but firmly, and looks up at me. There is no moon in the sky—just as the forecast had predicted—and I'm guessing her features rather than seeing them. Filling in the blanks. But it's her, my Alice. She looks at me from under the rim of a hood pulled down low.

'I did it, Mark. I did it.'

'What happened?'

She lets out a sigh. 'At first, it all went well. Not going into detail... you shouldn't know anything... I thought it was *over*, that she'd... but it wasn't. She fought back, Mark, fought a lot.' She pauses, then raises a hand in the air, waves it about gingerly. 'My wrist, I think it might be broken. I can't move the body on my own.'

I swallow. 'Move the body?' This wasn't part of the plan, was it?

'Yes, Mark,' she says, and there's the slightest note of exasperation in her voice. 'There's been a struggle, and they would know it was between two women. They have ways of figuring these things out. We can't have that, can we? They have to suspect that it was a man. Phil.' A brief pause, then, 'The body has to go, Mark. We have to take it away. *I* have to take it away.'

It seems so obvious now. I put my hands on her shoulders. I feel confident all of a sudden. 'It's all right,' I say. *Her wrist is broken. She can't move the body on her own. This is something I can fix.*

I turn, about to enter the house, but she grabs hold of me, and her grip is tight. *'Don't!'* she says, almost shouting. Then she fumbles with the thing she was holding and hands it to me. It's a dark, shapeless bundle, and at first I can't make it out. 'Wear this,' she says.

I reach out and take it. Plastic overalls. Only now do I notice that she's wearing the same. I hold them up, and something falls out, hits the ground. Looking down, I see two boat-shaped pieces of glinting plastic, like shower caps. 'For your shoes,' Alice explains as I kneel to pick them up.

I'm about to protest, saying there's no point in me wearing all this now, I'm already soaked through, but then I realise— of course. Of course. These aren't meant to keep me dry: they're meant to keep my prints, my DNA, off the crime scene. Off the body.

Getting them on is slow work. I can barely see anything in the dark, for one thing, and I'm not sure where to stick my arms, where my head is meant to go. Alice helps me, but it's tricky, the material slick and slimy with rain. I feel like I'm being wrapped and coated in oil. When it's finally done, shoe covers too, Alice says, 'Go in and bring her out here, OK? You should be able to carry her. In the meantime, I'll go and fetch the car.'

I turn towards my car, just yards from us, confused.

'No, not this one,' she says.

So there's another car, Alice's getaway car. 'Got it,' I say.

There's a moment of silence now. We stand there, peering at each other through the plastic hoods, and we both know that once this is done, we won't see one another for weeks. Months, even.

But we will eventually, her eyes seem to be telling me. *You and me, Mark. Together at last.*

She leans in and hugs me. It's a hurried, rushed motion, and I know I must forgive her for it. As much as I'd like it, there's no time for long, passionate embraces. We have to get this over with.

She releases me, then says, almost as a question, 'I'm going now.' *Can you handle this while I get the car?*

'Yes, you go. I'll be here when you get back.' *You can trust me, my love.*

She takes a step back, still looking at me. Then a quick nod, a deep breath, and she's running. Away from me, towards the trees, agile in the rain. I watch her go, her steps swift and confident, those of someone in control. She crosses into the woods, a shifting shadow among the leaves. An instant later, she's impossible to pinpoint, lost in the darkness, like a word that becomes undecipherable.

I strain my eyes, but she's gone. So completely gone, in fact, it feels to me she was never here at all.

You have a job to do, as has she. Get on with it.
I turn and enter Lilac House.

IN HERE, the dark is even thicker. I leave the door open, allowing what little light there is to filter through.

I'm in the living room, holding my breath, eyes wide, scanning the nothingness before me, left to right, then back again. And although I can't see much, I know I'm in the entrance. Except it's already morphing into something else: our cottage, but also now a crime scene. The idyllic seaside retreat, and a murderers' den. My Lilac House. A rotting place of corruption.

I reach out for the switch, blindly, and find it exactly where I knew it would be. I press it—but nothing. No lights. I try again, flicking it on and off, but it doesn't help (does it ever?).

It might be part of Alice's plan. Cutting the lights, Cecilia surprised by the sudden darkness, Alice gaining some advantage from it. It would make sense, wouldn't it?

Or it might simply be the storm.

I amble forward, arms raised, feet grazing the wooden floorboards to avoid tripping on something. The thought of striking Cecilia's lifeless ankle, falling down, finding myself lying next to her.

Do you think carrying her will be any easier?

I realise I don't know where Cecilia—where *her body*—is. It could be anywhere in the cottage. I should have asked Alice. But what a question to ask.

My eyes seem unable to adjust to the darkness. My limbs are part of it too, covered in these black overalls. But somehow, slowly, gradually, some details emerge: to my left, the vague outline of the sofa, its back towards me. Beyond it, the grey ghost of the fireplace. Next to it, the deeper darkness of the door leading to the corridor and the bedrooms. I turn to my right, and there's the kitchen and dining area, what is maybe the dull shine of a pot left on the hob.

I decide to check in front of the fireplace, as it is the most spacious area (wide enough, that is, for a body to be lying there). Turning left, I walk nervous little steps until I can reach out and find the sofa with my fingers. I lean down and pat the cushions, thinking Cecilia might somehow still be sprawled there, exactly where I left her. But no. No, she isn't.

Sticking to the edge of the sofa, I inch around it until I feel the carpet beneath my plastic shoe covers. There, opposite the sofa, is the fireplace. In it I see one single ember, buried deep in the ashes. It shines there, its light so weak it can't even dent the shadows gathered on the hearth.

I raise a foot ahead of me, drawing circles in the air with it, just above the floor. Then, feeling nothing, I put the foot down, move forwards, and do the same with the other. This whole area I explore, walking like that, but find nothing.

I circle the sofa, inspect the space that leads to the corridor, I even get down on my hands and knees, but there's no sign of Cecilia here.

Cautious, clumsy, blind, I move towards the dining area, walking past the open front door again, the storm raging outside. No sign of the moon behind the clouds.

I reach the dining area and navigate the space around me, thinking it's just too small, too narrow for Cecilia to be lying here. And I might be right, because I can't find her. What I do find are signs of the struggle that took place here—first the dining table (the same one I was sitting at only hours ago), now standing askew. Just a few degrees off from its usual position, but shifted enough now to be alien, unfamiliar. Beyond it, a chair lies on its back. My shoe strikes a fragment of something hard, sends it rattling across the kitchen floor. A shattered plate. There are other things, too: a fork... a glass, intact... a carving knife.

This was to be expected, of course, but I still find it surprising, coming across these scattered things. Unsettling, too—images of Alice and Cecilia, their bodies locked in a fight. The fear each must have felt, and Cecilia's perhaps deeper, more terrifying, because she was unaware of what was truly going on, of who the woman could be.

I retrace my steps, the soaked overalls squeaking horribly, and, after another quick feel around the living room, I walk into the corridor. Here the darkness is absolute, and I have to stretch my arms out at either side, fingers running along the surfaces of the walls, to get a sense of my position in space. The map in my head: bathroom straight ahead, at the end of the corridor. Before it, to my left, our bedroom. To my right, and closest to me, the empty room meant for my son. Just as I walk past it, I realise the door here is open, this door that is always closed. Not fully, but about halfway. I could turn and enter it first, but I keep going, decide to ignore this piece of information, heading towards our room. As I do, I utter a silent prayer, because I don't want Cecilia's corpse to be in there, because I want that room to stay pure, clean of the evil unfolding in Lilac House.

Not there. Please.

I push open the door to the master bedroom, and the moon, or a sliver of it, must have cut through the clouds and the rain, because a weak glow emanates from the surfaces in here. It is bright enough, at last, for me to see something: the bed, still made. Our suitcases on the floor, mine open, Cecilia's closed. No sign of Cecilia. There's an air of almost-normality in this room, only just polluted by the unnatural stillness and this spectral light.

Faster, now. I duck back into the corridor and head to the bathroom. It's a large, comfortable one, and one of the reasons we fell in love with the place. Lots of space on the floor. Lots of space, even, in the bathtub. I swallow before opening the door, preparing myself for what is likely to lie beyond. Will there be blood?

In the bathroom the moon shines even brighter, bouncing off the tiles. A single look is all it takes—Cecilia isn't here. Not on the floor, at least. Aware of my quickening pulse, I study the bath curtain, pulled to conceal the full length of the tub. Is this how I am to find her? Lying twisted in the bathtub?

Three swift paces and I'm grabbing a handful of curtain, wrenching it aside. And there, beneath me, stands the tub, perfectly empty and milky-white.

I let go of the curtain and curse. Dig my teeth deep into my cheek, make fists with my hands.

Why does she have to be in there? I ask myself. *Why there, of all places?* Then, pressingly: *Alice will be back any minute now. Carry her out of there and get this over with once and for all.*

Through the bathroom door and back into the corridor, holding my breath. Moonlight seeping in now, covering everything in a sheen of pale green. Everything but my black overalls, my murderer's outfit.

Here I am, in front of the door. There are voices in my head now, actual crazy-person voices. They are saying all sorts of things. I decide to ignore them.

My hand against this sad door, a gentle push, and I'm through.

50

And there it is.

It takes an instant for me to spot it—a strange, stretched-out instant that seems to sway through time. Past, present, future. Future, present, past. There it is, on the bed, this painfully small bed, its size enough to fill my eyes with tears. This bed, the very one we bought together, Cecilia and I, picking it among all those others, oddly lined up for inspection by prospective mums and dads. Each in a different style, covers featuring superheroes or cartoon characters or stylised animals with dots for eyes and Us for mouths. Our one, the one we went for, was simple, a wooden frame, with a comfortable mattress wrapped in warm, plain blue covers. This one here before me now.

And resting on those covers, there it is. Jarring, terrifyingly out of place in this untouched room. Not Cecilia's body, but a small white rectangle, about the size of a pencil case, there in the middle of the mattress.

I reach out, hesitantly, and pick it up. Just as I do (it feels like paper), I hear the distant sound of an engine approaching. And while that sound is reassuring—because Alice has all the answers, she can tell me where Cecilia is—I suddenly feel that something has gone horribly, horribly wrong.

Even with the light from the bathroom, it is too dark in here. I hold the small sheet of paper in my hand and walk back towards the living room. Yes, the car is coming. Approaching fast. The beam of a headlight appears through the window, throwing skeletal shadows of branches high on the walls, then creeping down.

I raise the sheet of paper to the light. Its texture is strange, uneven, rough, and I realise it's not a single sheet, but many small shreds taped together.

Of course, I know what it is. I know it before I can understand it. How could I ever forget?

But still, what can this mean?

Outside, the car is now in the driveway. I hear the driver's door opening, then slamming shut. The headlights stay on. It's strange, but it sounds like other doors open and close, too. There are noises, commotion. Voices. The shadows on the wall are now of people. Not just one. Two, maybe even three. They're running towards the open door of Lilac House. Towards me.

I turn to look at them; this must be a dream. Because it isn't Alice running through the door: it's Phil. There he stands, tall, skinny and drenched, dramatic in the doorway, the headlights behind him. His face, it takes me a second to read his expression. It's one I've never witnessed on him. Horror. It's so strange, this, I want to study it, but I'm distracted by something absurd: Clyde is here too. And Ed. They burst through the door, both wearing the same horrified expression as Phil. Mouths and eyes so wide as to appear unnatural.

My friends are here. It's almost comforting.

'Mark...' Phil says, bringing a hand to his lips. It's shaking. 'Where's Cecilia? What... Where is she?'

I can't answer. But I notice his gaze has drifted downwards, to my chest. I look down too and see that in the bright ray of the headlights, my overalls don't look black anymore. Not exactly. Nor are they wet with rain. Or rather—yes, they are black, and there is rainwater on them, but they are also matted in a dark red liquid. What I thought was rain.

But it isn't, is it? It's blood.

And there's blood elsewhere, too. I catch glimpses of it, flashes of red on the sofa, the wall, the kitchen floor.

'What have you done to her, Mark?' This is Clyde. He is breathing heavily, his chest heaving. He, too, is studying the blood on the walls, on me. Then our eyes meet, and I see his are filling with rage. I feel a rush of pity for him. *You really do love her, don't you, Clyde?*

'Is Alice outside?' I ask, feeling it is a pointless question, but wanting to ask nonetheless.

Phil looks at me as if I were insane. He might be right. 'Who's Alice?' he says.

Clyde shoves him aside, steps towards me screaming, 'Where is she, Mark? *WHERE IS CECILIA?*'

I feel guilty, because he looks so shaken, and that is a question I cannot answer. All I can do is look down at the paper I'm holding. Not a sheet of paper, actually, but a strip of old photographs, the kind you get at photo booths. Once in shreds, but now meticulously put back together with glue and tape. Hate too, perhaps.

In these photos, my own face and that of Claire, the woman with whom I cheated on my pregnant wife. Cheating in these very pictures, in fact. The ones I thought I had destroyed.

'I *told* you!' Clyde is shouting, speaking to the others now. 'She showed me the bruises... she was in danger. I told you...'

I feel dizzy. Around me, around us, a new set of lights has appeared. Intermittent, flashing red and blue. Another car is on its way. The police. I can hear the siren too, tearing through the storm.

My body is suddenly numb, and so is my mind, exhausted by the meaning, the implications of these photos. The world that must exist because *they* exist, undeniably, here in my hand. All is numbness.

But there is one thing that hurts. Ed's face, the sense of betrayal I can see there. The sadness with which he asks me, 'What have you done, Mark?'

And then: '*What have you done?*'

51

CECILIA

If I were to write to you, Mark, here's what I would say:

It was you who lost our child, not me. But you know that by now, don't you? I can imagine you quite clearly, sitting in a cell, chewing on your cheek the way you do, mulling over all that has happened in the past months, playing it through your mind on a loop. Sitting up straight all of a sudden, focusing on a detail that might be meaningful, developing complicated accounts to relay to your lawyer. Thinking maybe, just *maybe*, there might be a way to go back and mend things. Or, at least, to get you out of your current predicament. Out of jail.

Then, ultimately, returning to that single, simple truth: you lost our baby. You caused all this. And realising nothing can ever be mended again.

I hope it hurts.

I SAW YOU. You were standing in front of the kitchen window, your hands busy with the dustbin, but just out of view. And there was something in your posture, Mark, something about your throwing constant glances towards the door, that gave me pause. I ducked down, behind the hedge (no easy feat for a pregnant woman), the bags I was carrying spilling open at my sides, and studied you. My husband. You're an open book to me, Mark. Your mind is so simple.

When you'd finished, you poured yourself a glass of water and drank it fast, Adam's apple bobbing up and down. The glass quivered lightly, and I knew something was wrong.

It was hard, putting all those pieces together the next day. Fishing them out of the filth, wiping them clean and plotting their position among the other fragments. And as the pictures formed, it got harder. How I hated myself, Mark, crying like the damsel I've never been (never will be), bent over my bulging belly, piecing it all together. Your face, red with drink and lust. The woman, plump and vulgar and horny. You looked so witless, so predictable. So sad.

I would have forgiven you, had our baby been born. That's sad too, I suppose. I tried to put it all aside, forget what I saw, at least until the birth, but I couldn't. And it wasn't the heartbreak, Mark—please don't flatter yourself. Mostly, it was the rage. How could *you* betray *me*? The woman walking about with our child in my body. You hadn't even bothered to hide those photos well enough. Imagine that. You idiot.

And as much as it pains me to admit it, your betrayal (so casual, so careless) broke me. Your busying yourself to please me, after those photos, broke me too. Washing your ragged little conscience clean by massaging my feet, buying me expensive mother-to-be trinkets, wrapping me up in warm covers. Erasing your actions with a little bit of care for your pregnant wife. You felt like such a *good man*, didn't you? Your dim face beaming with new-found love and goodness. Revolting.

It broke me, and I lost the baby. Our baby, Mark. We

could have been so happy. From that moment onwards, I knew you had to pay. But how?

One thing I did know was *how much*: everything. I wanted you to lose everything. Me, your job, your friends, your reputation, your future. The obscenely positive opinion you have of yourself. Any future prospect of happiness. I could have killed you (and believe me, I pondered that long and hard), but that would have ruined my life, too. I don't deserve that, not again. I thought also about bringing the whole Michael Taylor incident to light somehow (more on that later), but it had happened too long ago, you might have found ways to fend off the accusations. It was *good*—you likely would have lost your job and maybe landed in jail. But it simply wasn't good enough.

And that's the way it might have gone had I not met Rebecca.

Oh, sorry. Silly me. You don't know who Rebecca is, do you?

You know her as *Alice*.

WE MET AT AN EXHIBITION. It was shortly after the miscarriage, and I was finding it difficult to entertain the visitors. As soon as I got the chance, I sneaked outside, eager to be alone for a minute. She followed me.

She's magnetic, isn't she? She seems so placid, so untroubled. I liked that about her. I'm sure you did too. 'What's wrong?' she asked me, and I loved the simplicity of the question, her genuine interest. I found myself, out there in a back street, London dark and noisy around us, telling her about the loss of our child, about what I'd been through. About the two empty rooms in our houses. And about you, too, Mark. What you had done. When I'd finished, she kissed me. She kissed me and said, 'I think he needs to pay.'

. . .

YOU'RE PAYING NOW. Beginning to, at least. In the papers, they describe me, your wife, as 'missing, presumed dead.' I can't tell you the sense of peace I get from reading those words. *Missing, presumed dead.* Out of the picture. A long way away.

I knew you'd fall for her. You've always been vulnerable to beauty and flattery. Rebecca—Alice—is blessed with the former and excels at the latter. We had it all planned out by the night of the party, that first time you met her, when you crept out for another of your sneaky cigarettes (you really thought I couldn't smell them on you?). She told you not to feel guilty about it, didn't she? That's because I told her to say so. To comfort you, let you know you're a *good boy*, Mark. That it's all someone else's fault. Signal that she'd forgive you anything in the world. And that she was willing to sleep with you, of course. You fell for it.

Boy, did you fall for it.

PHIL WAS HER IDEA, though. She understood that you were vain and weak, but she also sensed your pride. Someone taking your wife from you (the same one you had betrayed and would betray again), especially someone more handsome than you—*that* would really drive you mad. Especially if that someone were Phil.

The dullest part of carrying out this plan was having to hang out with Phil. How could you have thought I fancied him? So self-obsessed, so childish. And his art—soulless, all seen before. Still, it served the purpose.

So we constructed the new me: the distant, uncaring wife. The wife who would not even fuck you (no acting there). The wife who was now cheating on you, with one of your best buddies. A woman who is vindictive (I am) and could reveal the facts about Michael Taylor. Most of all (and this is the one thing Rebecca didn't perhaps fully appreciate or understand), a woman who would not give you a family, you who so desperately wanted one (as did I). How to deal with a woman like that?

How, Mark?

We led you all the way, simple as pushing buttons. Push this one, and Mark will accept your invitation for a coffee. Push this other one, and he'll take you to Lilac House. And this one here, if you push *that*, he'll agree to murder his wife.

CLYDE BELIEVED me the second I showed him the bruises. They didn't even look real. I had dug out a hammer from a drawer and struck my own arm, cursing you at every blow. Still, I couldn't get myself to hit hard enough, and I didn't want to ask Rebecca to do it (she was already doing enough). But Clyde bought it anyway. He's always been fond of me, and I knew he has nothing in his life, really. This would be something he could fill his time with.

You should have seen how delighted he was that first time I asked him if we could speak in private. It was gradual: the first few times, it was all about how I thought you didn't love me anymore. At this stage, he was concerned for both of us, I think. He cares (or, rather, *cared*) about you a lot, you know? He asked me if this had anything to do with the loss of our child. *I think so*, I said. I imagine he must have tried to reach out to you, broker the peace between us. That's not quite what I had in mind. So, after, came the hints of your mood swings, the threats of violence. How *different* you could be when it was just us two.

Finally, I told him how you had hit me on a couple of occasions. How there was something I knew that you wanted to keep hidden. And how you'd convinced yourself I was in some kind of secret relationship. Kept accusing me of cheating on you.

I don't know when Clyde started visiting our garden at night. It must have been quite early on. I didn't expect it, but it helped muddy the waters. Poor Clyde, hanging about out there in the dark, thinking he was watching over me. Hoping, no doubt, that he'd catch you in the act of striking me, so he could jump in, fat, lonely Clyde, and save the day. Such a silly male fantasy. He even 'convinced' me to end things with you. Remember that time you followed me after meeting with *Alice*? We timed that one to perfection, didn't we, Rebecca and I? We knew you'd misinterpret it all, my sobby talk with Clyde. You would think I was confessing my affair with Phil. Instead, what I *was* doing was accepting Clyde's suggestion: to leave you, drop the violent husband. I told him I would do so. Go to Lilac House with you, one last time, and tell you I was going to leave you.

I would apologise to him, if I could. I think it hurts him to think of me dead, hidden in some ditch you dug, or lying, rotting, at the bottom of the sea.

Once we were certain you'd fallen for *Alice*, everything else was easy. Getting you to agree to a plan (hers, of course, not yours), watching you carry it out, like a little robot, just as we'd expected. The timing was tricky, of course. We were worried Clyde and the others wouldn't get there in time, before you realised it was a trap. But they did: all it took was a quick phone call to Clyde the day before, telling him I was leaving with you to go to Lilac House, and that I was scared. He had me promise I'd call him if I felt something was up. And I did, from that pub along the way, the one where you had your little meltdown when you couldn't find me. Fearing your own plan wouldn't come to fruition, I imagine.

While you were away having your beer, Rebecca and I set the scene. The blood was the hardest part, because we knew it had to be real, of course. She cut me, sliced open my skin, and got to work. When she'd finished, she stitched me up, disinfected me and kissed me where the cut had been. 'Good job,' she said. She even had a fruit juice ready, like when one goes to donate blood. She's special.

BUT I'M NOT HERE to explain myself to you, Mark, although it would feel wonderful to watch your expression as I reveal it all. Witness your humiliation.

Anyway, you can figure the rest out. God knows you have the time. I'm sure you will, it's not that hard. You can even tell the police about it, if you like, but here's the thing—no one will believe you. Why would they? The truth is too outlandish, too unlikely. Why go with that messy story about the woman staging her own murder, the vanishing accomplice, when they have a husband covered in the blood of his missing wife? It's so much simpler.

THERE WAS one moment I thought I might call it all off. Not forgive you—how could I?—but spare you the murder accusations. Simply disappear and leave you alone, with neither me nor *Alice*.

It was that day you took me to that place, the Founder's Arms, for lunch. Remember? It was a set-up, of course, a last-chance test I had devised. I phoned just as you were preparing to meet Rebecca at your silly bench (do you romanticise about it? That would be funny). I proposed lunch and was slightly surprised when you accepted.

It was there that, for a very brief moment, you seemed to *understand* what I had been through. You looked at me, and I could actually see the love there. I must say, you almost had me. Then Rebecca appeared, and that was that. Immediately,

I was far from your thoughts. You sat there, squirming in your seat like an ill-behaved child, longing for nothing other than the hottie on the bench. That's when you lost me again, Mark. That's when I knew there was no way back.

I ALMOST FORGOT. Michael Taylor—the police *will* find out about that. I opened a separate email account from your computer, you see, and sent myself a string of emails in your name from there. Most of them are normal, some quite insane. In one you tell me that I'd... *better shut up about the Michael Taylor thing, because if anyone were to find out...* followed by a series of rather graphic threats. A bit blunt, isn't it? I agree, but I figure the inspectors have enough damning evidence against you for this to ring any alarm bells.

They seem to have had issues breaking into the account though, because I haven't read anything about this in the papers. But I suspect it's just a matter of time before they do.

I LOVED YOU, Mark. I really did. You were the one I was meant to start a family with. Grow old by your side, all that normal, beautiful stuff. Why couldn't you be the man I thought you were?

Farewell, husband.

I've found someone new.

They are strange, these paths love leads us down, aren't they?

52

MARK

My lawyer doesn't believe me.

I can read it in his expression, in the way I catch him looking at me sometimes. Like someone he would rather not spend time with. Like a murderer.

But he's a professional, and I think he's eager for the spotlight. So he sits and nods and scribbles notes. Even gives me some half-hearted encouragement at times. But that happens less and less now, and the more I speak, the more he seems concerned. That line between his eyebrows, it's getting deeper. He doesn't shake my hand before leaving anymore.

I wouldn't trust myself, either. Too much evidence against me, too easy to simply go with the good ol' husband-kills-wife story. That's usually the case, isn't it? Why would it be any different this time?

I've been framed. In so many ways it's almost impossible to juggle them all in my mind. My whole world has changed, and everything, *everything*, now appears different, under this harsh new light.

Alice?

Impossible to prove her existence. Strange that, but true. No one has seen her, no one has met her. My lawyer tenses up every time I mention her now. He's even suggested I stop doing it altogether. 'Pursue different avenues,' as he put it. 'Set that one aside.'

I think back to our letters, how I diligently burnt them after reading. I curse myself about thirty times a day for that. We weren't *spies*, and we weren't covering our tracks. She was covering hers. If I had at least kept a couple of those notes, it might help my case. It wouldn't be much, but it would be *something*. Because, as things stand, Alice is nothing. A ghost.

I've tried hard to prove she exists. I've asked my lawyer if we can pull any footage from the CCTV cameras near our bench or the coffee stand. As it turns out, they appear to be blind spots—no CCTV pointing at either of them. Funny that.

I remember being surprised by the odd routes we followed, walking through London, the few times we did. I believe now that there was nothing odd, nothing unpredictable about them. They had been meticulously studied by Alice, by Cecilia, to avoid her ending up on some tape somewhere. One day I thought I had it: I remembered she had walked into the office that very first time, to hand-deliver that note. There must be cameras all over the place in the building, right? Right. Except their contents are erased every three weeks. I somehow suspect Alice was aware of that, too.

One thing I did find was that very first note. The one that says:

A little bird told me this is where
you work.
Fancy a coffee?

-Alice

I've never heard Cecilia described as *a little bird*. It turns out the note was written with paper and pen from my own desk, back at home. According to my lawyer, this just sounds like a confusing dead end, at best. At worst, it suggests I've been fabricating evidence, and rather ineptly at that.

Talking about fabricating evidence: they found Phil's shoes, hair, and the dog-end packed neatly in the boot of my car. Alice must have slipped them in there while I was trying to find Cecilia's body.

'You were trying to pin it on your friend, weren't you?' an investigator (the bad cop) asked me during one of the many interrogations. What could I say?

THEY'VE SPOKEN TO EVERYONE. I used to hope that someone might be able to say something redeeming to the police, highlight an aspect that could magically unravel this whole situation. The opposite has been true, each chat more damning than the previous. At work, Bill said I had been acting unstable lately. He was surprised by the news, of course, but he had suspected something was off. BeeCreative distanced itself from me immediately. I don't blame them. They lost the Senesi account, too.

My dog-walking neighbour, Mr Banks, said he knew I was completely and utterly insane, pointing to my inexplicable assault on his person as evidence of this.

The people at the Queen Elizabeth remember me. I did indeed succeed in making myself memorable to them—as a mumbling, trembling stranger, who looked exactly like the sort who would down a couple of pints, then head off to murder his wife. That is, almost word for word, what one of them told the press.

My friends?

Phil has given a lot of interviews. The papers are all over

him. They love his good looks, his bad-boy vibe now
tempered, matured, following this tragedy. I read his art is
very much in demand. He told my lawyer he'd talk to me at
some point. He hasn't yet.

Clyde's been on the TV a lot. His media appeal is of a
different sort. He often cries, says he can't stop blaming
himself for what happened, as the interviewers nod mourn-
fully. He goes into the whole story, the bruises she showed
him, her confessing to being scared of me. All the way to the
shocking finale at the cove, me standing there, covered in my
wife's blood.

It is obvious, now, that he was the intruder. It might have
been obvious then too, had I been more aware of the world
beyond Alice. As strange as this may sound, I think all this
will do him good. He's lost a bit of weight, and I've never seen
him quite so driven. He hates me, of course. I can't help but
wish him well.

Ed is the one that hurts the most. He hasn't visited, hasn't
called. I wrote to him a few times, initially protesting my
innocence, and later simply trying to convey my affection for
him, his family. I haven't heard back, and I don't think I will. I
hope he is aware of how good he has it. I suspect he is.

FOR SOME REASON, I thought that inspector, Lombardi, would
be involved in the investigation. She isn't, although apparently Cecilia called her once, asking vague questions about
domestic violence, and what a woman should do if she fears
her husband might turn violent. Lombardi asked her if
anything had happened, but Cecilia was vague, and
Lombardi dropped the issue. She was busy with the murder
she was investigating at the time (completely unrelated, as it
turns out) and promised she would follow up at some point.
She never did. I think she's possessed by guilt now, because

she hangs about the corridor outside the interrogation room sometimes. She eyes me with such hostility I can only stare at my feet. Every time I see her, I wish I could explain.

I'VE PIECED IT TOGETHER, or I'm trying to. Everything that happened. Just like Cecilia, taping and gluing the evidence of my betrayal until she had the complete, appalling picture.

I've calculated the interval between her finding those photos and the loss of our unborn child. Time enough for the hurt to ripen inside her, bring the ruin it did. A ruin I brought on us, of course.

While I'm fighting this legal battle now, I doubt I can keep it up for much longer. I'm starting to think it might not be worth it. That maybe this is how it should end.

I got a message from my lawyer earlier today. He says they've found something on my computer, something significant, by the sound of his voice. He doesn't want to discuss it over the phone. I pin what hopes I have on this, maybe some element Cecilia has overlooked, some giveaway clue that could set me free.

Who was Alice? This is a question I've stopped asking myself. It fills me with remorse and pain and, mostly, shame. I still catch myself fantasising about her from time to time. Can you believe it? I still catch myself, head resting on my forearm and staring at the ceiling, whispering her name. Like an obscenity. Like an accusation. Like a curse.

At night, I lie awake on this hard mattress and think of my wife. *Cecilia*. The seething hatred she must have felt, the meticulousness of her revenge against me. Sometimes, I plot ways of getting back at her. Sometimes, I think I understand her. Mostly, I wonder where she is.

53

IN AMERICA, SOMEWHERE

A diner, along a highway, somewhere in America. One of those places in the middle of nowhere, a dot in the desert, an endless horizon.

Two women at a table. Their names have changed, as have their clothes. They sit opposite one another, and the taller of the two is gazing outside, cheek resting in her palm.

'All OK?' asks the other. She's younger, dark-haired.

Before replying, the fair-haired woman draws her eyes off the view and studies her companion. She does it with a gaze that you would want pointed at you, with thoughts you wish were for you. 'Yes,' she says simply. 'You?'

A smile, a dip of the chin. *Yes.*

'Can I refill those for you?' says a waitress, appearing by their side. Her *you* comes out as a *ya*. She is holding a pitcher of piping hot, black coffee, and her smile seems sincere. There is a warmth in her accent, one she is unaware of. The two women find it appealing and so different from their own, coming as they do from across the Atlantic.

'Thank you, yes.'

After the waitress has left, the woman who was once

called Cecilia leans forwards, lowering her voice and saying, 'Do you think he ever suspected anything?' She feels it's all right to ask such questions now, at this safe distance in both space and time.

The woman who has been known by two names, at least, gives this question some thought. Then, 'There was that time, in Dorset. You know, that old woman, telling us how wonderful we looked together. He asked me if I'd paid her to say that. The way he said it, it made me think he wasn't joking... not entirely.' She takes a sip from her coffee. 'I did, of course—pay her. I thought it would add a nice touch. Told the old woman it was for a bet or something. Didn't really make sense, as an explanation. But the money was reason enough for her. Other than that, I think he really believed me. I think he really wanted to.'

Cecilia nods, then she turns towards the view again. There's a long, comfortable pause, then she says, 'Let's not talk about him. Let's not mention him ever again.'

Alice, Rebecca, reaches out to hold her hand. She gives it a squeeze. Then suddenly retracts it and brings it to her stomach. She's closed her eyes tight, her lips twisted. Cecilia stands up and walks around the table, slides into the seat next to the other woman. This time it is she who reaches out, laying a comforting palm over Rebecca's. 'Kicking again, is he?' she asks.

'Yes. Ouch. He's busy in there today.'

Cecilia smiles. Her husband's single contribution to her happiness, growing healthily in Rebecca's womb. The child he always wanted and would never know about.

She entwines her fingers in Rebecca's, feeling his little movements, marvelling at them, so incredibly close beneath the skin. She can't wait to welcome him.

Cecilia leans her forehead against the other woman's and closes her eyes. Rocking gently, breathing deeply. She contemplates their two—*three*—bodies. Then the diner with its long L-shaped bar and busy waitress. Then from the outside, as if gliding above it. The dusty parking lot, the stretch of highway. And still farther: the endless expanse of space and sand and hills and towns and mountains and forests and cities and lakes and beaches and quiet places too. She holds the whole of this continent in her mind, then thinks of Rebecca, there next to her, bearing their child.

She considers her name, the sound of it. *Rebecca.* It seems to her a brave, confident name. One to be spoken aloud.

The child kicks, and what Cecilia feels against her palm is a hint of pressure, a delicate shifting. What Cecilia feels is peace and possibility and love.

ABOUT THE AUTHOR

Eliot Stevens grew up between Italy and the UK, studied philosophy, and works in the humanitarian sector. He's fascinated by the intricate coils of the human mind and tries to unravel them in his stories. He lives in the quiet countryside north of Rome with his beautiful family. When not writing, he mostly wishes he was. *The Woman on the Bench* is his first published novel.

Did you enjoy *The Woman on the Bench*? Please consider leaving a review to help other readers discover the book.

www.eliotstevens.com

Made in the USA
Columbia, SC
20 September 2022

67671141R00219